圖解

生活實用**英語**

人事物的種類構造

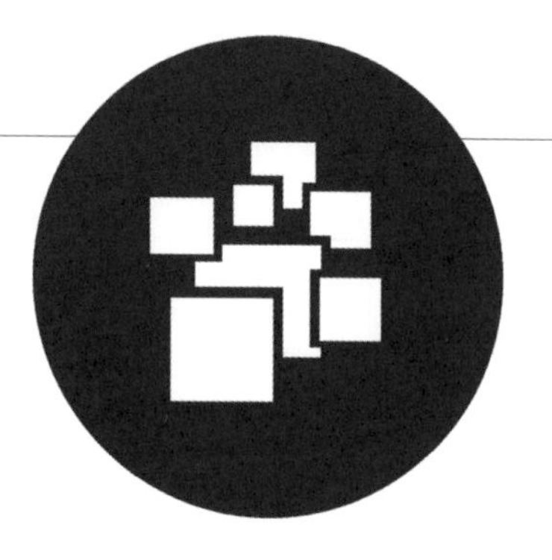

檸檬樹

出版前言

無邊無際的英文單字，如何有效歸納記憶？

【圖解生活實用英語】全系列三冊，
系統化整合龐雜大量的英文單字，分類為：

「眼睛所見」（具體事物）
「大腦所想」（抽象概念）
「種類構造」（生活經驗）

透過全版面的圖像元素，對應的單字具體呈現眼前；
達成「圖像化、視覺性、眼到、心到」的無負擔學習。

第 1 冊【舉目所及的人事物】：眼睛所見人事物的具體單字對應
第 2 冊【腦中延伸的人事物】：大腦所想人事物的具體單字對應
第 3 冊【人事物的種類構造】：生活所知人事物的具體單字對應

「人事物」的「種類、構造說法」與「生活經驗」實境呼應，
將英語學習導入日常生活，體驗物種結構的英文風景，

適合「循序自學」、「從情境反查單字」、「群組式串連記憶」。

第 1 冊：舉目所及的人事物

生活場景中，「常見人事物」的英文說法。

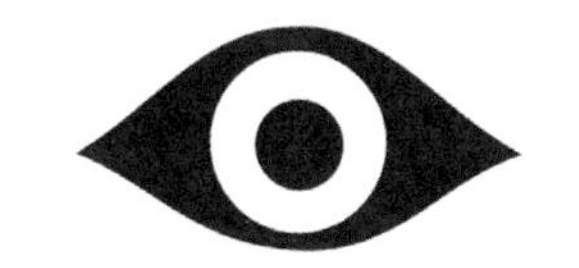

觀賞「馬戲團表演」，你會看到……

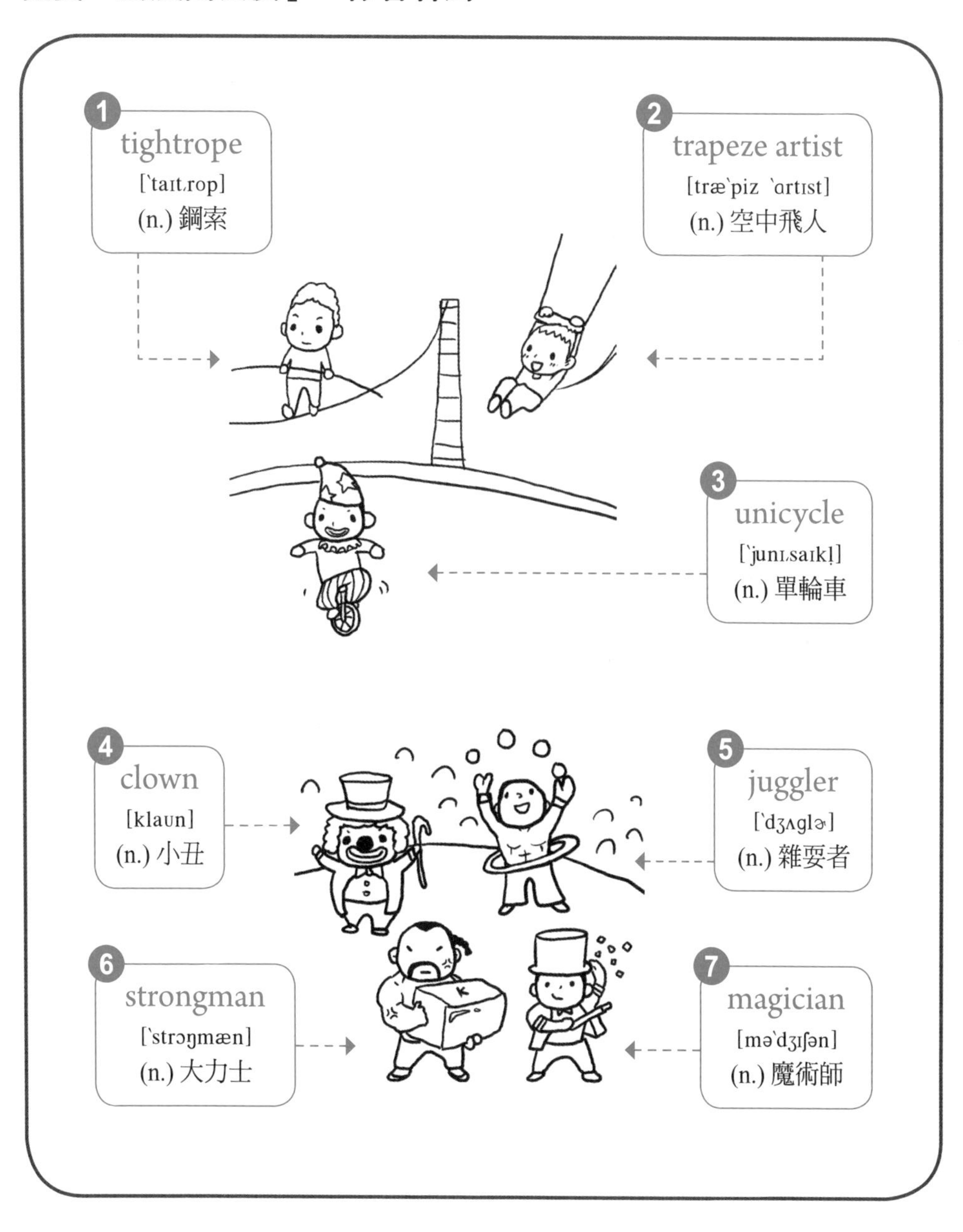

第 2 冊：大腦延伸的人事物

從這個主題，容易連想到的英文單字。

從「學生百態」，可能連想到……

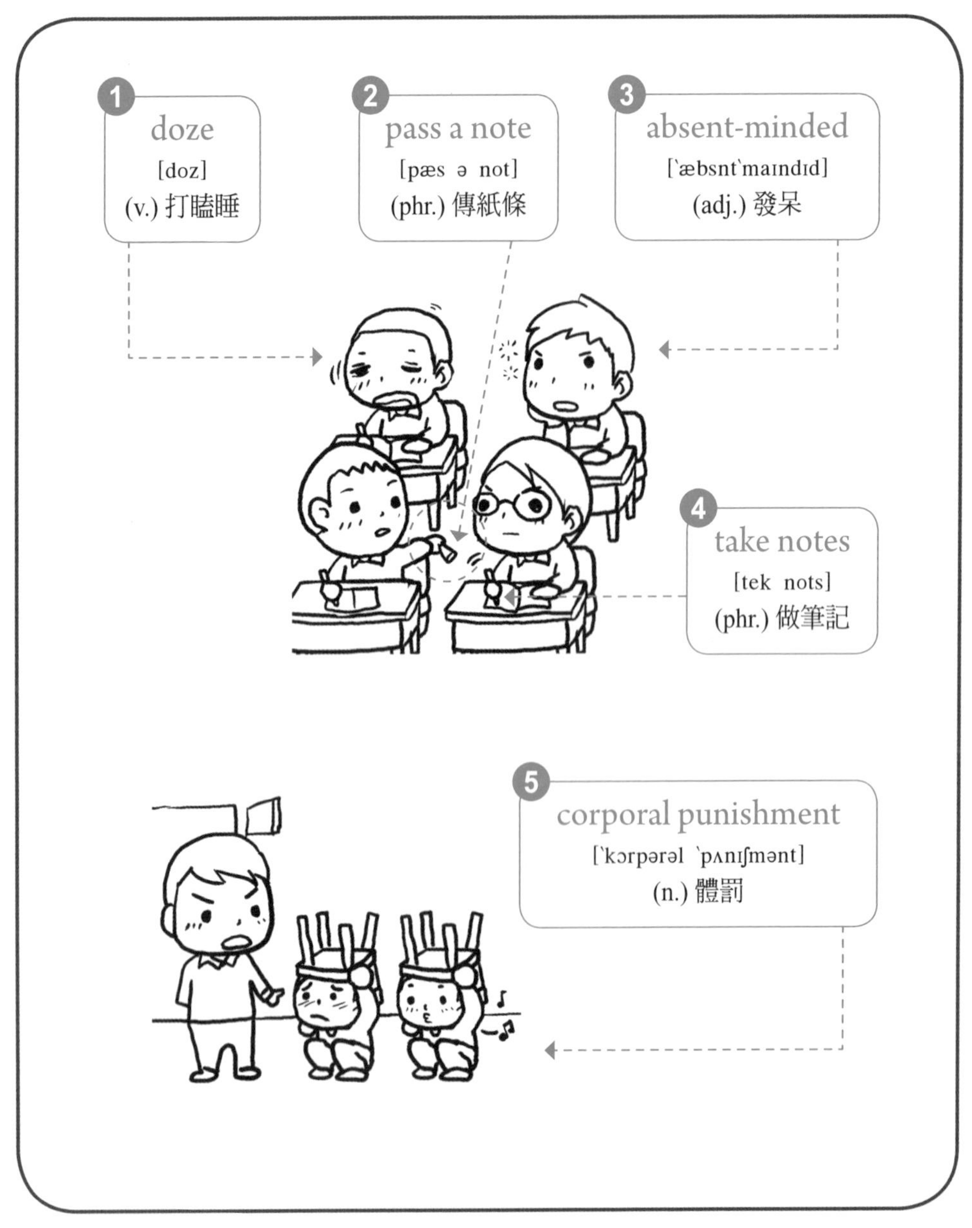

第 3 冊：人事物的種類構造

〔種類〕彙整「同種類、同類型事物」英文說法。

「奧運項目」的種類有……

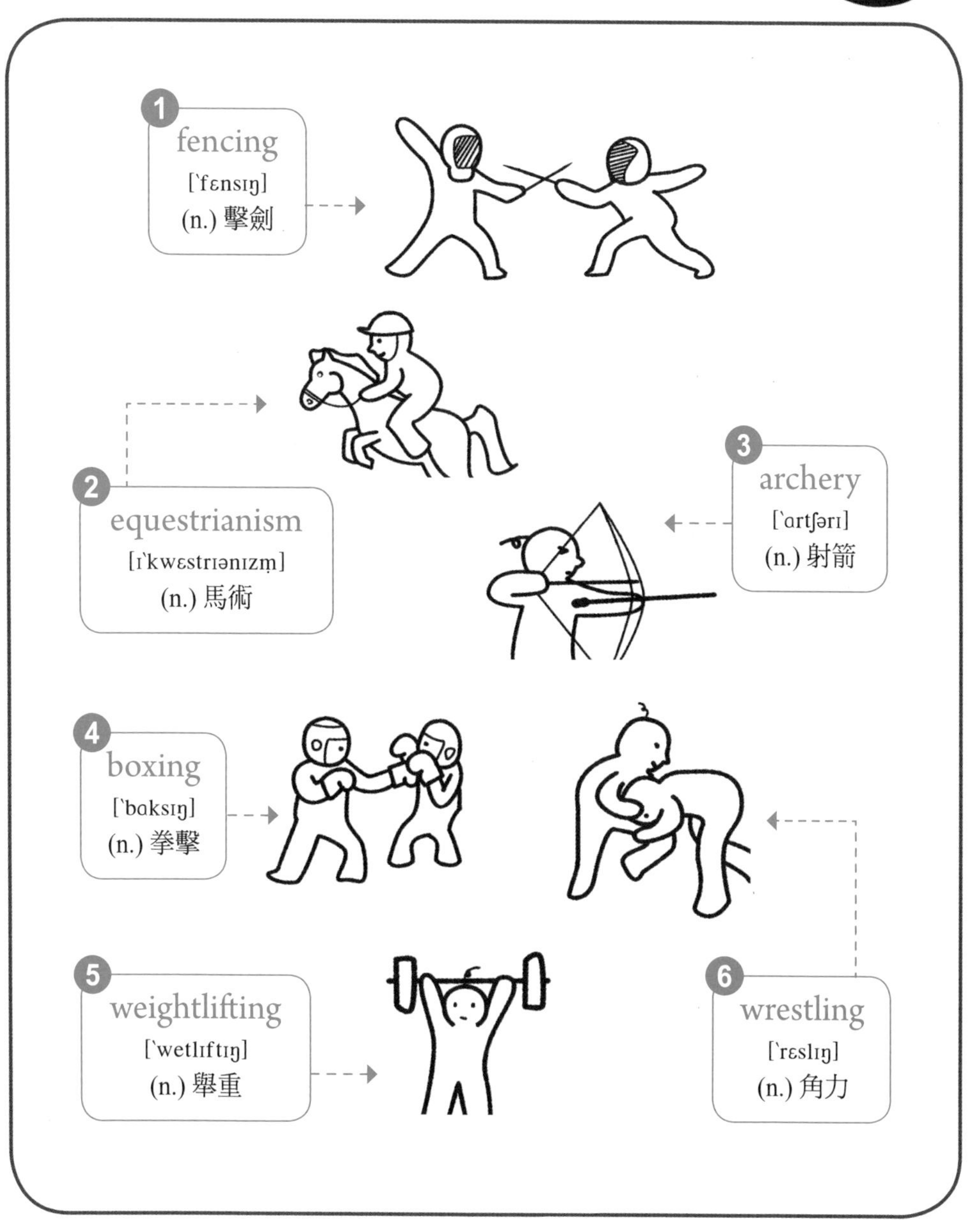

〔構造〕細究「事物組成結構」英文說法。

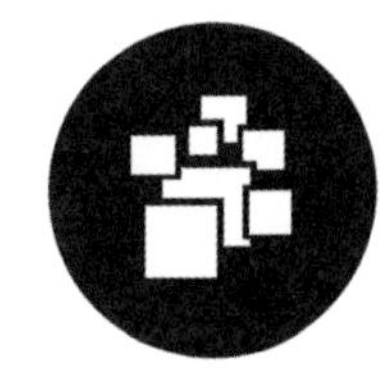

「腳踏車」的構造有……

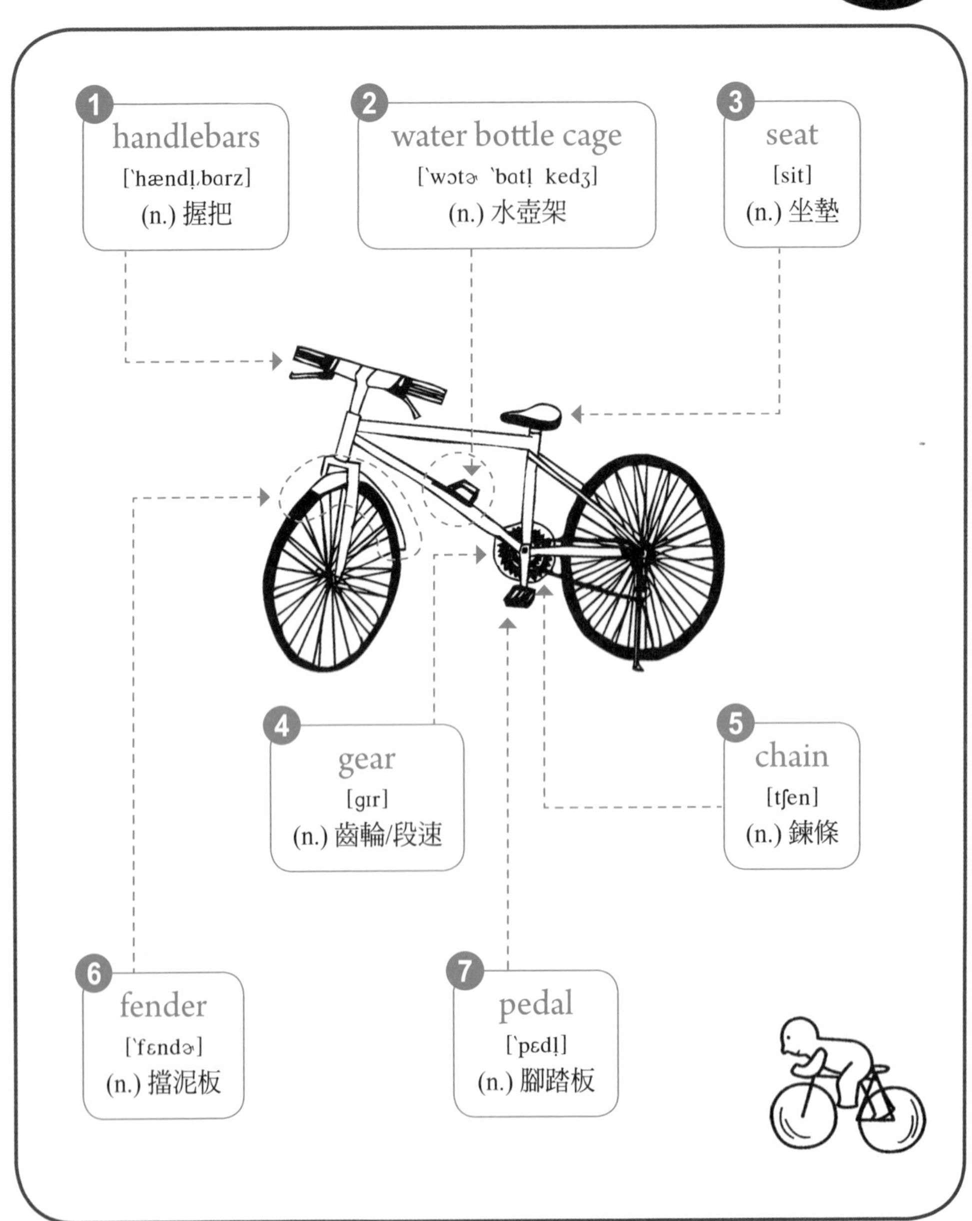

本書特色

【人事物的種類構造】：
「人事物」的「種類、構造說法」，與生活經驗實境呼應！

◎ 以插圖**【身體損傷的所有種類】**（單元 085、086、087）對應學習單字：
流血（bleed）、淤青（bruise）、擦傷（abrasion）、凍傷（frostbite）、燒燙傷（burn）、拉傷（stretch）、扭傷（sprain）、骨折（fracture）。

◎ 以插圖**【常見成藥的所有種類】**（單元 052、053）對應學習單字：
消炎藥（antiphlogistic）、胃藥（gastric drug）、退燒藥（antipyretic）、眼藥水（eye drops）、痠痛貼布（pain care patch）、止痛藥（painkiller）。

◎ 以插圖**【腳踏車的各部構造】**（單元 136、137）對應學習單字：
握把（handlebars）、坐墊（seat）、齒輪（gear）、鍊條（chain）、擋泥板（fender）、腳踏板（pedal）、水壺架（water bottle cage）。

各單元有「4 區域學習板塊」，點線面延伸完備的「生活單字＋生活例句」！

「透過圖像」對應單字，「透過例句」掌握單字用法，就能將英文運用自如。安排「4 區域學習板塊」達成上述功能：

1. **【單字圖解區】**：
   各單元約安排 5 ~ 7 個「具相關性的小群組單字」，以「全版面情境插圖」解說單字。

2. **【單字例句區】**：
   各單字列舉例句，可掌握單字用法、培養閱讀力，並強化單字印象。

3. **【延伸學習區】**：
   詳列例句「新單字、時態變化、重要片語」。

4. **【中文釋義區】**：
   安排在頁面最下方，扮演「輔助學習角色」，如不明瞭英文句義，再參考中譯。

採「全版面情境圖像」解說單字：
插圖清晰易懂，人事物的種類構造，留下具體英文印象！

【單字圖解區】
全版面情境插圖，對應的「人、事、物」單字具體呈現眼前。

【學習單字框】
包含「單字、KK音標、詞性、中譯」；並用虛線指引至插圖，不妨礙閱讀舒適度。

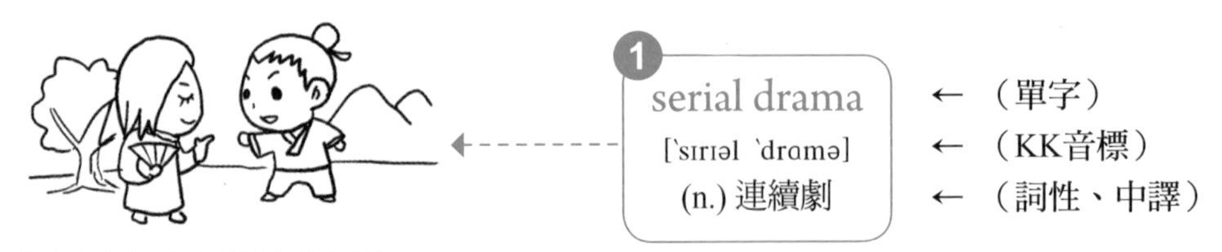

【小圖示另安排放大圖】
讓圖像構造清楚呈現。

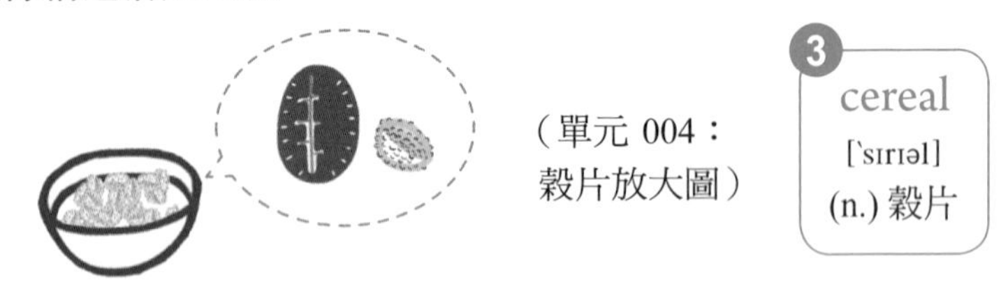

【情境式畫面學習】
透過插圖強化視覺記憶，能減輕學習負擔，加深單字印象。

可以「從情境主題查詢單字」，任意發想的單字疑問，都能找到答案！

全書「175 個生活情境」，「蘊藏 175 種英文風景」。生活中看到、想到的人事物，都能透過查詢主題，「呈現該場景蘊藏的英文風景」。

<u>最熟悉的生活百態，成為最實用的英語資源</u>。

適合親子共讀，利用插圖誘發學習興趣，將英語導入日常生活。

本書「以圖像對應英語」，「用英語認識生活中人事物的種類構造」，也適合親子共讀。可透過圖像誘發學習興趣，藉由「圖像英語」認識生活周遭，探索未接觸的世界，並增長英語知識。

單字加註背景知識，同步累積生活知識，提升英語力，豐富知識庫！

受限於生活經驗，許多生活中所知的人事物，可能「只知名稱、不知背景知識與內涵」。本書透過圖解指引英文單字，對於常聽聞、卻未必了解本質的單字，加註背景知識，有助於閱讀時加深單字印象。同步累積生活知識，對於聽說讀寫，更有助力。

◎ 單元 118【天然災害】的【hailstorm】（冰雹）：

對流雲系旺盛時，雲中水蒸氣凝結成冰粒降下。

◎ 單元 022【音樂類型】的【blues】（藍調）：

源自美國早期黑人音樂中的哀傷歌曲。由「blues」翻譯得名。

書末增列【全書單字附錄】：

詞性分類×字母排序，清楚知道「從這本書學到了哪些單字」！

依循「詞性分類＋字母排序」原則，將全書單字製作成「單字附錄總整理」。有別於本文的「情境式圖解」，「單字附錄」採取「規則性整理」，有助於學習者具體掌握「學了哪些單字、記住了哪些單字」。

讓所經歷的學習過程並非蜻蜓點水，而是務實與確實的學習紀錄。

目錄 Contents

※ 本書各單元 MP3 音軌 = 各單元序號

Part 1：所有種類名

飲食

娛樂

服飾 & 美容

日常場合

交通 & 通訊

身心狀態

學術 & 自然

職場&社會

Part 2：各部構造名

學術

交通

日常場合

人體

160	四肢 (2)	limbs (2)
161	頭部	head
162	眼睛	eye
163	鼻子	nose
164	嘴巴	mouth
165	人體組成 (1)	the human body (1)
166	人體組成 (2)	the human body (2)

飲食

167	蛋糕	cake
168	熱狗麵包 (1)	hot dog (1)
169	熱狗麵包 (2)	hot dog (2)
170	義大利麵	spaghetti
171	水果	fruit
172	蔬菜	vegetable

職場&社會

173	企業構成 (1)	cooperation structure (1)
174	企業構成 (2)	cooperation structure (2)
175	人口結構	composition of population

Part 1：
所有種類名

001~011
飲食

012~031
娛樂

032~043
服飾＆美容

044~059
日常場合

060~069
交通＆通訊

070~098
身心狀態

099~121
學術＆自然

122~127
職場＆社會

Part 2：
各部構造名

128~135
學術

136~142
交通

143~157
日常場合

158~166
人體

167~172
飲食

173~175
職場＆社會

001
餐具(1)

1
platter
[ˋplætɚ]
(n.) 大淺口盤
2
saucer
[ˋsɔsɚ]
(n.) 杯碟
3
plate
[plet]
(n.) 盤子

MP3 001

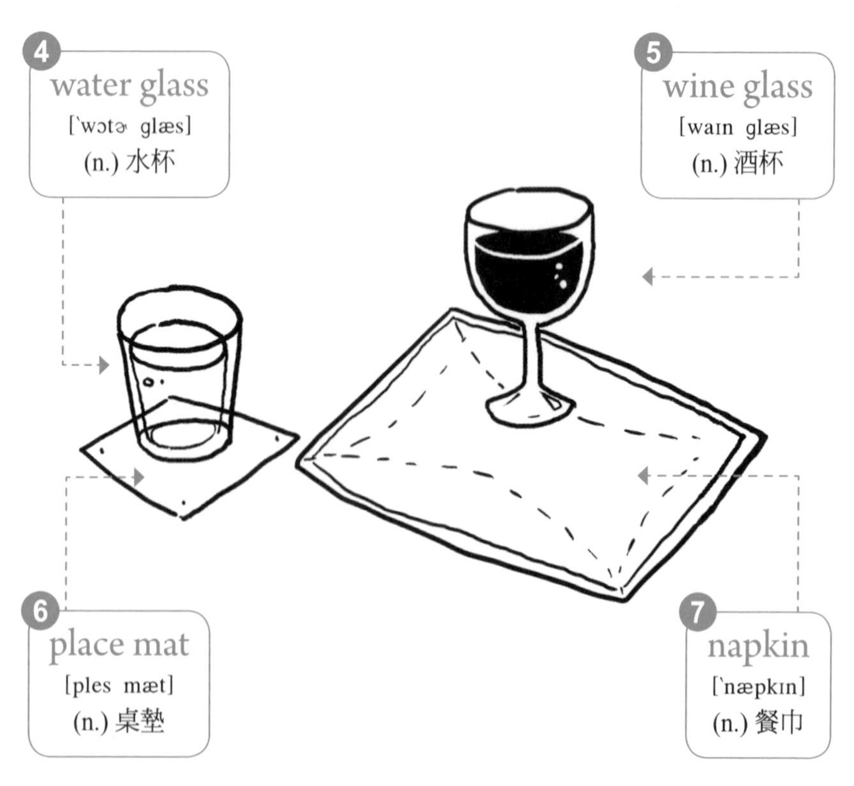
4
water glass
[ˋwɔtɚ glæs]
(n.) 水杯
5
wine glass
[waɪn glæs]
(n.) 酒杯
6
place mat
[ples mæt]
(n.) 桌墊
7
napkin
[ˋnæpkɪn]
(n.) 餐巾

❶ 大淺口盤

We ordered about five kinds of fried snacks, so they brought it all on a large platter.

點了五種油炸類的點心

❷ 杯碟

The man took a sip of tea and put his teacup back on the saucer.

喝了一小口茶

❸ 盤子

The food was put onto a large, flat plate.

❹ 水杯

The woman didn't drink wine, so she asked for a water glass to be brought to her table.

被拿來放到她的桌上

❺ 酒杯

Wine glasses usually have a long stem on a wide base.

長的杯腳連在寬的底座上

❻ 桌墊

There are six place mats on the table for the six diners.

❼ 餐巾

The girl used a napkin to wipe the sauce from her face.

擦掉她臉上的醬汁

學更多

❶ kind〈種類〉・fried〈油炸的〉・snack〈點心〉・brought〈bring（拿來）的過去式〉
❷ a sip of〈一小口〉・put back〈put back（把…放回原處）的過去式〉・teacup〈茶杯〉
❸ put〈put（放）的過去分詞〉・large〈大的〉・flat〈平淺的〉
❹ drink〈喝〉・asked〈ask（要求）的過去式〉・brought〈bring（帶來）的過去分詞〉
❺ wine〈酒〉・glass〈玻璃杯〉・stem〈高腳酒杯的腳〉・wide〈寬的〉・base〈底座〉
❻ place〈座位〉・mat〈墊子〉・diner〈用餐者〉
❼ used〈use（用）的過去式〉・wipe〈擦拭〉・sauce〈醬汁〉・face〈臉〉

中譯

❶ 我們點了五種油炸點心，所以送上來時，他們把所有點心都放在一個大淺口盤上。
❷ 那名男子喝了一小口茶，然後把茶杯放回杯碟上。
❸ 食物被放在一個又大又平淺的盤子上。
❹ 那位女士不飲酒，所以她要求拿一個水杯到桌上給她。
❺ 酒杯通常都是寬底座上，連接著長長的杯腳。
❻ 桌上有六個桌墊供六位用餐者使用。
❼ 那個女孩用餐巾擦掉沾在臉上的醬汁。

002 餐具(2)

MP3 002

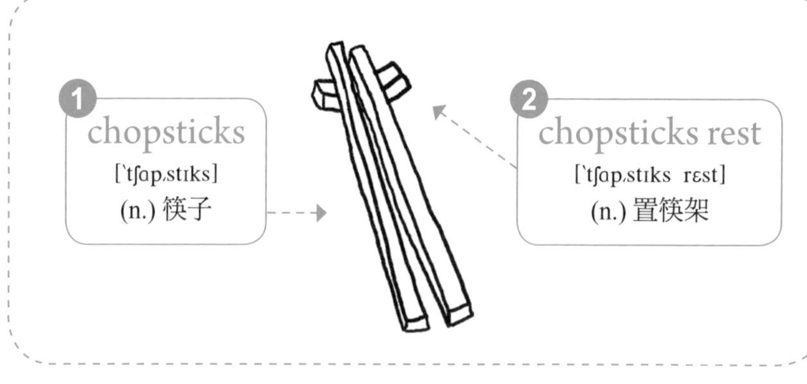

1 chopsticks [ˋtʃɑp͵stɪks] (n.) 筷子

2 chopsticks rest [ˋtʃɑp͵stɪks rɛst] (n.) 置筷架

3 bowl [bol] (n.) 碗

4 spoon [spun] (n.) 湯匙

5 fork [fɔrk] (n.) 叉子

6 butter knife [ˋbʌtɚ naɪf] (n.) 奶油刀

7 steak knife [stek naɪf] (n.) 牛排刀

❶ 筷子

Chinese restaurants always give their diners chopsticks to eat with.

用…來吃東西

❷ 置筷架

To keep her chopsticks off the table, she placed them on a chopsticks rest.

不讓她的筷子接觸到桌子

❸ 碗

I asked the waiter to bring me a large bowl of soup.

拿一大碗的湯給我

❹ 湯匙

The little boy got himself a big spoon to eat his ice cream with.

為他自己拿了一支大湯匙　用…吃他的冰淇淋

❺ 叉子

Most forks have three or four prongs.

❻ 奶油刀

Butter knives are not very sharp.

❼ 牛排刀

To cut the thick meat, you need a sharp steak knife.

學更多

❶ Chinese〈中國的〉・restaurant〈餐廳〉・always〈總是〉・diner〈用餐者〉
❷ keep off〈使…不接近〉・placed〈place（放置）的過去式〉・rest〈支撐物〉
❸ waiter〈服務生〉・bring〈拿來〉・large〈大的〉・soup〈湯〉
❹ got〈get（得到）的過去式〉・himself〈他自己〉・ice cream〈冰淇淋〉
❺ most〈大部分的〉・prong〈（叉子的）尖齒〉
❻ butter〈奶油〉・knives〈knife（刀子）的複數〉・sharp〈鋒利的〉
❼ cut〈切〉・thick〈厚的〉・meat〈肉〉・steak〈牛排〉

中譯

❶ 中式餐廳都會提供客人筷子來用餐。
❷ 為了不讓筷子接觸到桌面，她把筷子放在置筷架上。
❸ 我要求服務生給我一大碗湯。
❹ 那個小男孩拿了一支大湯匙來享用他的冰淇淋。
❺ 大部分的叉子都是三齒或四齒。
❻ 奶油刀不會非常鋒利。
❼ 要切開厚片肉，你需要一把鋒利的牛排刀。

003 西式早餐(1)

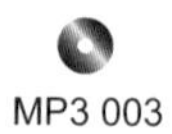
MP3 003

❶ 蛋
How do you like your eggs—boiled or fried?

❷ 烤吐司
The old man likes to spread butter and jam on his toast.
塗奶油和果醬在他的烤吐司上

❸ 法式吐司
French toast is soaked in egg before it's cooked.
法式吐司被浸泡在蛋液中

❹ 奶油
Hattie spread some butter on her toast.

❺ 果醬
Shane's favorite jam is strawberry jam.

❻ 三明治
Evan put some cheese between slices of bread and made a sandwich.
放一些起司在麵包夾層裡

學更多

❶ boiled〈煮熟的〉• fried〈油煎的〉
❷ old〈老的〉• spread〈塗〉
❸ French〈法國的〉• soaked〈soak（浸泡）的過去分詞〉• before〈在…之前〉• cooked〈cook（烹調）的過去分詞〉
❹ spread〈spread（塗）的過去式〉• some〈一些〉
❺ favorite〈特別喜愛的〉• strawberry〈草莓〉
❻ put〈put（放）的過去式〉• cheese〈起司〉• between〈在…之間〉• slice〈切片〉• bread〈麵包〉• made〈make（製作）的過去式〉

中譯

❶ 你想吃哪種蛋，水煮蛋或煎蛋？
❷ 這位老先生喜歡在烤吐司上塗抹奶油和果醬。
❸ 烹調法式吐司前，要先浸泡在蛋液裡。
❹ Hattie 在她的吐司上塗了一些奶油。
❺ Shane 最喜歡的果醬是草莓口味的。
❻ Evan 在麵包切片中間放了一些起司，做成一個三明治。

004 西式早餐(2)

MP3 004

❶ 培根

Bacon is quite a salty meat that comes from pigs.

相當鹹的肉

❷ 火腿

Ham is a popular sandwich meat. It comes from pigs.

它來自豬的身上

❸ 穀片

Corn flakes are a popular form of cereal.

玉米片

❹ 貝果

A bagel is a round piece of bread with a hole in the middle.

一塊圓形麵包

❺ 薯餅

Hash browns are little cakes made with potato.

用馬鈴薯做的

❻ 鬆餅

Waffles taste great with cream and honey.

❼ 鬆餅 / 薄煎餅

A stack of pancakes is my favorite thing to eat on Saturday mornings.

我最喜歡吃的東西

學更多

❶ quite〈相當〉・salty〈鹹的〉・meat〈肉〉・come from〈來自於〉・pig〈豬〉
❷ popular〈受歡迎的〉・sandwich〈三明治〉
❸ corn〈玉米〉・flake〈小薄片〉・form〈種類〉
❹ round〈圓形的〉・piece〈一塊〉・bread〈麵包〉・hole〈洞〉・middle〈中間〉
❺ hash〈剁碎的食物、肉末洋芋泥〉・brown〈褐色〉・little〈小的〉・cake〈餅狀食物〉
❻ taste〈吃起來〉・cream〈奶油〉・honey〈蜂蜜〉
❼ stack〈一疊〉・favorite〈特別喜愛的〉・Saturday〈星期六〉・morning〈早晨〉

中譯

❶ 培根是一種帶有重鹹味的豬肉。
❷ 火腿是一種受歡迎的三明治肉片。它是豬肉。
❸ 玉米片是一種受歡迎的穀片。
❹ 貝果是一種中間有洞的圓形麵包。
❺ 薯餅是用馬鈴薯做的餅狀食物。
❻ 鬆餅搭配奶油和蜂蜜，是相當美味的。
❼ 層層疊起的薄煎餅，是週六早晨我的最愛。

005 蛋

MP3 005

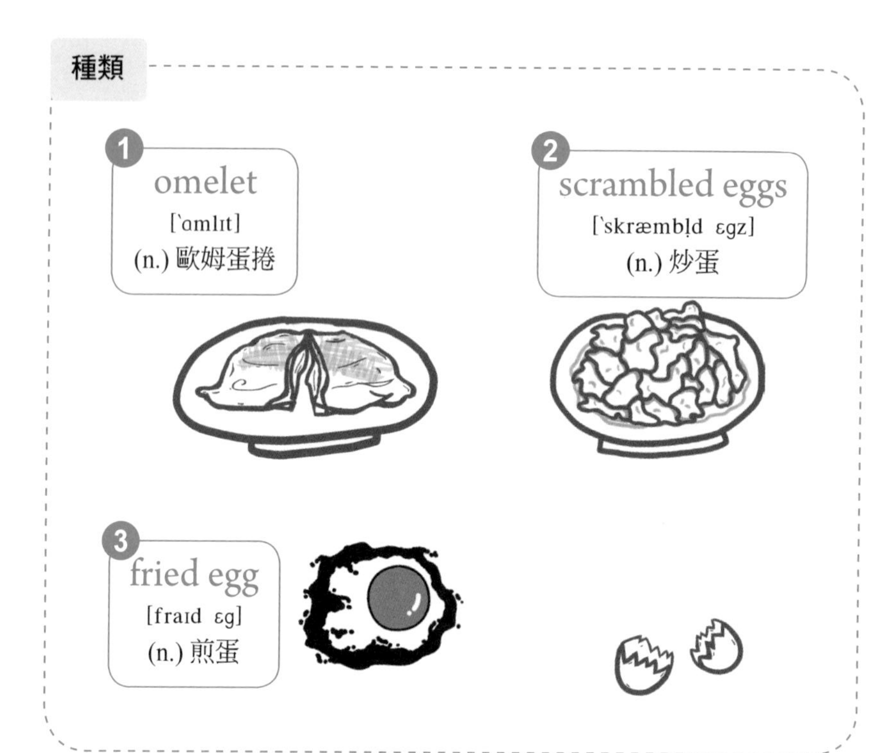

種類
1
omelet
[`ɑmlɪt]
(n.) 歐姆蛋捲
2
scrambled eggs
[`skræmbḷd ɛgz]
(n.) 炒蛋
3
fried egg
[fraɪd ɛg]
(n.) 煎蛋

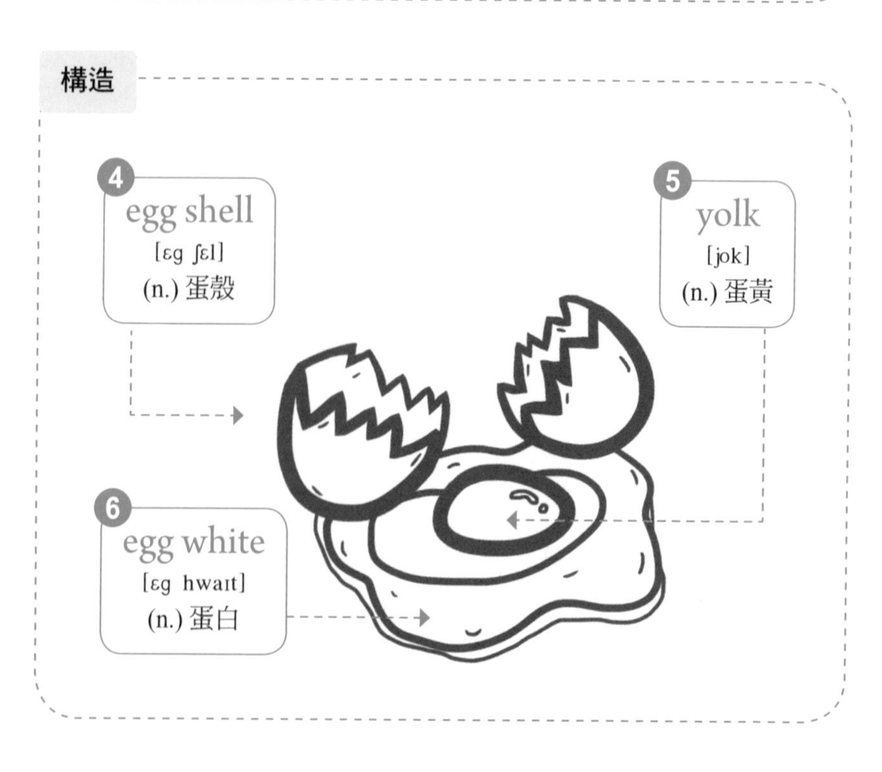

構造
4
egg shell
[ɛg ʃɛl]
(n.) 蛋殼
5
yolk
[jok]
(n.) 蛋黃
6
egg white
[ɛg hwaɪt]
(n.) 蛋白

❶ 歐姆蛋捲

To cook an omelet, beat some eggs and pour them into a hot frying pan.

攪拌一些雞蛋

❷ 炒蛋

To make scrambled eggs, keep beating the eggs while you cook them.

當你烹調它們的時候

❸ 煎蛋

Mrs. Brown is making fried egg in the frying pan.

❹ 蛋殼

Ryan peeled off the hard egg shell and ate his boiled egg.

剝掉硬的蛋殼　水煮蛋

❺ 蛋黃

The yolk is the yellow part in the middle of an egg.

在雞蛋的中央

❻ 蛋白

Frank hates egg whites; he only likes the yolks.

學更多

❶ cook〈烹調〉・beat〈攪拌〉・pour〈倒〉・hot〈熱的〉・frying pan〈平底鍋〉

❷ scrambled〈炒的〉・keep〈持續不斷〉・beating〈beat（攪拌）的 ing 型態〉

❸ making〈make（製作）的 ing 型態〉・fried〈油煎的〉

❹ peeled off〈peel off（去掉）的過去式〉・hard〈硬的〉・shell〈殼〉・ate〈eat（吃）的過去式〉・boiled〈煮熟的〉

❺ yellow〈黃色的〉・part〈部分〉・middle〈中間〉

❻ hate〈討厭〉・white〈蛋白〉・only〈只〉

中譯

❶ 要做歐姆蛋捲，你需要將雞蛋打勻，並倒入預熱的平底鍋。

❷ 要做一道炒蛋，你需要在烹調時持續不斷地翻炒蛋液。

❸ Brown 太太正用平底鍋做煎蛋。

❹ Ryan 剝掉硬蛋殼，享用了他的水煮蛋。

❺ 雞蛋中央的黃色部分就是蛋黃。

❻ Frank 討厭蛋白，他只喜歡吃蛋黃。

006

乳製品(1)

MP3 006

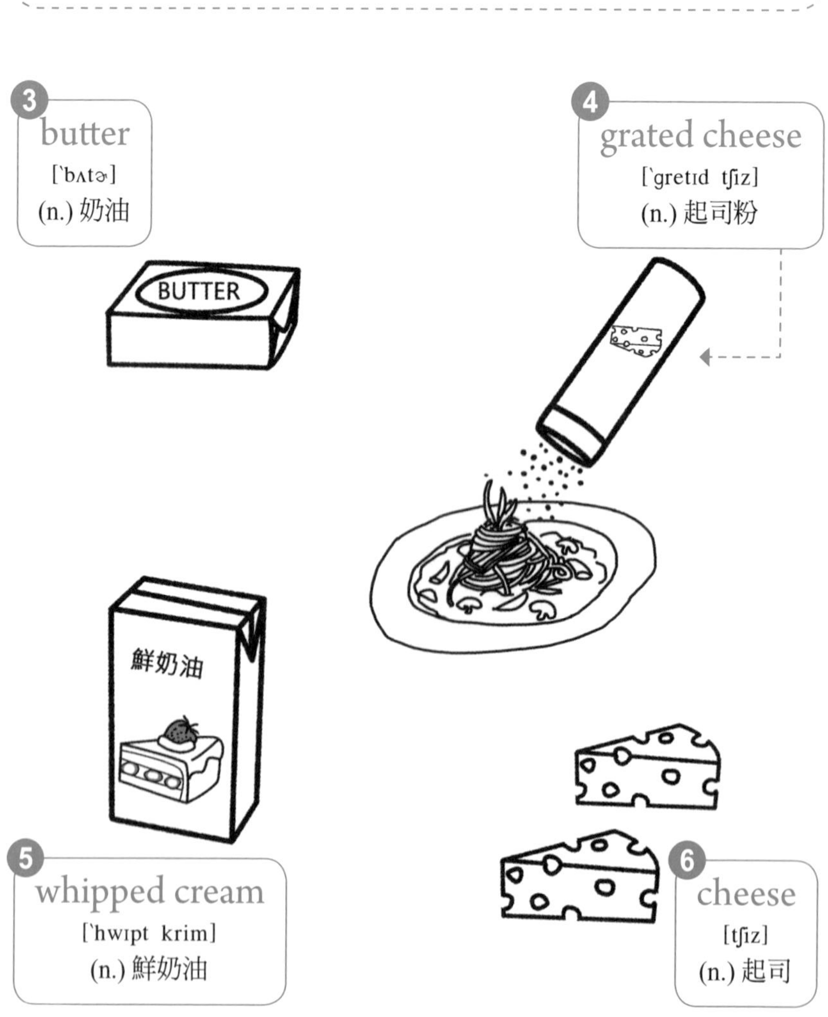

❶ 牛奶
Milk comes from cows.

❷ 奶粉
Milk powder is dried, so it doesn't go bad as quickly as real milk.
像真的牛奶一樣那麼快腐壞

❸ 奶油
Harry loves to spread salty, yellow butter on his toast.

❹ 起司粉
Grocery stores now sell bags of grated cheese for cooking.

❺ 鮮奶油
It's great to eat cake with whipped cream.
有鮮奶油的蛋糕

❻ 起司
Pizzas are usually topped with cheese.
通常…會被放在上層表面

學更多

❶ come from〈來自於〉‧cow〈乳牛〉
❷ powder〈粉末〉‧dried〈乾燥的〉‧go〈變成〉‧bad〈腐壞的〉‧as...as〈和…一樣〉‧quickly〈快速地〉‧real〈真正的〉
❸ spread〈塗〉‧salty〈鹹的〉‧yellow〈黃色〉‧toast〈烤吐司〉
❹ grocery store〈雜貨店〉‧sell〈販售〉‧bag〈一袋〉‧grated〈磨碎的〉‧cooking〈烹飪〉
❺ great〈極好的〉‧cake〈蛋糕〉‧whipped〈攪打過的〉
❻ pizza〈披薩〉‧usually〈通常〉‧topped〈top（蓋在…的上層表面）的過去分詞〉

中譯

❶ 牛奶來自於乳牛。
❷ 奶粉是乾燥的，所以它不像真的牛奶一樣那麼快腐壞。
❸ Harry 喜歡在烤吐司上面塗抹鹹味的黃奶油。
❹ 雜貨店現在都有販售成袋的起司粉供烹調使用。
❺ 享用鮮奶油蛋糕是一大樂事。
❻ 披薩的上層通常都是起司。

007 乳製品(2)

MP3 007

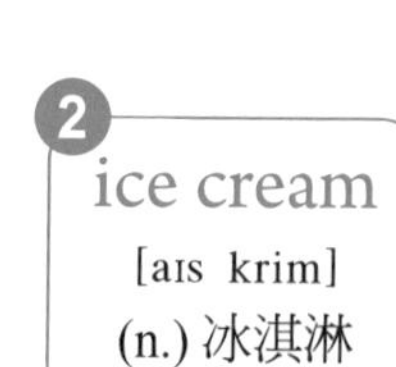

1 yogurt
[`jogət]
(n.) 優格

2 ice cream
[aɪs krim]
(n.) 冰淇淋

3 milk pudding
[mɪlk `pudɪŋ]
(n.) 鮮奶布丁

4 drinking yogurt
[`drɪŋkɪŋ `jogət]
(n.) 優酪乳

5 milkshake
[͵mɪlk`ʃek]
(n.) 奶昔

6 milk tea
[mɪlk ti]
(n.) 奶茶

❶ 優格
To make yogurt, you need to add bacteria to milk.
把菌種加入牛奶裡

❷ 冰淇淋
Polly loves to eat cold ice cream in the summer.

❸ 鮮奶布丁
Milk pudding is my favorite kind of pudding.
是我最喜愛的一種布丁

❹ 優酪乳
Drinking yogurt is thinner than regular yogurt.

❺ 奶昔
I mixed together strawberries, ice cream, and milk to make a thick milkshake.
一杯濃郁的奶昔

❻ 奶茶
I don't like milk tea, I drink my tea without milk or sugar.

學更多

❶ make〈製作〉・add〈添加〉・bacteria〈細菌〉・milk〈牛奶〉
❷ cold〈冰涼的〉・summer〈夏天〉
❸ pudding〈布丁〉・favorite〈特別喜愛的〉・kind〈種類〉
❹ drinking〈喝〉・thinner〈更稀薄的，thin（稀薄的）的比較級〉・regular〈一般的〉
❺ mixed〈mix（混合）的過去式〉・together〈一起〉・strawberry〈草莓〉・thick〈濃的〉
❻ drink〈喝〉・without〈沒有〉・sugar〈糖〉

中譯

❶ 要製作優格，你必須在牛奶裡添加菌種。
❷ Polly 喜愛在夏天吃清涼的冰淇淋。
❸ 鮮奶布丁是我最喜歡的一種布丁。
❹ 優酪乳比一般的優格來得稀薄。
❺ 我混合了草莓、冰淇淋和牛奶，做成一杯濃郁的奶昔。
❻ 我不喜歡奶茶。我喝茶都不加牛奶或糖。

008

常見蔬菜(1)

MP3 008

❶ 洋蔥
Please don't make me chop the onions!
不要讓我切

❷ 萵苣
That head of lettuce is wilting so you'd better not buy it.
你最好不要買它（= you had better not buy it）

❸ 高麗菜
Stir-fried cabbage is not only healthy, but also tasty!

❹ 青蔥
Adding a few shallots in a garden salad adds great flavor.
增添很棒的味道

❺ 韭菜
Have you tried the leek dumplings they serve here?
他們這裡供應的

❻ 竹筍
A popular ingredient in many Asian dishes is bamboo shoots.
常見的食材　亞洲料理

❼ 蘆筍
Asparagus is delicious, but it can be expensive out of season.
非產季時會很貴

學更多

❶ make〈使…做…〉・chop〈切〉
❷ head〈蔬菜的蒂頭〉・wilting〈wilt（枯萎）的 ing 型態〉・buy〈買〉
❸ stir-fried〈stir-fry（炒）的過去分詞〉・not only...but also...〈不僅…而且…〉・tasty〈可口的〉
❹ adding〈add（添加）的 ing 型態〉・garden salad〈田園沙拉〉・flavor〈味道〉
❺ tried〈try（試）的過去分詞〉・dumpling〈水餃〉・serve〈供應〉
❻ popular〈普遍的〉・ingredient〈原料〉・Asian〈亞洲的〉・bamboo〈竹〉・shoot〈幼芽〉
❼ delicious〈美味的〉・expensive〈昂貴的〉・out of season〈季節已過〉

中譯

❶ 拜託別讓我切洋蔥！
❷ 那顆萵苣的蒂頭開始枯萎了，所以你最好別買。
❸ 炒高麗菜不僅健康，還很可口！
❹ 在田園沙拉裡灑些青蔥，能增添美妙的風味。
❺ 你有吃過他們這邊賣的韭菜水餃嗎？
❻ 竹筍是許多亞洲料理中的常見食材。
❼ 蘆筍很好吃，不過在非產季時價格很昂貴。

009 常見蔬菜(2)

MP3 009

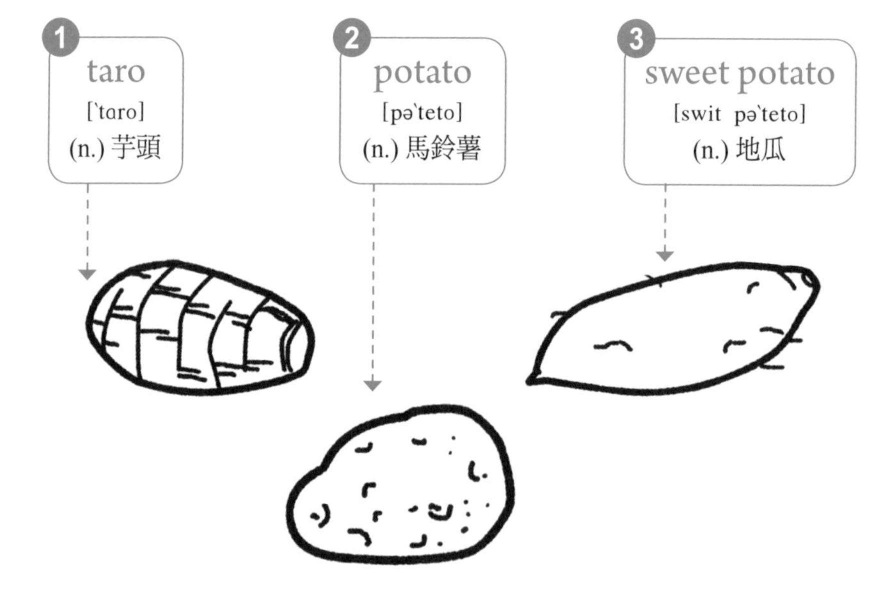

1 taro
[ˋtɑro]
(n.) 芋頭

2 potato
[pəˋteto]
(n.) 馬鈴薯

3 sweet potato
[swit pəˋteto]
(n.) 地瓜

4 burdock
[ˋbɝ͵dɑk]
(n.) 牛蒡

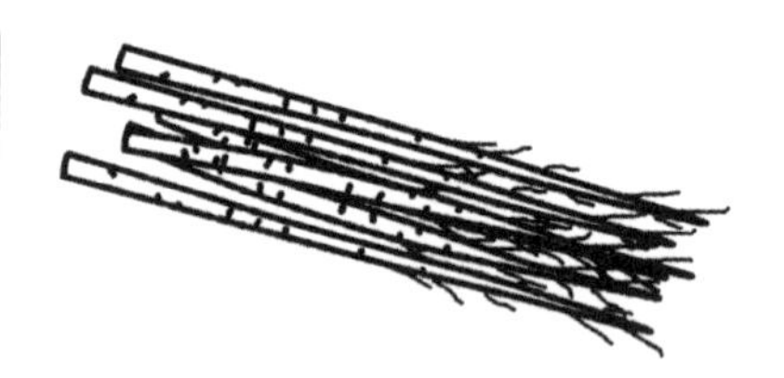

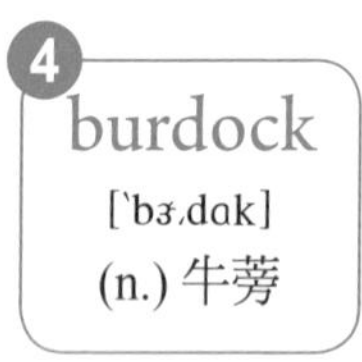

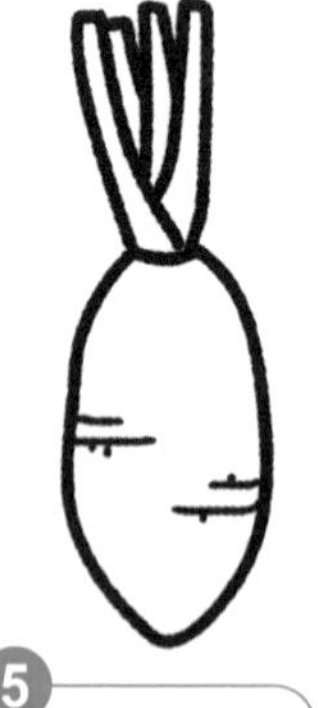

5 daikon
[ˋdɑɪkon]
(n.) 白蘿蔔

6 carrot
[ˋkærət]
(n.) 紅蘿蔔

❶ 芋頭
Taro is a root vegetable that is quite popular in East Asia.
東亞

❷ 馬鈴薯
Is there anything better than fried potatoes?
比炸馬鈴薯更好

❸ 地瓜
Delicious roasted sweet potatoes are often sold on the street in Taiwan.
常常在街上被販賣

❹ 牛蒡
Burdock is a root vegetable used primarily in Asian cuisines.
主要被用於亞洲料理

❺ 白蘿蔔
Daikon is the Japanese word for Asian white radishes.

❻ 紅蘿蔔
Everyone knows that rabbits love to eat carrots, right?
大家都知道…

學更多

❶ root〈根莖〉‧vegetable〈蔬菜〉‧quite〈很〉‧popular〈普及的〉‧Asia〈亞洲〉
❷ anything〈什麼東西〉‧better〈更好的〉‧fried〈油炸的〉
❸ delicious〈美味的〉‧roasted〈烤的〉‧sweet〈甜的〉‧sold〈sell（販賣）的過去分詞〉
❹ used〈use（使用）的過去分詞〉‧primarily〈主要地〉‧cuisine〈菜餚〉
❺ word〈單字〉‧Asian〈亞洲的〉‧white〈白色的〉‧radish〈小蘿蔔〉
❻ everyone〈每個人〉‧rabbit〈兔子〉

中譯

❶ 芋頭是東亞地區相當常見的根莖類蔬菜。
❷ 有比炸馬鈴薯更美味的食物嗎？
❸ 在台灣，路上經常能看到販售美味的烤地瓜。
❹ 牛蒡是主要用於亞洲料理的根莖類蔬菜。
❺ 亞洲的白蘿蔔，日文說法是「daikon」。
❻ 大家都知道兔子喜歡吃紅蘿蔔，對吧？

010

常見水果(1)

MP3 010

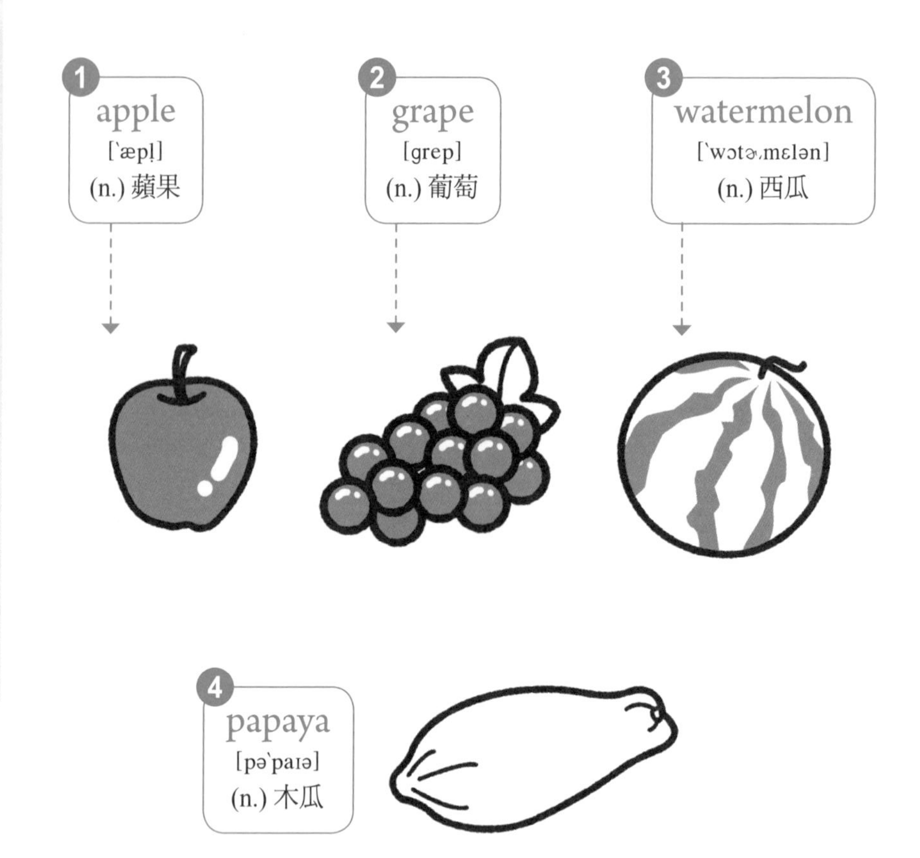
1
apple
[ˋæpḷ]
(n.) 蘋果
2
grape
[grep]
(n.) 葡萄
3
watermelon
[ˋwɔtɚ͵mɛlən]
(n.) 西瓜
4
papaya
[pəˋpaɪə]
(n.) 木瓜

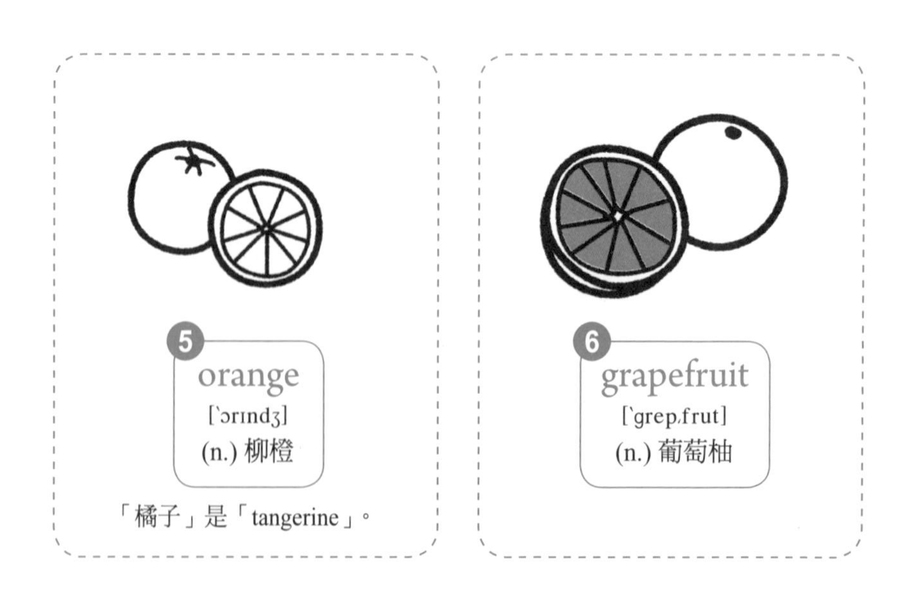
5
orange
[ˋɔrɪndʒ]
(n.) 柳橙
「橘子」是「tangerine」。
6
grapefruit
[ˋgrep͵frut]
(n.) 葡萄柚

❶ 蘋果

An apple a day keeps the doctor away unless you don't get enough sleep or eat junk food all the time.

一天一蘋果，醫生遠離我

一直吃垃圾食物

❷ 葡萄

Joanna popped some grapes into her mouth for a little after-school snack.

迅速地把幾顆葡萄放進她的嘴裡

課後點心

❸ 西瓜

Will you cut me a slice of watermelon, please?

一片西瓜

❹ 木瓜

Kyle's mom likes to give him papayas because they're so nutritious.

❺ 柳橙

I'm fighting a cold, so I'll eat more oranges for a while for the vitamin C.

我最近會多吃些柳橙

❻ 葡萄柚

Grapefruit is known to help dieters lose weight.

為⋯（人）所知

學更多

❶ away〈離開〉• unless〈除非〉• enough〈足夠的〉• sleep〈睡眠〉• junk food〈垃圾食物〉• all the time〈一直〉

❷ popped〈pop（把⋯迅速地放）的過去式〉• a little〈少量〉• after-school〈課後的〉

❸ cut〈切〉• slice〈切片〉• please〈請〉

❹ give〈給〉• because〈因為〉• nutritious〈有營養的〉

❺ fighting〈fight（搏鬥）的 ing 型態〉• cold〈感冒〉• for a while〈暫時〉• vitamin〈維他命〉

❻ known〈已知的、知名的〉• dieter〈減肥的人〉• lose weight〈減輕體重〉

中譯

❶ 除非你睡眠不足，或是一天到晚吃垃圾食物；否則一天一蘋果，就能讓你保持健康。

❷ Joanna 快速地吃了幾顆葡萄當作一點課後點心。

❸ 可以請你幫我切一片西瓜嗎？

❹ Kyle 的媽媽喜歡給他吃木瓜，因為木瓜很營養。

❺ 我正與感冒病毒搏鬥，所以我最近會多吃些柳橙來攝取維他命 C 。

❻ 葡萄柚有助於減肥的人減輕體重是眾所皆知的。

011 常見水果(2)

MP3 011

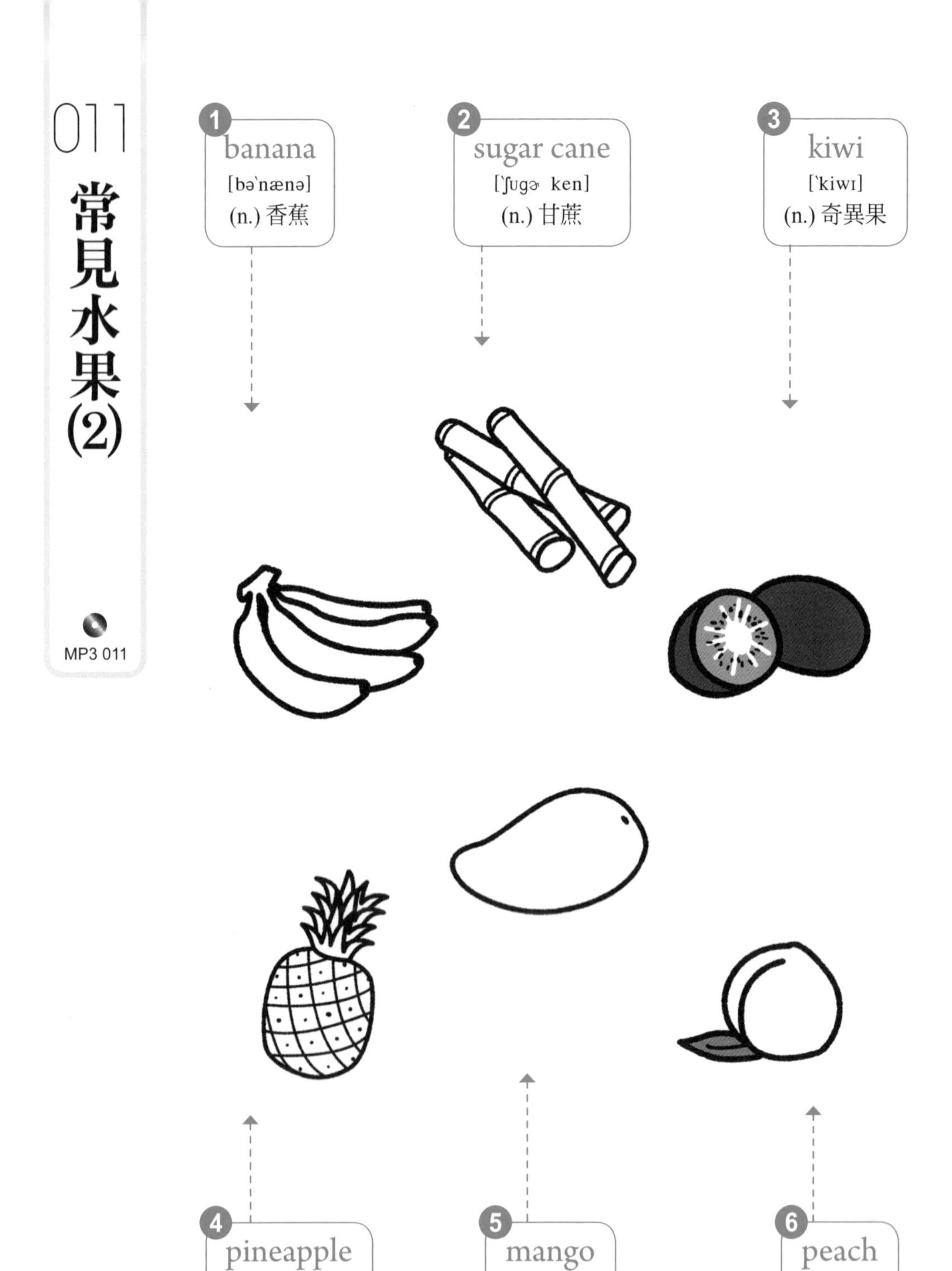

4 pineapple
[`paɪn.æpl̩]
(n.) 鳳梨

5 mango
[`mæŋgo]
(n.) 芒果

6 peach
[pitʃ]
(n.) 桃子

❶ 香蕉
Bananas are a great breakfast food.

❷ 甘蔗
If you want to protect your teeth, don't suck on sugar canes too often.
保護你的牙齒

❸ 奇異果
The skin on kiwi fruit is very fuzzy.
奇異果的果皮

❹ 鳳梨
Cutting up a pineapple requires a sharp knife.

❺ 芒果
Let's go to that drink stand and get a mango smoothie!
飲料店

❻ 桃子
Grandma's peach pie is the best dessert on the planet!
這個星球上最好吃的點心

學更多

❶ great〈極好的〉・breakfast〈早餐〉・food〈食物〉
❷ protect〈保護〉・teeth〈tooth（牙齒）的複數〉・suck〈吸吮〉・often〈常常〉
❸ skin〈外皮〉・fruit〈水果〉・fuzzy〈有絨毛的〉
❹ cutting up〈cut up（切開）的 ing 型態〉・require〈需要〉・sharp〈尖銳的〉・knife〈刀子〉
❺ drink〈飲料〉・stand〈攤子〉・smoothie〈果泥狀的飲品〉
❻ pie〈派〉・best〈最好的〉・dessert〈甜點〉・planet〈行星〉

中譯

❶ 香蕉是絕佳的早餐食物。
❷ 如果想要保護牙齒，就不要太常啃甘蔗。
❸ 奇異果的果皮毛茸茸的。
❹ 要切鳳梨，需要一把尖銳的刀子。
❺ 我們去那家飲料店買杯芒果果昔吧！
❻ 祖母的水蜜桃派，是世上最好吃的點心！

012

電影類型(1)

MP3 012

❶ 喜劇

Comedies are my favorite movie genre.

❷ 悲劇

While comedies might make you laugh, tragedies are more likely to make you cry.

喜劇可能讓你笑

❸ 動作片

Action movies contain exciting scenes involving car chases and explosions.

包含飛車追逐和爆破

❹ 冒險片

The characters in this adventure movie go on a long journey and fight monsters.

進行長途的旅程

❺ 武俠片

Bruce Lee is probably the biggest star ever of martial arts movies.

學更多

❶ favorite〈特別喜愛的〉‧movie〈電影〉‧genre〈體裁、類型〉

❷ laugh〈笑〉‧likely〈很可能的〉‧cry〈哭〉

❸ action〈活動〉‧contain〈包含〉‧exciting〈令人激動的〉‧scene〈場面〉‧involving〈involve（涉及）的 ing 型態〉‧chase〈追逐〉‧explosion〈爆破〉

❹ character〈角色〉‧adventure〈冒險〉‧journey〈旅程〉‧fight〈打鬥〉‧monster〈怪獸〉

❺ probably〈可能〉‧biggest〈最偉大的，big（偉大的）的最高級〉‧martial art〈武術〉

中譯

❶ 喜劇是我最喜歡的電影類型。

❷ 喜劇可能使你歡笑，而悲劇很可能使你落淚。

❸ 動作片包含驚心動魄的場面，像是飛車追逐和爆破。

❹ 這部冒險片裡的角色們會進行一趟長途旅行，並與怪獸作戰。

❺ 李小龍可能是歷來最偉大的武俠片演員。

013 電影類型(2)

MP3 013

1 biographical movie
[ˌbaɪəˋgræfɪkḷ ˋmuvɪ]
(n.) 傳記電影

2 documentary
[ˌdɑkjəˋmɛntərɪ]
(n.) 紀錄片

3 animation
[ˌænəˋmeʃən]
(n.) 動畫片

4 romantic movie
[rəˋmæntɪk ˋmuvɪ]
(n.) 浪漫愛情片

5 coming-of-age movie
[ˋkʌmɪŋ ɑv edʒ ˋmuvɪ]
(n.) 成長電影/青春勵志片

❶ 傳記電影

Biographical movies tell the stories of real people.

真人故事

❷ 紀錄片

Morgan Spurlock made a great documentary about what happened to him when he ate lots of fast food.

拍了一部很棒的紀錄片

❸ 動畫片

Animations feature drawings rather than real actors and actresses.

動畫片以圖畫為特色

❹ 浪漫愛情片

Wendy enjoys love stories so she always likes watching romantic movies.

❺ 成長電影 / 青春勵志片

In the coming-of-age movie, the main character realizes what kind of man he wants to be.

他想要成為哪種類型的人

學更多

❶ biographical〈傳記的〉・story〈故事〉・real〈真實的、現實的〉・people〈人們〉

❷ happened〈happen（發生）的過去式〉・ate〈eat（吃）的過去式〉・lots of〈很多〉・fast food〈速食〉

❸ feature〈以…為特色〉・drawing〈圖畫〉・rather than〈而不是…〉・actor〈男演員〉・actress〈女演員〉

❹ enjoy〈喜愛〉・love〈愛情〉・always〈總是〉・romantic〈浪漫的〉

❺ coming-of-age〈成熟〉・main〈主要的〉・character〈角色〉・realize〈了解〉・kind〈類型〉

中譯

❶ 傳記電影述說真人真事。

❷ Morgan Spurlock 拍了一部很棒的紀錄片，內容是關於他吃了大量速食之後所發生的事。

❸ 動畫片的特色在於圖畫，而非真人的男女演員。

❹ Wendy 喜歡愛情故事，所以她總愛看浪漫愛情片。

❺ 在這部青春勵志片裡，主角領悟到自己想要成為什麼樣的人。

014 電影類型(3)

MP3 014

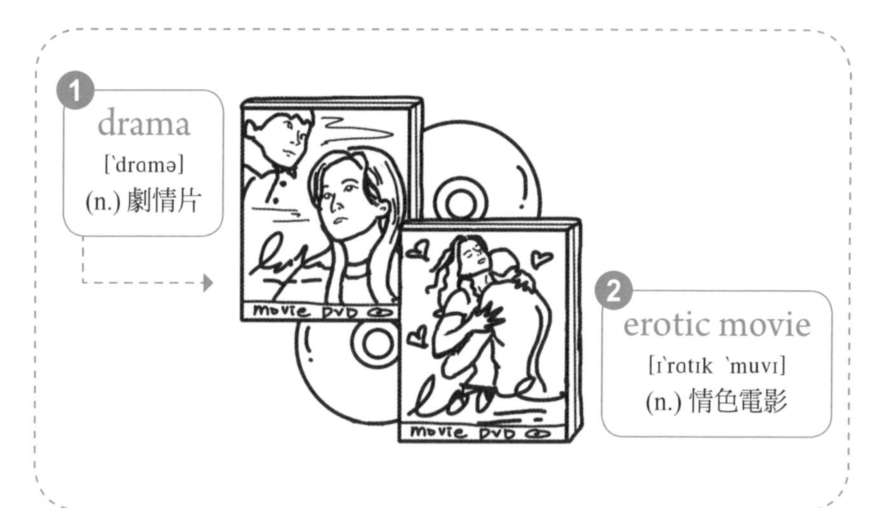

1 **drama**
[ˋdrɑmə]
(n.) 劇情片

2 **erotic movie**
[ɪˋrɑtɪk ˋmuvɪ]
(n.) 情色電影

3 **horror movie**
[ˋhɔrɚ ˋmuvɪ]
(n.) 恐怖片

4 **sci-fi movie**
[ˋsaɪˋfaɪ ˋmuvɪ]
(n.) 科幻片

「sci-fi」為「science fiction」的縮寫。

5 **war movie**
[wɔr ˋmuvɪ]
(n.) 戰爭片

6 **western**
[ˋwɛstɚn]
(n.) 美國西部片

❶ 劇情片
This is a wonderful drama. It tells a fascinating story.

❷ 情色電影
Children shouldn't watch erotic movies, because they contain scenes of people having sex.
包含人們性愛的場面

❸ 恐怖片
I hate being scared, so I try not to watch horror movies.
我討厭被驚嚇

❹ 科幻片
Sci-fi movies contain visions of the future.
包含對於未來的幻想

❺ 戰爭片
There were some real soldiers in that war movie.

❻ 美國西部片
Westerns feature cowboys.

學更多

❶ wonderful〈極好的〉・tell〈講述〉・fascinating〈吸引人的〉
❷ children〈child（兒童）的複數〉・erotic〈色情的〉・contain〈包含〉・scene〈場面〉・having〈have（進行）的 ing 型態〉・sex〈性愛〉
❸ hate〈討厭〉・scared〈scare（驚嚇）的過去分詞〉・try〈試圖〉・horror〈恐怖〉
❹ sci-fi〈科幻小說〉・vision〈幻想〉・future〈未來〉
❺ some〈一些〉・real〈真正的、實際的〉・soldier〈士兵〉・war〈戰爭〉
❻ feature〈以…為特色〉・cowboy〈牛仔〉

中譯

❶ 這是一部精彩的劇情片，它描述一個引人入勝的故事。
❷ 兒童不宜觀看情色電影，因為其中包含性愛場面。
❸ 我討厭被驚嚇，所以我盡量不看恐怖片。
❹ 科幻電影中蘊藏著對於未來世界的幻想。
❺ 那部戰爭片裡，有些是真正的士兵。
❻ 美國西部片的特色便是牛仔。

015 奧運項目(1)

MP3 015

❶ 籃球
Michael Jordan is one of the best basketball players of all time.

❷ 足球
In England, people call soccer "football."

❸ 排球
To play volleyball, you hit a ball over a high net with your hands or wrists.
把球打過網

❹ 曲棍球
There are two kinds of hockey—one is played on grass, and the other is played on ice.

❺ 壘球
Softball is similar to baseball, but the ball is bigger.
壘球和棒球相似

❻ 棒球
Many of the top baseball players play in the American Major Leagues.
頂尖棒球員

學更多

❶ best〈最好的〉・player〈球員〉・all time〈前所未有〉
❷ England〈英國〉・call〈稱呼〉・football〈足球〉
❸ hit〈打擊〉・over〈超過〉・net〈球網〉・hand〈手〉・wrist〈手腕〉
❹ kind〈種類〉・played〈play(打球)的過去分詞〉・grass〈草地〉・the other〈兩者中的另一個〉・ice〈冰〉
❺ similar〈相似的〉・ball〈球〉・bigger〈較大的,big(大的)的比較級〉
❻ many〈許多〉・top〈頂尖的〉・major〈主要的〉・league〈聯盟〉

中譯

❶ Michael Jordan 是有史以來最優秀的籃球運動員之一。
❷ 在英國,人們稱呼足球為「football」。
❸ 打排球時,你要用手或手腕將球擊飛過網。
❹ 曲棍球有兩種:一種在草地上進行,另一種則在冰上進行。
❺ 壘球和棒球很相似,但是壘球的球較大。
❻ 許多頂尖的棒球運動員都在美國大聯盟打球。

016 奧運項目(2)

MP3 016

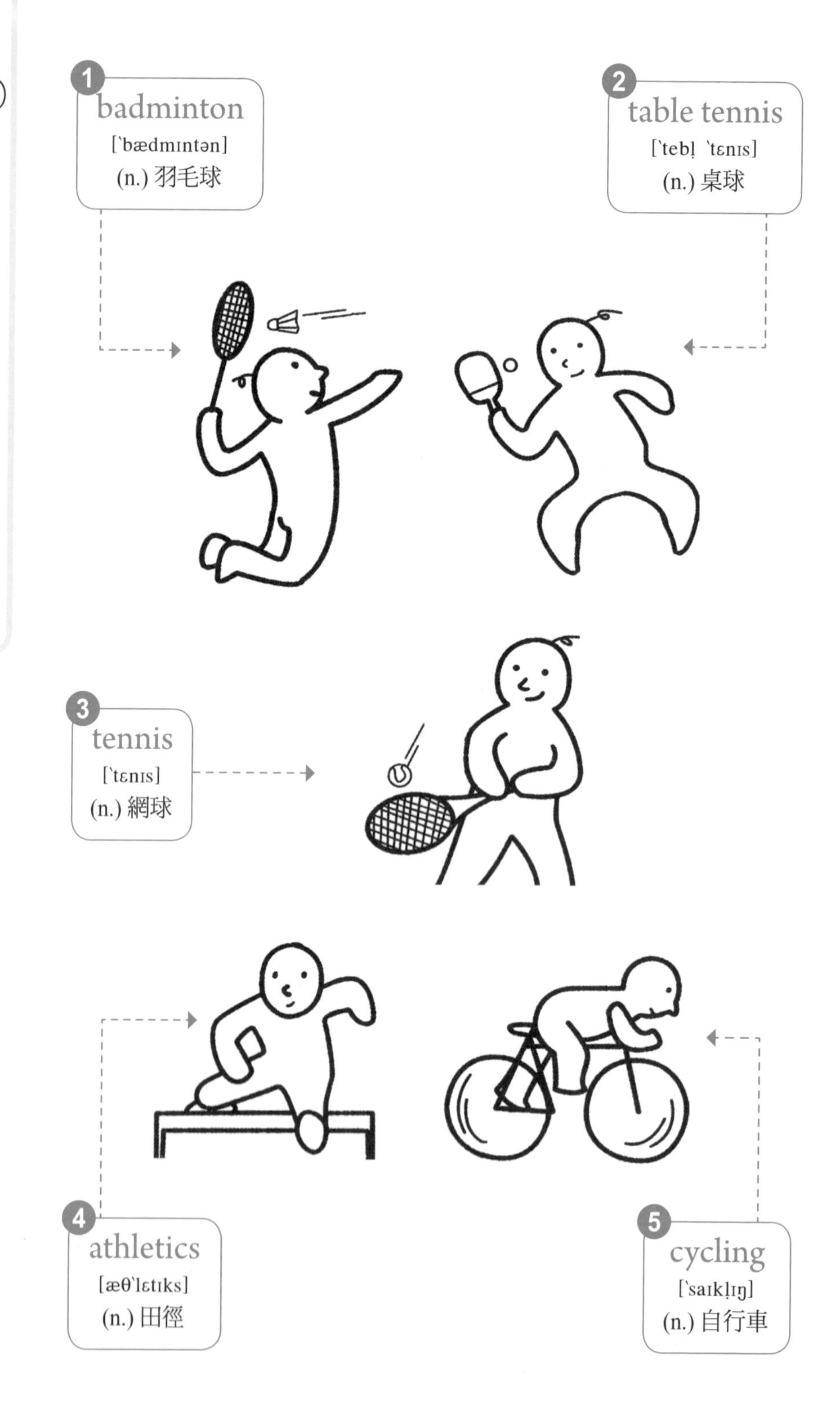

❶ 羽毛球
Badminton players hit a birdie across a high net.
把羽毛球打過高網

❷ 桌球
Table tennis is played with a small, light ball and small, hard paddles.

❸ 網球
Tennis can be played on grass, clay, and hard surfaces.
在草地、紅土和硬的地面上

❹ 田徑
I think athletics is really boring. I don't want to watch people running.

❺ 自行車
Sam's a cycling champion; he's very fast on a bike.

學更多

❶ hit〈打擊〉・birdie〈羽毛球〉・across〈越過〉・high〈高的〉・net〈網子〉
❷ table〈桌子〉・played〈play（打球）的過去分詞〉・light〈輕的〉・hard〈硬的〉・paddle〈球拍〉
❸ grass〈草地〉・clay〈泥土〉・surface〈地面〉
❹ really〈很〉・boring〈無聊的〉・running〈run（跑步）的 ing 型態〉
❺ champion〈冠軍〉・fast〈快的〉・bike〈自行車、腳踏車〉

中譯

❶ 羽毛球選手把羽毛球打過高網。
❷ 桌球是一種用輕巧的小球和堅硬的小型球拍來進行的運動。
❸ 網球可以在草地、紅土和硬地球場上進行。
❹ 我覺得田徑很無聊，我不想看人跑步。
❺ Sam 是自行車冠軍；他騎自行車的速度非常快。

017 奧運項目(3)

MP3 017

1 gymnastics
[dʒɪm`næstɪks]
(n.) 體操

2 synchronized swimming
[`sɪŋkrənaɪzd `swɪmmɪŋ]
(n.) 水上芭蕾

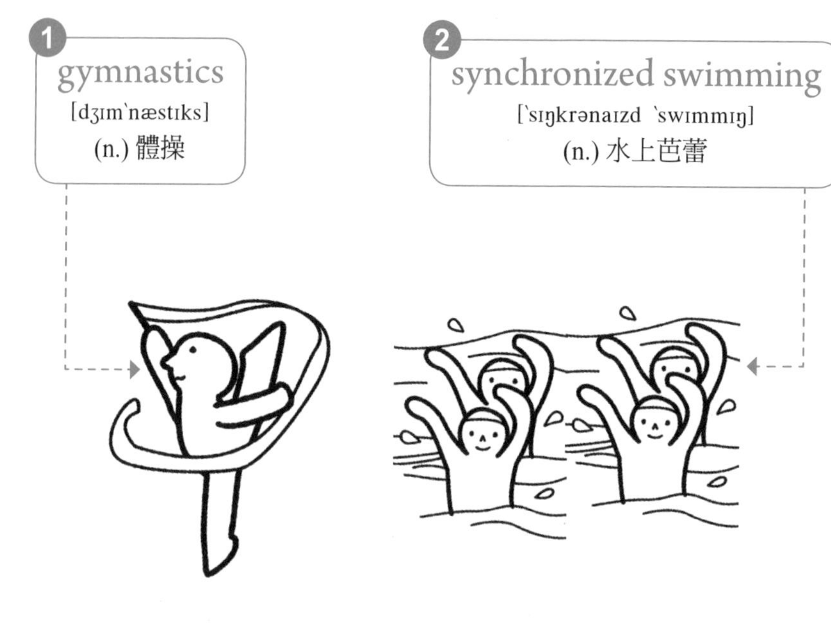

3 boat race
[bot res]
(n.) 划船比賽

4 swimming
[`swɪmɪŋ]
(n.) 游泳

5 diving
[`daɪvɪŋ]
(n.) 跳水

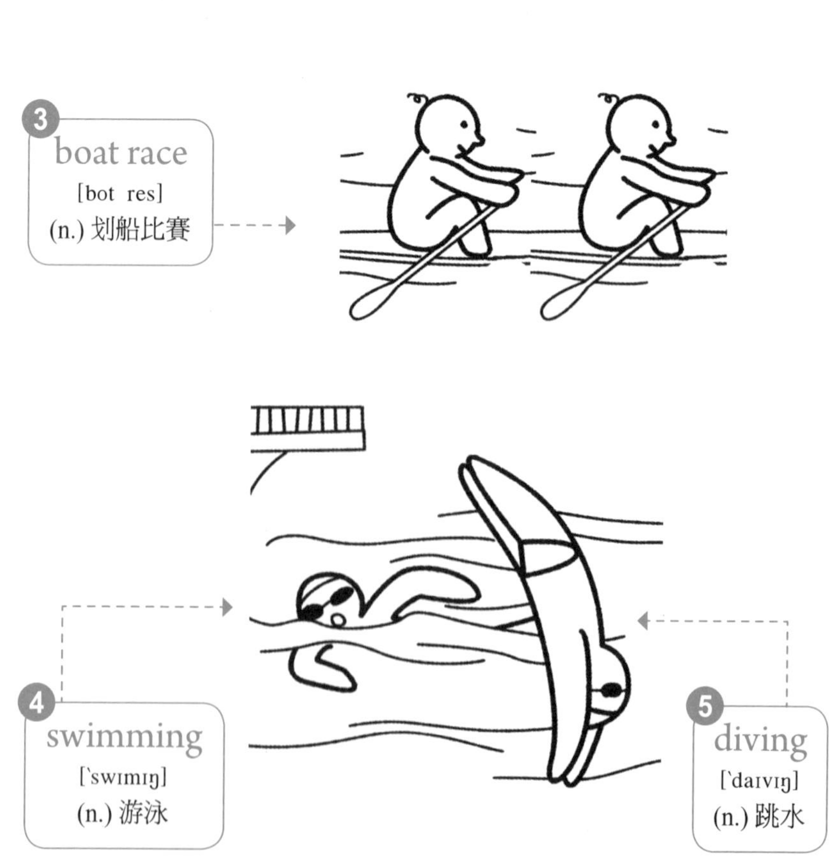

❶ 體操

Mary has been learning gymnastics for years, so she can now jump and swing on bars. It's great to watch.

已經持續學體操好幾年

在槓上跳躍與擺盪

❷ 水上芭蕾

In synchronized swimming, athletes make beautiful movements in a swimming pool.

運動員做很優美的動作

❸ 划船比賽

There are lots of different boat races with different types and sizes of boats.

不同的船型及大小

❹ 游泳

Swimming is my favorite type of exercise.

❺ 跳水

I love watching diving. Seeing people jump into water from great heights is very exciting.

從很高的地方跳入水裡

學更多

❶ learning〈learn（學習）的 ing 型態〉‧jump〈跳躍〉‧swing〈搖盪〉‧bar〈橫槓〉

❷ synchronized〈同步的、步驟一致的〉‧athlete〈運動員〉‧beautiful〈美麗的〉‧movement〈動作〉‧swimming pool〈游泳池〉

❸ different〈不同的、各種的〉‧boat〈小船〉‧race〈比賽〉‧type〈類型〉‧size〈大小〉

❹ favorite〈特別喜歡的〉‧exercise〈運動〉

❺ watching〈watch（觀看）的 ing 型態〉‧seeing〈see（看）的 ing 型態〉‧jump into〈跳入〉‧great〈程度超乎尋常的〉‧heights〈高處〉‧exciting〈令人興奮的〉

中譯

❶ Mary 已經持續學習體操許多年，所以她現在能在槓上騰躍與擺盪，看起來十分賞心悅目。

❷ 在水上芭蕾中，運動員會在泳池裡做出優美的動作。

❸ 因為船的類型及大小不同，有許多不同的划船比賽。

❹ 游泳是我最喜歡的運動項目。

❺ 我喜歡觀賞跳水。看人們從高處跳進水裡是很刺激的事。

018

奧運項目(4)

MP3 018

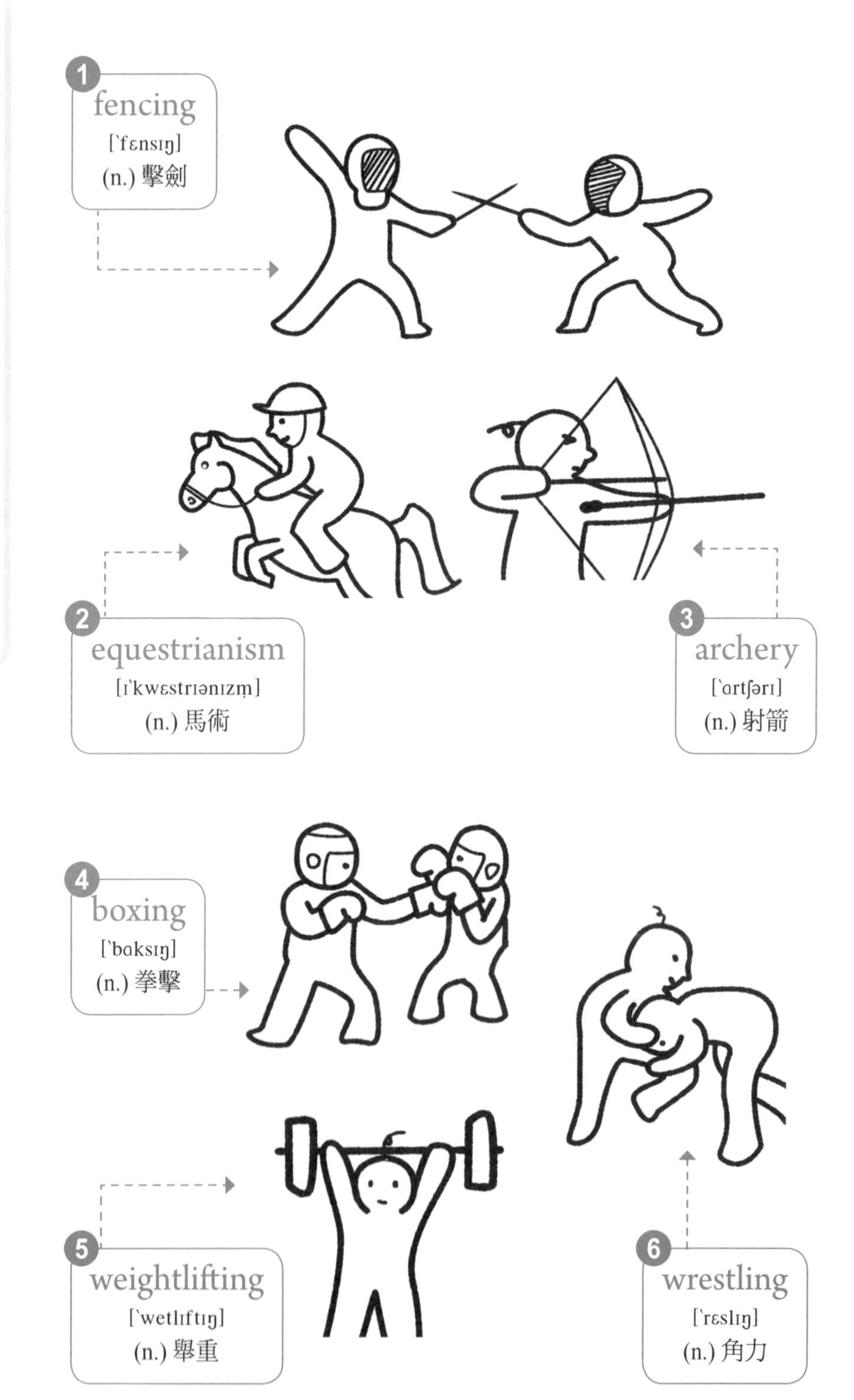

❶ 擊劍
In fencing, people use very thin, light swords.

❷ 馬術
In equestrianism, men and women display their skills with horses.
展示他們的騎馬技巧

❸ 射箭
In archery, people shoot arrows at a target.
把箭射向目標

❹ 拳擊
Some people think boxing is violent and should be banned.
應該被禁止

❺ 舉重
People who want to practice weightlifting have to be very strong.

❻ 角力
There are many kinds of wrestling, but wrestlers usually try to throw each other to the ground.
把對方摔倒在地

學更多

❶ use〈使用〉・thin〈薄的〉・light〈輕的〉・sword〈劍〉
❷ men〈man（男人）的複數〉・women〈woman（女人）的複數〉・display〈展示〉・skill〈技巧〉・horse〈馬〉
❸ shoot〈射〉・arrow〈箭〉・target〈目標〉
❹ violent〈暴力的〉・should〈應該〉・banned〈ban（禁止）的過去分詞〉
❺ practice〈練習〉・have to〈必須〉・strong〈強壯的〉
❻ wrestler〈角力選手〉・throw〈摔下〉・each other〈彼此〉・ground〈地面〉

中譯

❶ 在擊劍中，人們使用非常薄且輕巧的劍。
❷ 在馬術中，男士們和女士們展現他們的騎馬技巧。
❸ 在射箭中，大家把箭射向目標。
❹ 有些人認為拳擊很暴力，並且應該被禁止。
❺ 想要練習舉重的人必須很強壯。
❻ 角力有很多種，但角力選手通常都會試著把對手摔倒在地。

019 星座(1)

MP3 019

1 Aries
[ˋɛriz]
(n.) 牡羊座

3月21日 | 4月19日

2 Taurus
[ˋtɔrəs]
(n.) 金牛座

4月20日 | 5月20日

3 Gemini
[ˋdʒɛmə͵naɪ]
(n.) 雙子座

5月21日 | 6月20日

4 Cancer
[ˋkænsɚ]
(n.) 巨蟹座

6月21日 | 7月22日

5 Leo
[ˋlio]
(n.) 獅子座

7月23日 | 8月22日

6 Virgo
[ˋvɝgo]
(n.) 處女座

8月23日 | 9月22日

❶ 牡羊座

My brother's an Aries, so he's supposed to be energetic and creative.

他被認為應該是…

❷ 金牛座

She's a typical Taurus; she's stable and passive.

她很穩重、被動

❸ 雙子座

Frank is a Gemini, but he's not very versatile.

他不會非常反覆無常

❹ 巨蟹座

My mother is a Cancer, and, typically, she's very loyal and protective.

她很忠實且關切、保護別人

❺ 獅子座

Leos are supposed to be proud and fierce.

❻ 處女座

Virgos are supposed to be great students and communicators.

學更多

❶ be supposed to〈認為應該〉‧energetic〈充滿活力的〉‧creative〈有創造力的〉

❷ typical〈典型的〉‧stable〈穩定的〉‧passive〈被動的〉

❸ very〈非常〉‧versatile〈反覆無常的〉

❹ typically〈典型地〉‧loyal〈忠誠的〉‧protective〈對人很關切保護的〉

❺ proud〈驕傲的〉‧fierce〈凶狠的〉

❻ great〈優秀的〉‧student〈學生〉‧communicator〈溝通者〉

中譯

❶ 我弟弟是牡羊座，所以他應該是個充滿活力及創造力的人。

❷ 她是典型的金牛座，既穩重又被動。

❸ Frank 是雙子座，但他並不會非常反覆無常。

❹ 我母親是巨蟹座，且典型地個性非常忠實、對他人有強烈的保護欲。

❺ 獅子座一般被認為既驕傲又兇悍。

❻ 處女座一般被認為是優秀的學生，且善於溝通。

020 星座(2)

MP3 020

1 **Libra** [ˋlaɪbrə] (n.) 天秤座　9月23日｜10月22日

2 **Scorpio** [ˋskɔrpɪ.o] (n.) 天蠍座　10月23日｜11月21日

3 **Sagittarius** [.sædʒɪˋtɛrɪəs] (n.) 射手座　11月22日｜12月21日

4 **Capricorn** [ˋkæprɪkɔrn] (n.) 魔羯座　12月22日｜1月19日

5 **Aquarius** [əˋkwɛrɪəs] (n.) 水瓶座　1月20日｜2月18日

6 **Pisces** [ˋpɪsiz] (n.) 雙魚座　2月19日｜3月20日

❶ 天秤座

Like most Libras, Dave likes to put others at ease.

讓別人感覺輕鬆自在

❷ 天蠍座

A typical Scorpio should be reserved and secretive.

❸ 射手座

My big brother is a typical Sagittarius, which means he's quite spontaneous.

他相當率直

❹ 魔羯座

I'm a Capricorn, which means I should be responsible but mistrusting.

❺ 水瓶座

Those born in the sign of Aquarius are supposed to be clever and stubborn.

那些出生在水瓶星座的人（= those who are born in the sign of Aquarius）

❻ 雙魚座

She's a Pisces, so I guess she'll be compassionate.

她會很有同情心

學更多

❶ most〈大部分〉・put〈使處於某種狀態〉・others〈其他人〉・ease〈自在〉
❷ typical〈典型的〉・reserved〈沉默寡言的〉・secretive〈守口如瓶的〉
❸ big brother〈哥哥〉・mean〈表示…的意思〉・quite〈相當〉・spontaneous〈率直的〉
❹ responsible〈認真負責的〉・mistrusting〈不信任的、懷疑的〉
❺ be born〈出生〉・sign〈符號〉・clever〈聰明的〉・stubborn〈頑固的〉
❻ guess〈猜測〉・compassionate〈有同情心的〉

中譯

❶ 和大部分的天秤座一樣，Dave 喜歡讓別人感到輕鬆自在。
❷ 一個典型的天蠍座，應該是沉默寡言且守口如瓶的。
❸ 我哥哥是典型的射手座，這意味著他的個性相當率直。
❹ 我是魔羯座，這意味著我應該是認真負責，但對一切事物抱持著懷疑的個性。
❺ 那些出生在水瓶座的人，一般被認為是聰明且固執的。
❻ 她是雙魚座，所以我猜想她是個富有同情心的人。

021 星座(3)

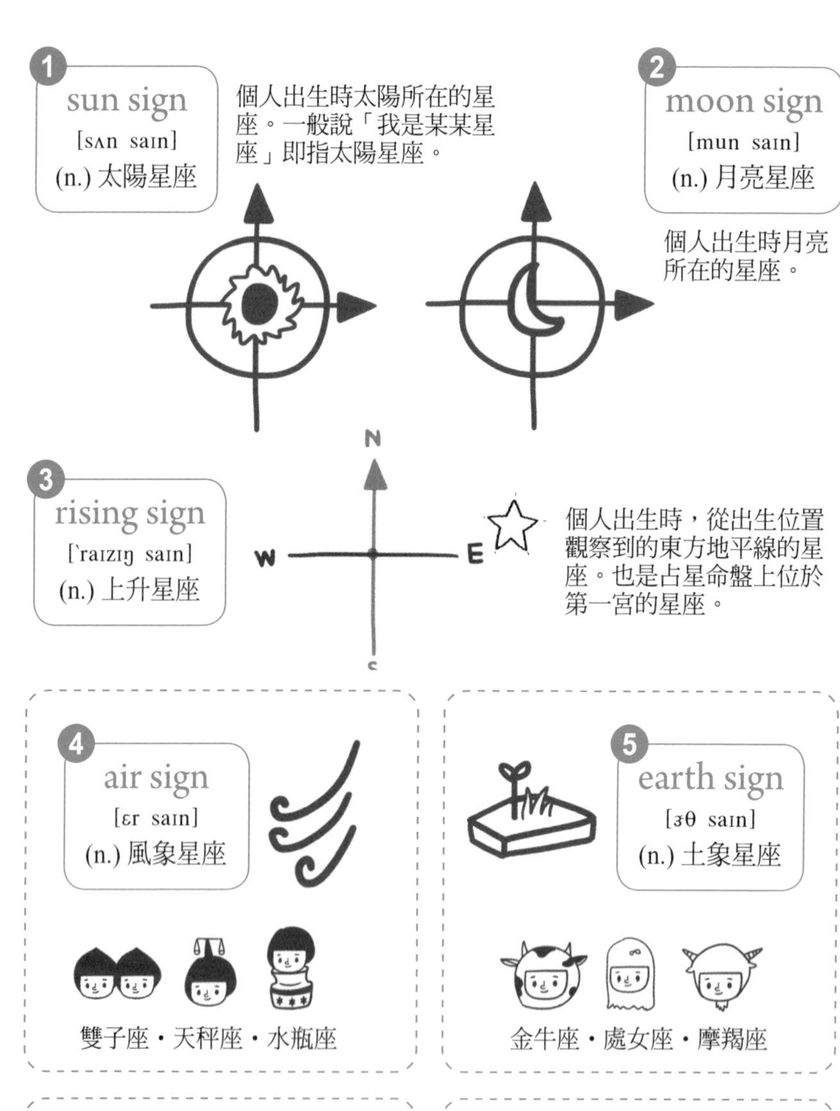

1 sun sign
[sʌn saɪn]
(n.) 太陽星座

個人出生時太陽所在的星座。一般說「我是某某星座」即指太陽星座。

2 moon sign
[mun saɪn]
(n.) 月亮星座

個人出生時月亮所在的星座。

3 rising sign
[\`raɪzɪŋ saɪn]
(n.) 上升星座

個人出生時，從出生位置觀察到的東方地平線的星座。也是占星命盤上位於第一宮的星座。

MP3 021

4 air sign
[ɛr saɪn]
(n.) 風象星座

雙子座・天秤座・水瓶座

5 earth sign
[ɝθ saɪn]
(n.) 土象星座

金牛座・處女座・摩羯座

6 fire sign
[faɪr saɪn]
(n.) 火象星座

牡羊座・獅子座・射手座

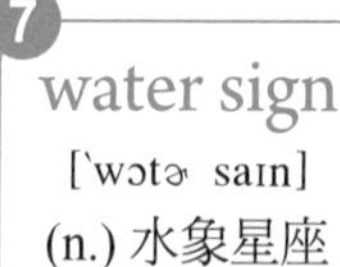

7 water sign
[\`wɔtɚ saɪn]
(n.) 水象星座

巨蟹座・天蠍座・雙魚座

❶ 太陽星座

The zodiac consists of 12 different sun signs. Yours is based on your birth date.

由 12 個不同的太陽星座構成

❷ 月亮星座

Moon signs help define our emotional development and personality.

❸ 上升星座

The rising sign is the zodiac sign rising in the east when you're born.

黃道 12 個宮位的各星座　當你出生時

❹ 風象星座

❺ 土象星座

Air signs are supposed to be outgoing, while earth signs are reserved.

❻ 火象星座

❼ 水象星座

Fire signs in the constellation have a forceful or powerful element to them, while water signs are more emotional in nature.

天生情感豐富

學更多

❶ zodiac〈黃道帶〉• consist〈構成〉• different〈不同的〉• sign〈符號〉• yours〈你的（東西）〉• be based on〈以…為根據〉• birth〈出生〉• date〈日期〉

❷ define〈定義〉• emotional〈感情的〉• development〈發展〉• personality〈性格〉

❸ rising〈上升的〉• rising〈rise（升起）的 ing 型態〉• east〈東方〉• be born〈出生〉

❹ ❺ air〈空氣〉• be supposed to〈認為應該〉• outgoing〈外向的〉• while〈然而〉• earth〈土〉• reserved〈沉默寡言的〉

❻ ❼ constellation〈星座〉• forceful〈堅強的〉• powerful〈強大的〉• element〈元素〉• emotional〈容易動感情的〉• nature〈天性〉

中譯

❶ 黃道帶由 12 個不同的太陽星座所構成；你的太陽星座是根據你的出生日期而定。

❷ 月亮星座有助於定義我們的情緒發展和性格。

❸ 上升星座是當你出生時，在東方升起的星座。

❹ ❺ 風象星座被認為是外向的，而土象星座則被認為是沉默寡言的。

❻ ❼ 在星座中，火象星座本身具有堅強、強大的元素；而水象星座則是天生情感豐富。

022 音樂類型(1)

MP3 022

1 blues [bluz] (n.) 藍調

源自美國早期黑人音樂中的哀傷歌曲。由「blues」翻譯得名。

2 jazz [dʒæz] (n.) 爵士

源自美國黑人音樂。即興演奏為其特色。

3 soul [sol] (n.) 靈魂樂

結合藍調與福音音樂的音樂型態。伴隨節奏拍掌、即興動作是其特徵。

4 country [ˋkʌntrɪ] (n.) 鄉村音樂

源於美國南部的音樂型態。歌詞描寫生活，琅琅上口。

5 folk [fok] (n.) 民謠

來自民間的純樸音樂，形式簡單、真情流露且具風土特色。

6 gospel [ˋgɑspḷ] (n.) 福音歌曲

7 spiritual music [ˋspɪrɪtʃuəl ˋmjuzɪk] (n.) 心靈音樂

❶ 藍調

The blues began with black people in America's Deep South.

美國深南部的黑人

❷ 爵士

Some jazz is very calm, but other kinds are wild and crazy.

❸ 靈魂樂

Soul music is full of emotion; it comes from the heart.

充滿感情

❹ 鄉村音樂

Taylor Swift is one of the world's biggest country music stars.

鄉村音樂歌手

❺ 民謠

Folk music is based on thoughtful, emotional words.

建立在…的基礎上、以…為起點

❻ 福音歌曲

Gospel is based on the music traditionally heard in Southern US churches.

傳統上會在美國南部教堂聽到的音樂

❼ 心靈音樂

Spiritual music should be gentle and soft, so that when you listen to it,

應該是和緩、輕柔的

you can think about God.

學更多

❶ black people〈黑人〉• Deep South〈深南部（美國南部的一個文化與地理區域名稱）〉
❷ calm〈平靜的〉• other〈其他的〉• kind〈種類〉• wild〈狂野的〉• crazy〈瘋狂的〉
❸ full of〈充滿…的〉• emotion〈感情〉• heart〈心靈〉
❹ world〈世界〉• biggest〈最受歡迎的，big（大受歡迎的）的最高級〉• star〈明星〉
❺ thoughtful〈富有思想的〉• emotional〈激起情感的〉• words〈言辭、歌詞〉
❻ traditionally〈傳統上〉• heard〈hear（聽）的過去分詞〉• southern〈南方的〉
❼ spiritual〈心靈的〉• gentle〈和緩的〉• soft〈輕柔的〉• listen〈聽〉• God〈上帝〉

中譯

❶ 藍調音樂起源於美國深南部的黑人。
❷ 有些爵士樂的風格很平靜，但有些則狂野又瘋狂。
❸ 靈魂樂充滿情感，它源自於心靈。
❹ Taylor Swift 是全球最受歡迎的鄉村音樂歌手之一。
❺ 歌詞富含寓意與情感，是民謠音樂的基本形式。
❻ 福音歌曲源自傳統上會在美國南部教堂聽到的音樂。
❼ 心靈音樂應該是和緩又輕柔的，以便於聆聽時，你可以在心裡想著上帝。

023 音樂類型(2)

MP3 023

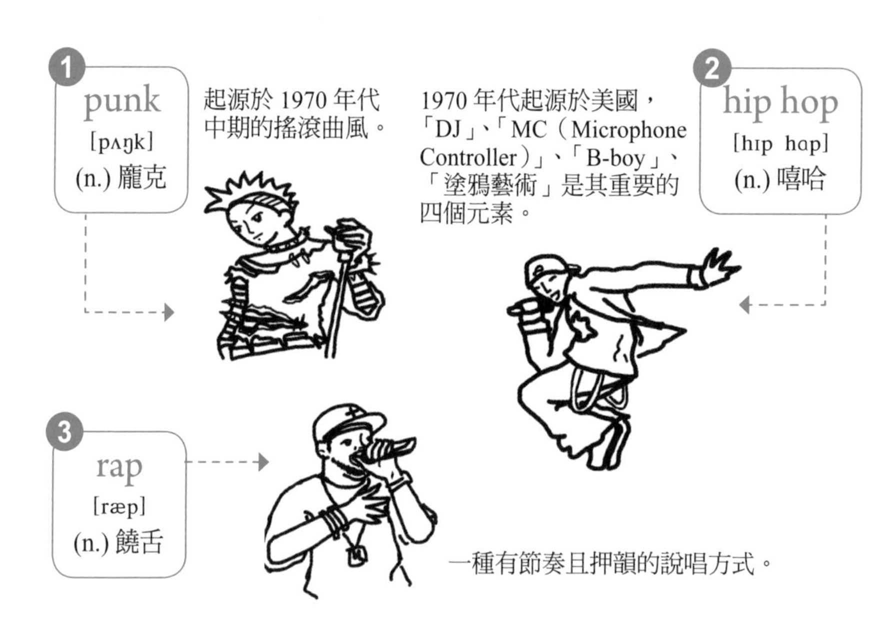

1 punk [pʌŋk] (n.) 龐克

起源於 1970 年代中期的搖滾曲風。

2 hip hop [hɪp hɑp] (n.) 嘻哈

1970 年代起源於美國，「DJ」、「MC（Microphone Controller）」、「B-boy」、「塗鴉藝術」是其重要的四個元素。

3 rap [ræp] (n.) 饒舌

一種有節奏且押韻的說唱方式。

4 rock & roll [rɑk ænd rol] (n.) 搖滾

5 heavy metal [ˋhɛvɪ ˋmɛtḷ] (n.) 重金屬

6 classical music [ˋklæsɪkḷ ˋmjuzɪk] (n.) 古典音樂

7 pop [pɑp] (n.) 流行音樂

❶ 龐克

Punk is usually very angry, rebellious music.

❷ 嘻哈

Hip hop is closely associated with breakdancing.
被緊密地和…連結

❸ 饒舌

The words in rap music are spoken rather than sung.
是被唸的而不是被唱的

❹ 搖滾

Rock and roll music usually features a lot of people playing electric guitars.
彈奏電吉他

❺ 重金屬

Heavy metal is usually fast, angry-sounding guitar music.
聽起來很憤怒

❻ 古典音樂

Mozart and Beethoven are two of the biggest names in classical music.
兩位最偉大的人物

❼ 流行音樂

Pop music is light, happy, and it's what most young teenagers prefer to listen to.
大部分年輕人比較喜歡聽的

學更多

❶ usually〈通常地〉・angry〈憤怒〉・rebellious〈叛逆的〉
❷ hip〈通曉的、嬉皮的〉・hop〈蹦跳〉・associated〈關聯的〉・breakdancing〈霹靂舞〉
❸ words〈歌詞〉・spoken〈speak（說）的過去分詞〉・sung〈sing（唱）的過去分詞〉
❹ rock〈搖滾〉・roll〈搖擺〉・feature〈以…為特色〉・electric〈電的〉・guitar〈吉他〉
❺ heavy〈沉重有力的〉・metal〈金屬〉・fast〈快的〉・sounding〈有…聲音的〉
❻ biggest〈最偉大的，big（偉大的）的最高級〉・name〈著名的人物〉・classical〈古典的〉
❼ light〈輕鬆的〉・young〈年輕的〉・teenager〈青少年〉・prefer〈更喜歡〉

中譯

❶ 龐克通常是非常憤怒、叛逆的音樂形式。
❷ 嘻哈和霹靂舞有密切的關聯。
❸ 饒舌音樂的歌詞是要用唸的，而非用唱的。
❹ 搖滾樂的特色，通常就是許多人彈奏電吉他
❺ 重金屬通常是節奏快速、聽起來感覺很憤怒的吉他音樂。
❻ 莫札特和貝多芬是古典音樂界裡兩位最偉大的人物。
❼ 流行音樂輕快又開心，是大部分年輕人比較喜歡聽的音樂類型。

024 電視節目(1)

MP3 024

❶ 連續劇

The serial drama told a story over 20 separate shows.

在不同的 20 集期間

❷ 迷你影集

A miniseries is a bit like a serial drama, but it's shorter.

迷你影集有點像連續劇

❸ 綜藝節目

On the variety show, lots of performers show off their skills.

賣弄

❹ 紀錄片

Dan enjoys documentaries, so he always watches Discovery or National Geographic.

探索頻道或國家地理頻道

❺ 實境節目

Reality television is supposed to show real people in real situations.

演出真人實境的內容

學更多

❶ serial〈連續的〉・drama〈戲劇〉・told〈tell（講述）的過去式〉・over〈在…期間〉・separate〈個別的、不同的〉

❷ a bit〈有點〉・shorter〈較短的，short（短的）的比較級〉

❸ variety〈綜藝表演〉・lots of〈很多〉・performer〈表演者〉・skill〈技巧〉

❹ discovery〈發現〉・national〈國家的〉・geographic〈地理的〉

❺ reality〈真實〉・television〈電視〉・be supposed to〈認為應該〉・show〈演出〉・real〈真正的〉・situation〈場景〉

中譯

❶ 那齣連續劇分成 20 集來敘述一個故事。

❷ 迷你影集有點像連續劇，但集數比較少。

❸ 在綜藝節目裡，許多表演者會刻意展現他們的技巧。

❹ Dan 喜歡看紀錄片，所以他總是看探索頻道或國家地理頻道。

❺ 實境節目會播出真人實境的演出內容。

025 電視節目(2)

MP3 025

1. **cooking show**
[ˋkʊkɪŋ ʃo]
(n.) 烹飪節目

2. **travel program**
[ˋtrævḷ ˋprogræm]
(n.) 旅遊節目

3. **game show**
[gem ʃo]
(n.) 益智遊戲節目

4. **animated series**
[ˋænə͵metɪd ˋsiriz]
(n.) 卡通

5. **children's television show**
[ˋtʃɪldrənz ˋtɛlə͵vɪʒən ʃo]
(n.) 兒童節目

❶ 烹飪節目
I learned how to make pasta by watching cooking shows.
如何做義大利麵

❷ 旅遊節目
My favorite shows on TV are the travel programs.

❸ 益智遊戲節目
I'm going on a game show to try and win some prizes.
我要參加益智遊戲節目

❹ 卡通
This animated series is beautifully drawn.

❺ 兒童節目
The little kids love the children's television show.

學更多

❶ learned〈learn（學習）的過去式〉・pasta〈義大利麵〉・cooking〈烹調〉
❷ favorite〈特別喜愛的〉・show〈節目〉・travel〈旅行〉・program〈節目〉
❸ game〈遊戲〉・try〈試圖〉・win〈贏得〉・prize〈獎品〉
❹ animated〈卡通片的〉・series〈系列〉・beautifully〈美麗地〉・drawn〈draw（畫）的過去分詞〉
❺ little〈幼小的〉・kid〈小孩〉・children〈child（小孩）的複數〉・television〈電視〉

中譯

❶ 我看烹飪節目學習如何烹調義大利麵。
❷ 我最喜歡的電視節目是旅遊節目。
❸ 我要參加益智遊戲節目，試著贏一些獎品回來。
❹ 這部卡通畫得很精美。
❺ 幼童都喜歡看兒童節目。

026 電視節目(3)

MP3 026

1. **news program** [njuz `progræm] (n.) 新聞節目
2. **sports** [spɔrts] (n.) 運動節目
3. **talk show** [tɔk ʃo] (n.) 談話性節目（脫口秀）
4. **reality competition show** [ri`ælətɪ ˏkɑmpə`tɪʃən ʃo] (n.) 選秀節目
5. **celebrity roast** [sɪ`lɛbrətɪ rost] (n.) 名人嘲諷秀

❶ 新聞節目

The old man watches news programs to find out what's going on in the world.

世界上發生了什麼事

❷ 運動節目

The man sat down and turned on ESPN to watch some sports.

❸ 談話性節目（脫口秀）

The talk show host interviews lots of big stars.

訪問很多大明星

❹ 選秀節目

American Idol is one of the world's biggest reality competition shows.

❺ 名人嘲諷秀

I hate Jim Carrey movies, but he's funny when he talks about other stars at celebrity roasts.

當他談論其他明星時

學更多

❶ old〈上了年紀的〉‧news〈新聞〉‧program〈節目〉‧find out〈得知〉‧world〈世界〉

❷ sat down〈sit down（坐下）的過去式〉‧turned on〈turn on（打開）的過去式〉

❸ talk〈談話〉‧host〈主持人〉‧interview〈訪問〉‧lots of〈很多〉‧big〈大受歡迎的〉‧star〈明星〉

❹ idol〈偶像〉‧biggest〈最受歡迎的，big（大受歡迎的）的最高級〉‧reality〈真實〉‧competition〈比賽〉

❺ hate〈不喜歡〉‧funny〈有趣的〉‧talk〈談論〉‧celebrity〈名人〉‧roast〈批評〉

中譯

❶ 那名年長者看新聞節目來知曉世界上發生了什麼事。

❷ 那名男子坐下來，並打開 ESPN 頻道觀賞運動節目。

❸ 那名脫口秀主持人會訪問許多大明星。

❹ 「美國偶像」是全球最受歡迎的選秀節目之一。

❺ 我不喜歡金凱瑞的電影，但他在名人嘲諷秀談論其他明星時，總是很逗趣。

027 電影工作人員(1)

MP3 027

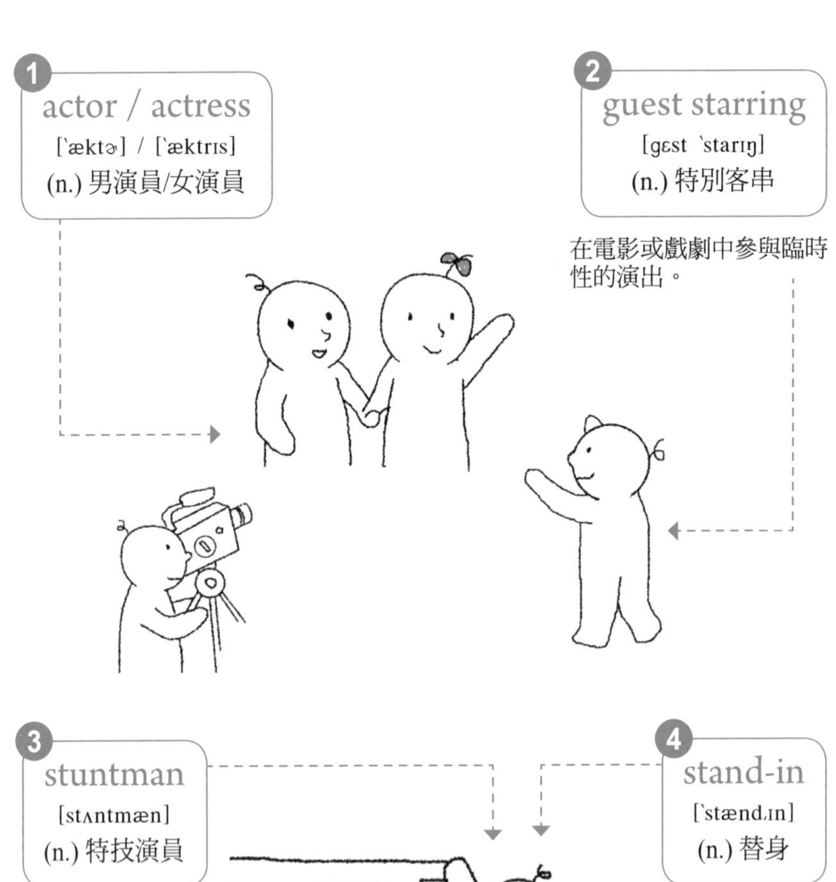

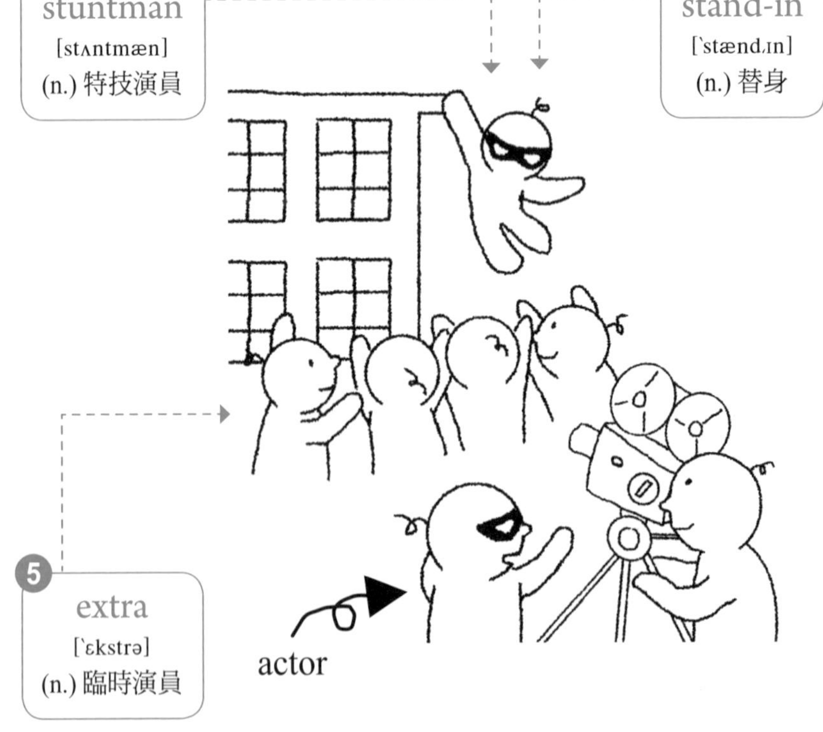

❶ 男演員 / 女演員

The romantic movie was terrible because I didn't believe the actor and actress loved each other.

男演員和女演員愛上了對方

❷ 特別客串

Matt Damon was guest starring in this movie.

❸ 特技演員

Stuntmen do dangerous things, so that actors won't get hurt.

❹ 替身

Stand-ins have to be ready to go on stage when the main actor or actress is sick.

必須隨時準備上場

❺ 臨時演員

Sandy works as an extra, and she appears as a minor character in several movies.

擔任臨時演員　當配角

學更多

❶ romantic〈浪漫的〉・terrible〈糟糕的〉・believe〈相信〉・each other〈對方〉

❷ guest〈特邀的〉・starring〈主演〉・movie〈電影〉

❸ dangerous〈危險的〉・get hurt〈受傷〉

❹ ready〈準備好的〉・stage〈舞台〉・main〈主要的〉・sick〈生病的〉

❺ work〈工作〉・as〈作為〉・appear〈出現〉・minor〈次要的〉・character〈角色〉・several〈一些〉

中譯

❶ 浪漫愛情電影很難看，因為我不相信男演員和女演員會愛上對方。

❷ Matt Damon 在這部電影裡擔綱特別客串演出。

❸ 危險的表演交給特技演員來做，所以演員們不會受傷。

❹ 當男女主角生病時，替身必須隨時準備上場。

❺ Sandy 的工作是擔任臨時演員，她在一些電影中飾演配角。

028 電影工作人員(2)

MP3 028

❶ 編劇

Tony would love to become a screenwriter and write movie scripts.

想要　寫電影劇本

❷ 武術指導

The stunt coordinator planned the action scenes in the movie.

設計武打場面

❸ 美術指導

The art director is trying to prepare the set for the movie.

❹ 服裝設計

The actress went to see the costume designer to talk about her dress.

❺ 化妝師

Ian is a makeup artist who specializes in making people look scary.

使得人們看起來很可怕

學更多

❶ become〈成為〉‧write〈寫〉‧movie〈電影〉‧script〈劇本〉

❷ stunt〈特技動作〉‧coordinator〈協調者〉‧planned〈plan（規劃）的過去式〉‧action〈動作〉‧scene〈場面〉

❸ art〈美術〉‧director〈指揮、負責人〉‧trying〈try（試圖、努力）的 ing 型態〉‧prepare〈準備〉‧set〈場景〉

❹ actress〈女演員〉‧costume〈服裝〉‧designer〈設計師〉‧dress〈服裝〉

❺ makeup〈化妝〉‧artist〈藝術家〉‧specialize〈專門從事〉‧scary〈可怕的〉

中譯

❶ Tony 想要成為編劇，寫些電影劇本。

❷ 武術指導設計了電影裡的武打場面。

❸ 那名美術指導正努力替電影安排場景。

❹ 那位女演員去找服裝設計，討論關於她的服裝。

❺ Ian 是名化妝師，專門替人們畫恐怖的妝容。

029 電影工作人員(3)

MP3 029

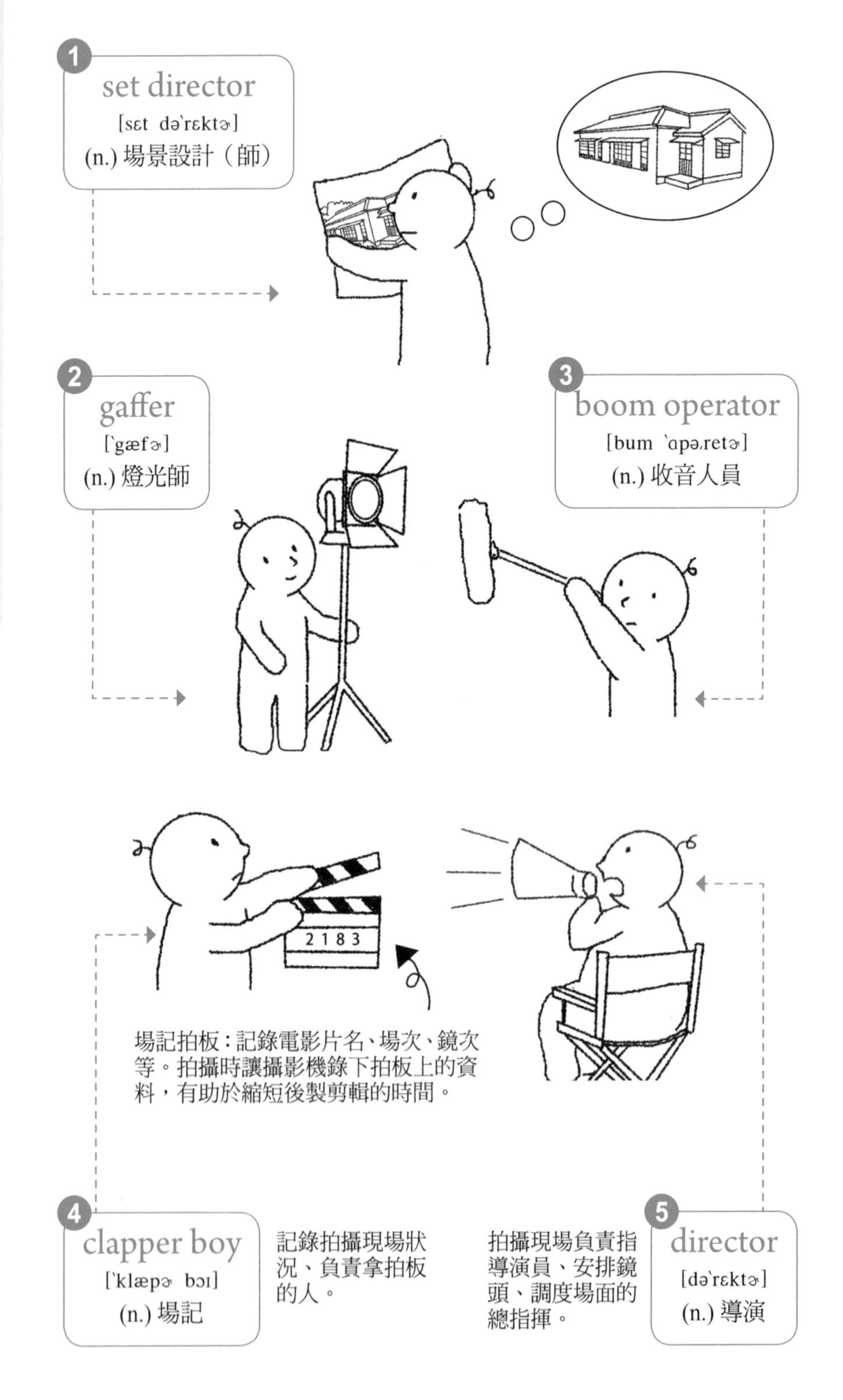

❶ 場景設計（師）

The director wasn't happy with how the set looked, so he fired the set director.

場景呈現的樣子

❷ 燈光師

My brother works as a gaffer for a famous Hollywood film studio.

❸ 收音人員

Boom operators need to be quite strong to hold the big microphone over the actors' heads all day.

在演員頭上舉大型麥克風

❹ 場記

The clapper boy has to announce that a scene is being filmed.

一個鏡頭正在進行拍攝

❺ 導演

The director told the leading actress to use more emotion in her acting.

女主角

學更多

❶ happy〈滿意的〉・set〈場景〉・fired〈fire（開除）的過去式〉

❷ brother〈兄弟〉・work〈工作〉・as〈作為〉・famous〈有名的〉・Hollywood〈好萊塢〉・film〈電影〉・studio〈工作室、電影攝影棚〉

❸ boom〈（話筒）吊杆〉・operator〈操作者〉・quite〈很〉・strong〈強壯的〉・hold〈托住〉・microphone〈麥克風〉・over〈在…上方〉・head〈頭〉・all day〈一整天〉

❹ clapper〈拍板〉・announce〈宣布〉・scene〈一個鏡頭〉・filmed〈film（拍攝）的過去分詞〉

❺ leading〈主要的〉・actress〈女演員〉・emotion〈感情〉・acting〈演技〉

中譯

❶ 導演對呈現的場景不滿意，所以開除了場景設計師。

❷ 我弟弟在一間知名的好萊塢電影攝影棚當燈光師。

❸ 收音人員必須很強壯，才能把大型麥克風舉在演員頭上一整天。

❹ 場記必須向現場人員宣布，目前正在進行某個鏡頭的拍攝。

❺ 導演告訴女主角要在演技中投入更多感情。

030 飯店設施(1)

MP3 030

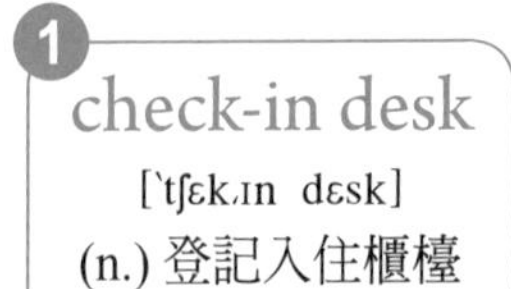
1 check-in desk
[ˋtʃɛk͵ɪn dɛsk]
(n.) 登記入住櫃檯

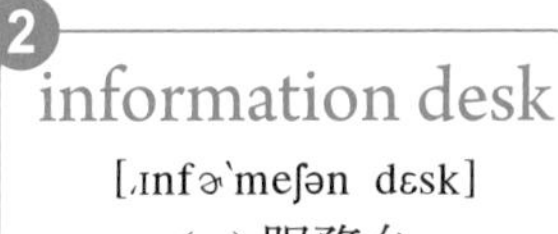
2 information desk
[͵ɪnfɚˋmeʃən dɛsk]
(n.) 服務台

3 hotel lobby
[hoˋtɛl ˋlɑbɪ]
(n.) 飯店大廳

4 parking lot
[ˋpɑrkɪŋ lɑt]
(n.) 停車場

5 atrium garden
[ˋɑtrɪəm ˋgɑrdn̩]
(n.) 中庭花園

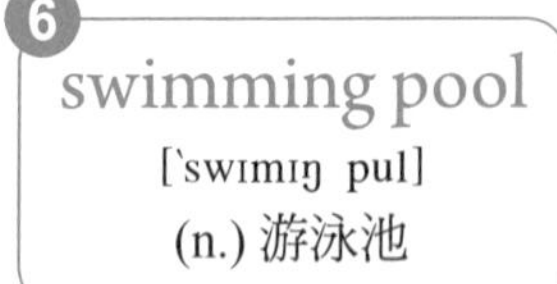
6 swimming pool
[ˋswɪmɪŋ pul]
(n.) 游泳池

7 room
[rum]
(n.) 房間/客房

❶ 登記入住櫃檯
Jasmine had to wait 20 minutes at the check-in desk when she arrived at the hotel.
必須等候 20 分鐘

❷ 服務台
Rich went to the information desk to get a map of the city.
索取一份市區地圖

❸ 飯店大廳
Wow, the hotel lobby in the Mandarin Oriental in New York City is spectacular!

❹ 停車場
He left his car in the parking lot and went into the hotel.
他把他的車子停在停車場

❺ 中庭花園
Tom sat by a large bush in the hotel's atrium garden.
Tom 坐在一棵大灌木樹旁

❻ 游泳池
The hotel has swimming pools inside and outside.

❼ 房間 / 客房
The businessman asked for a luxury room to sleep in.
睡在一間豪華客房裡

學更多

❶ check-in〈登記入住〉・desk〈櫃檯〉・arrived〈arrive（到達）的過去式〉
❷ went〈go（去）的過去式〉・information〈資訊〉・map〈地圖〉・city〈城市〉
❸ lobby〈大廳〉・Mandarin Oriental〈文華東方酒店〉・spectacular〈壯觀的〉
❹ left〈leave（留下）的過去式〉・parking〈停車〉・lot〈作特地用處的一塊地〉
❺ sat〈sit（坐）的過去式〉・by〈在…旁邊〉・bush〈灌木〉・atrium〈中庭〉
❻ swimming〈游泳〉・pool〈水池〉・inside〈在裡面〉・outside〈在外面〉
❼ businessman〈商人、企業家〉・asked〈ask（要求）的過去式〉・luxury〈奢華〉

中譯

❶ 當 Jasmine 抵達飯店，她必須先在登記入住櫃檯等候 20 分鐘。
❷ Rich 走到服務台索取了一份市區地圖。
❸ 哇！紐約市那家文華東方酒店的飯店大廳真是壯觀！
❹ 他把車子停在停車場，便進入了飯店。
❺ Tom 坐在飯店中庭花園的一棵大灌木樹旁。
❻ 那間飯店在室內及室外都有游泳池。
❼ 這名企業家要求入住豪華客房。

031 飯店設施(2)

MP3 031

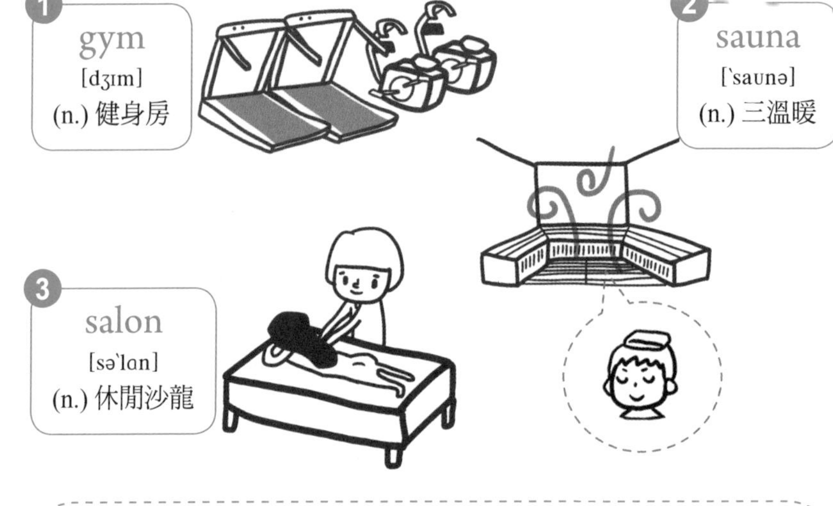

1 gym [dʒɪm] (n.) 健身房

2 sauna [ˋsaunə] (n.) 三溫暖

3 salon [səˋlɑn] (n.) 休閒沙龍

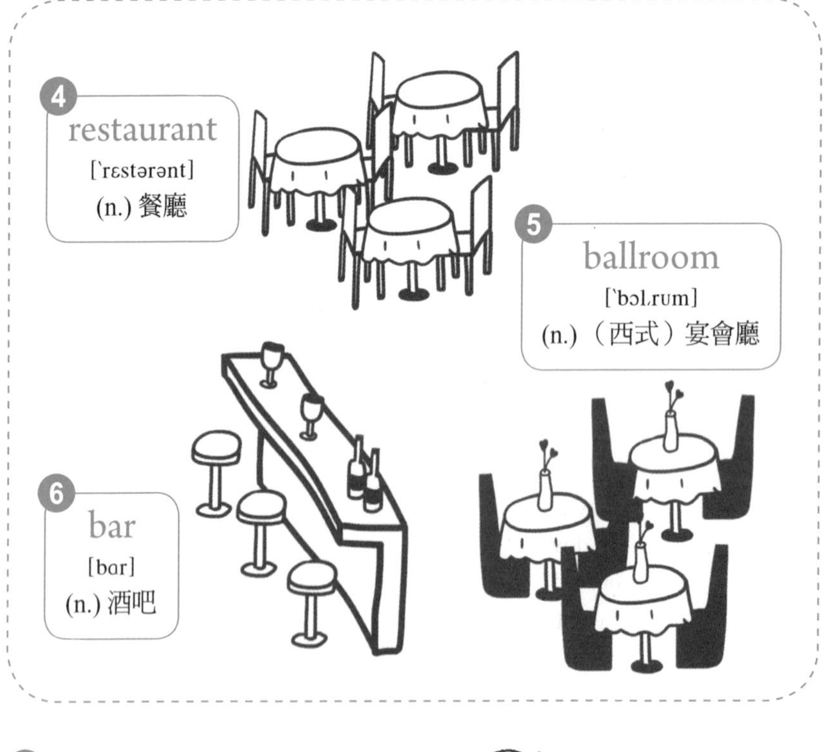

4 restaurant [ˋrɛstərənt] (n.) 餐廳

5 ballroom [ˋbɔl͵rum] (n.)（西式）宴會廳

6 bar [bɑr] (n.) 酒吧

7 safety box [ˋseftɪ bɑks] (n.) 保險箱

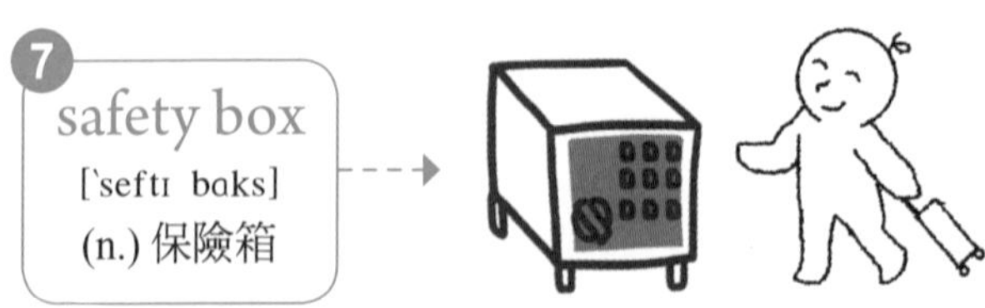

❶ 健身房

Eddie loves to exercise and lift weights in the gym.

舉重

❷ 三溫暖

Daisy was very sweaty after she left the sauna.

Daisy 全身是汗

❸ 休閒沙龍

Susan was in the salon for three hours having her hair done.

做頭髮

❹ 餐廳

There's a great Thai restaurant down the road if you're hungry.

沿著這條路

❺（西式）宴會廳

The ballroom is often hired out for wedding receptions.

宴會廳經常被出租

❻ 酒吧

Ivy couldn't sleep, so she went down to the bar to get a drink.

買一杯酒

❼ 保險箱

When you stay in a hotel, leave your valuable things in the safety box.

貴重物品

學更多

❶ love〈喜愛〉・exercise〈運動〉・lift〈舉起〉・weight〈重物〉

❷ sweaty〈滿身是汗的〉・after〈在…之後〉・left〈leave（離開）的過去式〉

❸ hour〈小時〉・having〈have（使、讓）的 ing 型態〉・done〈do（裝飾）的過去分詞〉

❹ Thai〈泰國的〉・down〈沿著〉・road〈路〉・hungry〈飢餓的〉

❺ hired out〈hire out（出租）的過去分詞〉・wedding〈婚禮〉・reception〈宴會〉

❻ sleep〈睡覺〉・went down〈go down（走下去）的過去式〉・drink〈酒、飲料〉

❼ stay〈暫住〉・hotel〈飯店〉・leave〈留下〉・valuable〈貴重的〉・safety〈安全〉

中譯

❶ Eddie 喜歡在健身房運動和舉重。

❷ Daisy 離開三溫暖後，全身都是汗。

❸ Susan 在沙龍裡待了三個小時做頭髮。

❹ 如果你餓了，這條路上有一間很棒的泰式餐廳。

❺ 宴會廳經常被出租作為婚宴場所。

❻ Ivy 睡不著，所以到樓下酒吧點了一杯酒。

❼ 當你投宿飯店時，要把貴重物品鎖進保險箱裡。

032
上衣樣式(1)

MP3 032

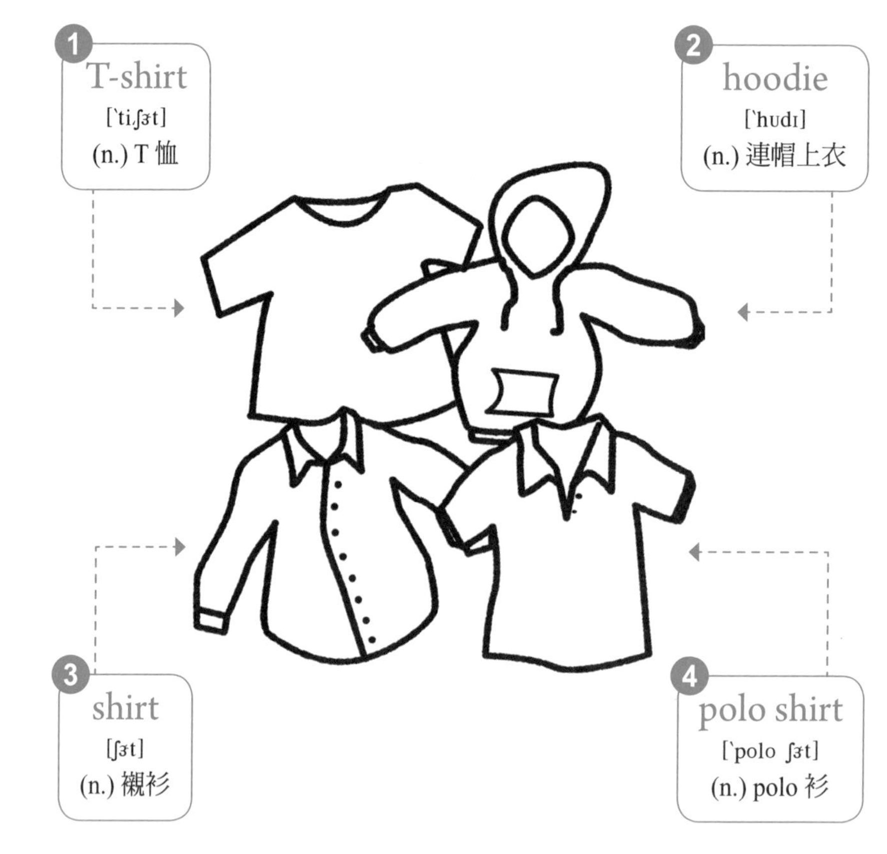
1 T-shirt
[ˋtiˌʃɝt]
(n.) T 恤
2 hoodie
[ˋhʊdɪ]
(n.) 連帽上衣
3 shirt
[ʃɝt]
(n.) 襯衫
4 polo shirt
[ˋpolo ʃɝt]
(n.) polo 衫

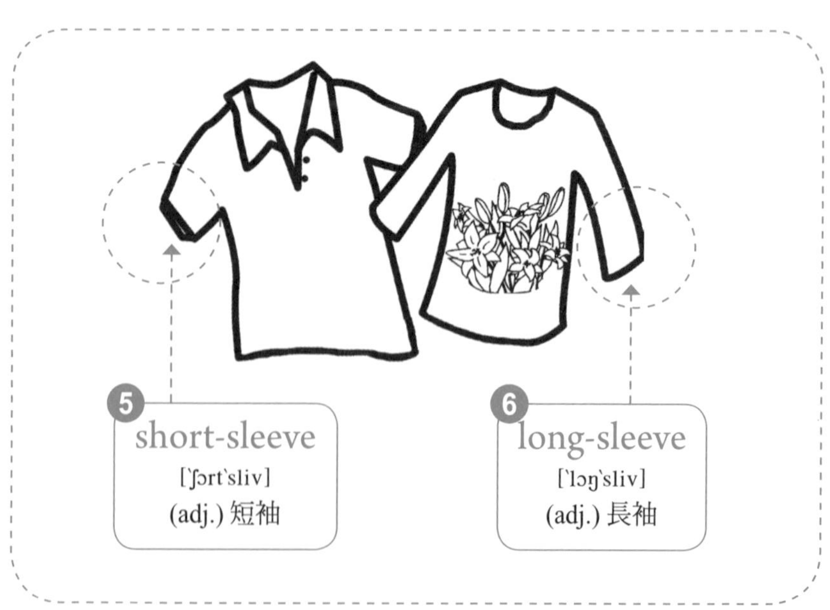
5 short-sleeve
[ˋʃɔrtˋsliv]
(adj.) 短袖
6 long-sleeve
[ˋlɔŋˋsliv]
(adj.) 長袖

❶ T 恤
T-shirts are light and comfortable, so they're perfect for playing sports in.
它們很適合運動時穿

❷ 連帽上衣
Tom felt very cold, so he pulled the hood of his hoodie over his head.
把連帽上衣的兜帽戴在頭上

❸ 襯衫
Dan bought a new white shirt to wear for his job interview.

❹ polo 衫
Polo shirts are T-shirts with collars, so they look a bit smarter than ordinary T-shirts.
有衣領的 T 恤

❺ 短袖
❻ 長袖
Short-sleeve shirts are more comfortable than long-sleeve ones in the hot, summer months.
長袖的（襯衫）

學更多

❶ light〈輕的〉‧comfortable〈舒服的〉‧perfect for〈對…最適當的〉‧sport〈運動〉
❷ felt〈feel（感覺）的過去式〉‧pulled〈pull（拉）的過去式〉‧hood〈兜帽〉
❸ bought〈buy（買）的過去式〉‧wear〈穿著〉‧job〈工作〉‧interview〈面試〉
❹ shirt〈襯衫〉‧collar〈衣領〉‧a bit〈有一點〉‧
smarter〈較時髦的，smart（時髦的）的比較級〉‧ordinary〈一般的〉
❺ ❻ short〈短的〉‧sleeve〈袖子〉‧long〈長的〉‧summer〈夏天〉‧month〈月〉

中譯

❶ T 恤既輕薄又舒適，所以很適合運動時穿。
❷ Tom 覺得非常冷，所以他戴上了連帽上衣的兜帽。
❸ Dan 為了工作的面試，買了一件新的白襯衫來穿。
❹ Polo 衫是有衣領的 T 恤，所以看起來比一般的 T 恤更時髦。
❺ ❻ 在炎熱的夏季月份，短袖襯衫會比長袖襯衫更舒適。

033 上衣樣式(2)

MP3 033

❶ 圓領

Round neck T-shirts are very casual, so you shouldn't wear them on formal occasions.

正式場合

❷ V 領

The front of the collar on V neck T-shirts looks like the letter V.

正面的衣領

❸ 立領

If you're going to be outside all day, wear a stand-up collar, as it will protect your neck from the sun.

保護你的脖子避免陽光

❹ U 領

Anna only buys scoop neck shirts and dresses because she feels they flatter her face shape.

那些衣服使得她的臉型更好看

❺ 露肩

The actress looks beautiful in her loose, off-the-shoulder top.

穿著她寬鬆的露肩上衣

學更多

❶ round〈圓的〉• neck〈脖子、衣領〉• casual〈休閒的〉• formal〈正式的〉• occasion〈場合〉

❷ front〈正面〉• collar〈衣領〉• look like〈看起來好像〉• letter〈字母〉

❸ outside〈在外面〉• stand-up〈直立的〉• as〈因為〉• protect A from B〈保護 A 免於 B〉• sun〈陽光〉

❹ scoop〈勺子〉• dress〈連衣裙〉• flatter〈使某人更加吸引人〉• shape〈形狀〉

❺ actress〈女演員〉• loose〈寬鬆的〉• shoulder〈肩膀〉• top〈上衣〉

中譯

❶ 圓領 T 恤非常休閒，所以你不該穿它們出席正式場合。

❷ V 領 T 恤的正面衣領，看起來很像字母 V。

❸ 如果你要一整天待在室外，就穿上立領的衣服，因為它可以保護你的脖子避免曬傷。

❹ Anna 只買 U 領的 T 恤和連身裙，因為她覺得穿那些衣服能使臉型更好看。

❺ 那位女演員穿著寬鬆的露肩上衣，看起來十分動人。

034 穿搭配件(1)

MP3 034

1 hat
[hæt]
(n.) 帽子

2 scarf
[skɑrf]
(n.) 圍巾

3 sunglasses
[ˋsʌn͵glæsɪz]
(n.) 太陽眼鏡

4 shawl
[ʃɔl]
(n.) 披肩

5 belt
[bɛlt]
(n.) 腰帶

6 glove
[glʌv]
(n.) 手套

❶ 帽子

Rich wears hats during the summer to protect his face from the sun.

❷ 圍巾

It's cold outside, so you might want to take a scarf.

❸ 太陽眼鏡

If your eyes are sensitive to sunlight, you should get yourself a pair of sunglasses. 你的眼睛對陽光敏感

❹ 披肩

The woman put a shawl around her shoulders when she started to feel cold. 在她的肩膀上圍了一條披肩

❺ 腰帶

My pants keep falling down; I think I need to get myself a belt.

一直往下掉 為我自己準備一條腰帶

❻ 手套

If you don't put on your gloves today, your hands will be really cold.

學更多

❶ wear〈戴著〉・during〈在…期間〉・protect A from B〈保護 A 免於 B〉・face〈臉〉・sun〈陽光〉

❷ cold〈冷的〉・outside〈外面〉・take〈拿取〉

❸ sensitive〈敏感的〉・sunlight〈陽光〉・get〈為…弄到〉・a pair of〈一副〉

❹ put〈put（放）的過去式〉・around〈環繞〉・shoulder〈肩膀〉

❺ pants〈褲子〉・keep〈持續不斷〉・falling〈fall（掉下）的 ing 型態〉

❻ put on〈戴上〉・hand〈手〉・really〈很〉

中譯

❶ 夏天時 Rich 都會戴上帽子，以免臉被曬傷。

❷ 外面很冷，所以你可能會想帶條圍巾。

❸ 如果你的眼睛對陽光敏感，你就該為自己準備一副太陽眼鏡。

❹ 當那位女士開始覺得冷時，她在肩上圍了一條披肩。

❺ 我的褲子一直往下掉；我想我需要一條腰帶。

❻ 如果你今天沒戴手套，你的手會非常冰冷。

035 穿搭配件(2)

MP3 035

1 bracelet
[`breslɪt]
(n.) 手鍊

2 watch
[watʃ]
(n.) 手錶

3 ring
[rɪŋ]
(n.) 戒指

4 necklace
[`nɛklɪs]
(n.) 項鍊

5 earring
[`ɪr,rɪŋ]
(n.) 耳環

6 hairpin
[`hɛr,pɪn]
(n.) 髮夾

❶ 手鍊

Neil put the bracelet on his girlfriend's wrist.

把手鍊戴在他女朋友的手腕上

❷ 手錶

Ever since I lost my watch I haven't had any idea what the time is.

現在是幾點

❸ 戒指

The girl has rings on almost all of her fingers.

❹ 項鍊

The princess wore a beautiful diamond necklace at the event.

戴了一條漂亮的鑽石項鍊

❺ 耳環

Wow, that man must have at least ten earrings in his right ear.

他的右耳至少有 10 支耳環

❻ 髮夾

The lady used a hairpin to hold her hair in position.

固定她的頭髮

學更多

❶ put on〈put on（戴上）的過去式〉・girlfriend〈女朋友〉・wrist〈手腕〉

❷ ever since〈從…的時候開始〉・lost〈lose（遺失）的過去式〉・had〈have（有）的過去分詞〉・idea〈想法〉

❸ almost〈幾乎〉・all〈全部的〉・finger〈手指〉

❹ princess〈公主〉・wore〈wear（戴）的過去式〉・diamond〈鑽石〉・event〈重大事件〉

❺ must〈一定〉・at least〈至少〉・right〈右邊的〉・ear〈耳朵〉

❻ lady〈小姐〉・hold〈保持某種姿態〉・hair〈頭髮〉・position〈適當的位置〉

中譯

❶ Neil 把手鍊戴在女朋友的手腕上。

❷ 自從我弄丟了手錶，我就不知道現在是幾點了。

❸ 那個女孩幾乎每根手指上都戴著戒指。

❹ 公主在重大場合上戴了一條美麗的鑽石項鍊。

❺ 哇！那個男人的右耳一定至少戴了 10 支耳環。

❻ 那位小姐用髮夾固定她的頭髮。

036 化妝品(1)

MP3 036

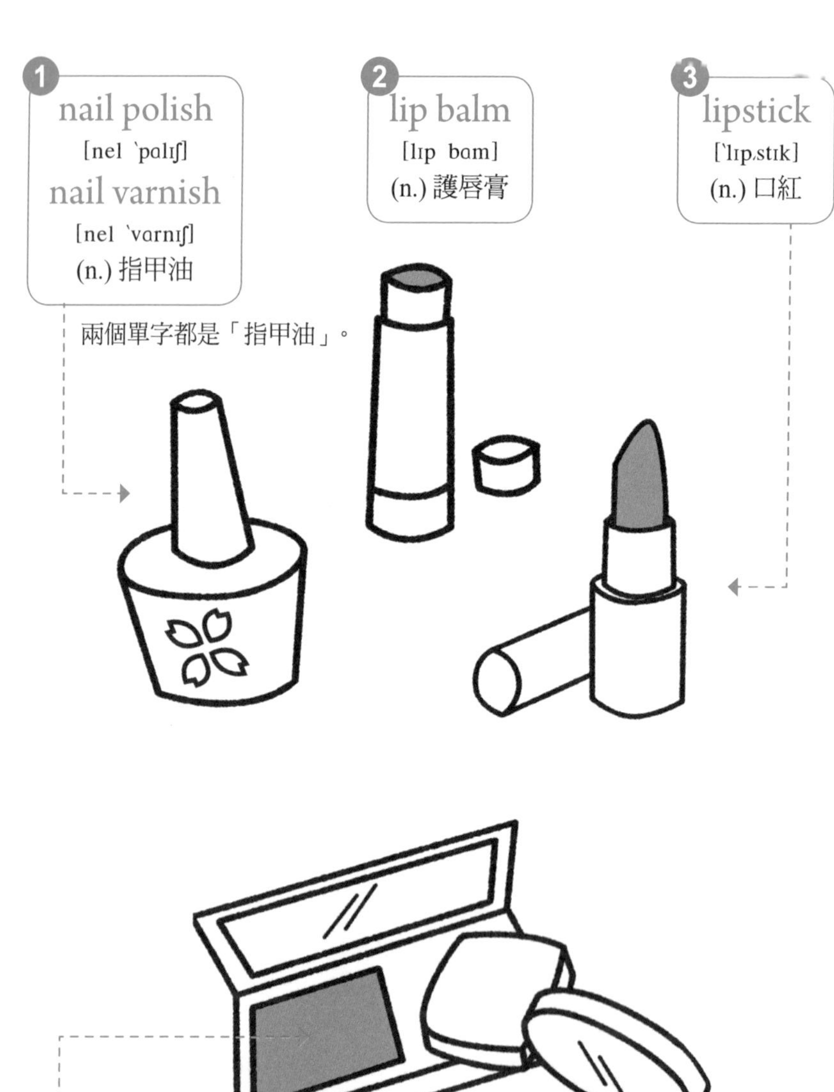

❶ 指甲油
Beth is an unusual girl, and she often uses green nail polish on her finger nails.

❷ 護唇膏
Your lips look very dry; you should rub some lip balm on them.
在嘴唇上擦點護唇膏

❸ 口紅
The lady usually wears red lipstick when she goes to work.
擦紅色口紅

❹ 粉餅 / 粉底
The girl put foundation powder all over her face before putting on any other makeup.
在她臉上塗抹粉底

❺ 腮紅
Rachel used blush to make her cheeks look a little bit more pink.
讓她的臉頰看起來更粉嫩一點

學更多

❶ unusual〈特別的〉・green〈綠色的〉・nail〈指甲〉・polish〈擦亮劑〉・finger〈手指〉・varnish〈亮光漆〉
❷ lip〈嘴唇〉・dry〈乾燥的〉・rub〈擦上〉・balm〈軟膏〉
❸ lady〈女士〉・wear〈塗抹〉・red〈紅色的〉・work〈工作〉
❹ put〈put（塗抹）的過去式〉・foundation〈粉底霜〉・powder〈化妝用的粉〉・all over〈到處〉・makeup〈化妝品〉
❺ cheek〈臉頰〉・a little bit〈有一點〉・more〈更多〉・pink〈粉紅色〉

中譯

❶ Beth 是個與眾不同的女孩，而且她常在手指甲塗上綠色的指甲油。
❷ 你的嘴唇看起來很乾燥。你應該擦點護唇膏。
❸ 那位女士經常擦紅色口紅去上班。
❹ 上妝前，那個女孩先在臉上撲上粉底。
❺ Rachel 用腮紅讓她的臉頰看起來更粉嫩一點。

037

化妝品(2)

MP3 037

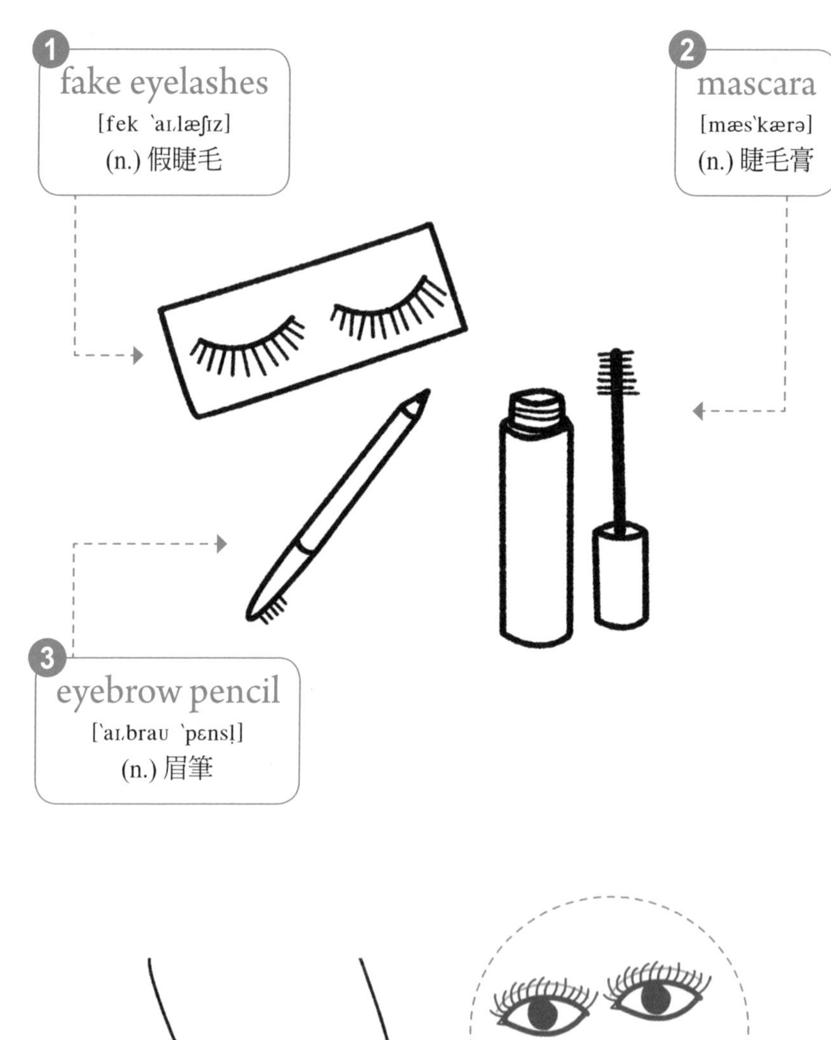

1. fake eyelashes [fek ˋaɪˏlæʃɪz] (n.) 假睫毛
2. mascara [mæsˋkærə] (n.) 睫毛膏
3. eyebrow pencil [ˋaɪˏbraʊ ˋpɛnsḷ] (n.) 眉筆

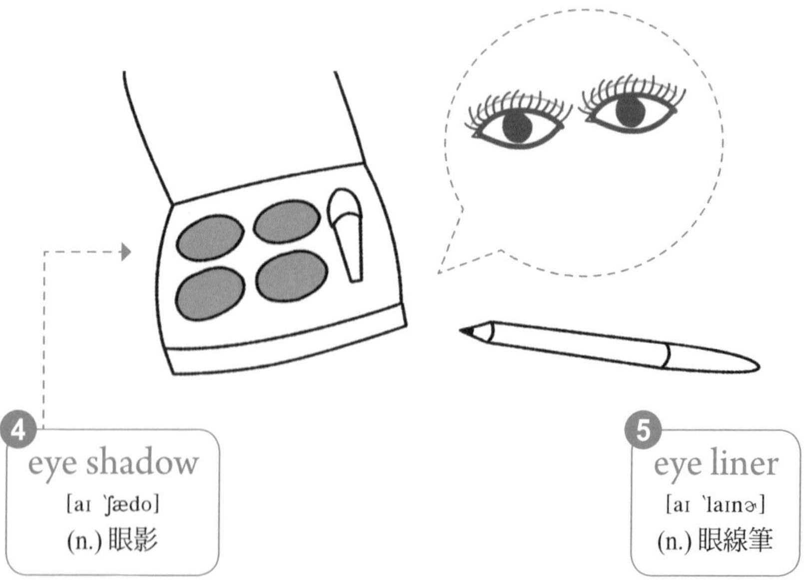

4. eye shadow [aɪ ˋʃædo] (n.) 眼影
5. eye liner [aɪ ˋlaɪnɚ] (n.) 眼線筆

❶ 假睫毛

Fake eyelashes are all the rage in Asia. It seems like most young women wear them.
在亞洲非常流行 似乎

❷ 睫毛膏

Mascara is used to make eyelashes look thicker, longer, and darker.
被用來

❸ 眉筆

People use eyebrow pencils to make their eyebrows seem thicker or longer.

❹ 眼影

The fashion model likes to wear a dark eye shadow around her eyes.
畫深色眼影

❺ 眼線筆

She used an eye liner to draw black lines around her eyes.
在她的眼睛周圍畫上黑線

學更多

❶ fake〈假的〉・eyelash〈睫毛〉・all the rage〈非常流行〉・most〈大部分的〉・young〈年輕的〉・women〈woman（女人）的複數〉・wear〈戴著〉

❷ make〈使得〉・thicker〈較為濃密的，thick（濃密的）的比較級〉・darker〈較黑的，dark（黑的）的比較級〉

❸ eyebrow〈眉毛〉・pencil〈筆狀物〉・seem〈看來好像〉

❹ fashion〈時裝〉・model〈模特兒〉・wear〈塗抹〉・dark〈深色的〉・shadow〈陰影〉

❺ liner〈眼線筆〉・draw〈畫〉・line〈線條〉・around〈圍繞〉

中譯

❶ 假睫毛在亞洲非常風行，似乎大部分的年輕女性都會戴著它們。

❷ 睫毛膏用來使睫毛看起來更濃密、更細長、更黑。

❸ 人們利用眉筆，讓他們的眉毛看起來更濃密或更長。

❹ 時裝模特兒喜歡在眼睛周圍畫上深色的眼影。

❺ 她用眼線筆在她的眼睛周圍畫上黑線。

038 皮膚清潔保養品(1)

MP3 038

1 **toner** [ˋtonɚ] (n.) 化妝水

2 **moisturizing mist** [ˋmɔɪstʃəˏraɪzɪŋ mɪst] (n.) 保濕噴霧

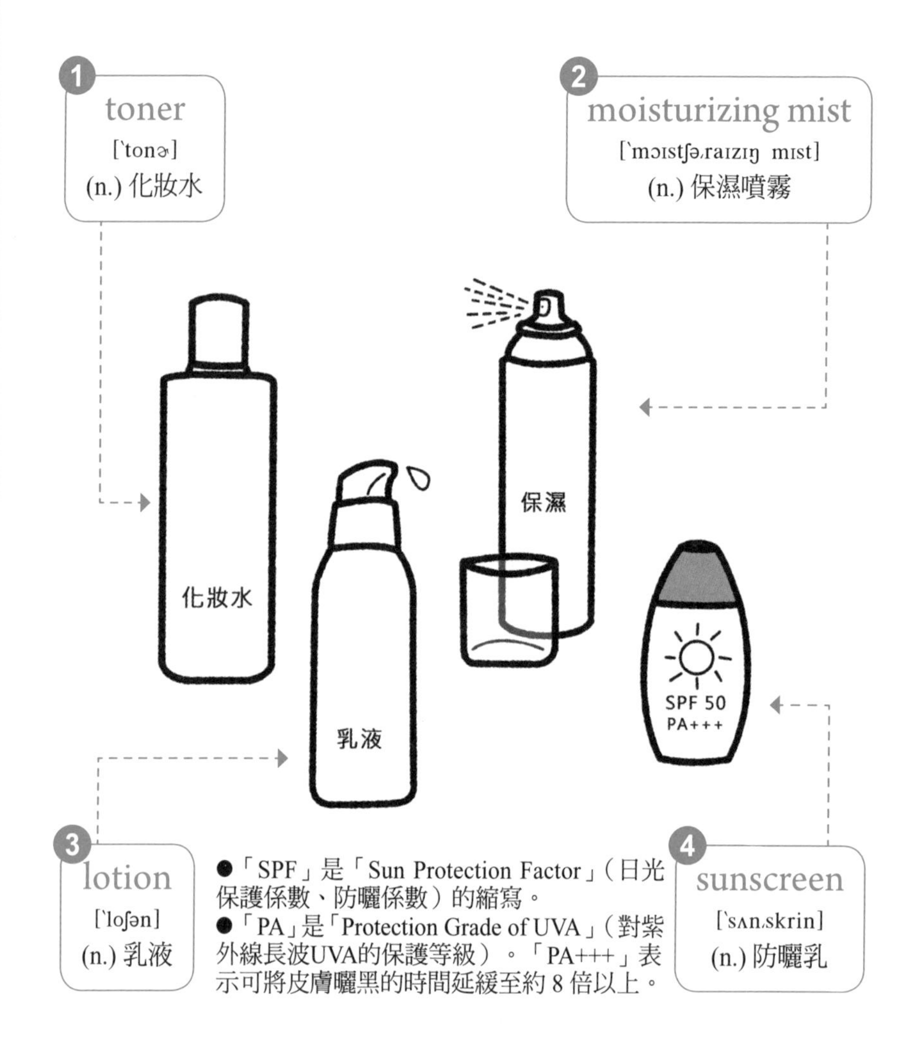

3 **lotion** [ˋloʃən] (n.) 乳液

4 **sunscreen** [ˋsʌnˏskrin] (n.) 防曬乳

● 「SPF」是「Sun Protection Factor」（日光保護係數、防曬係數）的縮寫。
● 「PA」是「Protection Grade of UVA」（對紫外線長波UVA的保護等級）。「PA+++」表示可將皮膚曬黑的時間延緩至約 8 倍以上。

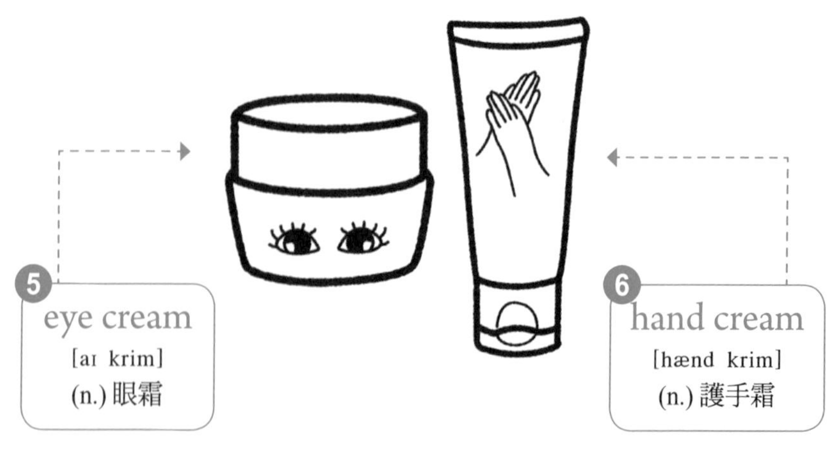

5 **eye cream** [aɪ krim] (n.) 眼霜

6 **hand cream** [hænd krim] (n.) 護手霜

❶ 化妝水
My girlfriend uses a toner every day to tighten the skin on her face.
緊實她的臉部肌膚

❷ 保濕噴霧
I always spray a moisturizing mist onto my face on sunny days.
在我的臉上噴保濕噴霧

❸ 乳液
Experts say that you should use lotion regularly to keep your skin moisturized.
經常擦乳液

❹ 防曬乳
You should apply sunscreen about 20 minutes before going out into the sun.

❺ 眼霜
I haven't had much sleep lately, so I need to use eye cream to keep myself looking good.
我最近睡眠不足

❻ 護手霜
Rose likes her hands to be soft so she uses a hand cream every day.

學更多

❶ girlfriend〈女朋友〉・tighten〈使繃緊〉・skin〈皮膚〉・face〈臉〉
❷ spray〈噴〉・moisturizing〈濕潤的〉・mist〈噴霧〉・sunny〈陽光充足的〉
❸ expert〈專家〉・regularly〈經常地〉・keep〈保持某一狀態〉・moisturized〈moisturize（使濕潤）的過去分詞〉
❹ apply〈塗抹〉・about〈大約〉・going out〈go out（外出）的 ing 型態〉
❺ had〈have（有）的過去分詞〉・sleep〈睡眠〉・lately〈最近〉・cream〈乳霜〉
❻ hand〈手〉・soft〈柔軟的〉・use〈使用〉

中譯

❶ 我的女朋友每天擦化妝水來緊實臉部肌膚。
❷ 在陽光普照的日子，我一定會在臉上噴保濕噴霧。
❸ 專家表示：應該勤擦乳液，以保持你的皮膚濕潤。
❹ 大約在外出曝曬於太陽下的前 20 分鐘，你就應該塗抹防曬乳。
❺ 我最近都睡眠不足，所以我需要擦眼霜來讓自己有好氣色。
❻ Rose 喜歡讓她的雙手保持柔嫩，所以她每天都擦護手霜。

039

皮膚清潔保養品(2)

MP3 039

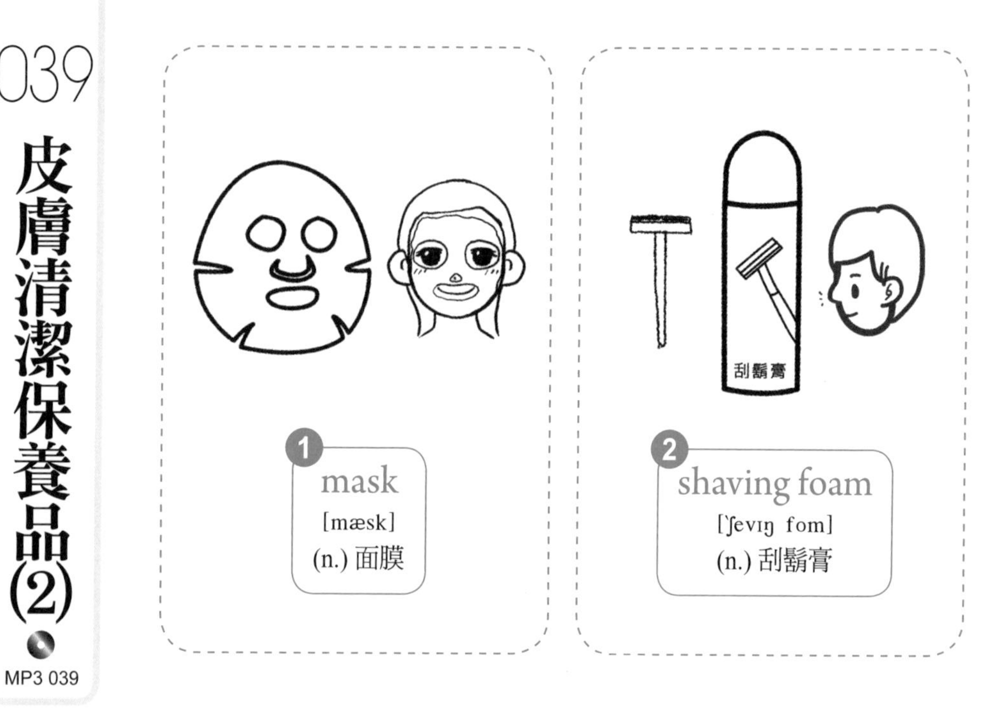

1 mask
[mæsk]
(n.) 面膜

2 shaving foam
[ˋʃevɪŋ fom]
(n.) 刮鬍膏

3 cleansing cotton
[ˋklɛnzɪŋ ˋkɑtn̩]
(n.) 卸妝棉

4 makeup remover
[ˋmek͵ʌp rɪˋmuvɚ]
(n.) 卸妝油

5 cleanser
[ˋklɛnzɚ]
(n.) 洗面乳

❶ 面膜

I think the easiest way to keep my face moisturized is by using a face mask.

讓我的臉保持濕潤

❷ 刮鬍膏

Shaving foam moisturizes your skin and helps to prevent it from getting cut.

防止肌膚被刮傷

❸ 卸妝棉

Cleansing cotton is great for removing makeup.

❹ 卸妝油

As makeup is quite oily, you'll need a makeup remover to take it off.

卸除它（化妝品）

❺ 洗面乳

After removing her makeup, Mandy used a cleanser on her face.

學更多

❶ easiest〈最簡單的，easy（簡單的）的最高級〉・way〈方式〉・keep〈保持某一狀態〉・moisturized〈moisturize（使濕潤）的過去分詞〉・using〈use（使用）的 ing 型態〉

❷ shaving〈刮鬍子〉・foam〈泡沫〉・moisturize〈使濕潤〉・skin〈皮膚〉・prevent A from B〈防止 A 避免 B〉・cut〈cut（刮）的過去分詞〉

❸ cleansing〈清洗的〉・cotton〈棉〉・great〈極好的〉・makeup〈化妝品〉

❹ as〈因為〉・quite〈相當〉・oily〈含油的〉・remover〈去除劑〉・take off〈移去〉

❺ after〈在…之後〉・removing〈remove（卸除）的 ing 型態〉・face〈臉〉

中譯

❶ 要讓自己的臉保持濕潤，我認為最簡單的方法就是敷臉部面膜。

❷ 刮鬍膏會濕潤你的皮膚，並有助於防止皮膚被刮傷。

❸ 卸妝棉能有效卸除化妝品。

❹ 因為化妝品很油，所以你需要卸妝油來卸除它。

❺ 卸除化妝品之後，Mandy 用洗面乳來洗臉。

040 袋子(1)

MP3 040

1 plastic bag
[ˋplæstɪk bæg]
(n.) 塑膠袋

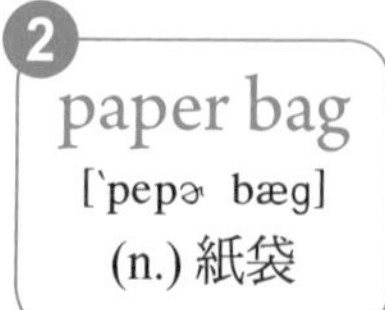

2 paper bag
[ˋpepɚ bæg]
(n.) 紙袋

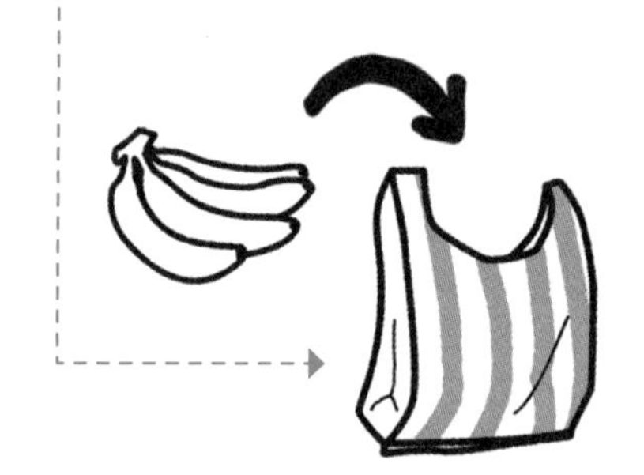

3 shopping bag
[ˋʃɑpɪŋ bæg]
(n.) 購物袋

4 trash bag
[træʃ bæg]
(n.) 垃圾袋

5 zipper bag
[ˋzɪpɚ bæg]
(n.) 夾鍊袋

6 insulated lunch bag
[ˋɪnsjʊˏletɪd lʌntʃ bæg]
(n.) 保溫袋

❶ 塑膠袋
You usually have to pay for plastic bags in supermarkets and convenience stores.
必須付錢買塑膠袋

❷ 紙袋
I don't like paper bags as I worry that they're not strong enough.
它們不夠堅固

❸ 購物袋
I like to reuse my shopping bags to try and help the environment.

❹ 垃圾袋
We really need to throw away that trash bag; it's starting to smell.
丟掉那個垃圾袋

❺ 夾鍊袋
The little boy always takes sandwiches to school in a zipper bag.

❻ 保溫袋
By putting my food in an insulated lunch bag, I was able to keep it warm till lunch time.
讓它到午餐時間還保持溫熱

學更多

❶ plastic〈塑膠的〉・supermarket〈超級市場〉・convenience store〈便利商店〉
❷ paper〈紙的〉・as〈因為〉・worry〈擔心〉・strong〈堅固的〉・enough〈足夠〉
❸ reuse〈重複使用〉・shopping〈購物〉・try〈嘗試〉・environment〈環境〉
❹ throw away〈丟掉〉・trash〈垃圾〉・starting〈start（開始）的 ing 型態〉・smell〈發臭〉
❺ take〈帶去〉・sandwich〈三明治〉・zipper〈拉鍊〉・bag〈袋子〉
❻ putting〈put（放置）的 ing 型態〉・insulated〈被隔熱的〉・able〈能〉・keep〈保持某一狀態〉・warm〈溫熱的〉・till〈直到…為止〉・lunch〈午餐〉

中譯

❶ 在超級市場和便利商店，通常你必須付錢購買塑膠袋。
❷ 我不喜歡紙袋，因為我擔心它們不夠堅固。
❸ 我喜歡重複利用我的購物袋，試著為保護環境付出心力。
❹ 我們真的要丟掉那個垃圾袋，它開始發臭了。
❺ 那個小男孩總是用夾鍊袋裝三明治帶到學校去。
❻ 我把食物裝進保溫袋，就能保溫到午餐時間。

041
袋子(1)

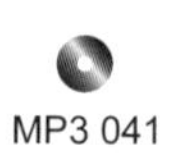

MP3 041

1
space bag
[spes bæg]
(n.) 真空收納袋
2
wash bag
[wɑʃ bæg]
(n.) 洗衣袋
3
shockproof notebook bag
[`ʃɑk͵pruf `not͵bʊk bæg]
(n.) 筆記型電腦防震袋
4
dustproof bag
[`dʌst`pruf bæg]
(n.) 防塵袋

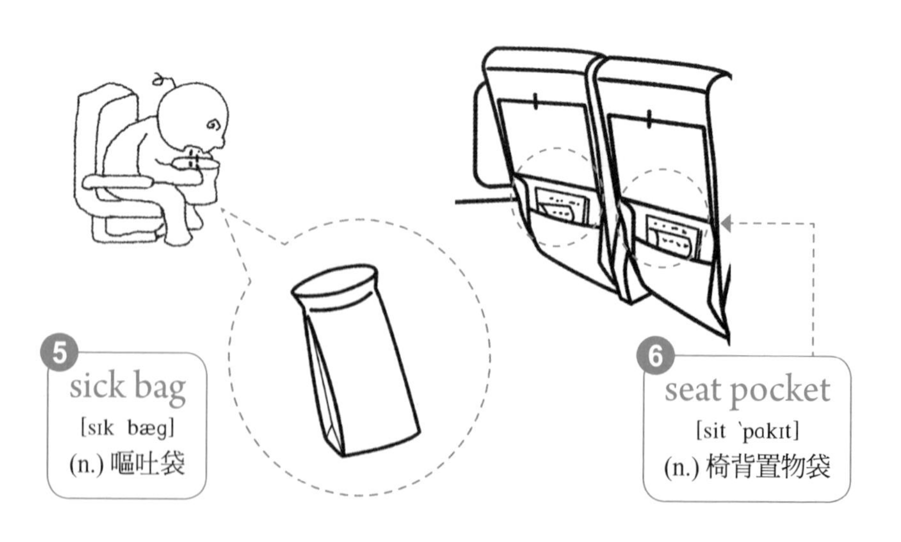

5
sick bag
[sɪk bæg]
(n.) 嘔吐袋
6
seat pocket
[sit `pɑkɪt]
(n.) 椅背置物袋

❶ 真空收納袋
Space bags are great for storing blankets because they take up less room.
因為它們佔用較少的空間

❷ 洗衣袋
When washing delicate clothes, you should put them in a wash bag.

❸ 筆記型電腦防震袋
After his old notebook computer broke, Mark always uses a shockproof notebook bag now.

❹ 防塵袋
The man bought a lot of dustproof bags to store his old photos in.
把他的舊照片保存在裡面

❺ 嘔吐袋
If you suffer with travel sickness, you should always make sure you take sick bags with you on journeys.
如果你會暈車　確保你有帶著嘔吐袋

❻ 椅背置物袋
Tim found his train seat, sat down, and put his magazines in the seat pocket in front of him.
把他的雜誌放進椅背置物袋

學更多

❶ storing〈store（收納）的 ing 型態〉・blanket〈毯子〉・take up〈佔用〉・room〈空間〉
❷ washing〈wash（清洗）的 ing 型態〉・delicate〈需要小心處理的〉
❸ notebook〈筆記型電腦〉・broke〈break（弄壞）的過去式〉・shockproof〈防震的〉
❹ bought〈buy（購買）的過去式〉・dustproof〈防塵的〉・store〈保存〉・photo〈照片〉
❺ suffer〈受苦〉・travel sickness〈暈車、暈機、暈船〉・journey〈旅途〉
❻ sat down〈sit down（坐下）的過去式〉・magazine〈雜誌〉・in front of〈在…的前面〉

中譯

❶ 真空收納袋在收納毯子時很好用，因為它們佔用較少的空間。
❷ 清洗那些需要小心處理的衣物時，你應該把它們放進洗衣袋。
❸ 當那台老舊的筆記型電腦摔壞之後， Mark 現在都會使用筆記型電腦防震袋。
❹ 那個男人買了許多防塵袋來保存他的舊照片。
❺ 如果你會暈車，就應該確保旅途中隨身攜帶著嘔吐袋。
❻ Tim 找到他的火車座位之後便坐了下來，並把他的雜誌放進前方的椅背置物袋。

042 隨身提包(1)

MP3 042

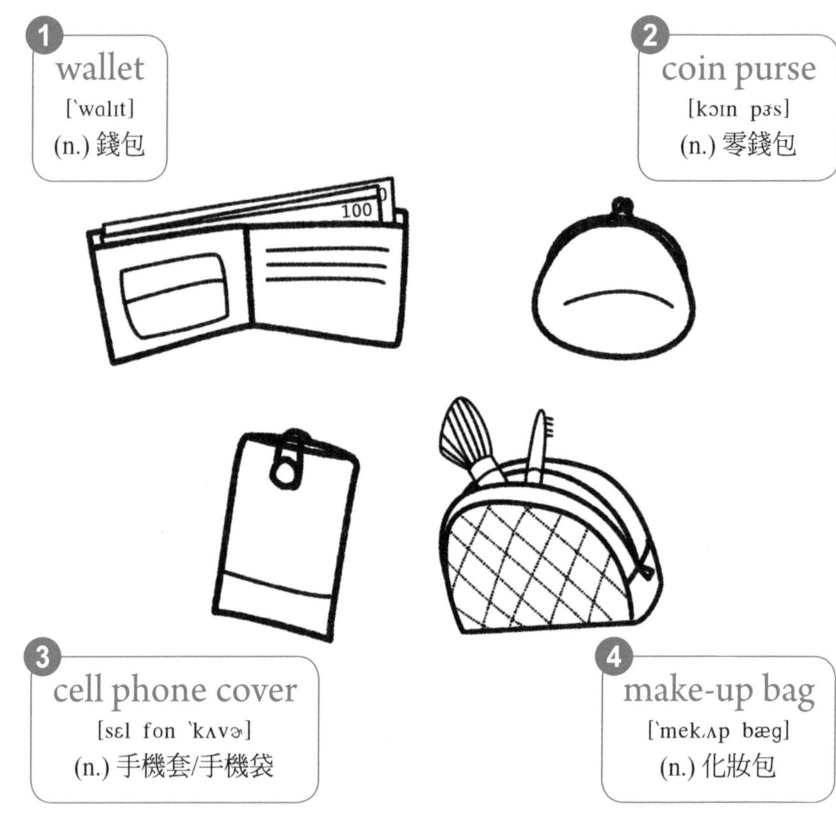

1. wallet
[ˋwɑlɪt]
(n.) 錢包

2. coin purse
[kɔɪn pɝs]
(n.) 零錢包

3. cell phone cover
[sɛl fon ˋkʌvɚ]
(n.) 手機套/手機袋

4. make-up bag
[ˋmek͵ʌp bæg]
(n.) 化妝包

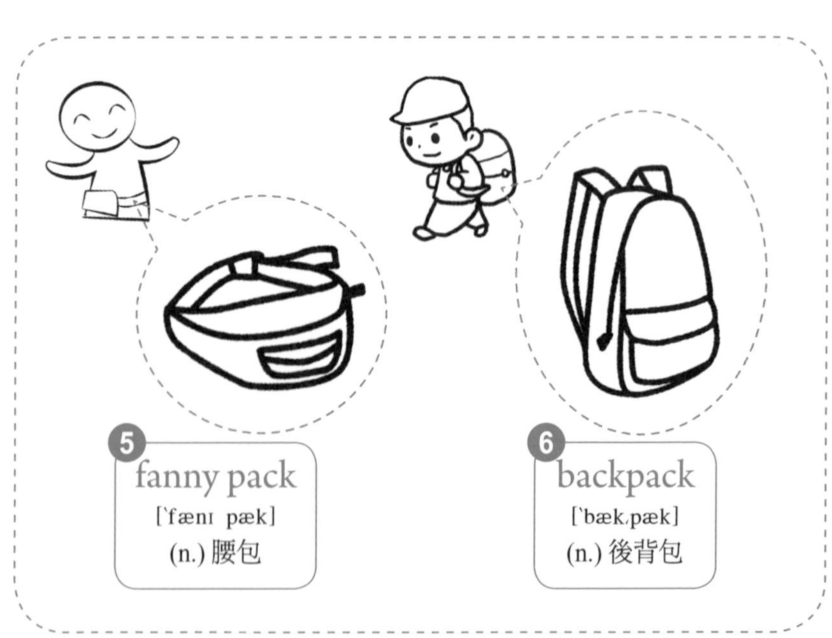

5. fanny pack
[ˋfænɪ pæk]
(n.) 腰包

6. backpack
[ˋbæk͵pæk]
(n.) 後背包

❶ 錢包
After paying for dinner, my dad closed his wallet and put it in his back pocket.
放進他的後面口袋

❷ 零錢包
My sister's always losing her change, so I bought her a coin purse.
買了一個零錢包給她

❸ 手機套 / 手機袋
Cell phone covers not only look great, but also help protect cell phones from getting scratched.
看起來很棒　保護手機避免被刮到

❹ 化妝包
To make sure she didn't lose any of her make-up, Kitty put it all into a make-up bag.

❺ 腰包
Fanny packs are really convenient when you go traveling as you can keep your passport and tickets next to you all the time.
讓護照和機票在你身邊

❻ 後背包
When I go hiking, I carry my food, water, and clothes in a backpack.

學更多

❶ paying〈pay（付款）的 ing 型態〉‧closed〈close（蓋上）的過去式〉‧back〈後面的〉
❷ losing〈lose（遺失）的 ing 型態〉‧change〈零錢〉‧coin〈硬幣〉‧purse〈錢包〉
❸ cell phone〈手機〉‧cover〈套子〉‧not only A but also B〈不僅 A 而且 B〉‧scratched〈scratch（刮）的過去分詞〉
❹ make sure〈確定〉‧make-up〈化妝品〉‧put〈put（放）的過去式〉
❺ fanny〈屁股〉‧pack〈包〉‧convenient〈方便的〉‧as〈因為〉‧all the time〈一直〉
❻ go hiking〈去遠足〉‧carry〈攜帶〉‧food〈食物〉‧water〈水〉‧clothes〈衣服〉

中譯

❶ 付完晚餐錢之後，爸爸就闔上錢包，並放進褲子後面的口袋。
❷ 我妹妹總是會弄丟零錢，所以我買了一個零錢包給她。
❸ 手機袋不僅美觀，還有助於保護手機不被刮傷。
❹ 為了確保自己不弄丟任何化妝品，Kitty 把它們全都放入化妝包。
❺ 當你去旅行時，腰包真的很方便，因為你可以隨時把護照和機票帶在身邊。
❻ 當我去遠足時，我會把食物、水和衣服裝進後背包。

043 隨身提包(2)

MP3 043

1. **handbag** [ˋhænd͵bæg] (n.) 手提包
2. **briefcase** [ˋbrif͵kes] (n.) 公事包
3. **travel bag** [ˋtrævḷ bæg] (n.) 旅行袋
4. **suitcase** [ˋsut͵kes] (n.) 行李箱

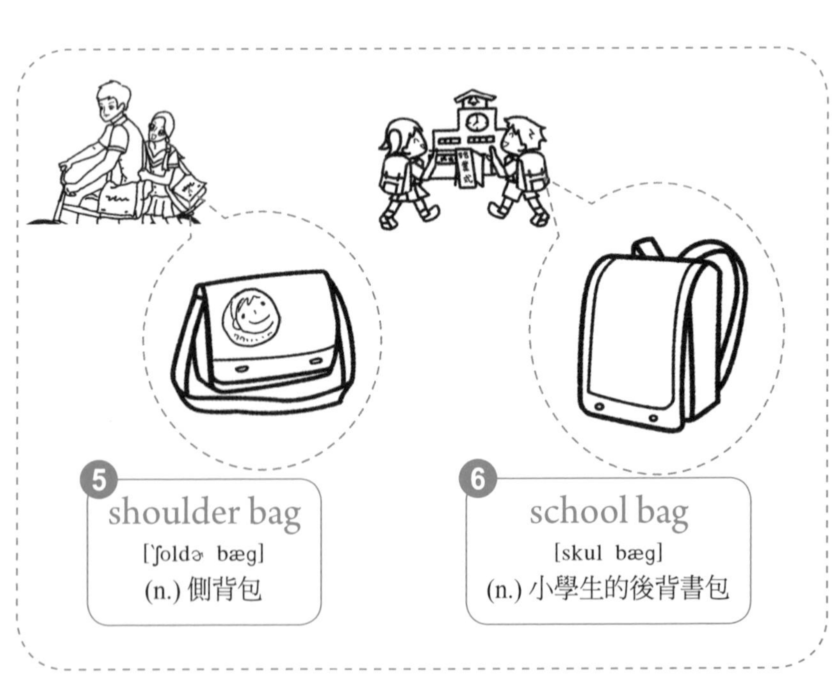

5. **shoulder bag** [ˋʃoldɚ bæg] (n.) 側背包
6. **school bag** [skul bæg] (n.) 小學生的後背書包

❶ 手提包

Handbags were invented for women, as their clothing often didn't have pockets.

手提包是為了女性而被發明的

❷ 公事包

Business people often carry briefcases as they stop papers from getting folded or torn.

避免文件被摺到或被撕破

❸ 旅行袋

The woman packed her travel bag before going on her overseas business trip.

國外出差

❹ 行李箱

As soon as they got to the hotel, the travelers took all their clothes out of their suitcase.

一…就…

從行李箱拿出他們所有的衣服

❺ 側背包

Some college students carry their books in shoulder bags to look cool.

❻ 小學生的後背書包

Many students have the name of their school on their school bags.

他們學校的名字

學更多

❶ invented〈invent（發明）的過去分詞〉• as〈因為〉• clothing〈衣服〉• pocket〈口袋〉
❷ business people〈business person（商務人士）的複數〉• stop〈阻止〉• papers〈文件〉• folded〈fold（摺疊）的過去分詞〉• torn〈tear（撕破）的過去分詞〉
❸ packed〈pack（打包）的過去式〉• overseas〈國外的〉• business trip〈出差〉
❹ got〈get（到達）的過去式〉• hotel〈飯店〉• traveler〈旅客〉• clothes〈衣服〉
❺ college〈大學〉• carry〈攜帶〉• shoulder〈肩膀〉
❻ student〈學生〉• name〈姓名〉• school〈學校〉

中譯

❶ 手提包是為女性發明的，因為她們的衣服通常沒有口袋。
❷ 商務人士通常攜帶公事包，因為公事包能避免文件造成摺痕或破損。
❸ 在前往國外出差之前，那位女士打包了她的旅行袋。
❹ 旅客一到達飯店，就從行李箱把所有的衣服拿出來。
❺ 有些大學生用側背包裝書，讓自己看起來很酷。
❻ 許多學生的後背書包上，都有他們學校的校名。

044 時間(1)

MP3 044

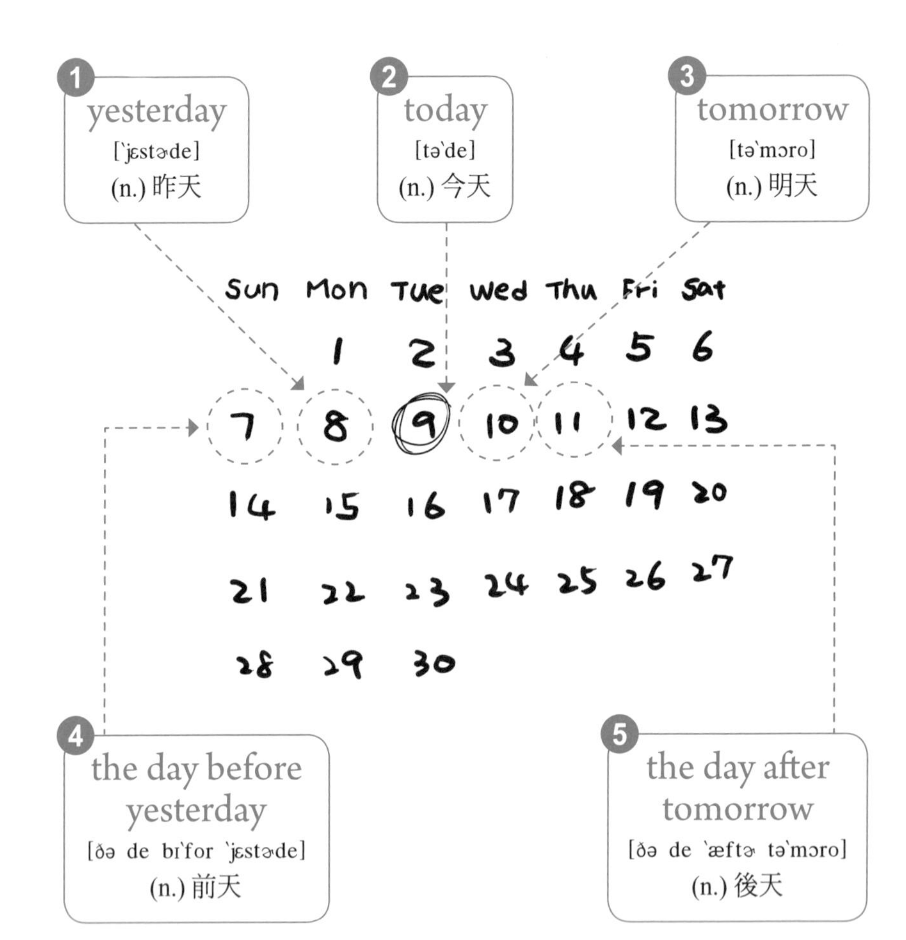

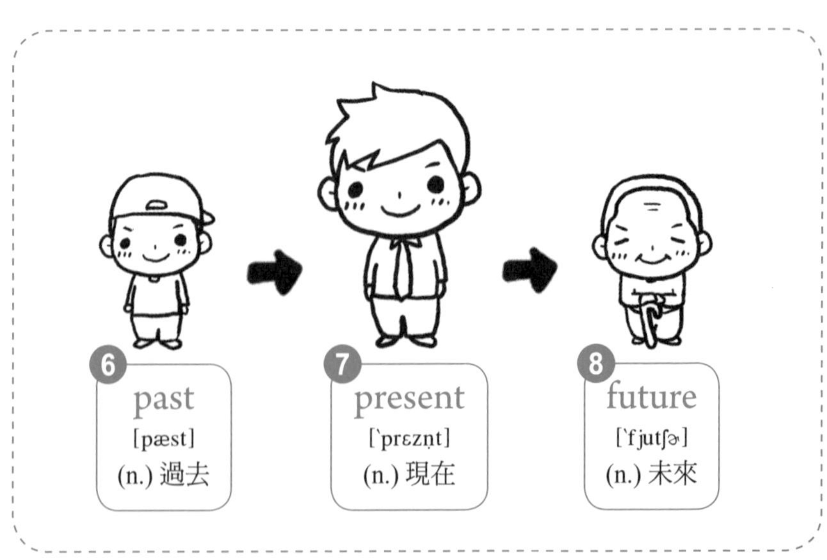

❶ 昨天
I ate some bad food yesterday, so I'm feeling ill now.

❷ 今天
I slept well last night and woke up today feeling great.
感覺很棒

❸ 明天
It's Friday today. Tomorrow is Saturday.

❹ 前天
The day before yesterday was Saturday. Today is Monday.

❺ 後天
I'll see her the day after tomorrow. That gives me 48 hours to get ready.

❻ 過去
Things that happened yesterday are in the past.

❼ 現在
Forget about the past and future. Focus on the present.
專注當下

❽ 未來
Tom's thinking about tomorrow. He's always thinking about the future.

學更多

❶ ate〈eat（吃）的過去式〉・bad〈腐壞的〉・food〈食物〉・ill〈不健康的〉
❷ slept〈sleep（睡）的過去式〉・well〈很好地〉・woke up〈wake up（起床）的過去式〉
❸ Friday〈星期五〉・Saturday〈星期六〉
❹ before〈在…之前〉・Monday〈星期一〉
❺ see〈見面〉・after〈在…之後〉・get〈成為某種狀態〉・ready〈準備好的〉
❻ thing〈事情〉・happened〈happened（發生）的過去式〉
❼ forget〈忘記〉・focus on〈集中於…〉
❽ thinking〈think（思索）的 ing 型態〉・always〈總是〉

中譯

❶ 我昨天吃到一些壞掉的食物，現在覺得不太舒服。
❷ 我昨晚睡得很好，而且今天起床覺得神清氣爽。
❸ 今天是星期五，明天是星期六。
❹ 前天是星期六，今天是星期一。
❺ 我後天要跟她見面，還有 48 個小時可以做準備。
❻ 昨天所發生的事，都是過去了。
❼ 忘卻過去與未來，專注於當下。
❽ Tom 正思索著明天的事。他總是遙想著未來。

045 時間(2)

MP3 045

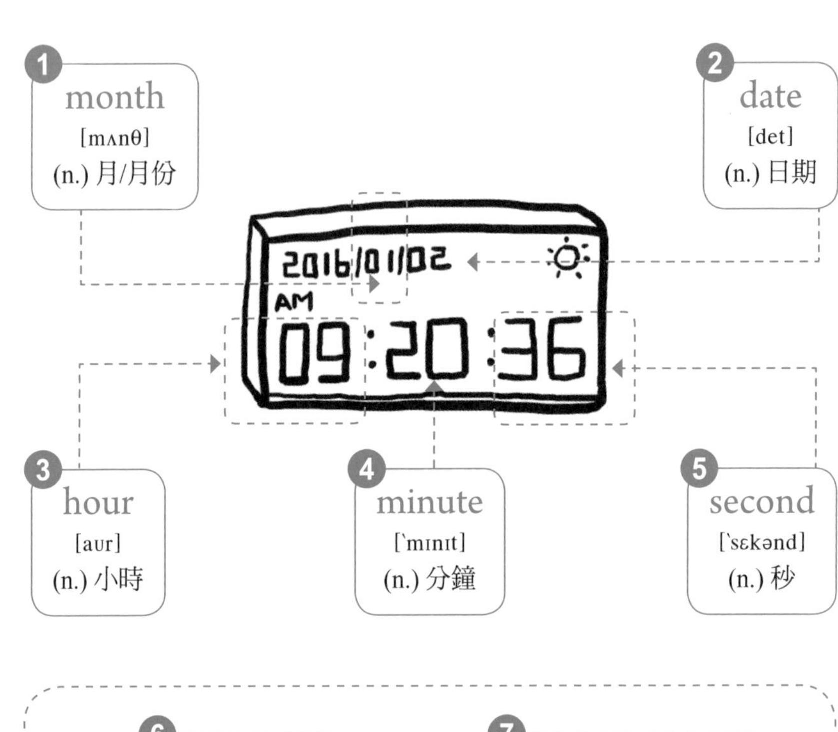

❶ 月／月份

July is my favorite month.

❷ 日期

On what date were you born?

❸ 小時

The exam will last for three hours.

持續三個小時

❹ 分鐘

Rob lives near Olivia. It takes him five minutes to get to her house.

花費他五分鐘的時間

❺ 秒

There are 60 seconds in a minute.

❻ 當地時間

The plane will land in 20 minutes, and the local time is 6:30.

20 分鐘後

❼ 時差

There's a time difference between Taiwan and the US. When it's night here, it's the morning over there.

❽ 時間到

At the end of the exam, the teacher said "Time's up."

學更多

❶ July〈七月〉・favorite〈特別喜愛的〉
❷ be born〈出生〉
❸ exam〈考試〉・last〈持續〉
❹ live〈居住〉・near〈接近〉・take〈花費〉・get〈到達〉・house〈房子〉
❺ there are...〈有…〉
❻ plane〈飛機〉・land〈降落〉・local〈當地的〉・time〈時間〉
❼ difference〈差異〉・between〈在…之間〉・over there〈在那裡〉
❽ end〈最後部分〉・teacher〈老師〉・said〈say（說）的過去式〉

中譯

❶ 七月是我最喜愛的月份。
❷ 你的出生日期是哪一天？
❸ 考試時間為三個小時。
❹ Rob 和 Olivia 住得很近，只需五分鐘就能到她家。
❺ 一分鐘有六十秒。
❻ 飛機將在 20 分鐘後降落，當地時間為 6 點 30 分。
❼ 台灣和美國有時差，當一邊是晚上時，另一邊則是早上。
❽ 在考試的尾聲，老師說：「時間到」。

046 方向&位置(1)

MP3 046

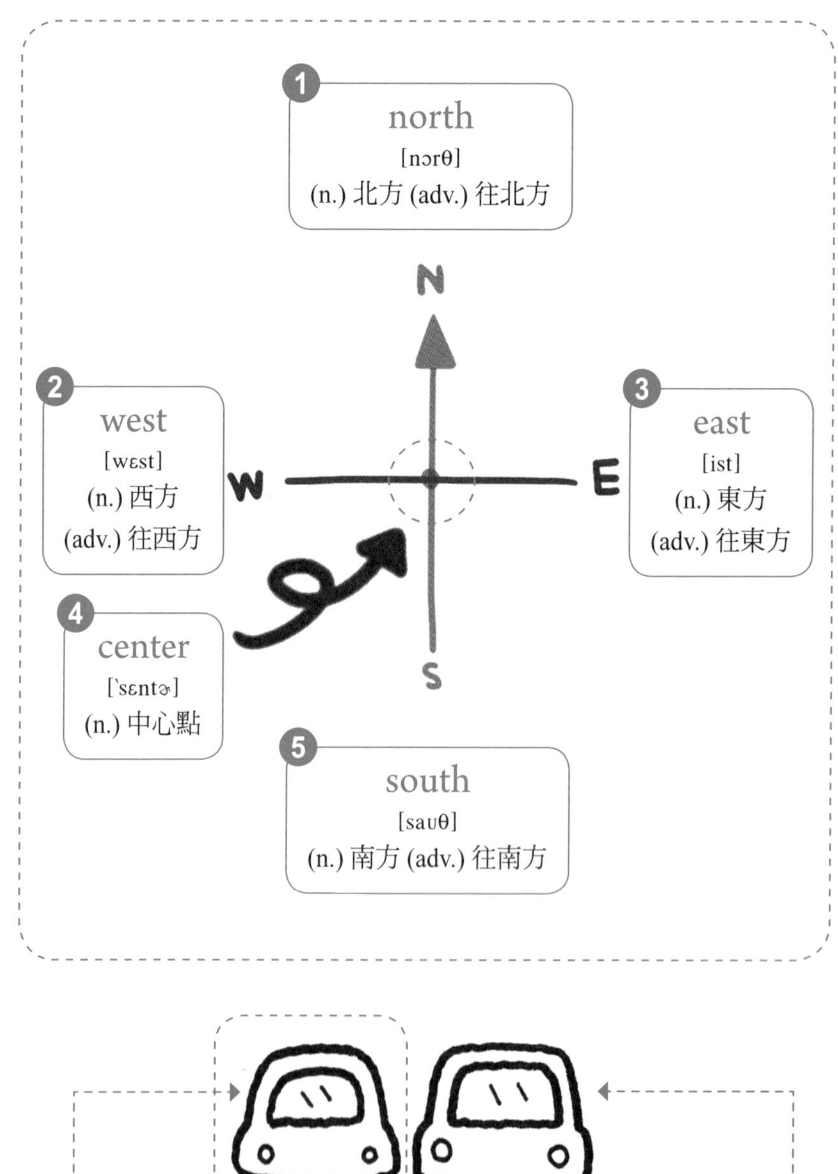

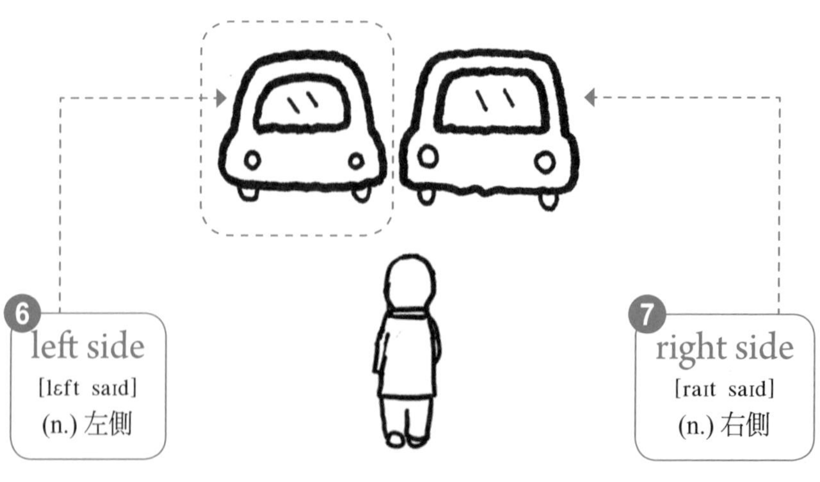

❶ 北方 / 往北方
If you walk north on Fuxing South Road for 30 minutes from Heping East Road, you'll go past Breeze Mall.
復興南路 和平東路 微風廣場

❷ 西方 / 往西方
My bedroom window faces west, which makes my room really hot during the summer.
在夏天時

❸ 東方 / 往東方
Five minutes east of my apartment is my favorite restaurant.

❹ 中心點
The umpire stood in the center of the court at the start of the game.
比賽的開端

❺ 南方 / 往南方
I'm flying south from France to Africa tonight.
往南方飛行

❻ 左側
That picture on the wall is hanging crooked. Its left side is lower than its right.
比它的右側低

❼ 右側
In Taiwan, people drive on the right side of the road.

學更多

❶ walk〈走〉• minute〈分鐘〉• past〈經過〉• breeze〈微風〉• mall〈購物中心〉
❷ bedroom〈臥室〉• face〈朝向〉• make〈使〉• room〈房間〉• during〈在…期間〉
❸ apartment〈公寓〉• favorite〈特別喜愛的〉• restaurant〈餐廳〉
❹ umpire〈裁判〉• stood〈stand（站）的過去式〉• court〈球場〉• game〈比賽〉
❺ flying〈fly（飛行）的 ing 型態〉• France〈法國〉• Africa〈非洲〉
❻ picture〈圖畫〉• wall〈牆壁〉• hanging〈hang（懸掛）的 ing 型態〉• crooked〈歪的〉
❼ people〈人們〉• drive〈駕駛〉• right〈右的〉• side〈邊〉• road〈道路〉

中譯

❶ 如果你從和平東路往北方走到復興南路，走 30 分鐘你就會經過微風廣場。
❷ 我臥室的窗戶朝向西方，這使得我的房間在夏天時真的非常熱。
❸ 我最喜歡的一間餐廳，是在我的公寓往東方五分鐘路程的地方。
❹ 比賽開始時，裁判站到球場的中心點。
❺ 今晚我要搭機從法國往南方飛至非洲。
❻ 牆上的那幅畫掛歪了，它的左側比右側低。
❼ 在台灣，人們行駛於道路的右側。

047 方向&位置(2)

MP3 047

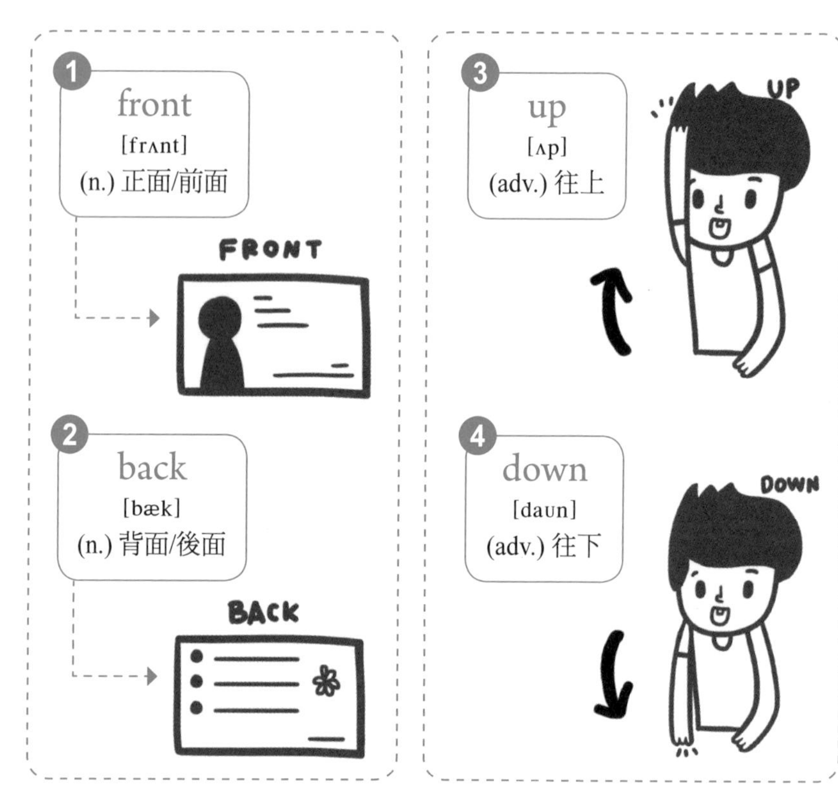

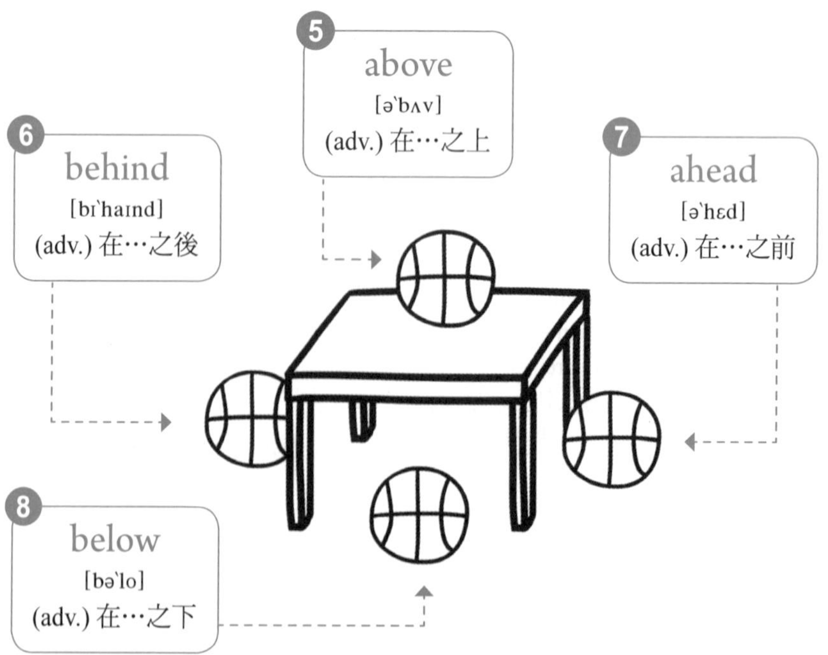

❶ 正面／前面
❷ 背面／後面
There's a picture on the front of my T-shirt; there's nothing on the back.
背面什麼都沒有

❸ 往上
My favorite restaurant is located on the second floor of this building, so
位於
I have to walk up some stairs to get there.

❹ 往下
The stairs going down to the basement are very steep. Be careful or you might stumble.
小心一點

❺ 在…之上
The person living in the apartment above me is noisy. He keeps
住在我的公寓樓上
jumping up and down.
跳上跳下

❻ 在…之後
I turned around because I thought I heard someone behind me.
我聽到了有人在我後面

❼ 在…之前
Gina is faster than us, so she always walks ahead of us.
她總是走在我們前面

❽ 在…之下
Daisy keeps a trash can below her sink.

學更多

❶❷ picture〈圖片〉・T-shirt〈T 恤〉・nothing〈沒什麼〉
❸ second〈第二的〉・floor〈樓層〉・building〈建築物〉・get〈到達〉
❹ stairs〈樓梯〉・basement〈地下室〉・steep〈陡峭的〉・or〈否則〉・stumble〈絆倒〉
❺ person〈人〉・apartment〈公寓〉・noisy〈吵鬧的〉・keep〈持續不斷〉
❻ turned around〈turn around（轉身）的過去式〉・thought〈think（認為）的過去式〉
❼ faster〈較快的，fast（快的）的比較級〉・always〈總是〉・walk〈走〉
❽ keep〈使留在某處〉・trash can〈垃圾桶〉・sink〈水槽〉

中譯

❶❷ 我的 T 恤的前面有一張圖，背面則什麼都沒有。
❸ 我最喜歡的餐廳位於這棟建築物的二樓，所以我必須往上爬些階梯才能到那裡。
❹ 那個往下通往地下室的樓梯非常陡峭，你得小心一點，否則可能會跌倒。
❺ 住在我公寓樓上的人很吵，他老是跳上跳下的。
❻ 我回頭看，因為我覺得有聽到有人在我後面。
❼ Gina 走路的速度比我們快，所以她總是走在我們前面。
❽ Daisy 把垃圾桶放在水槽下面。

048 天氣(1)

MP3 048

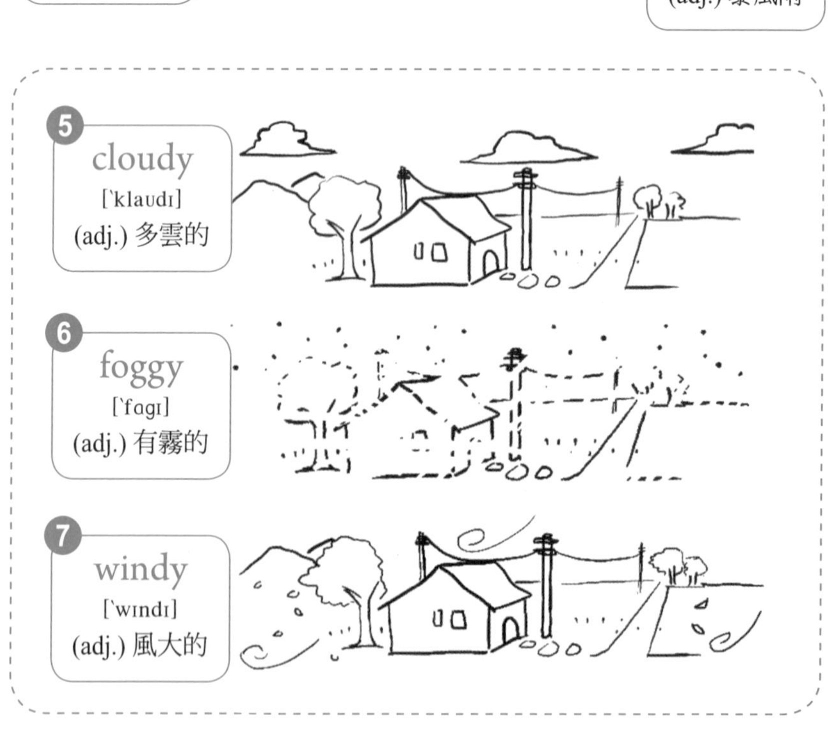

❶ 下雪的
I love snowy weather. It's beautiful when everything is white.
當一切都是雪白的

❷ 融雪 / 融化
The ice on the river thawed when the weather warmed up.
河面上的冰融化了

❸ 下雨的
It's a rainy day. You'll need your umbrella.

❹ 暴風雨
My mom gets scared in stormy weather. She doesn't like the lightning.

❺ 多雲的
It's too cloudy to see any stars tonight.

❻ 有霧的
It's really foggy in the mountains. You won't be able to see very far.

❼ 風大的
It's a windy day, and leaves are being blown into my house.
樹葉被吹進

學更多

❶ weather〈天氣〉・beautiful〈漂亮的〉・everything〈一切事物〉・white〈雪白的〉
❷ ice〈冰〉・river〈河〉・warmed up〈warm up（變暖）的過去式〉
❸ need〈需要〉・umbrella〈雨傘〉
❹ get〈變得〉・scared〈恐懼的〉・lightning〈閃電〉
❺ too...to...〈太…以致於無法…〉・see〈看〉・any〈任何一個〉・star〈星星〉
❻ really〈非常〉・mountain〈山〉・able〈能〉・far〈遠〉
❼ leaves〈leaf（葉子）的複數〉・blown〈blow（吹）的過去分詞〉

中譯

❶ 我喜歡下雪的天氣，當一切都覆蓋一層雪白時很美。
❷ 當天氣變得暖和，河面的冰就融化了。
❸ 今天是個下雨的日子，你會需要你的雨傘。
❹ 我媽媽害怕暴風雨的天氣，她不喜歡閃電。
❺ 今天晚上非常多雲，以致於看不到任何一顆星。
❻ 整座山都是有霧的，你無法看到很遠的地方。
❼ 今天是個風大的日子，樹葉都被吹進家裡。

049 天氣(2)

MP3 049

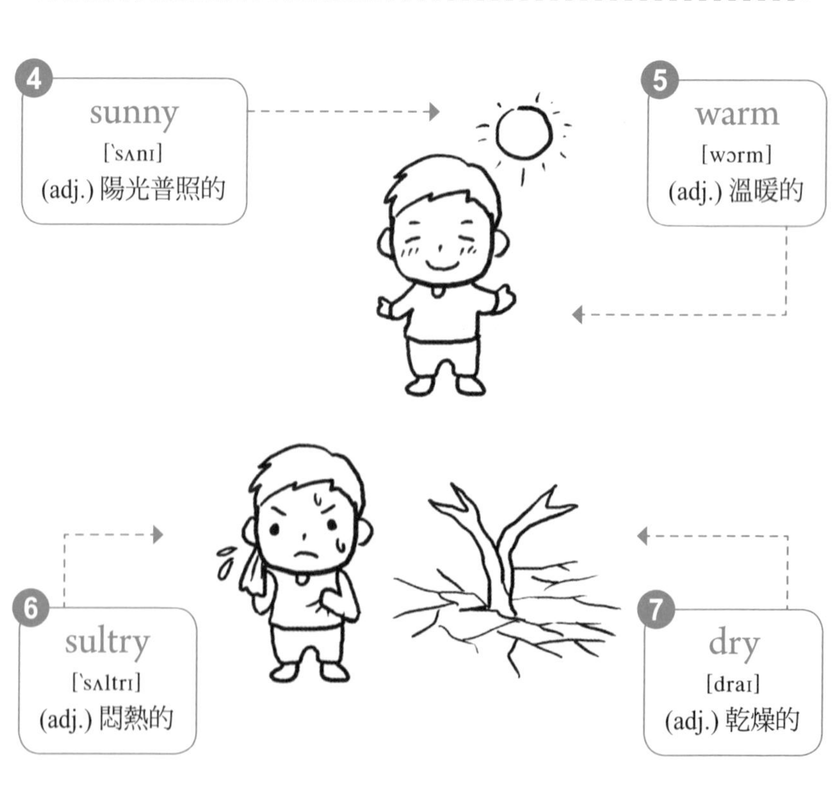

❶ 寒冷的
It's a bit chilly out here; I need a sweater.
在外面這裡

❷ 微涼的
It was warm in the day, but it's quite cool now.
現在比較涼

❸ 結冰
The river froze last night because it was so cold.

❹ 陽光普照的
I love going to the beach on sunny days.

❺ 溫暖的
You won't need a sweater. It's quite warm out here.

❻ 悶熱的
I'm sweating so much in these sultry conditions.
我汗流不止

❼ 乾燥的
It rarely rains in the desert; it's very dry.
沙漠裡很少下雨

學更多

❶ a bit〈有點〉・need〈需要〉・sweater〈毛衣〉
❷ warm〈溫暖的〉・day〈白天〉・quite〈相當、比較〉
❸ river〈河〉・froze〈freeze（結冰）的過去式〉・last night〈昨天晚上〉・cold〈冷的〉
❹ love〈喜愛〉・beach〈海灘〉・day〈日子〉
❺ out〈在外面〉・here〈這裡〉
❻ sweating〈sweat（流汗）的 ing 型態〉・conditions〈環境〉
❼ rarely〈很少〉・rain〈下雨〉・desert〈沙漠〉

中譯

❶ 外面這裡有點冷，我需要加件毛衣。
❷ 白天很溫暖，但現在比較涼。
❸ 這條河流昨天晚上結冰了，因為當時天氣非常寒冷。
❹ 我喜歡在陽光普照的日子去海邊。
❺ 你不需要穿毛衣，外面這裡很溫暖。
❻ 在這悶熱的環境裡，我汗流不止。
❼ 沙漠裡很少下雨，天氣非常乾燥。

050 常見商店(1)

MP3 050

1. grocery store
[ˋgrosərɪ stor]
(n.) 雜貨店

2. convenience store
[kənˋvinjəns stor]
(n.) 便利商店

3. supermarket
[ˋsupɚˏmarkɪt]
(n.) 超級市場

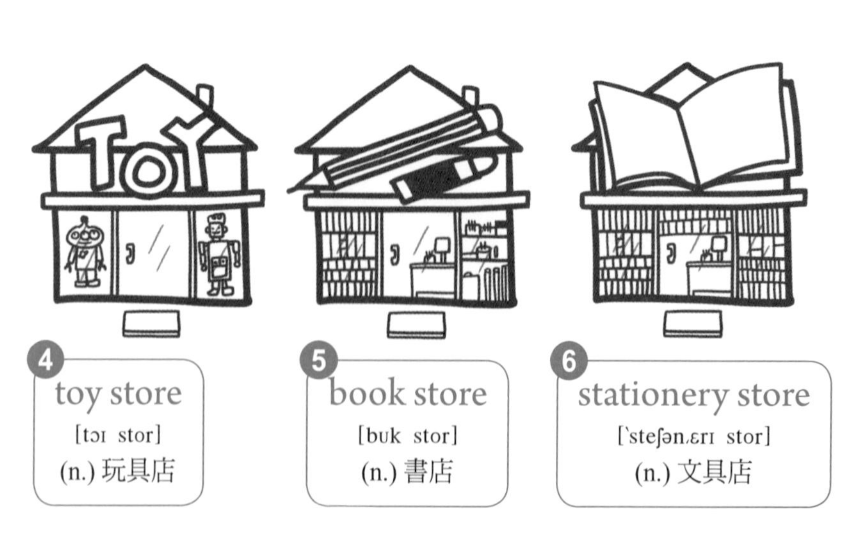

4. toy store
[tɔɪ stor]
(n.) 玩具店

5. book store
[buk stor]
(n.) 書店

6. stationery store
[ˋsteʃənˏɛrɪ stor]
(n.) 文具店

❶ 雜貨店

Rich went to the grocery store to pick up some food.

買一些食物

❷ 便利商店

Sam buys drinks from the convenience store on the corner.

❸ 超級市場

Supermarkets have a lot of items at pretty low prices.

有很多商品

❹ 玩具店

Kids love looking at all the toys in the toy store.

❺ 書店

The student bought some textbooks in the book store.

❻ 文具店

Ian bought pens and pencils in the stationery store.

學更多

❶ went〈go（去）的過去式〉• grocery〈食品雜貨店〉• store〈店〉• pick up〈買東西〉• some〈一些〉• food〈食物〉

❷ drink〈飲料〉• convenience〈方便〉• corner〈街角〉

❸ item〈物品〉• pretty〈相當〉• low〈低的〉• price〈價格〉

❹ love〈喜愛〉• looking at〈look at（看…）的 ing 型態〉• all〈所有的〉• toy〈玩具〉

❺ bought〈buy（買）的過去式〉• textbook〈教科書〉• book〈書籍〉

❻ pen〈原子筆〉• pencil〈鉛筆〉• stationery〈文具〉

中譯

❶ Rich 到雜貨店買了一些食物。

❷ Sam 在街角的便利商店買飲料。

❸ 超級市場裡有許多價格低廉的商品。

❹ 孩子們喜歡看玩具店裡的所有玩具。

❺ 那名學生在書店買了幾本教科書。

❻ Ian 在文具店買了一些原子筆和鉛筆。

051 常見商店(2)

MP3 051

1. **food stand** [fud stænd] (n.) 小吃攤
2. **restaurant** [ˋrɛstərənt] (n.) 餐廳
3. **online store** [ˋɑnˌlaɪn stor] (n.) 線上商店
4. **shopping mall** [ˋʃɑpɪŋ mɔl] (n.) 購物中心
5. **second-hand store** [ˋsɛkəndˋhænd stor] (n.) 二手商店
6. **boutique** [buˋtik] (n.) 精品店
7. **bargain shop** [ˋbɑrgɪn ʃɑp] (n.) 平價商店

❶ 小吃攤
They make dumplings at this food stand.
做餃子

❷ 餐廳
After shopping, Gail likes to eat in a restaurant.

❸ 線上商店
I don't go out to do my shopping. I just visit online stores.
購物

❹ 購物中心
There are so many different kinds of shops in the shopping mall.
各種不同類型的商店

❺ 二手商店
Everything in the second-hand store has been used before.
以前就已經被使用過

❻ 精品店
The little boutique sells fashionable clothes.
流行服飾

❼ 平價商店
I love bargain shops. Everything's so cheap!

學更多

❶ make〈做〉・dumpling〈餃子〉・stand〈攤子〉
❷ shopping〈shop（購物）的 ing 型態〉・eat〈用餐〉
❸ go out〈外出〉・shopping〈購物〉・just〈只〉・visit〈拜訪〉・online〈線上〉
❹ different〈不同的〉・kind〈種類〉・shop〈商店〉
❺ second-hand〈二手的〉・used〈use（使用）的過去分詞〉・before〈以前〉
❻ little〈小的〉・sell〈販售〉・fashionable〈流行的〉・clothes〈衣服〉
❼ love〈喜愛〉・bargain〈便宜商品〉・everything〈一切事物〉・cheap〈便宜的〉

中譯

❶ 他們在這家小吃攤賣餃子。
❷ 逛街之後，Gail 喜歡到餐廳用餐。
❸ 我不出門購物，我只逛網路商店。
❹ 購物中心裡有許多各類型的商店。
❺ 二手商店販賣的所有商品，都是之前有人使用過的。
❻ 這間小型的精品店販售流行服飾。
❼ 我愛平價商店，裡面所有的商品都超便宜！

052 常見成藥(1)

MP3 052

1 anti-inflammatory
[ˌæntɪɪn`flæməˌtorɪ]
(n.) 消炎藥 (adj.) 消炎的

2 painkiller
[penˌkɪlɚ]
(n.) 止痛藥

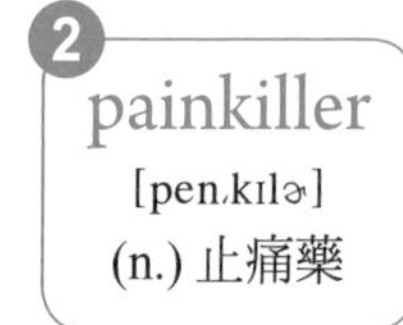

3 gastric drug
[`gæstrɪk drʌg]
(n.) 胃藥

4 aspirin
[`æspərɪn]
(n.) 阿斯匹靈

5 antipyretic
[ˌæntɪpaɪ`rɛtɪk]
(n.) 退燒藥 (adj.) 退燒的

6 cough syrup
[kɔf `sɪrəp]
(n.) 咳嗽糖漿

❶ 消炎藥 / 消炎的

The doctor gave Sarah an anti-inflammatory drug for her fever.

❷ 止痛藥

My back's really hurting me. I need to take a painkiller.

服用止痛藥

❸ 胃藥

This is a gastric drug. It will help your stomach to feel better.

❹ 阿斯匹靈

Aspirin can help you in lots of ways; it's very good if you have a headache.

在許多方面幫助你 如果你頭痛

❺ 退燒藥 / 退燒的

I asked the doctor for some antipyretic medicine, like ibuprofen, for my fever.

我向醫生要求

❻ 咳嗽糖漿

The man took some cough syrup to treat his sore throat.

喝了一些咳嗽糖漿 喉嚨痛

學更多

❶ gave〈give（給）的過去式〉・inflammatory〈發炎的〉・drug〈藥〉・fever〈發燒〉

❷ back〈背部〉・hurting〈hurt（使疼痛）的 ing 型態〉・take〈服藥〉

❸ gastric〈胃的〉・help〈幫助〉・stomach〈胃〉・feel〈感覺〉・better〈比較好〉

❹ lots of〈許多〉・way〈方面〉・if〈如果〉・headache〈頭痛〉

❺ asked〈ask（要求）的過去式〉・like〈像〉・ibuprofen〈布洛芬，一種消炎止痛的退燒藥〉・medicine〈藥〉

❻ cough〈咳嗽〉・syrup〈糖漿〉・treat〈治療〉・sore〈疼痛發炎的〉・throat〈喉嚨〉

中譯

❶ 醫生開給 Sarah 消炎的藥來治療發燒。

❷ 我的背真的好痛。我需要服用止痛藥。

❸ 這是胃藥。它有助於讓你的胃舒服一點。

❹ 阿斯匹靈可以在許多時候派上用場；如果你頭痛，它非常有效。

❺ 我跟醫生要了一些退燒的藥——像是布洛芬，來治療我的發燒。

❻ 那位男士喝了些咳嗽糖漿來治療他的喉嚨痛。

053 常見成藥(2)

MP3 053

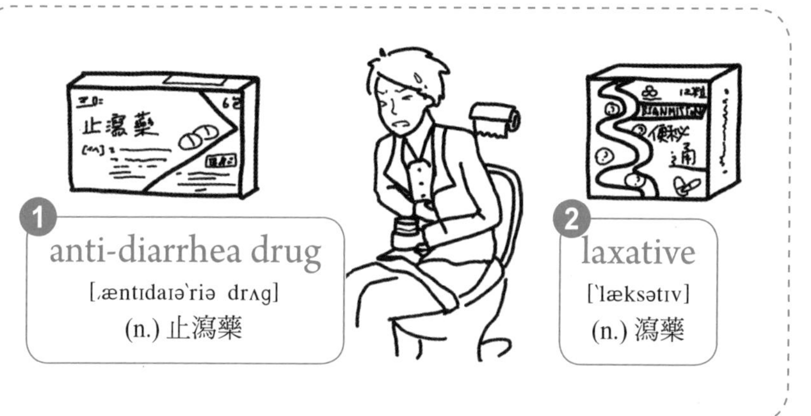

❶ **anti-diarrhea drug**
[ˌæntɪdaɪəˋriə drʌg]
(n.) 止瀉藥

❷ **laxative**
[ˋlæksətɪv]
(n.) 瀉藥

❸ **eye drops**
[aɪ drɑps]
(n.) 眼藥水

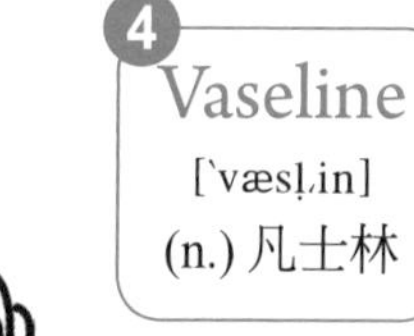

❹ **Vaseline**
[ˋvæsḷˌin]
(n.) 凡士林

兩個單字都是「香港腳藥膏」。

❺ **athlete's foot cream**
[ˋæθlits fʊt krim]
athlete's foot lotion
[ˋæθlits fʊt ˋloʃən]
(n.) 香港腳藥膏

❻ **pain care patch**
[pen kɛr pætʃ]
(n.) 痠痛貼布

❶ 止瀉藥

My stomach feels terrible and I keep rushing to the toilet. I really need an anti-diarrhea drug.

我不斷衝去廁所

❷ 瀉藥

After taking a strong laxative, Dan had to rush to the toilet.

必須衝去廁所

❸ 眼藥水

Neil's eyes were itchy, so he used some eye drops to ease the soreness.

他用了幾滴眼藥水

❹ 凡士林

You can use Vaseline to keep your skin moisturized.

使你的肌膚保持濕潤

❺ 香港腳藥膏

After wearing wet shoes all day, my feet are itchy, so I've got some athlete's foot cream for them.

穿著濕鞋子一整天　我為我的腳擦了一些香港腳藥膏

❻ 痠痛貼布

After carrying heavy boxes all day, he put some pain care patches on his muscles.

搬運沉重的箱子　貼了一些痠痛貼布

學更多

❶ stomach〈胃〉‧terrible〈極糟的〉‧keep〈持續不斷〉‧
rushing to〈rush to（衝向⋯）的 ing 型態〉‧anti〈反抗〉‧diarrhea〈腹瀉〉

❷ taking〈take（服藥）的 ing 形態〉‧strong〈強烈的〉‧toilet〈廁所〉

❸ eye〈眼睛〉‧itchy〈癢的〉‧drops〈滴劑〉‧ease〈減輕〉‧soreness〈疼痛〉

❹ keep〈保持某一狀態〉‧skin〈皮膚〉‧moisturized〈moisturize（使濕潤）的過去分詞〉

❺ wet〈濕的〉‧athlete〈運動員〉‧cream〈藥用乳膏〉‧lotion〈藥膏〉

❻ heavy〈沉重的〉‧pain〈疼痛〉‧care〈照料〉‧patch〈貼片〉‧muscle〈肌肉〉

中譯

❶ 我的胃很不舒服，而且一直跑廁所，我真的很需要止瀉藥。

❷ 服用強效瀉藥後，Dan 必須衝去廁所。

❸ Neil 的眼睛很癢，所以他滴了幾滴眼藥水來減輕疼痛。

❹ 你可以用凡士林讓你的肌膚保持濕潤。

❺ 穿著濕鞋子一整天之後，我的腳很癢，所以我擦了些香港腳藥膏。

❻ 搬重箱子一整天之後，他在肌肉上貼了一些痠痛貼布。

054

居家隔間(1)

MP3 054

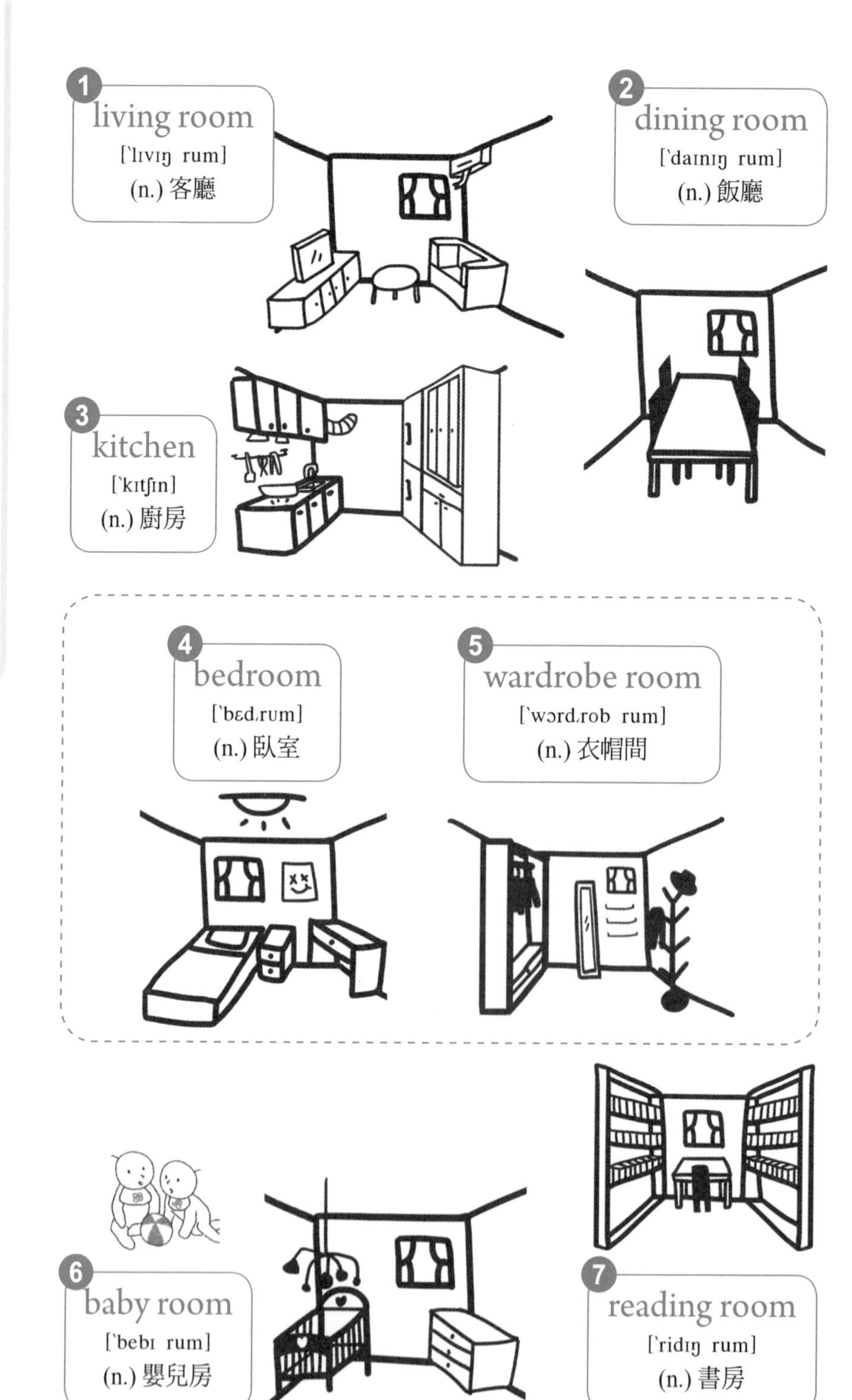

❶ 客廳

When I get home from work, I like to sit down and watch TV in the living room.

我下班回到家

❷ 飯廳

The woman always likes to entertain dinner guests in the dining room.

在飯廳招待客人晚餐

❸ 廚房

Gary loves cooking, so he spends lots of time in the kitchen.

❹ 臥室

I like my bedroom to be dark, cool, and quiet when I go to sleep at nighttime.

❺ 衣帽間

The rich lady has a lot of clothes, so she wants a home with its own wardrobe room.

貴婦　一個有獨立衣帽間的家

❻ 嬰兒房

As soon as she knew that she was pregnant, the woman started talking about decorating the baby room.

她一知道自己懷孕之後　開始討論…

❼ 書房

The man has converted one of the bedrooms into a reading room where he can look through newspapers, books, and magazines.

學更多

❶ work〈工作〉‧sit down〈坐下〉‧watch〈觀看〉‧living〈生活〉‧room〈房間〉
❷ entertain〈招待〉‧dinner〈晚餐〉‧guest〈客人〉‧dining〈進餐〉
❸ cooking〈烹飪〉‧spend〈花費〉‧lots of〈許多〉‧time〈時間〉
❹ dark〈黑暗的〉‧cool〈涼快的〉‧quiet〈安靜的〉‧nighttime〈夜間〉
❺ rich〈有錢的〉‧a lot of〈許多〉‧clothes〈衣服〉‧own〈自己的〉‧wardrobe〈衣櫥〉
❻ as soon as〈一…就…〉‧pregnant〈懷孕的〉‧decorating〈decorate（裝飾）的 ing 型態〉
❼ converted〈convert（改裝）的過去分詞〉‧look through〈瀏覽〉‧magazine〈雜誌〉

中譯

❶ 當我下班回到家，我喜歡坐在客廳看電視。
❷ 那名女子總是喜歡在飯廳招待客人享用晚餐。
❸ Gary 喜歡烹飪，所以他花很多時間待在廚房。
❹ 晚上睡覺時，我喜歡臥室是幽暗、涼爽又安靜的。
❺ 那位貴婦擁有許多衣服，所以她希望家裡有一個獨立的衣帽間。
❻ 這位女士一知道自己懷孕後，便開始討論要如何佈置嬰兒房。
❼ 那個男人把其中一間臥室改成書房，讓自己能在裡面看報、讀書、以及翻閱雜誌。

055 居家隔間(2)

MP3 055

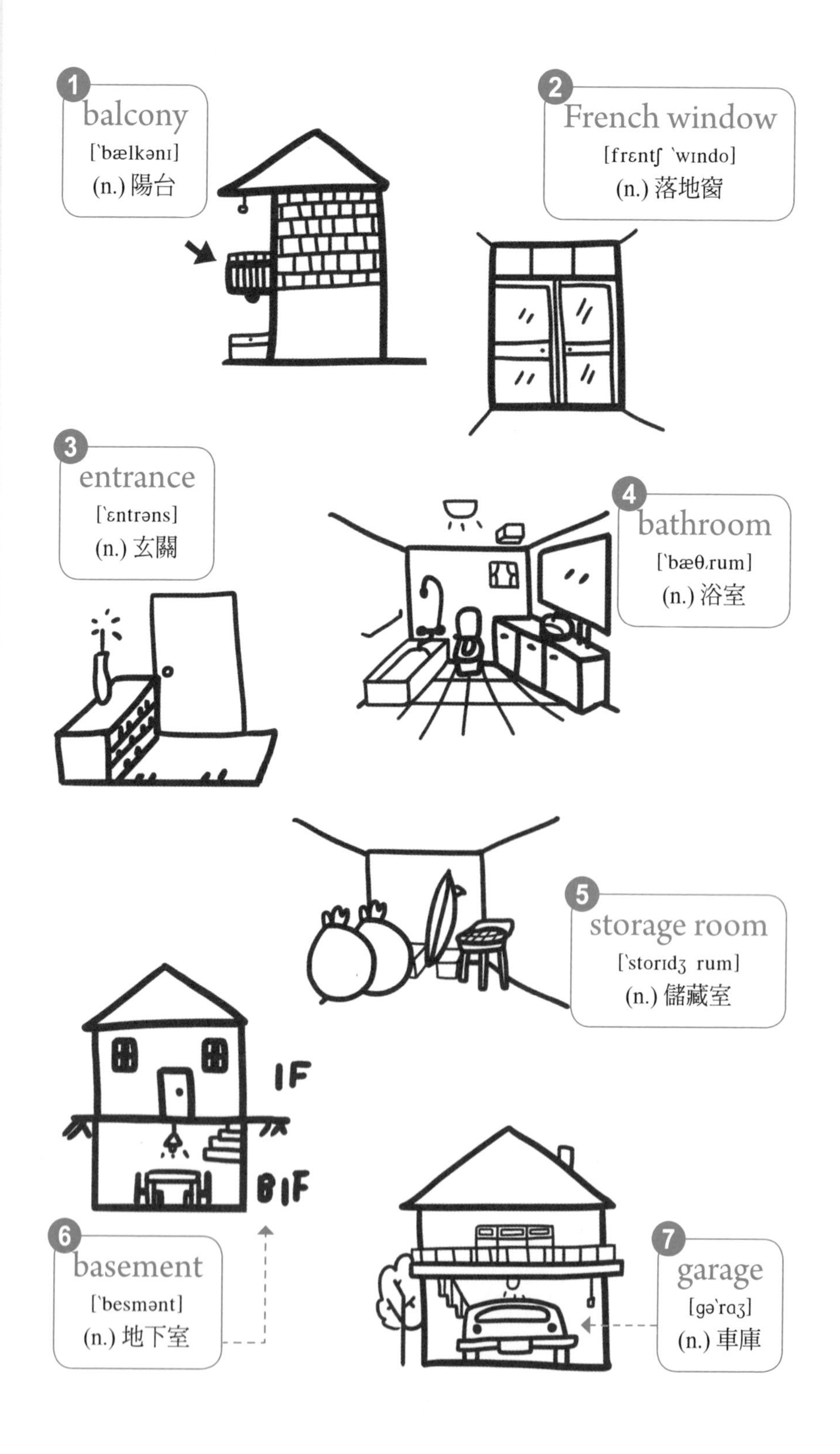

❶ 陽台

The couple stood out on the balcony and enjoyed the cool, evening air.

站在外面的陽台上

❷ 落地窗

This room has French windows, so it's always very bright in here.

❸ 玄關

Guests are usually asked to take off their shoes and leave them in the house's entrance.

脫掉他們的鞋子

❹ 浴室

Mrs. Harris is taking a long, hot shower in the bathroom.

❺ 儲藏室

The family's storage room is full of boxes, old toys, and sports equipment.

❻ 地下室

The family stores the things they don't use under the house in the basement.

儲存他們不用的東西

❼ 車庫

The garage is big enough for two cars.

大到可以停放兩輛車子

學更多

❶ couple〈夫妻〉・out〈在外面〉・cool〈涼快的〉・evening〈傍晚〉・air〈空氣〉
❷ French〈法國的〉・window〈窗戶〉・always〈總是〉・bright〈明亮的〉
❸ usually〈通常地〉・asked〈ask（要求）的過去分詞〉・take off〈脫掉〉・leave〈留下〉
❹ taking〈take（做）的 ing 型態〉・long〈長久的〉・hot〈熱的〉・shower〈淋浴〉
❺ storage〈儲藏〉・be full of〈充滿…的〉・sports〈運動的〉・equipment〈器具〉
❻ family〈家庭〉・store〈儲藏〉・use〈使用〉・under〈在…下方〉・house〈房子〉
❼ big〈大的〉・enough〈足夠地〉・car〈車子〉

中譯

❶ 那對夫妻站在屋外的陽台，享受傍晚涼爽的空氣。
❷ 這個房間有落地窗，所以房間裡總是非常明亮。
❸ 客人通常會被要求脫鞋，並放在房子的玄關處。
❹ Harris 太太正在浴室洗一個長時間的熱水澡。
❺ 這個家庭的儲藏室堆滿了箱子、舊玩具和運動器材。
❻ 這家人把他們不用的東西，都存放在屋子下方的地下室。
❼ 這個車庫大到可以停放兩輛車。

056
掃除用具(1)

MP3 056

1 floor wax
[flor wæks]
(n.) 地板蠟
2 vacuum cleaner
[ˋvækjʊəm ˋklinɚ]
(n.) 吸塵器

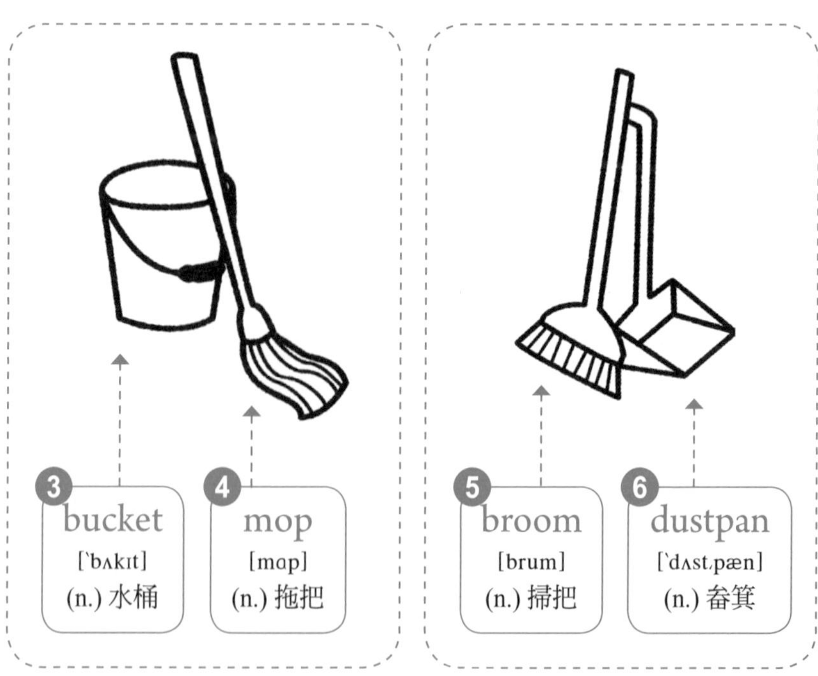
3 bucket
[ˋbʌkɪt]
(n.) 水桶
4 mop
[mɑp]
(n.) 拖把
5 broom
[brum]
(n.) 掃把
6 dustpan
[ˋdʌst͵pæn]
(n.) 畚箕

❶ 地板蠟
Floor wax makes floors look shiny and clean.

❷ 吸塵器
Vacuum cleaners suck dirt and dust up from the floor.
吸起汙物和灰塵

❸ 水桶
You can put water in this bucket when you mop the floors.
把水裝進這個水桶

❹ 拖把
Frank wet the mop and used it to clean the floor.

❺ 掃把
The mother asked her son to sweep the floor with the broom.
用掃把掃地

❻ 畚箕
After sweeping up all the dust, the boy brushed it into a dustpan.
掃進畚箕裡

學更多

❶ wax〈蠟〉・make〈使得〉・shiny〈發光的、有光澤的〉・clean〈乾淨的〉
❷ vacuum〈真空裝置〉・cleaner〈吸塵器〉・suck up〈吸收〉・dirt〈汙物〉・dust〈灰塵〉
❸ put〈放〉・mop〈用拖把拖〉・floor〈地板〉
❹ wet〈wet（弄濕）的過去式〉・used〈use（使用）的過去式〉・clean〈清掃〉
❺ asked〈ask（要求）的過去式〉・sweep〈掃〉
❻ sweeping〈sweep（掃）的 ing 型態〉・brushed〈brush（拂去）的過去式〉

中譯

❶ 地板蠟讓地板看起來既閃亮又乾淨。
❷ 吸塵器能吸起地板上的汙物及灰塵。
❸ 當你拖地時，可以用這個水桶來裝水。
❹ Frank 把拖把弄濕，然後用來擦地板。
❺ 那位媽媽叫她的兒子用掃把掃地。
❻ 掃完所有灰塵後，男孩把它掃進畚箕裡。

057 掃除用具(2)

MP3 057

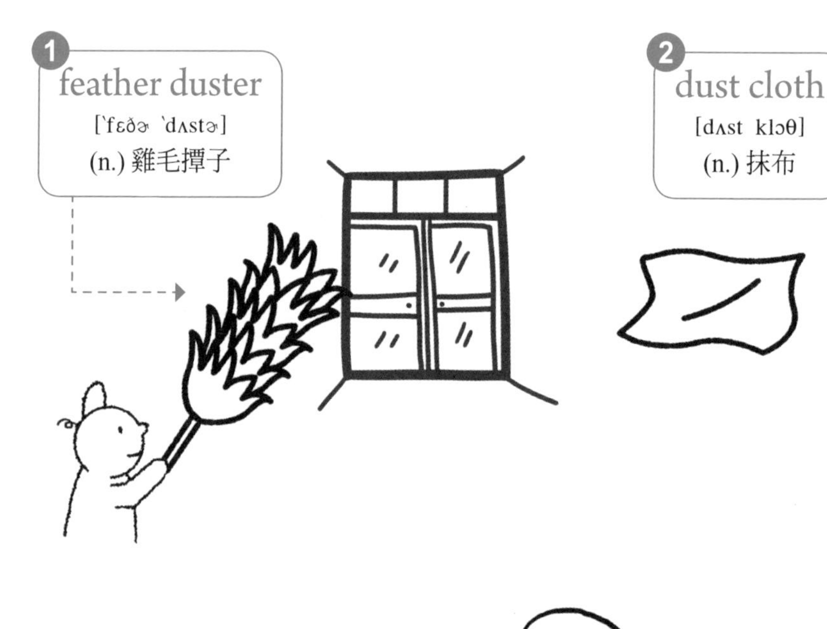

1 feather duster
[ˋfɛðɚ ˋdʌstɚ]
(n.) 雞毛撢子

2 dust cloth
[dʌst klɔθ]
(n.) 抹布

3 working gloves
[ˋwɝkɪŋ glʌvz]
(n.) 家事手套

4 cleaning brush
[ˋklinɪŋ brʌʃ]
(n.) 清潔刷

5 cleanser
[ˋklɛnzɚ]
(n.) 清潔劑

❶ 雞毛撢子

Not many people still use feather dusters to clean their houses.

很少人

❷ 抹布

Emily used a dust cloth to wipe the dust off her tables and shelves.

擦掉她的桌子及書架的灰塵

❸ 家事手套

To protect your hands when you're cleaning, you might want to use working gloves.

❹ 清潔刷

It's best to use a cleaning brush when you clean your toilet.

最好使用清潔刷

❺ 清潔劑

People usually use cleansers to clean their kitchens and bathrooms.

學更多

❶ still〈仍然〉‧feather〈羽毛〉‧duster〈撢子〉‧clean〈打掃〉

❷ dust〈灰塵〉‧cloth〈布〉‧wipe off〈擦掉〉‧shelves〈shelf（書架架子）的複數〉

❸ protect〈保護〉‧hand〈手〉‧cleaning〈clean（打掃）的 ing 型態〉‧use〈使用〉‧working〈工作〉‧glove〈手套〉

❹ best〈最好的〉‧cleaning〈打掃〉‧brush〈刷子〉‧toilet〈馬桶〉

❺ usually〈經常〉‧kitchen〈廚房〉‧bathroom〈浴室〉

中譯

❶ 現在很少人還在使用雞毛撢子清掃家裡。

❷ Emily 用抹布擦掉她桌上及書架的灰塵。

❸ 打掃時為了保護雙手，你可能需要戴上家事手套。

❹ 清洗馬桶時，你最好使用清潔刷。

❺ 人們經常使用清潔劑，來清潔廚房和浴室。

058 寵物用品(1)

MP3 058

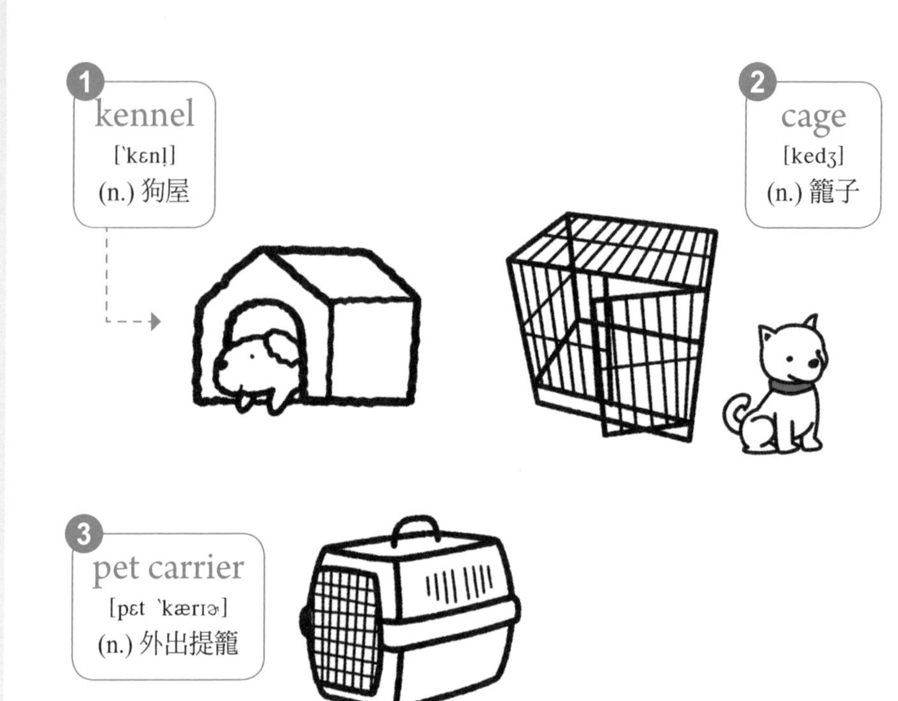

1 kennel [ˋkɛnl̩] (n.) 狗屋

2 cage [kedʒ] (n.) 籠子

3 pet carrier [pɛt ˋkærɪɚ] (n.) 外出提籠

4 pet food [pɛt fud] (n.) 飼料

5 bowl [bol] (n.) 飼料碗

6 pet cookie [pɛt ˋkʊkɪ] (n.) 寵物餅乾

❶ 狗屋

Frank doesn't like to keep the dog in the house, so the animal has to sleep in a kennel outside.

讓狗待在屋子裡　必須睡在外面的狗屋裡

❷ 籠子

I keep my pet bird in a large cage.

❸ 外出提籠

She loves her little dog and takes it everywhere in a pet carrier.

帶著牠到處走

❹ 飼料

You should be careful when you buy pet food; make sure you get good-quality food.

❺ 飼料碗

Jessie likes buying things for her dog. She bought her a new bowl last weekend.

美國人習慣用「he」和「she」稱呼寵物，也可以用「it」。

❻ 寵物餅乾

I give my dog pet cookies when he behaves well.

表現良好

學更多

❶ keep〈使留在某處〉・animal〈動物〉・sleep〈睡覺〉・outside〈在外面〉
❷ pet〈寵物〉・bird〈鳥〉・large〈大的〉
❸ little〈小的〉・everywhere〈到處〉・carrier〈搬運工具〉
❹ careful〈小心的〉・make sure〈確定〉・get〈買到〉・quality〈品質〉
❺ buying〈buy（買）的 ing 型態〉・bought〈buy（買）的過去式〉・weekend〈週末〉
❻ give〈給〉・cookie〈甜餅乾〉・behave〈表現〉・well〈很好地〉

中譯

❶ Frank 不喜歡讓狗待在屋子裡，所以牠必須睡在外面的狗屋。
❷ 我把我的寵物鳥關在一個大籠子裡。
❸ 她很愛她的小狗，還會把牠放進外出提籠，帶牠到處走。
❹ 買飼料時要小心一點，要確認你買的是品質良好的飼料。
❺ Jessie 喜歡買東西給她的小狗。上週末她買了一個新的飼料碗給牠。
❻ 當我的狗狗表現良好時，我會給牠寵物餅乾。

059 寵物用品(2)

MP3 059

1 cat litter
[kæt `lɪtɚ]
(n.) 貓砂
2 pet clothes
[pɛt kloz]
(n.) 寵物衣服
3 pet collar
[pɛt `kɑlɚ]
(n.) 項圈
4 pet leash
[pɛt liʃ]
(n.) 牽繩
除蚤劑
5 anti-flea spray
[`æntɪˌfli spre]
(n.) 除蚤噴劑

❶ 貓砂

It's important to use cat litter if you don't want your house to smell bad.

你的房子聞起來有異味

❷ 寵物衣服

My girlfriend thinks pet clothes look cute, but I don't want to dress up my dog.

❸ 項圈

I bought my dog a pet collar after he ran away the first time.

美國人習慣用「he」和「she」稱呼寵物，也可以用「it」。

❹ 牽繩

Mandy keeps her dog on a pet leash when she takes it on a walk.

幫她的狗繫上牽繩

❺ 除蚤噴劑

I think it's time to buy some more anti-flea spray; the dog keeps scratching himself.

狗一直在抓癢

學更多

❶ important〈重要的〉・litter〈貓砂〉・smell〈聞起來〉・bad〈不好的〉

❷ pet〈寵物〉・clothes〈衣服〉・look〈看起來〉・cute〈可愛的〉・dress up〈打扮〉

❸ bought〈buy（買）的過去式〉・collar〈項圈〉・after〈在…之後〉・ran away〈run away（跑掉）的過去式〉・first〈第一的〉・time〈次〉

❹ leash〈拴狗用的皮帶〉・walk〈散步〉

❺ anti〈抵抗〉・flea〈跳蚤〉・spray〈噴劑〉・keep〈持續不斷〉・scratching〈scratch（抓癢）的 ing 型態〉

中譯

❶ 如果你不希望屋子聞起來有異味，使用貓砂是很重要的。

❷ 我的女朋友覺得寵物衣服看起來很可愛，但我不想讓我的狗穿衣服。

❸ 我的狗第一次跑掉之後，我就買了一個項圈給牠戴。

❹ Mandy 溜狗時，她會幫狗繫上牽繩。

❺ 我想是時候多買些除蚤噴劑了；家裡的狗一直在抓癢。

060 通訊設備(1)

MP3 060

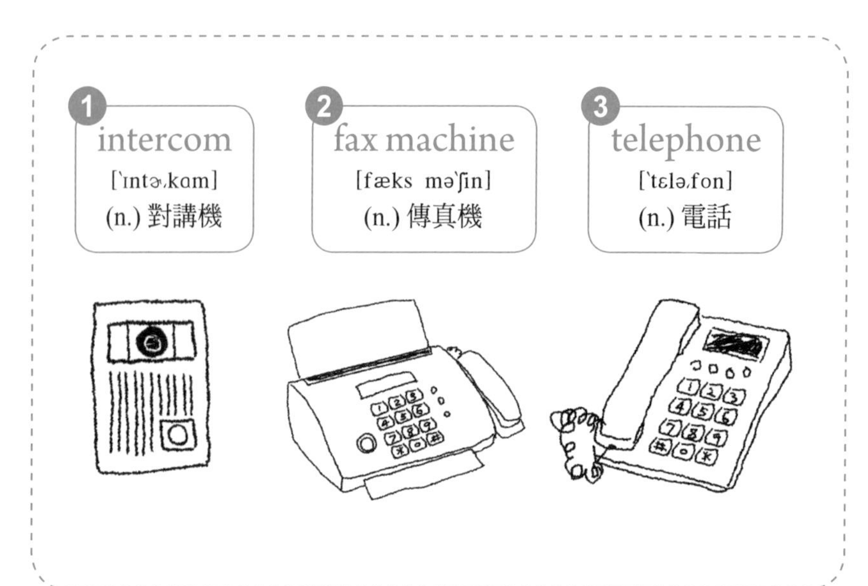

1. **intercom** [ˋɪntɚˏkɑm] (n.) 對講機
2. **fax machine** [fæks məˋʃin] (n.) 傳真機
3. **telephone** [ˋtɛləˏfon] (n.) 電話

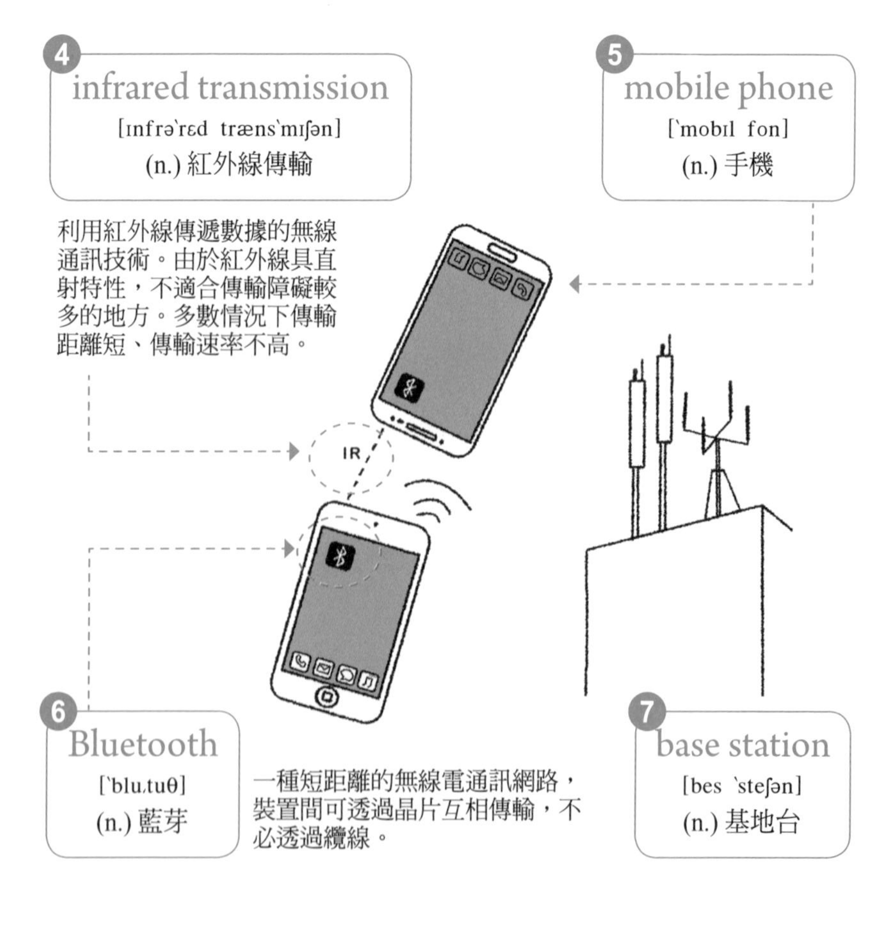

4. **infrared transmission** [ɪnfrəˋrɛd trænsˋmɪʃən] (n.) 紅外線傳輸

利用紅外線傳遞數據的無線通訊技術。由於紅外線具直射特性，不適合傳輸障礙較多的地方。多數情況下傳輸距離短、傳輸速率不高。

5. **mobile phone** [ˋmobɪl fon] (n.) 手機
6. **Bluetooth** [ˋbluˏtuθ] (n.) 藍芽

一種短距離的無線電通訊網路，裝置間可透過晶片互相傳輸，不必透過纜線。

7. **base station** [bes ˋsteʃən] (n.) 基地台

❶ 對講機

The boss used the office intercom to ask his secretary a question.

❷ 傳真機

Do you have a fax machine in your office? I need to send you some documents.

發送一些文件給你

❸ 電話

Give me your telephone number. I'd like to call you over the weekend.

我想打電話給你（= I would like to call you）

❹ 紅外線傳輸

My laptop is currently linked to my desktop via an infrared transmission.

現在正被連結到… 透過紅外線傳輸

❺ 手機

Neil can't make any calls because he dropped his mobile phone and broke it.

不能打電話 摔落他的手機並且弄壞了

❻ 藍芽

Jean uses a Bluetooth headset when she drives. It allows her to talk on the phone without using her hands.

❼ 基地台

There's a base station in the taxi company's main office. The manager uses

計程車行的總公司

it to keep in contact with his drivers.

保持聯繫

學更多

❶ boss〈老闆〉・office〈辦公室〉・secretary〈秘書〉・question〈問題〉
❷ fax〈傳真〉・machine〈機器〉・send〈寄、發送〉・document〈文件〉
❸ number〈號碼〉・call〈打電話〉・over〈在…期間〉・weekend〈週末〉
❹ laptop〈筆記型電腦〉・desktop〈桌上型電腦〉・via〈透過〉・infrared〈紅外線的〉
❺ dropped〈drop（掉落）的過去式〉・mobile〈移動式的〉・broke〈break（弄壞）的過去式〉
❻ headset〈耳機〉・drive〈開車〉・allow〈使成為可能〉・without〈沒有〉
❼ taxi〈計程車〉・company〈公司〉・main〈主要的〉・manager〈負責人〉

中譯

❶ 老闆利用辦公室的對講機問秘書一個問題。
❷ 你的辦公室裡有傳真機嗎？我需要傳送一些文件給你。
❸ 給我你的電話號碼，我想在週末打電話給你。
❹ 我的筆記型電腦透過紅外線傳輸，現在正連結到我的桌上型電腦。
❺ Neil 不能打電話，因為他摔壞了他的手機。
❻ Jean 開車時會使用藍芽耳機，這使她不需要用到手就能講電話。
❼ 計程車行的總公司裡有一個基地台，車行負責人用它來和他的司機們保持聯繫。

061

通訊設備(2)

MP3 061

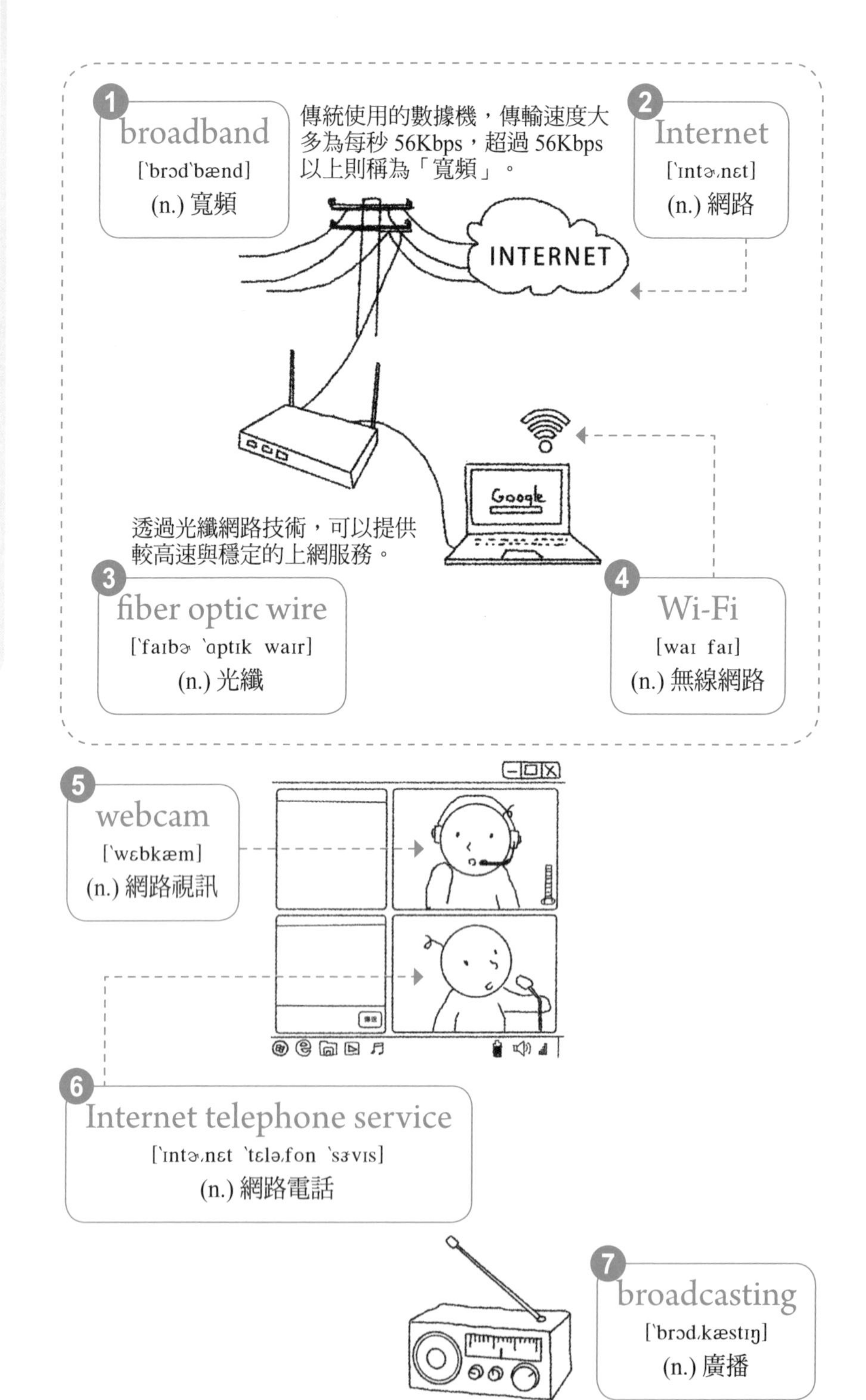

❶ 寬頻

People with broadband Internet connections are able to access websites more quickly.

寬頻網路連接

❷ 網路

I love looking for information on the Internet. You can find anything on there.

❸ 光纖

Fiber optic wires can transport much more information than copper wires.

傳遞更多的資訊

❹ 無線網路

My dad has Wi-Fi in his home and can use his laptop in any room

❺ 網路視訊

The young lovers use webcams to see one another when they chat on the Internet.

使用網路視訊看對方

❻ 網路電話

When I'm overseas, I use an Internet telephone service to talk with my family, because it's cheaper than regular telephone networks.

一般的電話網路

❼ 廣播

The BBC produces radio and TV programs, and it is one of the world's oldest broadcasting companies.

學更多

❶ connection〈連接〉・access〈讀取〉・website〈網頁〉・quickly〈迅速地〉
❷ looking for〈look for（尋找）的 ing 型態〉・find〈找到〉・anything〈任何東西〉
❸ fiber〈纖維物質〉・optic〈光學的〉・wire〈電線〉・transport〈運輸〉・copper〈銅〉
❹ dad〈爸爸〉・home〈家〉・use〈使用〉・laptop〈筆記型電腦〉・room〈房間〉
❺ young〈年輕的〉・lover〈情人〉・one another〈彼此〉・chat〈聊天〉
❻ overseas〈在國外〉・family〈家人〉・regular〈一般的〉・network〈網路〉
❼ produce〈製作〉・program〈節目〉・oldest〈最長時間的，old（長時間的）的最高級〉

中譯

❶ 使用寬頻網路連線的人，能更快速地讀取網頁。
❷ 我喜歡透過網路搜尋資訊，你能在網路上找到任何東西。
❸ 相較於銅線，光纖能傳遞更多資訊。
❹ 我爸在家裡裝了無線網路，他能在任何一個房間使用他的筆記型電腦。
❺ 年輕情侶們上網聊天時，會使用網路視訊看對方。
❻ 當我在國外時，我會使用網路電話和家人說話，因為它的費用比一般的電話網路便宜。
❼ BBC 製作廣播及電視節目，它是全球歷史最悠久的廣播公司之一。

062 交通工具(1)

MP3 062

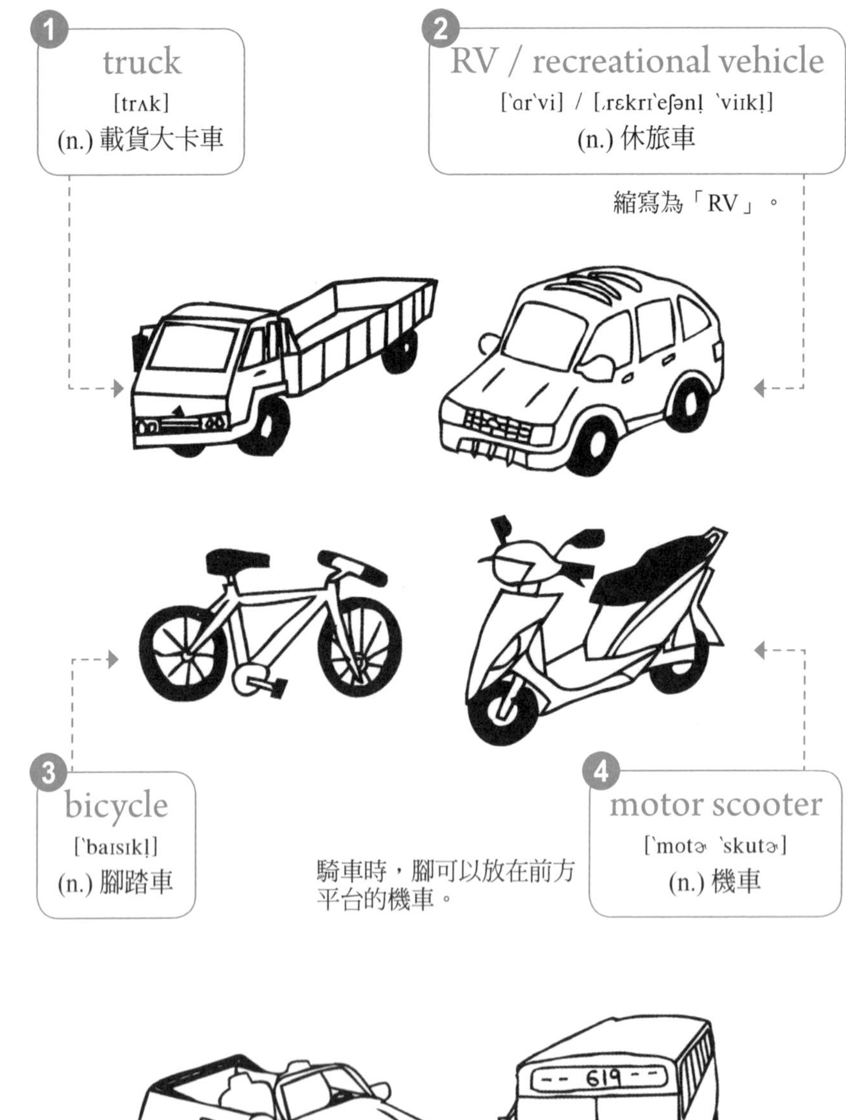

1 truck
[trʌk]
(n.) 載貨大卡車

2 RV / recreational vehicle
[ˋɑrˋvi] / [ˏrɛkrɪˋeʃənḷ ˋviɪkḷ]
(n.) 休旅車

縮寫為「RV」。

3 bicycle
[ˋbaɪsɪkḷ]
(n.) 腳踏車

4 motor scooter
[ˋmotɚ ˋskutɚ]
(n.) 機車

騎車時，腳可以放在前方平台的機車。

5 convertible
[kənˋvɝtəbḷ]
(n.) 敞篷車

6 bus
[bʌs]
(n.) 公車

❶ 載貨大卡車
Trucks deliver most of the goods we buy in the supermarket.

❷ 休旅車
My grandparents bought an RV to travel around the US.
在美國各地環遊

❸ 腳踏車
Oh no! My bicycle has a flat tire.
輪胎沒氣了

❹ 機車
Ron's new motor scooter is trendy and fast.

❺ 敞篷車
Russell bought a new convertible to impress the ladies.
讓女士們留下深刻印象

❻ 公車
Riding the bus instead of driving helps save gas.
以搭公車代替開車

學更多

❶ deliver〈運送〉・most〈大部分的〉・goods〈商品〉・supermarket〈超市〉
❷ grandparents〈祖父母〉・bought〈buy（買）的過去式〉・travel〈旅遊〉
❸ flat〈洩了氣的〉・tire〈輪胎〉
❹ new〈新的〉・trendy〈時髦的〉・fast〈快的〉
❺ impress〈留下深刻的印象〉・lady〈女士〉
❻ riding〈ride（搭乘）的 ing 型態〉・instead of〈代替〉・driving〈駕駛〉・save〈節省〉・gas〈汽油〉

中譯

❶ 我們在超市所買的商品，大多是載貨大卡車運送的。
❷ 我的祖父母買了一部休旅車，他們開著它在美國各地遊覽。
❸ 喔不！我的腳踏車輪胎沒氣了。
❹ Ron 的新機車外觀時髦，速度也很快。
❺ 為了讓女士們留下深刻印象，Russell 買了一輛新的敞篷車。
❻ 以搭公車取代自己開車，有助於節省汽油。

063 交通工具(2)

MP3 063

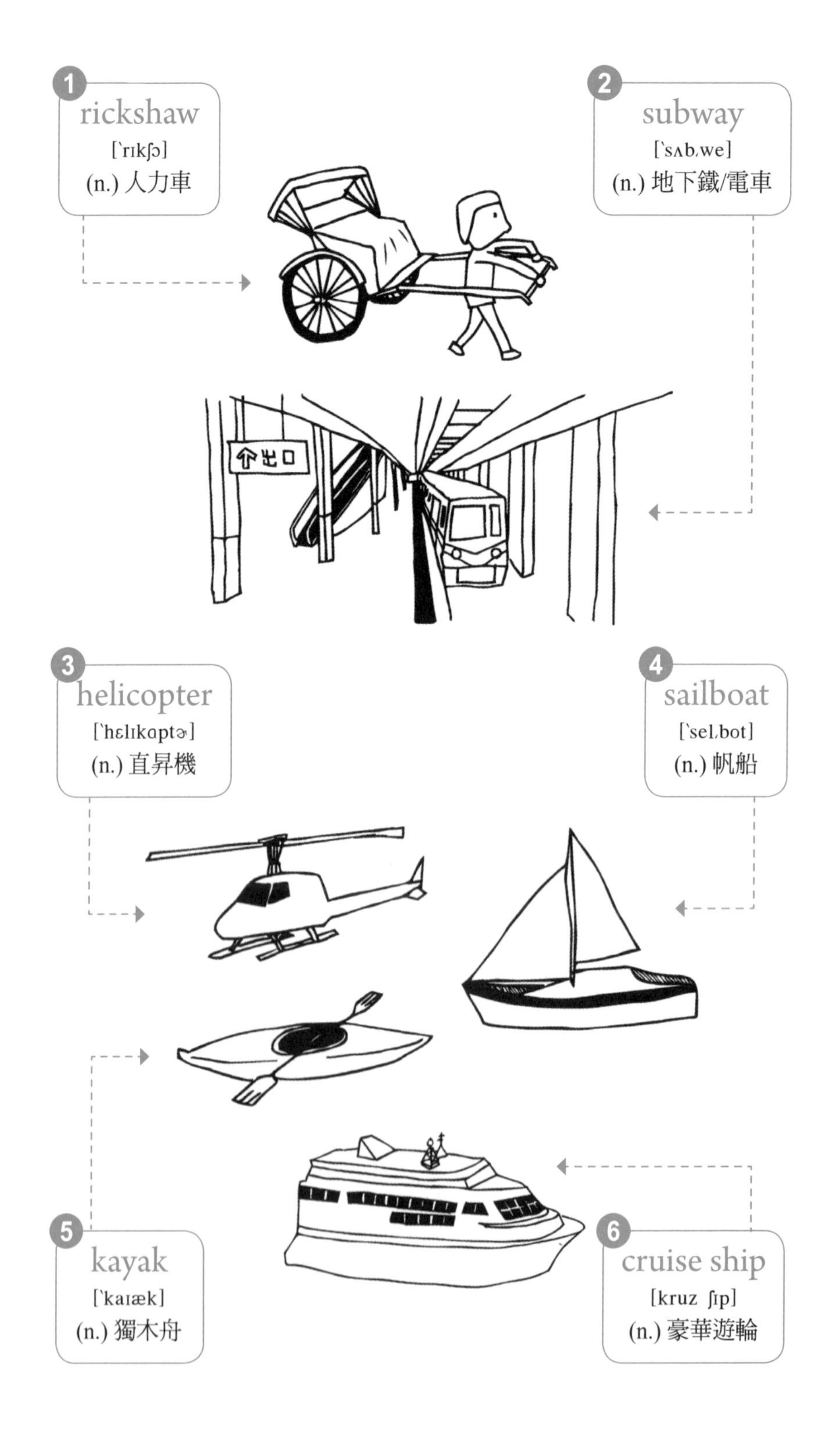

❶ 人力車
In China, you can still see people renting rickshaws to get around.
租人力車到處移動

❷ 地下鐵 / 電車
The Technology Building station is very close, so I always take the subway to work.
搭電車去上班

❸ 直昇機
News agencies often use helicopters to report the news.
報導新聞

❹ 帆船
Although I can't afford to buy my own sailboat, I can rent one for a day.
買不起

❺ 獨木舟
Kayaks can be fun, though paddling in them is not easy.
在裡面划船不容易

❻ 豪華遊輪
Cruise ships offer a surprising number of activities for passengers.
驚人的數量

學更多

❶ still〈仍然〉・renting〈rent（租用）的 ing 型態〉・get around〈到處走動〉
❷ technology〈科技〉・station〈車站〉・close〈近的〉・always〈總是〉
❸ news agency〈新聞通訊社〉・use〈利用〉・report〈報導〉・news〈新聞〉
❹ although〈雖然〉・afford〈買得起、能做〉・own〈自己的〉
❺ fun〈有趣的〉・though〈雖然〉・paddling〈paddle（用槳划船）的 ing 型態〉
❻ cruise〈坐船旅行〉・ship〈船〉・offer〈提供〉・surprising〈驚人的〉・number〈數量〉・activity〈活動〉・passenger〈旅客〉

中譯

❶ 在中國，你還看得到有人租人力車四處移動。
❷ 科技大樓站很近，所以我都搭電車去上班。
❸ 新聞通訊社經常利用直昇機來報導新聞。
❹ 雖然我買不起屬於自己的帆船，但我可以租一艘來玩一整天。
❺ 獨木舟可以很好玩，雖然坐在裡面用槳划船並不容易。
❻ 豪華遊輪為遊客準備了數量驚人的活動。

064 交通號誌(1)

MP3 064

1 no left turn

[no lɛft tɝn]

(phr.) 禁止左轉

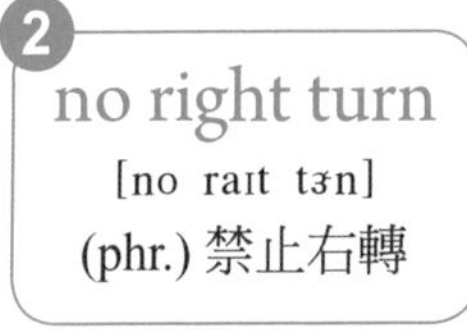

2 no right turn

[no raɪt tɝn]

(phr.) 禁止右轉

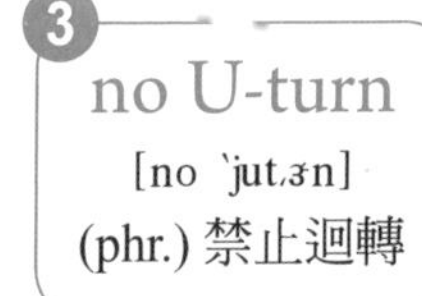

3 no U-turn

[no ˋjuˏtɝn]

(phr.) 禁止迴轉

4 one-way street

[ˋwʌnˏwe strit]

(n.) 單行道

5 highway traffic sign

[ˋhaɪˏwe ˋtræfɪk saɪn]

(n.) 高速公路號誌

6 school zone traffic sign

[skul zon ˋtræfɪk saɪn]

(n.)（前有）學校號誌

❶ 禁止左轉

There's no left turn here, so you'll have to go right instead.
你必須改成右轉

❷ 禁止右轉

Danny got angry when he saw the "no right turn" sign. The shop he wanted was down the road on the right.
他想去的商店在這條路上

❸ 禁止迴轉

Realizing I was driving in the wrong direction, I turned around, but then a police officer stopped me and said: "No U-turns here, sir."

❹ 單行道

You can't drive in this direction; this is a one-way street!

❺ 高速公路號誌

Highway traffic signs give directions and mileage to upcoming destinations to drivers.

❻ （前有）學校號誌

You'd better watch out for school zone traffic signs because if you're caught speeding, the ticket is expensive!
如果你被抓到超速駕駛

學更多

❶ left〈左邊〉・turn〈轉彎〉・have to〈必須〉・right〈右邊〉・instead〈作為替代〉
❷ angry〈生氣〉・sign〈標誌〉・shop〈商店〉・down〈沿著〉・road〈道路〉
❸ realizing〈realize（意識到）的 ing 型態〉・turned around〈turn around（迴轉）的過去式〉
❹ drive〈駕駛〉・direction〈方向〉・one-way〈單向的〉・street〈街道〉
❺ highway〈公路〉・traffic〈交通〉・mileage〈英里數〉・upcoming〈即將來臨的〉・destination〈目的地〉
❻ watch out〈注意〉・zone〈區域〉・caught〈catch（逮捕）的過去分詞〉・ticket〈罰單〉

中譯

❶ 這裡禁止左轉，所以你必須改成右轉。
❷ 看到「禁止右轉」號誌時 Danny 很生氣，他想去的商店是在這條路的右側。
❸ 發現開錯方向後我便迴轉，但隨及警察把我攔下並說：「先生，這裡禁止迴轉」。
❹ 你不能把車往這個方向開，這是單行道！
❺ 高速公路號誌提供駕駛人行車方向，以及距離下一個目的地的英里數。
❻ 你最好要注意學校號誌，因為如果在那個區域被抓到超速，罰單金額會很高。

065 交通號誌(2)

MP3 065

❶ 速限

Phil got into trouble with the police for driving over the speed limit.

招惹到警察

❷ 方向標示 / 方向

Which direction should I go – left or right?

我應該往哪個方向走

❸ 行人通行號誌

Stand here for a minute; the crosswalk light is still red.

一會兒

❹ 測速照相機

You no longer need to be caught speeding by police, a speed camera can catch you!

❺ 斑馬線

Be careful! You should not cross here because there is no zebra crossing.

不該穿越這裡

學更多

❶ got into trouble〈get into trouble（惹上麻煩）的過去式〉‧police〈警察〉‧driving〈drive（駕駛）的 ing 型態〉‧over〈超過〉‧limit〈限制〉

❷ should〈應該〉‧left〈左邊〉‧right〈右邊〉

❸ minute〈分鐘〉‧crosswalk〈行人穿越道〉‧light〈燈〉‧still〈仍然〉

❹ no longer〈不再〉‧caught〈catch（逮捕）的過去分詞〉‧speeding〈超速駕駛〉

❺ careful〈小心的〉‧cross〈穿越〉‧there is no...〈沒有…〉‧zebra〈有斑紋的〉

中譯

❶ Phil 因為開車超過速限而惹上麻煩，被警察開罰。

❷ 我該往哪個方向走——左邊還是右邊？

❸ 在這裡站了一會兒，行人通行號誌仍是紅燈。

❹ 用不著警察抓你超速，一台測速照相機就能逮到你了。

❺ 小心！你不應該在這裡穿越馬路，因為這裡沒有斑馬線。

066 交通號誌(3)

MP3 066

❶ 小心落石

You'll often see signs warning of falling rocks ahead on mountain roads.

小心落石的警告標示

❷ 路面顛簸

This is a bumpy road, so you should slow down.

❸ 車輛改道

There are men working on the road ahead, so you'll need to take a detour down that road.

在前方路段施工　改道

❹ 施工中

Alex said the bridge is under construction, so he had to take the tunnel instead.

他必須改走隧道

❺ 禁止進入

We can't go in there; there's a "Do not enter" sign.

學更多

❶ warning〈warn（警告）的 ing 型態〉・falling〈落下的〉・rock〈岩石〉・ahead〈在前面〉・mountain〈山〉

❷ bumpy〈顛簸的〉・should〈應該〉・slow down〈減速〉

❸ working〈work（工作）的 ing 型態〉・need〈需要〉・down〈沿著〉・road〈道路〉

❹ bridge〈橋〉・under〈處於…情況〉・construction〈建造〉・tunnel〈隧道〉・instead〈作為替代〉

❺ enter〈進入〉・sign〈標誌〉

中譯

❶ 在山路上，你常會看到「小心落石」的警告標示。

❷ 這裡路面顛簸，所以你應該減速慢行。

❸ 前方路段有人員在施工，所以你要改道行駛另一條路。

❹ Alex 說橋梁還在施工中，所以他必須改走隧道。

❺ 我們不能進去裡面，那裡有「禁止進入」的標示。

067 駕車狀況(1)

MP3 067

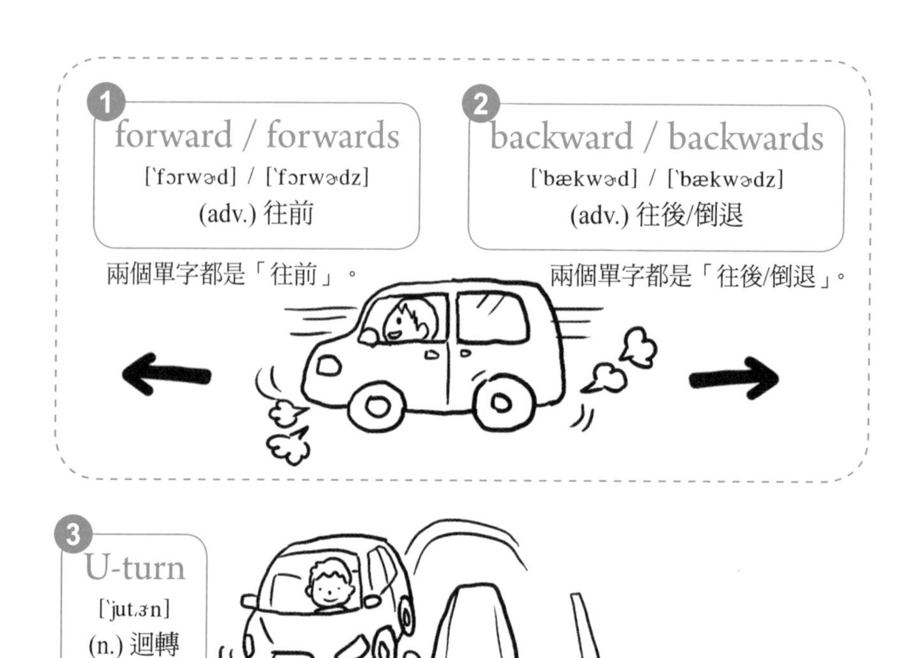

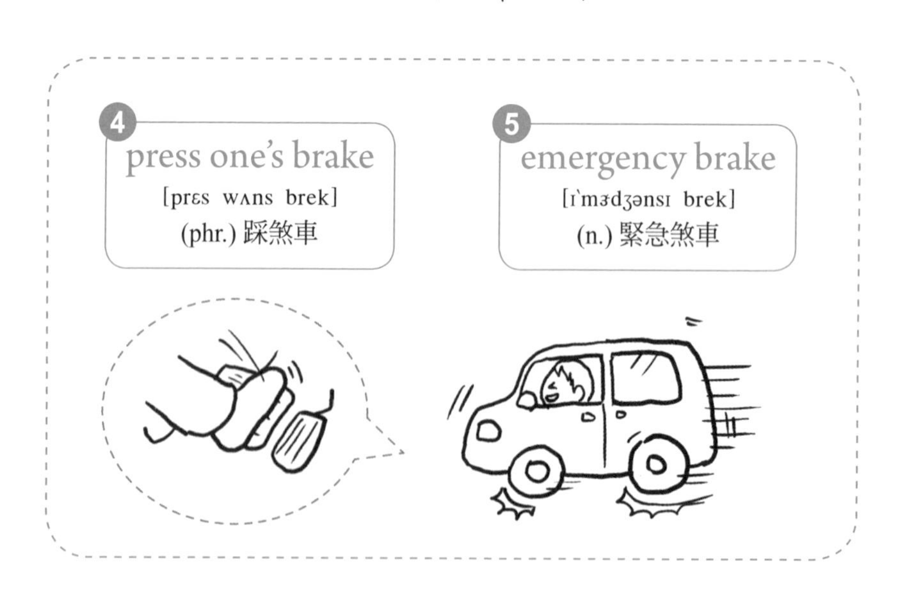

❶ 往前
❷ 往後 / 倒退
Instead of going forward, Lillian put her car in reverse and drove backward down the street.

❸ 迴轉
Tom thought he was going the wrong way, so he made a U-turn.

❹ 踩煞車
When a little boy ran out into the road, the driver pressed his brakes hard.
駕駛很用力的踩煞車

❺ 緊急煞車
You don't need to do an emergency brake unless you have to stop very quickly.

❻ 停車
Jeff was feeling sick, so he decided to stop his car and get out.
停下他的車子

學更多

❶ ❷ Instead of〈代替〉• put〈put（使…處於某種狀態）的過去式〉• in reverse〈反向〉• drove〈drive（駕駛）的過去式〉• down〈沿著〉• street〈街道〉
❸ thought〈think（認為）的過去式〉• wrong〈錯誤的〉• made〈make（做）的過去式〉
❹ ran〈run（跑）的過去式〉• out〈向外面〉• pressed〈press（重壓）的過去式〉• brake〈煞車〉• hard〈猛力地〉
❺ emergency〈緊急情況〉• unless〈除非〉• stop〈停止〉• quickly〈迅速地〉
❻ sick〈生病的〉• decided〈decide（決定）的過去式〉• get out〈下車〉

中譯

❶ ❷ Lillian 不把車往前開，而是讓車子反向，倒退開在路上。
❸ Tom 認為他走錯路了，所以他把車子迴轉。
❹ 當一名小男孩跑到馬路上，駕駛人猛力地踩了煞車。
❺ 你不需要緊急煞車，除非你必須馬上停下來。
❻ Jeff 覺得不舒服，所以他決定停車，並走出車外。

068 駕車狀況(2)

MP3 068

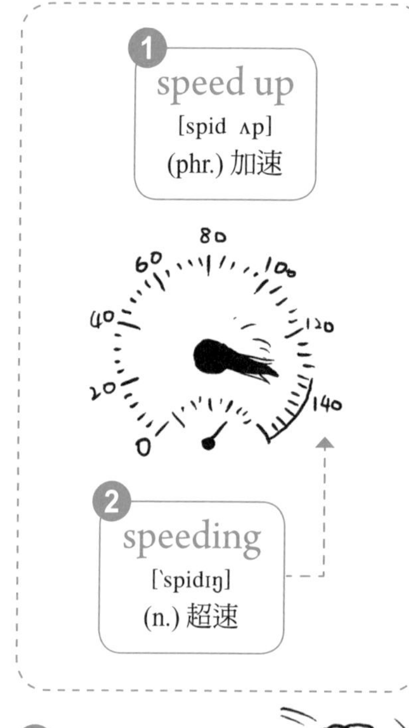

1 speed up
[spid ʌp]
(phr.) 加速

2 speeding
[ˋspidɪŋ]
(n.) 超速

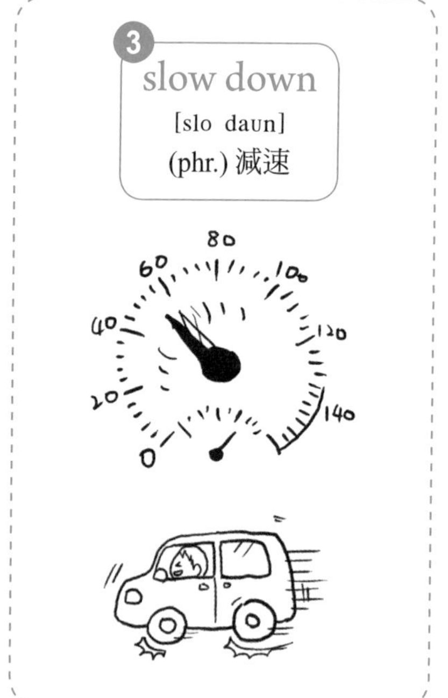

3 slow down
[slo daʊn]
(phr.) 減速

4 shift gears
[ʃɪft gɪrz]
(phr.) 換檔

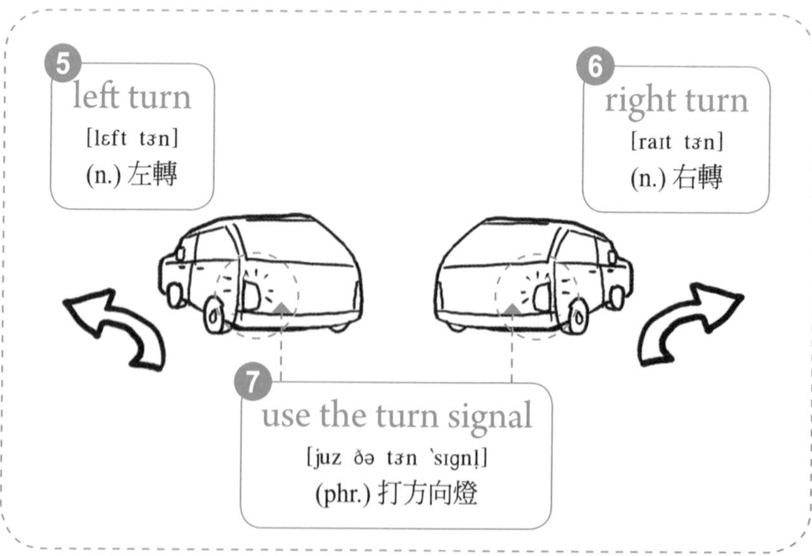

5 left turn
[lɛft tɝn]
(n.) 左轉

6 right turn
[raɪt tɝn]
(n.) 右轉

7 use the turn signal
[juz ðə tɝn ˋsɪgn̩]
(phr.) 打方向燈

❶ 加速

If you want to win this race, you'd better speed up. Everyone's passing you!

❷ 超速

James got into trouble when he was caught speeding.
當他被抓到超速

❸ 減速

Betty realized she was driving too fast, so she slowed down.
她開車太快

❹ 換檔

With an automatic car, you don't have to shift gears.
自排車

❺ 左轉

Some people don't look around them before making a left turn, but that's dangerous.

❻ 右轉

Up ahead, you need to make a right turn at the stoplight.

❼ 打方向燈

Use the turn signal before making a turn so that other drivers know what you're going to do.
在轉彎之前　其他駕駛人
你打算要做什麼

學更多

❶ win〈獲勝〉‧race〈競賽〉‧speed〈速度〉‧passing〈pass（超過）的 ing 型態〉
❷ got into trouble〈get into trouble（惹上麻煩）的過去式〉‧
caught〈catch（抓到）的過去分詞〉
❸ realized〈realize（意識到）的過去式〉‧driving〈drive（駕駛）的 ing 型態〉
❹ automatic〈自動的〉‧shift〈轉換〉‧ gear〈汽車排檔〉
❺ look around〈環顧四周〉‧left〈左邊的〉‧turn〈轉彎〉‧dangerous〈危險的〉
❻ up ahead〈在前面〉‧right〈右邊的〉‧stoplight〈紅綠燈〉
❼ use〈使用〉‧signal〈信號〉‧making〈make（做）的 ing 型態〉‧driver〈駕駛〉

中譯

❶ 如果你想在這場競賽中勝出，你最好加速前進。其他人快要超越你了！
❷ James 被抓到超速時，身陷麻煩了。
❸ Betty 意識到自己把車開得太快，所以她減速了。
❹ 開自排車的話，你就不需要換檔。
❺ 有些人要左轉前並不會環顧四周，但這是危險的。
❻ 在前方紅綠燈處你需要右轉。
❼ 轉彎前要先打方向燈，這樣其他駕駛人才知道你要做什麼。

069 駕車狀況(3)

MP3 069

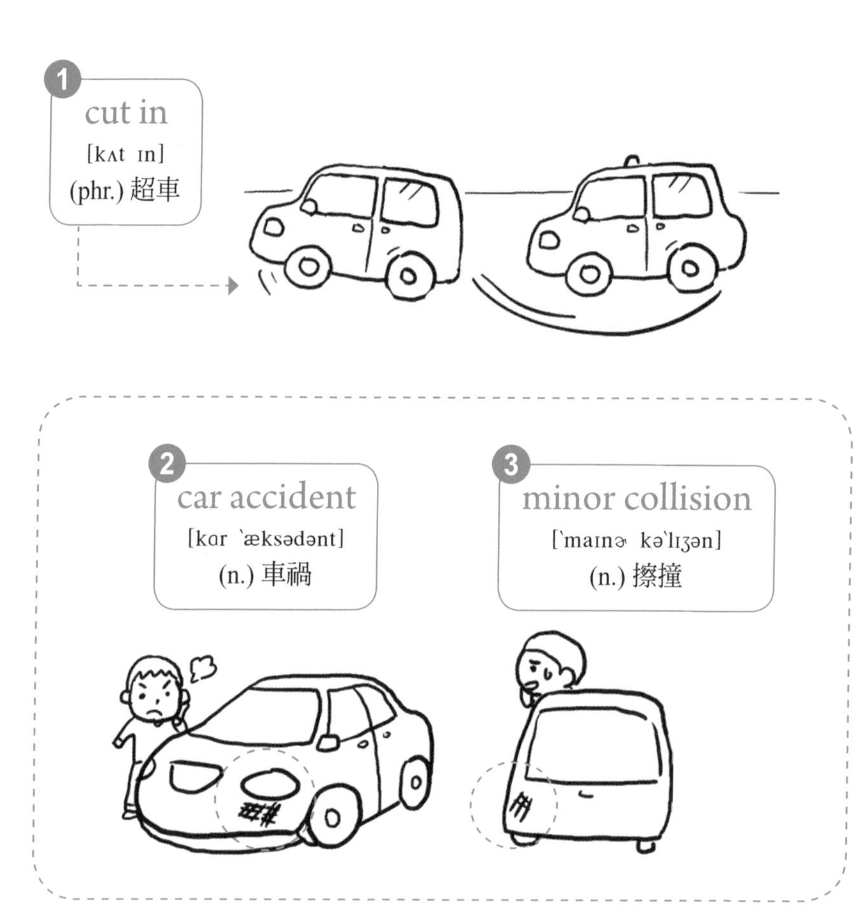

1 cut in
[kʌt ɪn]
(phr.) 超車

2 car accident
[kɑr `æksədənt]
(n.) 車禍

3 minor collision
[`maɪnɚ kə`lɪʒən]
(n.) 擦撞

4 collision
[kə`lɪʒən]
(n.) 碰撞/相撞

5 break down
[brek daʊn]
(phr.) 拋錨

❶ 超車
I hate it when other drivers cut in right in front of me. I think it's very rude.
正好就在我前面

❷ 車禍
Rachel called the police and an ambulance after she saw a car accident.

❸ 擦撞
Jerry was so grateful that the minor collision he had with another motor scooter did not damage his scooter too much.
他和另一台機車發生的擦撞

❹ 碰撞／相撞
My car was involved in a collision, so some of its parts are broken.
我的車受到一場碰撞的牽連

❺ 拋錨
The woman was scared when her car broke down at night time on the quiet road.

學更多

❶ hate〈討厭〉・driver〈駕駛人〉・right〈正好〉・in front of〈在…的前面〉・rude〈無禮的〉
❷ called〈call（打電話）的過去式〉・police〈警察〉・ambulance〈救護車〉・saw〈see（看到）的過去式〉・accident〈事故〉
❸ grateful〈感激的〉・minor〈輕微的〉・motor scooter〈機車〉・damage〈毀壞〉
❹ involved〈involve（牽涉）的過去分詞〉・part〈零件〉・broken〈損壞的〉
❺ scared〈恐懼的〉・broke down〈break down（拋錨）的過去式〉・quiet〈安靜的〉・road〈道路〉

中譯

❶ 我討厭其他駕駛人超車到我前面，我覺得這樣很沒有禮貌。
❷ Rachel 目睹車禍發生之後，打電話呼叫警察和救護車。
❸ Jerry 慶幸自己和另一台機車的擦撞，並沒有讓自己的機車受到太多損害。
❹ 我的車遭受碰撞，所以有些零件損壞了。
❺ 當深夜時分車子在寂靜無聲的馬路上拋錨時，那名女子感到很害怕。

070
個性（正面）(1)

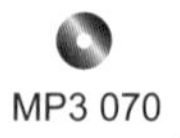
MP3 070

1
optimistic
[ˌɑptəˋmɪstɪk]
(adj.) 樂觀的
2
active
[ˋæktɪv]
(adj.) 積極的/活潑的
3
confident
[ˋkɑnfədənt]
(adj.) 自信的
S

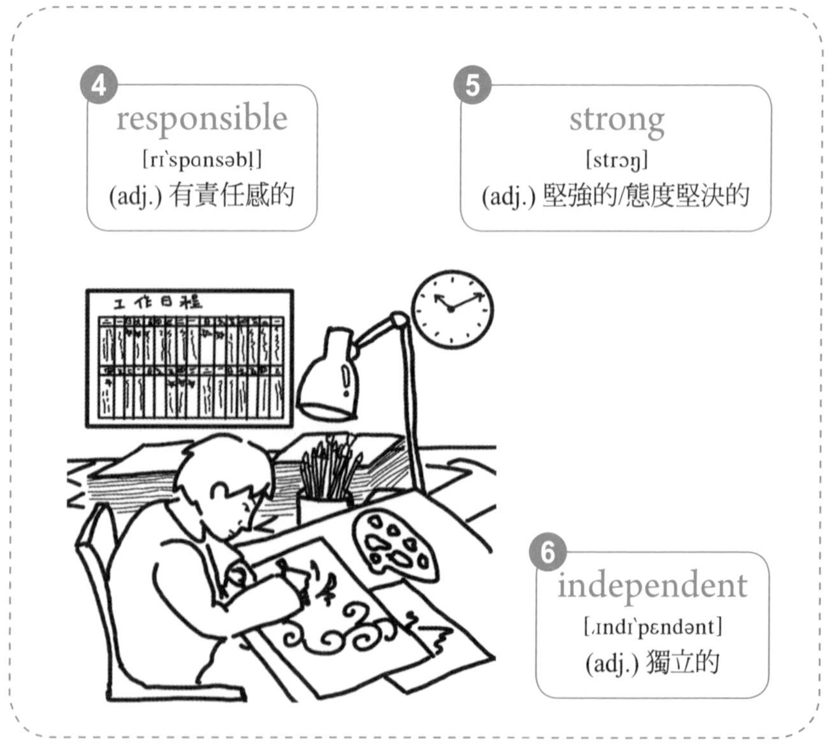
4
responsible
[rɪˋspɑnsəbḷ]
(adj.) 有責任感的
5
strong
[strɔŋ]
(adj.) 堅強的/態度堅決的
工作日程
6
independent
[ˌɪndɪˋpɛndənt]
(adj.) 獨立的

❶ 樂觀的

Josh is an optimistic person and always looks on the bright side of things.

看到光明的一面

❷ 積極的 / 活潑的

Sally is an active person, and she loves exercising.

❸ 自信的

I wish I were more confident; I always get nervous around people I don't know.

我希望我更有自信（與現在事實相反的表現句型）　我不認識的人

❹ 有責任感的

You can't rely on Lindsey to do anything; she's really not very responsible.

你不能信賴 Lindsey

❺ 堅強的 / 態度堅決的

He's a strong person and always sticks to his principles.

堅持他的原則

❻ 獨立的

The little boy is very independent and likes to do things without his parents.

學更多

❶ person〈人〉・always〈總是〉・bright〈明亮的〉・side〈面〉

❷ love〈喜愛〉・exercising〈exercise（運動）的 ing 型態〉

❸ wish〈希望〉・get〈變得〉・nervous〈緊張不安的〉・around〈在…附近〉

❹ rely on〈信賴〉・anything〈任何事情〉・really〈實在〉

❺ stick〈堅持〉・principle〈原則〉

❻ little〈幼小的〉・without〈沒有〉・parents〈雙親〉

中譯

❶ Josh 是個樂觀的人，而且總是把事情往好的方面想。

❷ Sally 是個活潑的人，而且喜歡運動。

❸ 我希望自己能夠更有自信；在不認識的人面前我總會變得很緊張。

❹ 你不能指望 Lindsey 做任何事，她實在很沒有責任感。

❺ 他是個態度堅決的人，而且總是堅守自己的原則。

❻ 那個小男孩非常獨立，喜歡自己做事而不倚靠父母。

071 個性（正面）(2)

MP3 071

① open-minded
[ˋopənˋmaɪndɪd]
(adj.) 心胸開闊的

② honest
[ˋɑnɪst]
(adj.) 誠實的/正直的

③ humorous
[ˋhjumərəs]
(adj.) 幽默的

④ easygoing
[ˋizɪˏgoɪŋ]
(adj.) 隨和的

⑤ passionate
[ˋpæʃənɪt]
(adj.) 熱心的/熱情的

⑥ friendly
[ˋfrɛndlɪ]
(adj.) 友善的/親切的

❶ 心胸開闊的
My grandfather is quite open-minded, and he's always ready to try new things.

❷ 誠實的 / 正直的
She thinks I'm not honest, so she doesn't trust me at all.
她完全不信任我

❸ 幽默的
I laugh a lot when I'm with Ruth as she's so humorous.
當我和 Ruth 在一起時

❹ 隨和的
I think I'm an easygoing person, so I don't worry about things very much.

❺ 熱心的 / 熱情的
Brenda is a passionate person, and she likes to show her boyfriend how much she loves him.
她有多麼愛他

❻ 友善的 / 親切的
Everyone at work is very friendly, so it was nice to meet everyone.

學更多

❶ grandfather〈祖父〉・quite〈很〉・ready〈樂意的〉・try〈嘗試〉
❷ think〈認為〉・trust〈信任〉・at all〈根本〉
❸ laugh〈笑〉・a lot〈許多〉・as〈因為〉
❹ person〈人〉・worry〈擔心〉
❺ show〈表明〉・boyfriend〈男朋友〉・how much〈多少〉
❻ everyone〈每個人〉・at work〈在工作〉・nice〈好的〉・meet〈認識〉

中譯

❶ 我的祖父非常心胸開闊，總是樂意嘗試新事物。
❷ 她認為我不誠實，所以她完全不信任我。
❸ 和 Ruth 相處時我很常笑，因為她很幽默。
❹ 我認為自己是個隨和的人，所以什麼事都不太擔心。
❺ Brenda 是個熱情的人，她喜歡讓她男朋友知道自己有多麼愛他。
❻ 每位同事都很友善，能夠認識大家是件美好的事。

072 個性（負面）(1)

MP3 072

❶ 悲觀的

The pessimistic young man always thinks bad things will happen to him.
壞事會發生在他身上

❷ 懦弱的

The only problem with Wayne is that he's quite weak, so people often get him to do things he doesn't want to do.
叫他做事情

❸ 多疑的

Don't worry what Rick says. He's a suspicious person and doesn't trust anyone.

❹ 沒耐性的

My boss is quite impatient, so I need to make sure I finish my work on time.
設法確保我在時間內完成我的工作

❺ 沒有責任感的

Don't share any secrets with Ann. She's irresponsible and can't be trusted.
不能被信任

❻ 懶散的

Ian's a nice man, but he's sloppy, so his home is quite messy.

學更多

❶ young〈年輕的〉・always〈總是〉・bad〈壞的〉・happen〈發生〉
❷ only〈唯一的〉・problem〈問題〉・quite〈相當〉・often〈常常〉・get〈使得〉
❸ worry〈擔心〉・say〈說〉・person〈人〉・trust〈信任〉・anyone〈任何人〉
❹ quite〈很〉・make sure〈設法確保〉・finish〈完成〉・on time〈準時〉
❺ share〈分享〉・secret〈祕密〉・trusted〈trust（信任）的過去分詞〉
❻ nice〈好的〉・home〈家〉・messy〈凌亂的〉

中譯

❶ 那個悲觀的年輕人總認為壞事會發生在他身上。
❷ Wayne 唯一的問題就是他很懦弱，所以大家會經常叫他去做那些他不想做的事。
❸ 別在意 Rick 說的話。他生性多疑，不相信任何人。
❹ 我的老闆很沒耐性，所以我得設法確保自己準時完成工作。
❺ 別和 Ann 分享任何祕密。她沒有責任感，不能信任。
❻ Ian 是個不錯的人，但他很懶散，所以他家裡很凌亂。

073 個性（負面）(2)

MP3 073

1 **arrogant** [ˋærəgənt] (adj.) 傲慢的

2 **violent** [ˋvaɪələnt] (adj.) 殘暴的

3 **selfish** [ˋsɛlfɪʃ] (adj.) 自私的

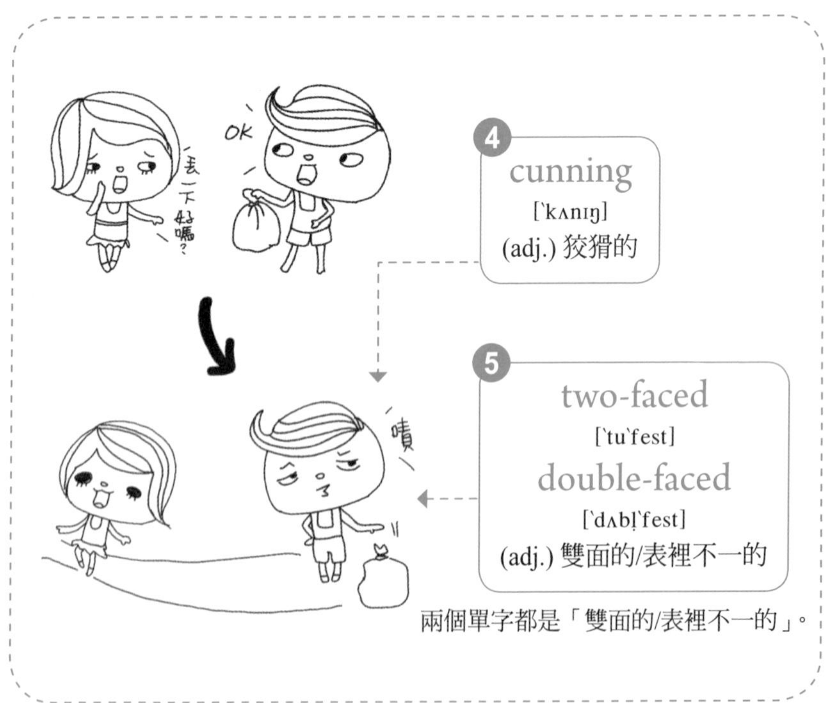

4 **cunning** [ˋkʌnɪŋ] (adj.) 狡猾的

5 **two-faced** [ˋtuˋfest]
double-faced [ˋdʌblฺˋfest]
(adj.) 雙面的/表裡不一的

兩個單字都是「雙面的/表裡不一的」。

❶ 傲慢的

She's so arrogant! She thinks she's better than everyone else.

比其他人都好

❷ 殘暴的

I didn't realize Mark was violent until I saw him hit my brother.

❸ 自私的

The older boy is selfish and never shares anything with his sister.

❹ 狡猾的

Ben's very cunning and always uses tricks to make sure he gets what he wants.

他想要的事物

❺ 雙面的 / 表裡不一的

Claire is two-faced. She'll be nice when she's talking to you, but then she'll say bad things about you when you're not there.

但接著她會說你的壞話

學更多

❶ think〈認為〉‧better〈更好的〉‧else〈其他〉

❷ realize〈了解、意識到〉‧until〈直到…為止〉‧saw〈see（看）的過去式〉‧hit〈hit（打）的過去式〉

❸ older〈年紀較大的，old（年紀大的）的比較級〉‧never〈從未〉‧share〈分享〉‧sister〈姊妹〉

❹ always〈總是〉‧trick〈詭計〉‧make sure〈設法確保〉‧get〈得到〉

❺ nice〈友好的〉‧talking〈talk（談話）的 ing 型態〉‧double〈雙層的〉

中譯

❶ 她真是傲慢！她認為自己比任何人都優秀。

❷ 我一直不知道 Mark 是個殘暴的人，直到我看到他打我弟弟。

❸ 那個哥哥很自私，從來都不跟妹妹分享任何東西。

❹ Ben 非常狡猾，總是利用詭計來確保他能得到自己想要的東西。

❺ Claire 是個表裡不一的人。和你說話時，她會表現得很友善；但當你不在場時，她就會說你的壞話。

074 情緒（正面）

MP3 074

❶ 冷靜的

Tracy is always calm and never gets excited or nervous.

變得激動

❷ 自豪的

Tom thinks he's better than anyone else; he's very proud.

比其他任何人都好

❸ 喜出望外的

Jan was overjoyed to discover her granddaughter, Lily, was engaged.

❹ 滿懷希望的

I'm hopeful that the situation will improve soon.

情況很快會改善

❺ 知足的 / 滿足的

It can be satisfying to work hard on something and do a good job.

做得很棒

❻ 感激的

I'm grateful for everything you've done for me.

你為我做的

❼ 安心的

People usually feel more secure when they're with close friends.

親密好友

學更多

❶ always〈總是〉・never〈從未〉・excited〈激動的〉・nervous〈緊張不安的〉
❷ think〈認為〉・better〈更好的〉・else〈其他〉
❸ discover〈發現〉・granddaughter〈孫女〉・engaged〈已訂婚的〉
❹ situation〈情況〉・improve〈改善〉・soon〈很快地〉
❺ work hard〈努力工作〉・good〈好的〉・job〈成果〉
❻ everything〈每件事〉・done〈do（做）的過去分詞〉
❼ people〈人們〉・usually〈通常〉・feel〈感覺〉・close〈親密的〉

中譯

❶ Tracy 總是很冷靜，從不激動或緊張。
❷ Tom 覺得自己比任何人都優秀，他非常自豪。
❸ 當 Jan 發現自己的孫女 Lily 訂婚了，他感到喜出望外。
❹ 我滿懷希望認為情況會很快獲得改善。
❺ 認真做事，而且把它做好，就能令人感到滿足。
❻ 我很感激你為我做的每件事。
❼ 人們和親密好友相處時，通常會感到比較安心。

075 情緒（負面）(1)

MP3 075

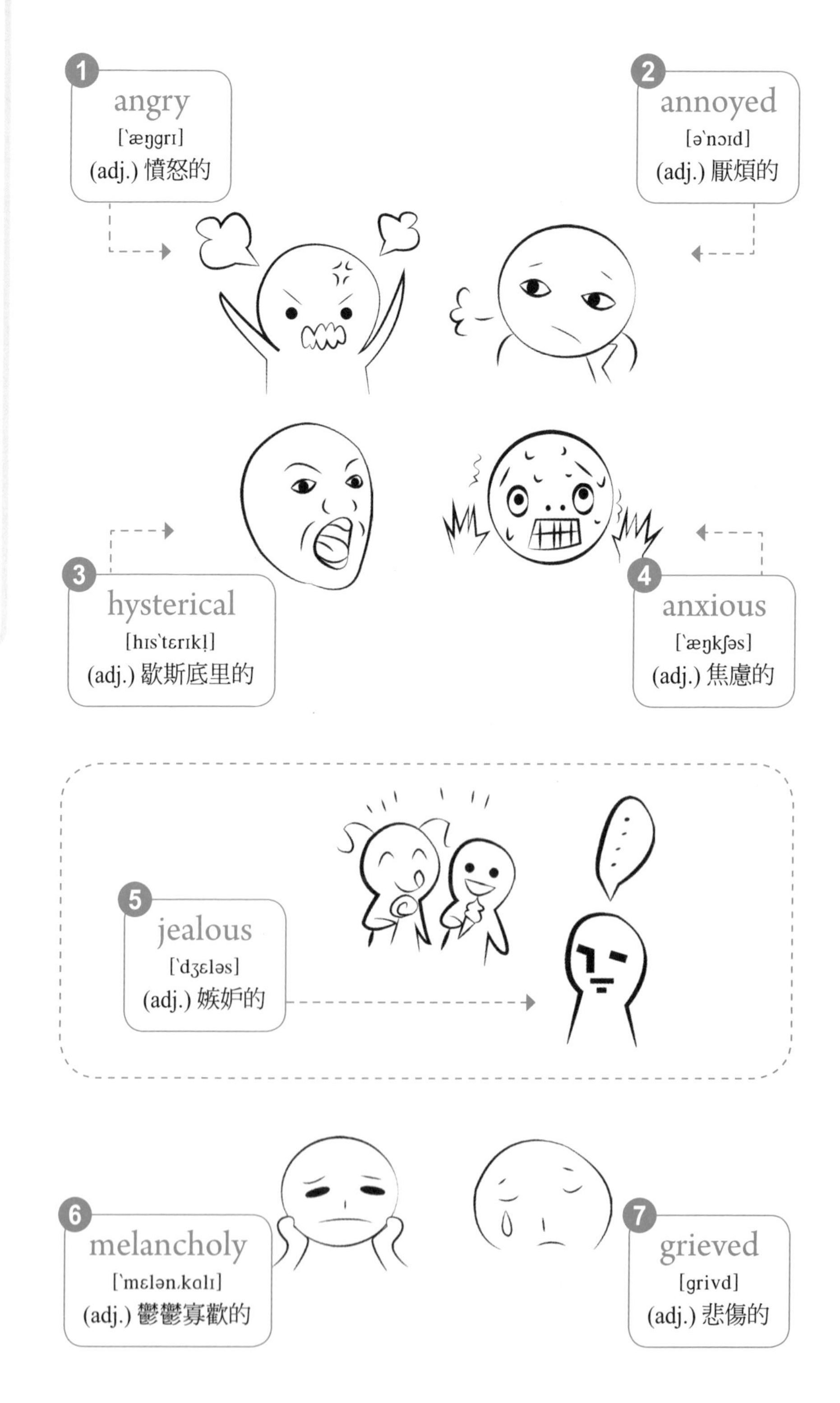

❶ 憤怒的
My mom gets really angry when the house is messy.

❷ 厭煩的
Sometimes she is annoyed about doing laundry. Why can't she just put all the clothes in the washing machine with laundry detergent?

洗衣服

把全部的衣服丟進洗衣機

❸ 歇斯底里的
Rachel was hysterical when she heard the news. She wouldn't stop crying.

停止哭泣

❹ 焦慮的
The father got quite anxious when his daughter didn't come home on time.

父親變得很焦慮　準時回家

❺ 嫉妒的
My friend has a beautiful sports car. I'm totally jealous of him.

我非常嫉妒他

❻ 鬱鬱寡歡的
I'm having a melancholy day as I have nothing to do.

❼ 悲傷的
The old man was grieved by the death of his pet dog.

學更多

❶ get〈變得〉・really〈十分〉・house〈房子〉・messy〈凌亂的〉
❷ laundry〈要洗的衣服、洗好的衣服〉・put〈放〉・laundry detergent〈洗衣精〉
❸ heard〈hear（聽）的過去式〉・news〈消息〉・crying〈cry（哭泣）的 ing 型態〉
❹ quite〈很〉・daughter〈女兒〉・come home〈回家〉・on time〈準時〉
❺ beautiful〈漂亮的〉・sports car〈跑車〉・totally〈完全〉
❻ having〈have（經歷）的 ing 型態〉・as〈因為〉・nothing〈沒什麼〉
❼ old〈上了年紀的〉・death〈死亡〉・pet〈寵物〉

中譯

❶ 當屋子一團亂的時候，我媽就會變得很憤怒。
❷ 有時候她對洗衣服感到厭煩。為什麼她不能把所有的衣服和洗衣精一起丟進洗衣機就好呢？
❸ 當 Rachel 聽到那個消息時就變得歇斯底里，她無法停止哭泣。
❹ 當女兒沒有準時回家時，那位父親變得很焦慮。
❺ 我朋友有一輛很漂亮的跑車，我非常嫉妒他。
❻ 我今天過得鬱鬱寡歡，因為我無事可做。
❼ 那個老人因為所養的狗過世了而感到悲傷。

076 情緒（負面）(2)

MP3 076

❶ 失望的
The girl was disappointed that she didn't pass the test.

❷ 後悔的
Rex felt regretful after telling his girlfriend she needed to lose weight.
減肥

❸ 挫敗的
Paul was frustrated by his flight's 24-hour delay caused by a typhoon.
被颱風造成的

❹ 內疚的
I felt very guilty about breaking my friend's pen.

❺ 尷尬的
I was so embarrassed when my mom told me she loved me in front of my friends.

❻ 羞愧的
I'm ashamed of myself for eating my mother's birthday cake.
我對我自己感到羞愧

❼ 恐懼的
Suzy hated Halloween because she was fearful of ghosts.

學更多

❶ girl〈女孩〉・pass〈通過〉・test〈測驗〉
❷ felt〈feel（感覺）的過去式〉・telling〈tell（告訴）的 ing 型態〉
❸ flight〈班機〉・delay〈延遲〉・caused〈cause（引起）的過去分詞〉・typhoon〈颱風〉
❹ breaking〈break（弄壞）的 ing 型態〉・pen〈筆〉
❺ told〈tell（說）的過去式〉・in front of〈在…的前面〉
❻ myself〈我自己〉・birthday cake〈生日蛋糕〉
❼ hated〈hate（討厭）的過去式〉・ghost〈鬼、幽靈〉

中譯

❶ 那個女孩很失望，因為她沒通過考試。
❷ Rex 告訴女朋友她需要減肥之後，就感到後悔了。
❸ Paul 的班機受颱風影響延誤了 24 個小時，這使他感到挫敗。
❹ 把朋友的筆弄壞了，我覺得非常內疚。
❺ 當我媽在我的朋友面前說她愛我時，我覺得很尷尬。
❻ 我吃掉了媽媽的生日蛋糕，我對自己感到羞愧。
❼ Suzy 討厭過萬聖節，因為她對幽靈感到恐懼。

077 品德(1)

MP3 077

1. brave
[brev]
(adj.) 勇敢

2. justice
[ˋdʒʌstɪs]
(n.) 正義

3. wise
[waɪz]
(adj.) 聰明

4. gentle
[ˋdʒɛntḷ]
(adj.) 溫和

5. forgiveness
[fɚˋgɪvnɪs]
(n.) 寬恕

6. fair
[fɛr]
(adj.) 公正

❶ 勇敢
Our firefighters are some of the bravest people working today.

❷ 正義
Sometimes, I think that there is no justice in the world. Bad things keep happening to good people.
一直發生在好人身上

❸ 聰明
My teacher is very wise. She always knows what the right thing to do is.
什麼是正確該做的事

❹ 溫和
My grandmother is a gentle woman, so she's good at looking after babies.
她擅於照顧小嬰兒

❺ 寬恕
You need to learn forgiveness. You can't stay angry with people forever.
永遠都在對人生氣

❻ 公正
It wasn't fair of you to shout at me. I didn't do anything wrong.

學更多

❶ firefighter〈消防隊員〉‧bravest〈最勇敢，brave（勇敢）的最高級〉‧working〈work（工作）的 ing 型態〉
❷ sometimes〈有時〉‧think〈認為〉‧world〈世界〉‧keep〈持續不斷〉‧happening〈happen（發生）的 ing 型態〉
❸ teacher〈老師〉‧always〈總是〉‧right〈正確的〉
❹ be good at〈擅長…〉‧looking after〈look after（照顧）的 ing 型態〉
❺ learn〈學習〉‧stay〈繼續、保持〉‧angry〈生氣的〉‧forever〈永遠〉
❻ shout〈喊叫〉‧anything〈任何事情〉‧wrong〈錯誤的〉

中譯

❶ 我們的消防隊員，是現今最勇敢的工作者之一。
❷ 有時候，我覺得世界上並沒有正義，壞事總是發生在好人身上。
❸ 我的老師非常聰明，她總是知道哪些是正確且該做的事。
❹ 我的祖母是位溫和的女性，所以她擅於照顧小嬰兒。
❺ 你需要學習寬恕，你不能永遠都在生別人的氣。
❻ 你對我大吼大叫並不公平，我沒有做錯任何事。

078 品德(2)

MP3 078

❶ 謹慎

Barbara shows a lot of prudence; she's always careful about what she does.

表現很謹慎 / 她做的事情

❷ 純潔

The little girl never has any bad thoughts. She's very pure.

❸ 善良

Kind people always think about other people's feelings.

❹ 無私

My mother's very unselfish, and she does things for me even when she's tired.

甚至是在她疲憊的時候

❺ 謙遜

It's good to be modest; don't go around telling everyone how good you are.

不要到處告訴別人

❻ 誠懇

He isn't lying; I think he's sincere.

學更多

❶ show〈展現〉‧a lot of〈很多〉‧always〈總是〉‧careful〈小心的〉

❷ little〈幼小的〉‧never〈從未〉‧bad〈不好的〉‧thought〈想法〉

❸ think〈想〉‧other〈其他的〉‧feeling〈感受〉

❹ very〈非常〉‧even〈甚至〉‧tired〈疲倦的〉

❺ around〈到處〉‧telling〈tell（告訴）的 ing 型態〉‧everyone〈每個人〉

❻ lying〈lie（說謊）的 ing 型態〉‧think〈認為〉

中譯

❶ Barbara 展現十足的謹慎，她做事總是很小心。

❷ 那個小女孩從來沒有任何不好的念頭，她非常純潔。

❸ 善良的人總是會顧慮到別人的感受。

❹ 我媽媽非常無私，即使疲憊的時候，也會為我做一些事。

❺ 謙虛是項美德，別到處對人說自己有多優秀。

❻ 他沒有在說謊，我覺得他很誠懇。

079 減肥方式(1)

MP3 079

❶ medical weight loss clinic
[ˋmɛdɪkḷ wet lɔs ˋklɪnɪk]
(n.) 減重門診

❷ weight-loss diet
[ˋwetˋlɔs ˋdaɪət]
(n.) 減肥餐

❸ low-carbohydrate
[lo ˏkɑrbəˋhaɪdret]
(adj.) 低醣

❹ low-calorie
[lo ˋkælərɪ]
(adj.) 低卡路里

❺ slimming diet
[ˋslɪmɪŋ ˋdaɪət]
(n.) 代餐

❶ 減重門診

I work at a medical weight loss clinic, so I advise people how to lose weight in a healthy way.

如何用健康的方法來減重

❷ 減肥餐

I'm getting a little fat, so I need to go on a weight-loss diet.

吃減肥餐

❸ 低醣

To lose weight, try eating low-carbohydrate foods like celery.

低醣食物

❹ 低卡路里

I usually have low-calorie drinks like diet sodas.

低卡飲料

❺ 代餐

Karen's already very thin, but she still wants to go on a slimming diet.

繼續吃代餐

學更多

❶ medical〈醫療的〉・weight〈體重〉・loss〈失去〉・clinic〈診所〉・advise〈建議〉・healthy〈健康的〉・way〈方法〉

❷ getting〈get（變得）的 ing 型態〉・a little〈一點〉・fat〈肥胖的〉・go on〈開始、繼續進行〉・diet〈飲食〉

❸ lose weight〈減輕體重〉・try〈嘗試〉・low〈低的〉・carbohydrate〈碳水化合物、醣〉・celery〈芹菜〉

❹ usually〈通常〉・have〈喝〉・calorie〈卡路里，是熱量的單位〉・drink〈飲料〉・diet soda〈無糖汽水〉

❺ already〈已經〉・thin〈瘦的〉・still〈仍然〉・slimming〈減肥〉

中譯

❶ 我在減重門診工作，因此我會建議人們如何用健康的方法來減重。

❷ 我有點變胖了，所以我需要開始吃減肥餐。

❸ 為了減重，要試著吃低醣食物，像是芹菜。

❹ 我通常喝低卡飲料，像是無糖汽水。

❺ Karen 已經很瘦了，但她仍然想要繼續吃代餐控制飲食。

080 減肥方式(2)

MP3 080

1 **gym**
[dʒɪm]
(n.) 健身房

2 **expend one's energy**
[ɪkˋspɛnd wʌns ˋɛnɚdʒɪ]
(phr.) 消耗熱量

3 **exercise**
[ˋɛksɚˏsaɪz]
(v.) 運動

4 **diet**
[ˋdaɪət]
(n.) 節食

5 **diet program**
[ˋdaɪət ˋprogræm]
(n.) 減肥計劃

❶ 健身房
Ken spends hours in the gym every week. He loves lifting weights.
舉重

❷ 消耗熱量
Fiona goes jogging every day to expend her energy.

❸ 運動
I play sports most days as I love to exercise.
我大部分的時間都在運動

❹ 節食
I hate going on diets because I love eating different foods.
我討厭節食

❺ 減肥計劃
My doctor gave me a good diet program that he said wouldn't damage my body.
一個他說不會傷害我的身體的優質減肥計劃

學更多

❶ spend〈花費〉・hour〈小時〉・lifting〈lift（舉起）的 ing 型態〉・weight〈重物〉
❷ jogging〈jog（慢跑）的 ing 型態〉・every day〈每天〉・expend〈消耗〉・energy〈能量〉
❸ sport〈運動〉・most〈大部分的〉・as〈因為〉
❹ hate〈討厭〉・going on〈go on（開始、繼續進行）的 ing 型態〉・different〈不同的〉
❺ doctor〈醫生〉・gave〈give（給）的過去式〉・program〈計劃〉・damage〈損害〉・body〈身體〉

中譯

❶ Ken 每星期都花數小時在健身房。他喜歡舉重。
❷ Fiona 每天都去慢跑以消耗熱量。
❸ 我大部分的時間都在運動，因為我愛運動。
❹ 我討厭節食，因為我喜歡品嚐各種食物。
❺ 我的醫生給了我一個不傷身體的優質減肥計劃。

081 減肥方式(3)

MP3 081

1 slimming and beauty center
[ˋslɪmɪŋ ænd ˋbjutɪ ˋsɛntɚ]
(n.) 瘦身美容中心

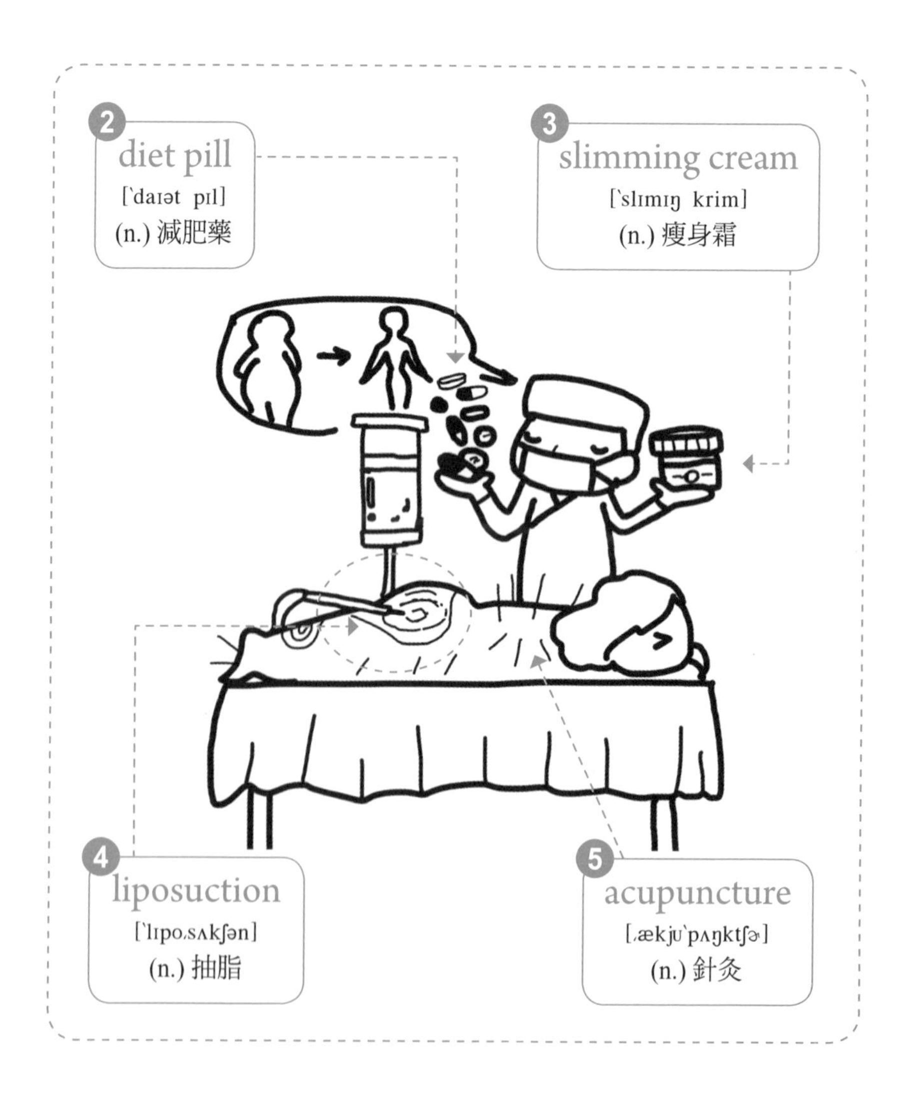

2 diet pill
[ˋdaɪət pɪl]
(n.) 減肥藥

3 slimming cream
[ˋslɪmɪŋ krim]
(n.) 瘦身霜

4 liposuction
[ˋlɪpo͵sʌkʃən]
(n.) 抽脂

5 acupuncture
[͵ækjʊˋpʌŋktʃɚ]
(n.) 針灸

❶ 瘦身美容中心

I'm going over to the slimming and beauty center later to buy some slimming drinks.

瘦身飲料

❷ 減肥藥

These diet pills are supposed to help you lose weight quickly.

❸ 瘦身霜

I rub a slimming cream on my stomach every night to try and lose weight.

擦瘦身霜在我的肚子上

❹ 抽脂

At liposuction centers, people have the fat sucked out of their bodies.

人們讓脂肪從…被抽出

❺ 針灸

More and more people in Europe are using acupuncture to relieve pain.

學更多

❶ over〈從一方至另一方〉・slimming〈減肥〉・beauty〈美麗〉・center〈中心〉・later〈較晚地〉・drink〈飲料〉

❷ pill〈藥丸、藥片〉・be supposed to〈認為應該〉・lose weight〈減重〉・quickly〈迅速地〉

❸ rub〈擦上〉・cream〈乳霜〉・stomach〈肚子〉・try〈嘗試〉

❹ have〈使得〉・sucked〈suck（吸）的過去分詞〉・out of〈從…拿出來〉

❺ more and more〈越來越〉・Europe〈歐洲〉・relieve〈減輕〉・pain〈疼痛〉

中譯

❶ 我等等想去瘦身美容中心買一些瘦身飲料。

❷ 這些減肥藥應該能幫助你快速減輕體重。

❸ 我每天晚上都在肚子塗抹瘦身霜試著減重。

❹ 在抽脂中心，人們讓脂肪從自己身體被抽取出來。

❺ 在歐洲，越來越多人都在利用針灸減輕疼痛。

082 身體不適(1)

MP3 082

1 sneeze
[sniz]
(v.) 打噴嚏

2 nasal congestion
[`nezḷ kən`dʒɛstʃən]
(n.) 鼻塞

3 runny nose
[`rʌnɪ noz]
(n.) 流鼻水

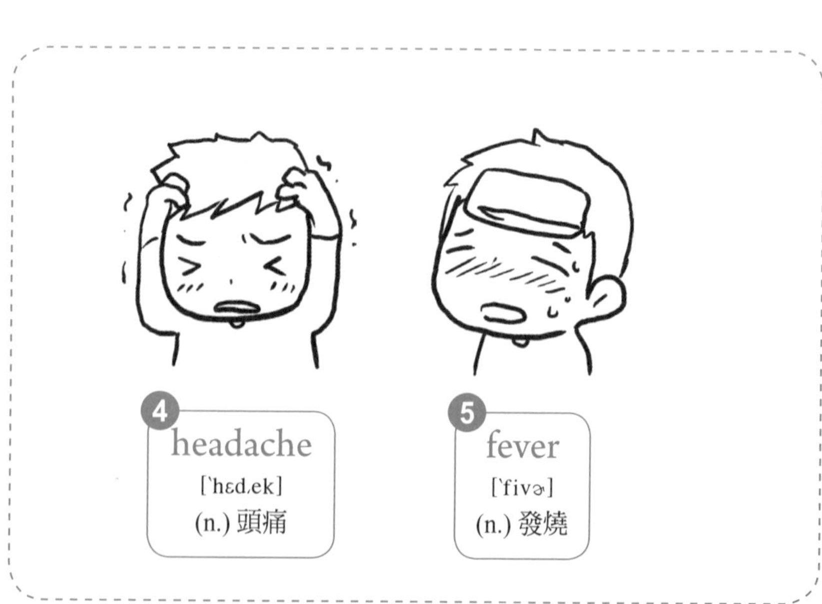

4 headache
[`hɛd͵ek]
(n.) 頭痛

5 fever
[`fivɚ]
(n.) 發燒

❶ 打噴嚏
Can you give me a tissue? I'm going to sneeze.

❷ 鼻塞
I can't breathe through my nose because of my nasal congestion.
用鼻子呼吸

❸ 流鼻水
I have a runny nose, so I keep having to wipe it.
我要一直擦它

❹ 頭痛
The man asked his family to speak quietly because he had a headache.

❺ 發燒
The little girl had a fever of 102 degrees.

學更多

❶ give〈給〉・tissue〈衛生紙〉・be going to〈將要〉
❷ breathe〈呼吸〉・through〈憑藉〉・nose〈鼻子〉・nasal〈鼻的〉・congestion〈阻塞〉
❸ runny〈流鼻涕的〉・keep〈繼續不斷〉・having to〈have to（必須）的 ing 型態〉・wipe〈擦〉
❹ asked〈ask（要求）的過去式〉・family〈家人〉・speak〈說話〉・quietly〈輕聲地〉
❺ little〈幼小的〉・degree〈度〉

中譯

❶ 可以給我一張衛生紙嗎？我快要打噴嚏了。
❷ 我不能用鼻子呼吸，因為我鼻塞了。
❸ 我流鼻水，所以我必須一直擦鼻涕。
❹ 那名男子要求他的家人輕聲細語，因為他頭痛。
❺ 那個小女孩發燒到（華氏）102 度。

083 身體不適(2)

MP3 083

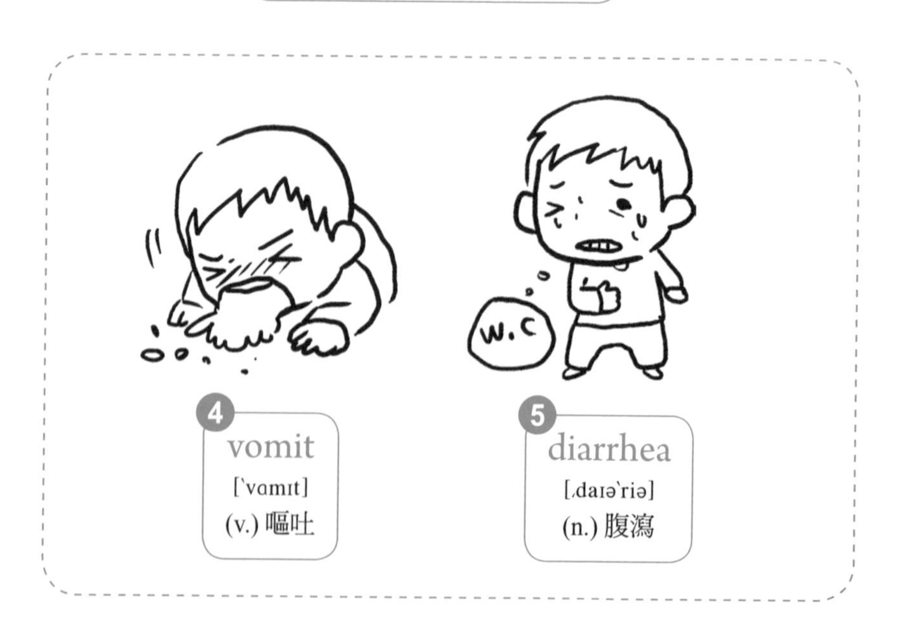

❶ 咳嗽
I have a terrible cough; my throat feels awful.
我咳嗽咳得很嚴

❷ 喉嚨痛
It hurts to talk right now because I have a sore throat.

❸ 喉嚨有痰
I know it's disgusting to keep spitting, but I have phlegm in my throat.
一直吐痰很噁心

❹ 嘔吐
The little boy ate too much ice cream, and now he needs to vomit.

❺ 腹瀉
That food has given me diarrhea, and I keep going to the toilet.
那個食物讓我腹瀉

學更多

❶ terrible〈嚴重的〉・throat〈喉嚨〉・feel〈感覺〉・awful〈不舒服的〉
❷ hurt〈帶來痛苦〉・talk〈講話〉・right now〈就是現在〉・sore〈疼痛發炎的〉
❸ disgusting〈令人作嘔的〉・spitting〈spit（吐痰）的 ing 型態〉・phlegm〈痰〉
❹ ate〈eat（吃）的過去式〉・ice cream〈冰淇淋〉・need〈需要〉
❺ food〈食物〉・given〈give（帶來）的過去分詞〉・keep〈繼續不斷〉・toilet〈廁所〉

中譯

❶ 我咳嗽咳得很嚴重，我的喉嚨很不舒服。
❷ 我現在說話會很不舒服，因為我喉嚨痛。
❸ 我知道一直吐痰很噁心，但是我的喉嚨有痰。
❹ 那個小男孩吃了太多冰淇淋，所以他現在得去嘔吐。
❺ 那個食物讓我腹瀉，所以我一直跑廁所。

084 身體不適(3)

MP3 084

❶ 寒顫
Pass me my sweater, please. I have the chills.

❷ 全身痠痛
Jeff has been feeling ill all week, and he still has an aching body.
Jeff 一整個星期都覺得不舒服

❸ 呼吸困難
Dan has difficulty in breathing and even climbing the stairs is hard for him.
爬樓梯

❹ 失去意識
Alice was knocked unconscious when she hit her head on the table.
Alice 被撞到失去意識

❺ 昏迷
Some people believe that when you go into a coma you can still hear things.

學更多

❶ pass〈傳遞〉・sweater〈毛衣〉・please〈請〉
❷ feeling〈feel（感覺）的 ing 型態〉・ill〈生病的〉・all〈整個的〉・week〈週〉・aching〈疼痛的〉・body〈身體〉
❸ difficulty〈困難〉・breathing〈呼吸〉・even〈甚至〉・climbing〈climb（爬）的 ing 型態〉・stairs〈樓梯〉・hard〈困難的〉
❹ knocked〈knock（撞成…）的過去分詞〉・hit〈hit（碰撞）的過去式〉・head〈頭〉
❺ believe〈相信〉・still〈仍然〉・hear〈聽〉

中譯

❶ 請把毛衣拿給我，我打寒顫了。
❷ Jeff 一整個星期都覺得不舒服，他現在仍然全身痠痛。
❸ Dan 有呼吸困難的問題，甚至連爬樓梯對他而言都很不容易。
❹ Alice 的頭撞到桌子之後，她就失去意識了。
❺ 有些人相信，當你昏迷時，你仍然可以聽到聲音。

085

身體損傷(1)

MP3 085

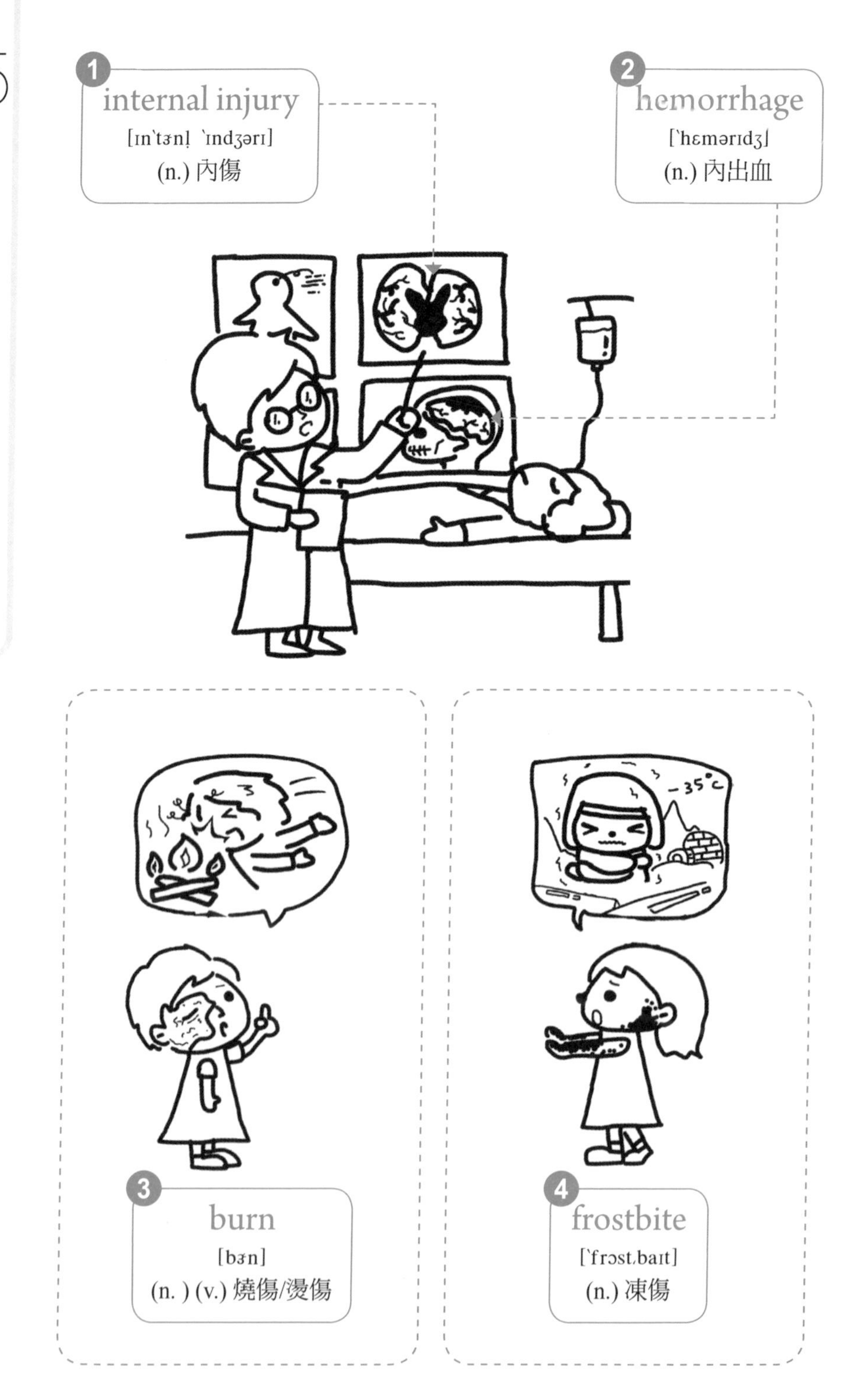

❶ 內傷

Although she looks fine, she has several internal injuries.

她看起來很健康

❷ 內出血

The man fell into a coma after suffering a brain hemorrhage.

陷入昏迷

❸ 燒傷／燙傷

You'll burn your finger if you put it in that boiling water.

如果你把手指放進滾燙的熱水

❹ 凍傷

The mountain climber has frostbite on his fingers because it was so cold

登山客的手指頭凍傷了

on top of the mountain.

在山頂上

學更多

❶ although〈雖然〉‧look〈看起來〉‧fine〈健康的〉‧several〈數個的〉‧internal〈內部的〉‧injury〈損傷〉

❷ fell into〈fall into（陷入）的過去式〉‧coma〈昏迷〉‧after〈在…之後〉‧suffering〈suffer（受苦）的 ing 型態〉‧brain〈腦〉

❸ finger〈手指〉‧if〈如果〉‧put〈放入〉‧boiling〈沸騰的〉‧water〈水〉

❹ mountain climber〈登山客〉‧cold〈冷的〉‧top〈頂部〉‧mountain〈山〉

中譯

❶ 雖然她看起來很健康，但是她有多處內傷。

❷ 那名男子在腦部內出血之後，就陷入了昏迷。

❸ 如果你把手指放入滾燙的熱水，你的手指就會燙傷。

❹ 這名登山客的手指頭凍傷了，因為山頂上太冷了。

086 身體損傷(2)

MP3 086

❶ 拉傷／伸展

His muscles were stretched a bit too much and now he's in pain.

他的肌肉伸展得有點過頭了　他很痛

❷ 扭傷

Dawn fell over and sprained her ankle; she's now having trouble walking.

她現在走路有困難

❸ 脫臼

She suffered a dislocation of her wrist, so the bones are in the wrong position.

她的手腕脫臼了　在不對的位置

❹ 骨折

A fracture is a crack in your bones.

你的骨頭有裂痕

學更多

❶ muscle〈肌肉〉・stretched〈stretch（拉傷、伸展）的過去分詞〉・a bit〈稍微〉・in pain〈在痛苦中〉

❷ fell over〈fall over（跌倒）的過去式〉・sprained〈sprain（扭傷）的過去式〉・ankle〈腳踝〉・having trouble〈have trouble（做…有困難）的 ing 型態〉・walking〈walk（走）的 ing 型態〉

❸ suffered〈suffer（受苦）的過去式〉・wrist〈手腕〉・wrong〈不對的〉・position〈位置〉

❹ crack〈裂痕〉・bone〈骨頭〉

中譯

❶ 他的肌肉伸展得有點過頭了，所以他現在覺得很痛。

❷ Dawn 跌倒了，還扭傷了腳踝；她現在走路有點困難。

❸ 她的手腕脫臼了，所以骨頭的位置跑掉了。

❹ 骨折就是你的骨頭上有裂痕。

087 身體損傷(3)

MP3 087

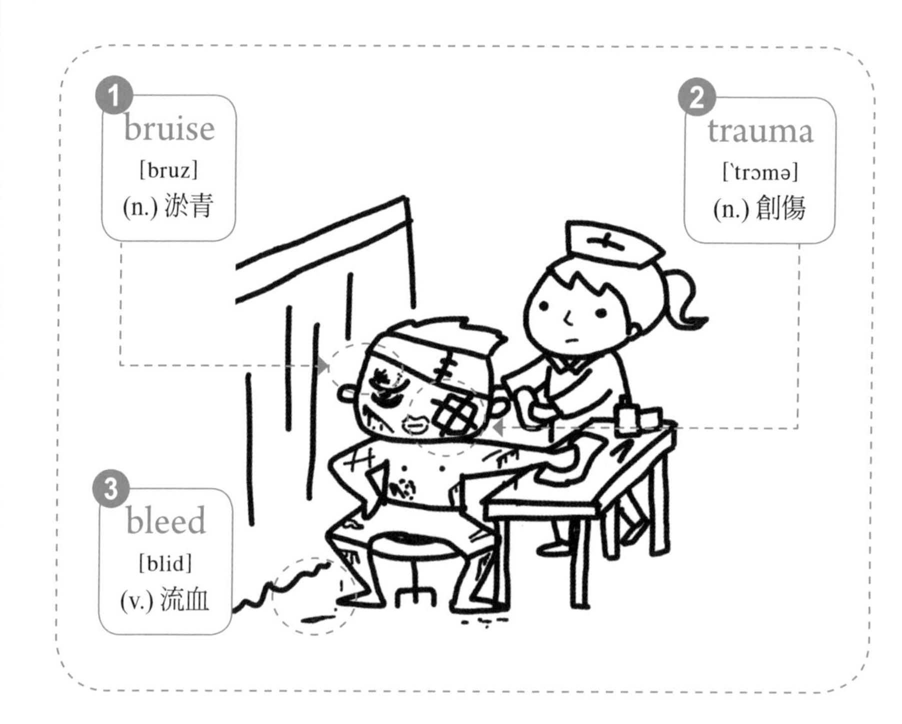

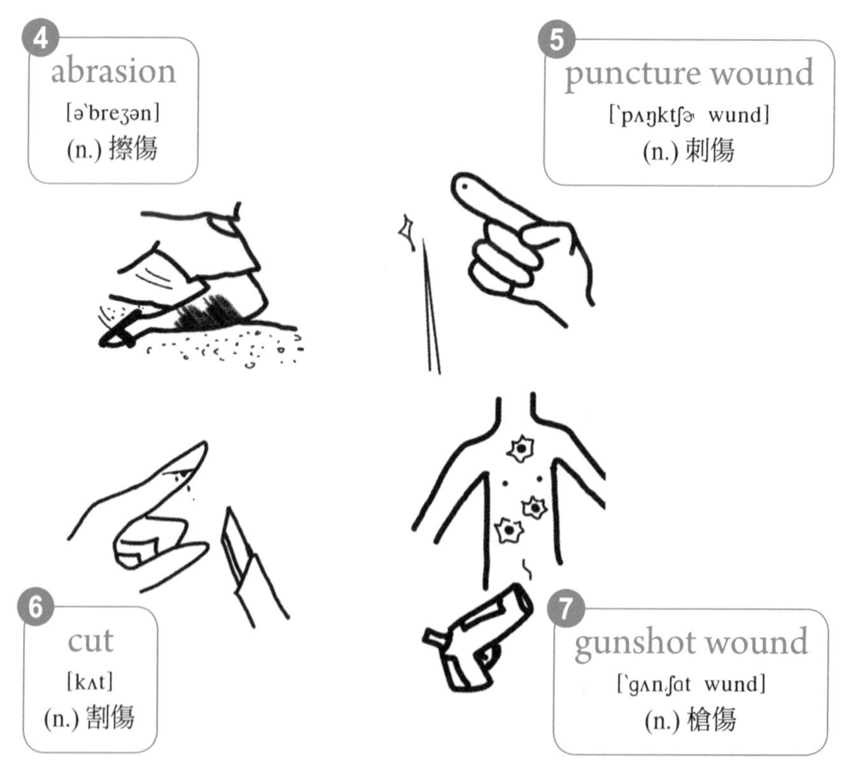

❶ 淤青

I have a bruise on my leg from where I was kicked.

我被踢到的地方

❷ 創傷

The patient was in trauma after the terrible car crash.

❸ 流血

I just cut my finger, and it's bleeding badly.

現在流血流得很嚴重

❹ 擦傷

After scraping his hand on the rock, he has a bad abrasion.

❺ 刺傷

He has a puncture wound from where the knife entered his arm.

刀刺進他的手臂的地方

❻ 割傷

She has a cut on her finger after slipping when chopping vegetables.

❼ 槍傷

The policeman received a gunshot wound when the criminal started shooting.

受到槍傷　開始射擊

學更多

❶ leg〈腿〉・kicked〈kick（踢）的過去分詞〉
❷ patient〈病人〉・after〈在…之後〉・terrible〈嚴重的〉・car crash〈車禍〉
❸ just〈剛才〉・cut〈cut（割）的過去式〉・finger〈手指〉・badly〈嚴重地〉
❹ scraping〈scrape（刮擦）的 ing 型態〉・hand〈手〉・rock〈石頭〉・bad〈嚴重的〉
❺ puncture〈刺〉・wound〈傷口〉・entered〈enter（進入）的過去式〉・arm〈手臂〉
❻ slipping〈slip（滑倒）的 ing 型態〉・chopping〈chop（切）的 ing 型態〉
❼ received〈receive（受到）的過去式〉・gunshot〈射擊〉・criminal〈罪犯〉

中譯

❶ 我的腿被踢到的地方，有一個淤青。
❷ 那位病患在嚴重的車禍中受到創傷。
❸ 我剛剛割傷手指，現在流血流得很嚴重。
❹ 他的手擦到石頭之後，造成嚴重的擦傷。
❺ 刀子刺進他手臂的地方，有一個刺傷的傷口。
❻ 她在切蔬菜的時候滑倒，割傷自己的手指。
❼ 當嫌犯開始射擊時，員警受到了槍傷。

088 手的動作(1)

MP3 088

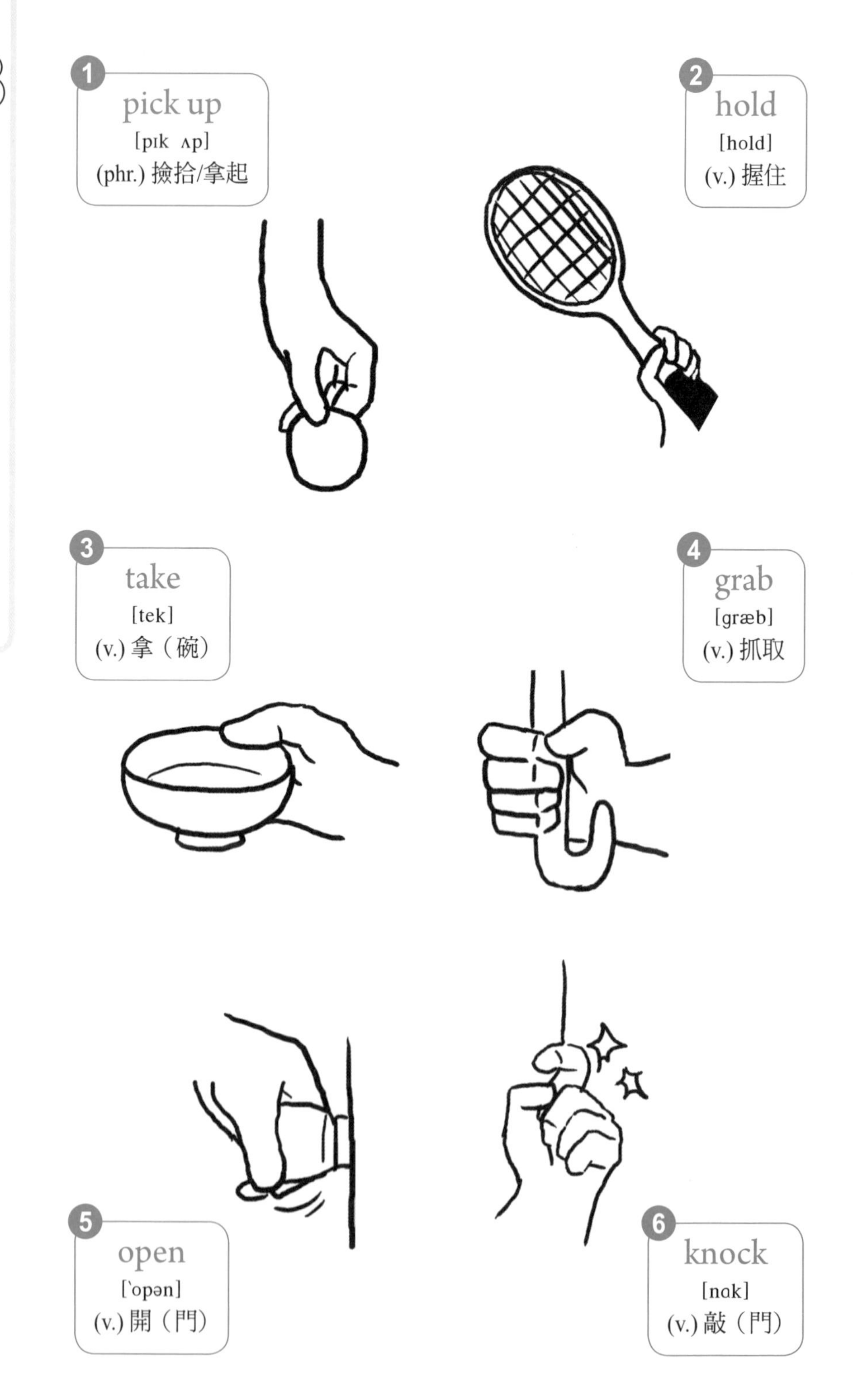

❶ 撿拾 / 拿起
Could you pick up my bag please? It's just over there.

❷ 握住
You should hold on to something if you have to stand on the train.
握住某個東西

❸ 拿（碗）
I always take a business card from restaurants I like.
拿名片　我喜歡的餐廳

❹ 抓取
Andy quickly grabbed his keys and left the house.
出門

❺ 開（門）
Could you open the door, please? My hands are full.
我的手拿滿了東西

❻ 敲（門）
I'll knock on the door to see if there's anyone here.
是否有任何人在這裡

學更多

❶ bag〈包包〉．please〈請〉．over there〈在那裡〉
❷ have to〈必須〉．stand〈站立〉．train〈火車〉
❸ always〈總是〉．business card〈名片〉．restaurant〈餐廳〉
❹ quickly〈迅速地〉．grabbed〈grab（抓握）的過去式〉．key〈鑰匙〉．left〈leave（離開）的過去式〉
❺ door〈門〉．hand〈手〉．full〈滿的〉
❻ see〈知道〉．if〈是否〉．anyone〈任何人〉

中譯

❶ 可以請你把我的包包拿起來嗎？它就在那。
❷ 如果你必須在火車上站立，就應該要握住某個東西。
❸ 我都會從喜歡的餐廳裡拿張名片。
❹ Andy 迅速地抓取了他的鑰匙，然後就出門了。
❺ 可以請你開門嗎？我兩手都是東西。
❻ 我會敲門，這樣就知道有沒有人在這裡。

089 手的動作(2)

MP3 089

1. **hold hands**
[hold hændz]
(phr.) 牽手

2. **shake hands**
[ʃek hændz]
(phr.) 握手

3. **make a fist**
[mek ə fɪst]
(phr.) 握拳

4. **point**
[pɔɪnt]
(v.)（用手）指出

5. **lift hand**
[lɪft hænd]
(v.) 舉手

6. **wave**
[wev]
(v.) 揮舞

❶ 牽手
The young lovers always hold hands.

❷ 握手
When you meet people, it's polite to shake hands.

❸ 握拳
Whenever the girl gets angry she makes a fist.
每當那個女孩生氣時

❹（用手）指出
Which one is your house? Can you point to it?

❺ 舉手
❻ 揮舞
OK, everyone, if you like this song, lift your hands and wave them in the air.

學更多

❶ young〈年輕的〉・lover〈情侶〉・always〈總是〉・hold〈握著〉・hand〈手〉
❷ meet〈遇見〉・polite〈有禮貌的〉・shake〈握手〉
❸ whenever〈每當〉・get〈變得〉・angry〈生氣的〉・fist〈拳〉
❹ your〈你的〉・house〈房子〉
❺ ❻ everyone〈每個人〉・song〈歌曲〉・lift〈舉起〉・air〈空中〉

中譯

❶ 年輕的情侶們總是牽著手。
❷ 與人見面時，握手是種禮貌。
❸ 每當那個女孩生氣時，她都會握拳。
❹ 哪一間房子是你家？你可以指出來嗎？
❺ ❻ 好，各位，如果你喜歡這首歌，就舉起你的手在空中揮舞吧。

090 手的動作(3)

MP3 090

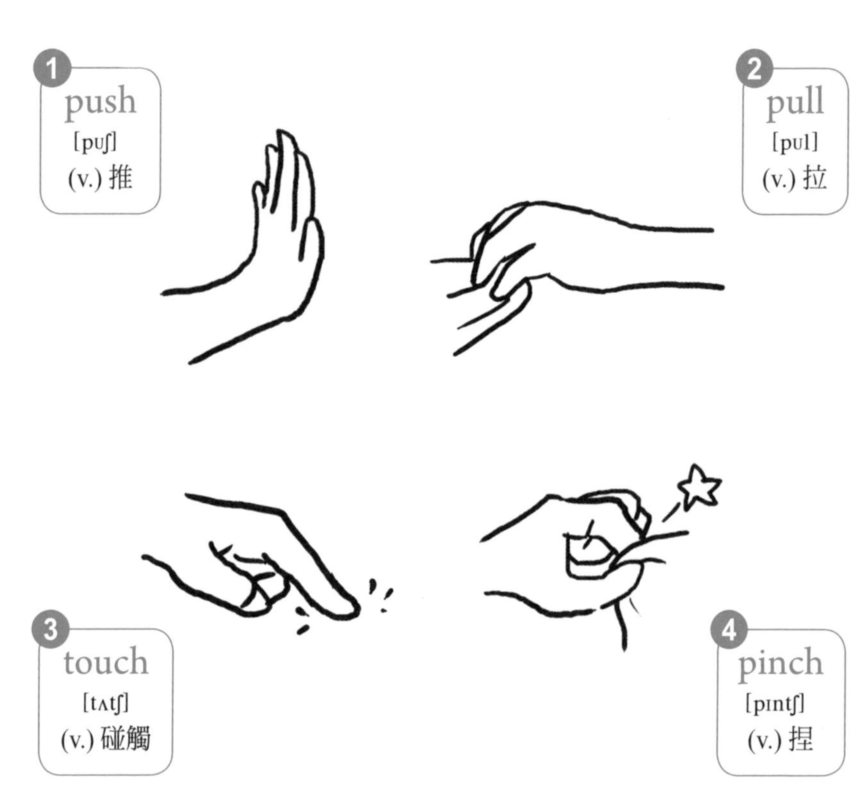

1. push [pʊʃ] (v.) 推
2. pull [pʊl] (v.) 拉
3. touch [tʌtʃ] (v.) 碰觸
4. pinch [pɪntʃ] (v.) 捏

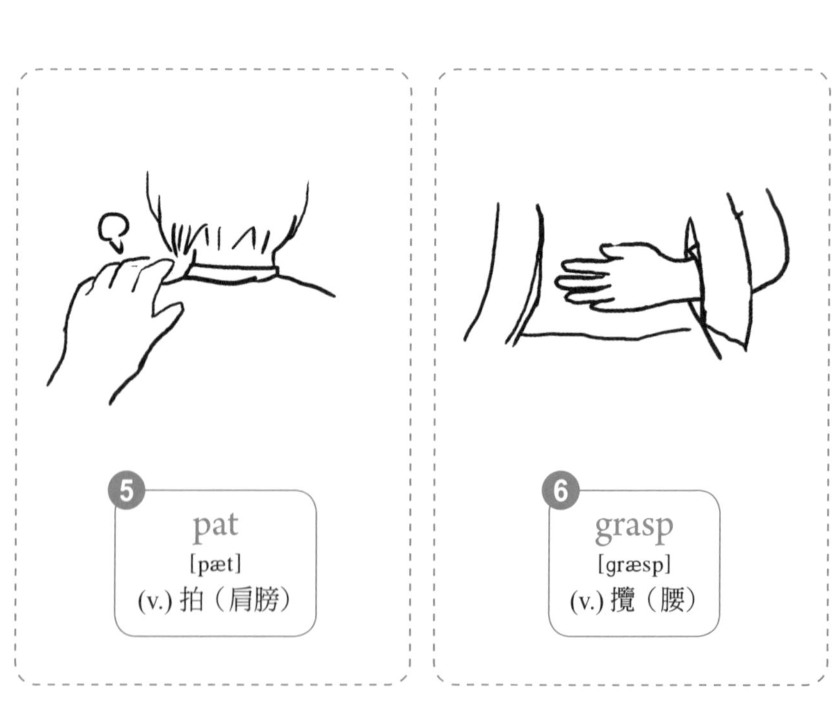

5. pat [pæt] (v.) 拍（肩膀）
6. grasp [græsp] (v.) 攬（腰）

❶ 推

Don't push it towards me; pull it towards you.

❷ 拉

The boy pulled my sleeve to get my attention.

引起我的注意

❸ 碰觸

Whenever you touch something, your fingers leave fingerprints.

你的手指頭會留下指紋

❹ 捏

Please don't pinch me. If you want my attention, you can just touch my arm gently.

輕輕觸碰我的手臂

❺ 拍（肩膀）

I always pat my dog when he's good.

❻ 攬（腰）

Tom said he saw Kevin grasp his girlfriend's waist.

Kevin 攬了他女朋友的腰

學更多

❶ toward〈朝向〉
❷ pulled〈pull（拉）的過去式〉・sleeve〈袖子〉・attention〈注意〉
❸ whenever〈每當〉・finger〈手指頭〉・leave〈留下〉・fingerprint〈指紋〉
❹ want〈想要〉・just〈只是〉・arm〈手臂〉・gently〈輕輕地〉
❺ always〈總是〉・dog〈狗〉・good〈乖的〉
❻ said〈say（說）的過去式〉・saw〈see（看見）的過去式〉・waist〈腰部〉

中譯

❶ 別把它推向我，要把它拉向你。
❷ 那個小男孩拉我的袖子，企圖引起我的注意。
❸ 每當你碰觸到東西，你的手指都會留下指紋。
❹ 別捏我。如果你要引起我的注意，只要輕碰我的手臂就好。
❺ 當我的狗表現良好時，我總會拍拍牠。
❻ Tom 說他看見 Kevin 攬了女朋友的腰。

091
腿的動作(1)

MP3 091

❶ 追趕

The little boy ran off, so the man had to chase him down the road.

必須沿路追趕他

❷ 跑

Most large dogs can run much faster than humans.

大部分的大型狗

❸ 跳躍

Instead of walking around the fence, the man just jumped over it.

繞著柵欄走

❹ 爬行

Babies start to crawl before they can walk.

❺ 走 / 散步

The old woman likes to go for a walk after eating dinner.

❻ 站立

❼ 坐下

There wasn't any room to sit down on the MRT, so he had to stand up.

沒有位置

學更多

❶ ran off〈run off（跑走）的過去式〉・down〈沿著〉・road〈路〉

❷ most〈大部分的〉・faster〈比較快地，fast（快地）的比較級〉・human〈人〉

❸ instead of〈代替〉・walking around〈walk around（沿著、繞著…的外面行走）的 ing 型態〉・fence〈柵欄〉・over〈越過〉

❹ baby〈嬰兒〉・start〈開始〉・before〈在…之前〉

❺ old〈上了年紀的〉・after〈在…之後〉・dinner〈晚餐〉

❻ ❼ any〈任何一個〉・room〈位置〉・MRT〈捷運〉・had to〈have to（必須）的過去式〉

中譯

❶ 那個小男孩跑走了，所以那個男人必須沿路追趕他。

❷ 大部分的大型狗可以跑得比人類還快。

❸ 那名男子沒有沿著柵欄走，而是跳過了柵欄。

❹ 嬰兒在能夠行走之前，他們會先開始爬行。

❺ 那位上了年紀的的女士喜歡在晚餐後散步。

❻ ❼ 捷運裡沒有空位可以坐，所以他只好站著。

092

腿的動作(2)

MP3 092

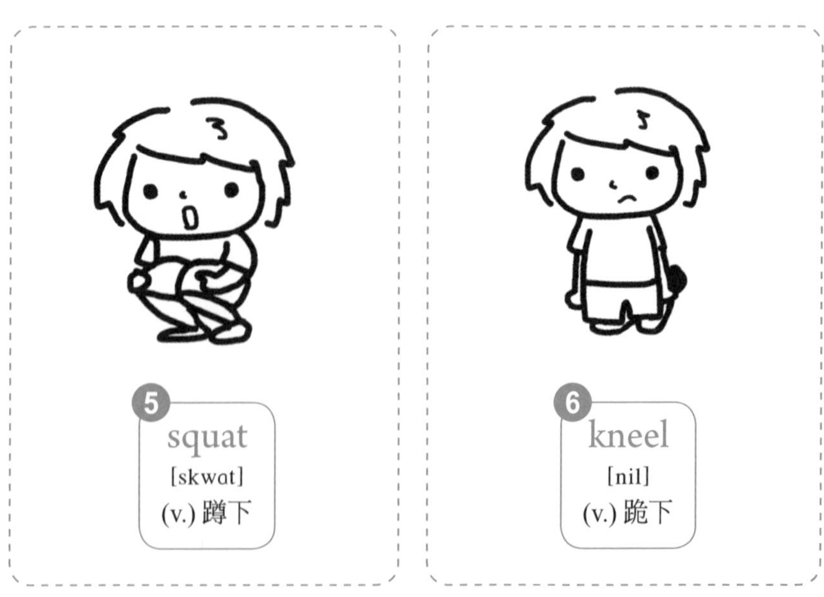

❶ 跨越
The man always hurdles the small fence near his house when he goes running.
他家附近的小柵欄

❷ 抬 / 舉
Steve lifted up the TV and carried it to his bedroom.

❸ 踩踏 / 行走
The stairs are so steep on the Great Wall of China, you have to step very high as you climb up.
長城
當你爬上去時

❹ 踢
The player kicked the soccer ball and stepped backwards.
往後邁步

❺ 蹲下
When picking up heavy objects, you should bend your knees and squat.
當拿起重物時

❻ 跪下
The man knelt down in church and began to pray.
跪下

學更多

❶ small〈小的〉・fence〈柵欄〉・near〈在…附近〉・running〈run（跑步）的 ing 型態〉
❷ lifted〈lift（抬、舉）的過去式〉・carried〈carry（搬運）的過去式〉・bedroom〈臥室〉
❸ stairs〈樓梯〉・steep〈陡峭的〉・great〈規模大的〉・wall〈城牆〉・climb〈登上〉
❹ player〈球員〉・kicked〈kick（踢）的過去式〉・soccer ball〈足球〉・backwards〈向後〉
❺ heavy〈重的〉・object〈物體〉・bend〈彎曲〉・knee〈膝蓋〉
❻ knelt〈kneel（跪下）的過去式〉・down〈向下〉・church〈教堂〉・
began〈begin（開始）的過去式〉・pray〈祈禱〉

中譯

❶ 那名男子在跑步時，都會跨越他家附近的小柵欄。
❷ Steve 抬起電視，搬到他的臥室裡。
❸ 長城的階梯很陡峭，當你攀登時，腳必須踩踏得非常高。
❹ 那位球員踢了足球，並向後移動。
❺ 當你要拿起重物時，應該先曲膝並蹲下。
❻ 那位男士在教堂裡跪下，並開始禱告。

093 身體的動作

MP3 093

1 handstand
[ˋhænd.stænd]
(n.) 倒立

2 stretch
[strɛtʃ]
(v.) 伸展

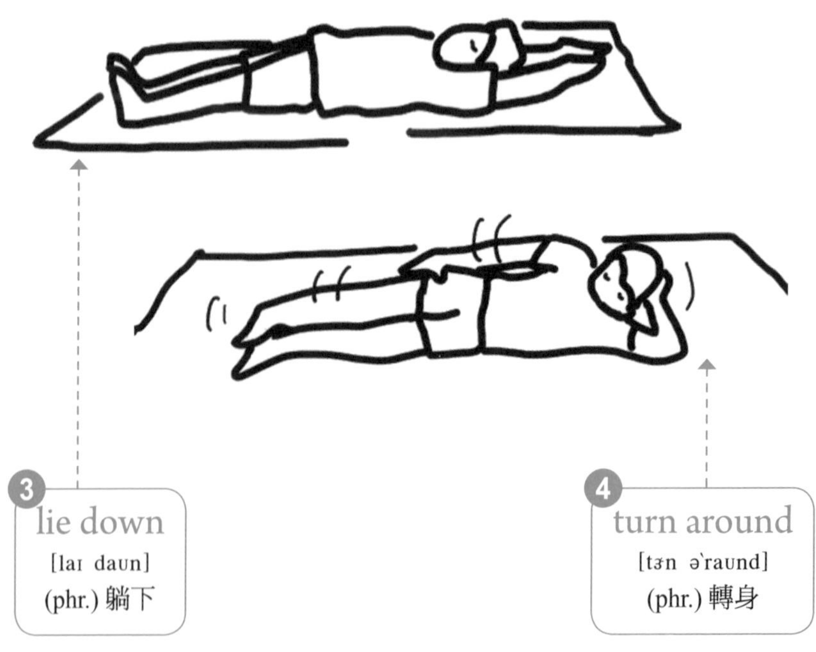

3 lie down
[laɪ daʊn]
(phr.) 躺下

4 turn around
[tɝn əˋraʊnd]
(phr.) 轉身

❶ 倒立

Not many people can keep themselves upside-down in a handstand.

保持他們自己是顛倒的狀態

❷ 伸展

You should always stretch your muscles before doing any sport.

伸展你的肌肉

❸ 躺下

Harry felt sick, so he decided to lie down on the floor.

躺在地上

❹ 轉身

Could you turn around and look at me, please?

轉身看著我

學更多

❶ many〈許多的〉・keep〈保持某一狀態〉・themselves〈他們自己〉・upside-down〈顛倒的〉

❷ always〈總是〉・muscle〈肌肉〉・before〈在…之前〉・doing〈do（做）的 ing 型態〉・any〈任一〉・sport〈運動〉

❸ felt〈feel（感覺）的過去式〉・sick〈病的〉・decided〈decide（決定）的過去式〉・lie〈躺〉・floor〈地板〉

❹ turn〈轉〉・around〈向相反方向〉・look at〈看〉・please〈請〉

中譯

❶ 能夠倒立讓自己保持上下顛倒的人並不多。

❷ 做任何運動之前，你都必須伸展肌肉。

❸ Harry 覺得不舒服，所以他決定躺在地上。

❹ 可以請你轉身看著我嗎？

094 形容身材(1)

MP3 094

① **pear-shaped**
[ˋpɛr͵ʃept]
(adj.) 梨型

② **apple-shaped**
[ˋæpl̩͵ʃept]
(adj.) 蘋果型

③ **hourglass figure**
[ˋaur͵glæs ˋfɪgjɚ]
(n.) 沙漏型身材

④ **V-shaped**
[ˋvi͵ʃept]
(adj.) 倒三角形

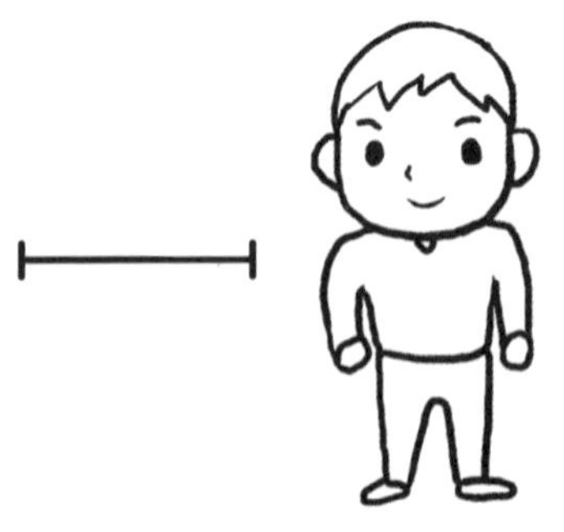

⑤ **broad-shouldered**
[brɔd ˋʃoldɚd]
(adj.) 肩膀寬闊的

⑥ **wide-hipped**
[waɪd hɪpt]
(adj.) 寬臀的/臀部寬的

❶ 梨型
Dawn has big hips and a small chest. She's pear-shaped.
大屁股和一個小胸部

❷ 蘋果型
The boy's really overweight. He has an apple-shaped figure.

❸ 沙漏型身材
She's very curvy. She has an hourglass figure.

❹ 倒三角形
Rob is very strong, so his chest is V-shaped.
他的胸膛是倒三角型

❺ 肩膀寬闊的
Sam looks very strong. He's very broad-shouldered.

❻ 寬臀的 / 臀部寬的
Rebecca has trouble finding pants that fit her because she's so wide-hipped.
Rebecca 很難找到適合她的褲子

學更多

❶ big〈大的〉・hip〈屁股〉・small〈小的〉・pear〈洋梨〉
❷ overweight〈超重的〉・apple〈蘋果〉・shaped〈某種形狀的〉
❸ curvy〈曲線美的〉・hourglass〈沙漏〉・figure〈體型〉
❹ very〈非常〉・strong〈強壯的〉・chest〈胸部〉
❺ look〈看起來〉・broad〈寬闊的〉・shouldered〈有…肩膀的〉
❻ have trouble〈做某事有困難〉・finding〈find（找到）的 ing 型態〉・pants〈褲子〉・fit〈適合〉・wide〈寬的〉・hipped〈有…臀部的〉

中譯

❶ Dawn 有個大屁股、小胸部，她屬於梨型身材。
❷ 那個男孩實在是過重，他有個蘋果型身材。
❸ 她的曲線優美，擁有一副沙漏型身材。
❹ Rob 非常強壯，他的胸膛呈現倒三角形。
❺ Sam 看起來非常強壯，他的肩膀非常寬闊。
❻ Rebecca 很難找到適合她的褲子，因為她的臀部很寬。

095 形容身材(2)

MP3 095

1 muscular
[ˋmʌskjələ]
(adj.) 肌肉發達

2 flabby
[ˋflæbɪ]
(adj.) 肌肉鬆弛

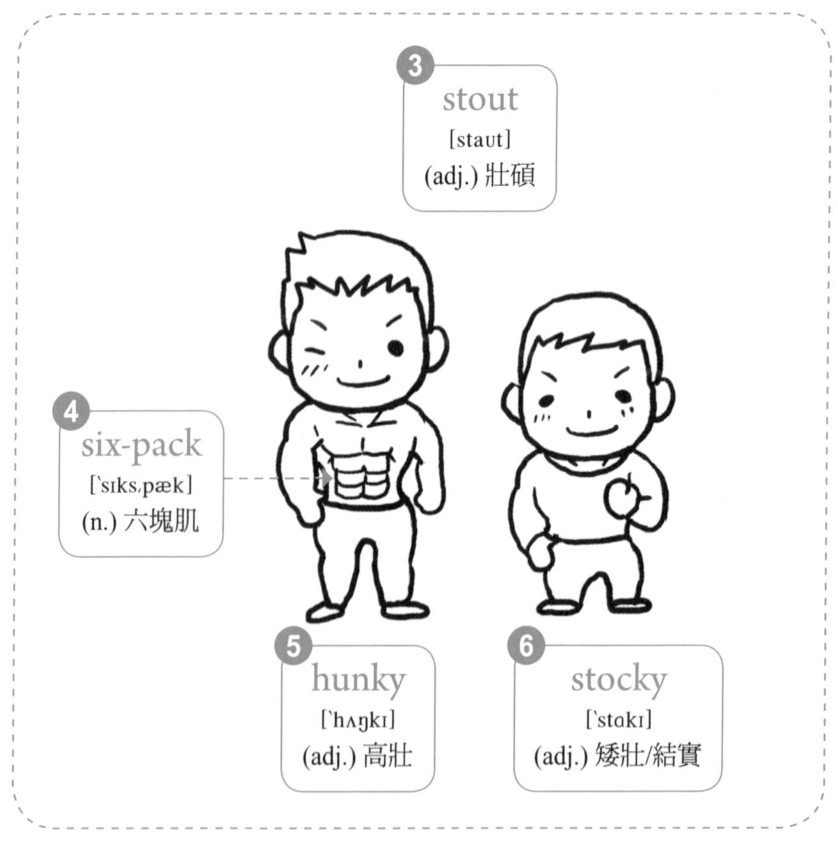

❶ 肌肉發達

He must lift weights; he's very muscular.

他一定有練舉重

❷ 肌肉鬆弛

You should do some exercise; you're looking a bit flabby.

你看起來有點肌肉鬆弛

❸ 壯碩

I wouldn't say he's fat, but he is pretty stout.

❹ 六塊肌

The man lifted up his T-shirt to show off his six-pack.

掀起他的 T 恤

❺ 高壯

He's a hunky man. All the girls wanted to know who he is.

他是誰

❻ 矮壯／結實

Ian is short and stocky. He looks quite strong.

他看起來挺壯的

學更多

❶ must〈一定〉・lift weight〈舉重〉・very〈非常〉
❷ exercise〈運動〉・looking〈look（看起來）的 ing 型態〉・a bit〈有點〉
❸ say〈說〉・ fat〈胖的〉・pretty〈相當〉
❹ lifted up〈lift up（掀起）的過去式〉・show off〈炫耀〉
❺ man〈男人〉・all〈所有的〉・girl〈女孩〉・know〈知道〉
❻ short〈矮的〉・quite〈相當〉・strong〈強壯的〉

中譯

❶ 他一定有練舉重，他的肌肉非常發達。
❷ 你應該做些運動，你看起來有點肌肉鬆弛。
❸ 我不會說他很胖，但是他的身材挺壯碩的。
❹ 那個男人掀起了 T 恤，炫耀他的六塊肌。
❺ 他是一個高壯的男人，所有的女孩都想知道他是誰。
❻ Ian 個子矮、身材結實，看起來挺壯的。

096 形容身材(3)

MP3 096

1 **slim**
[slɪm]
(adj.) 苗條/瘦得好看

2 **curvy**
[ˋkɝvɪ]
(adj.) 窈窕/曲線優美

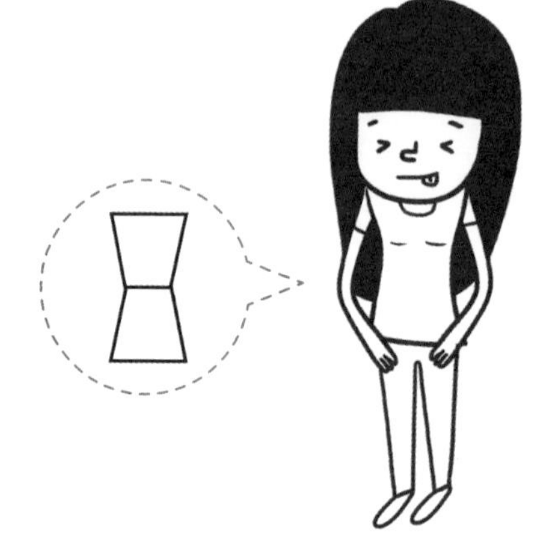

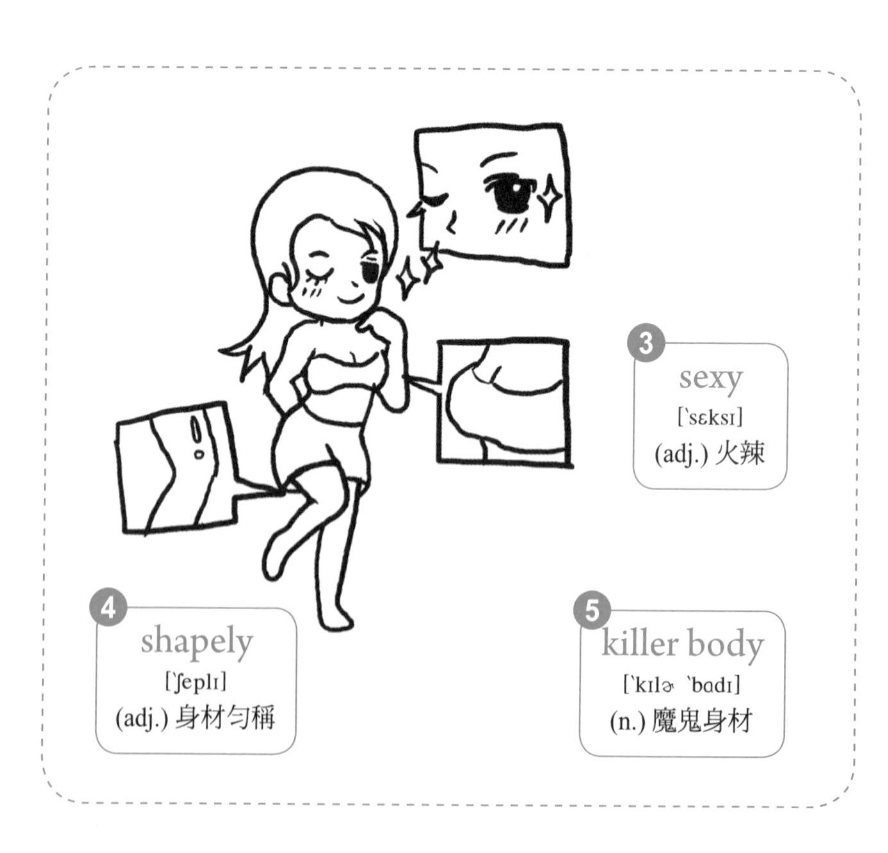

3 **sexy**
[ˋsɛksɪ]
(adj.) 火辣

4 **shapely**
[ˋʃeplɪ]
(adj.) 身材勻稱

5 **killer body**
[ˋkɪlɚ ˋbɑdɪ]
(n.) 魔鬼身材

❶ 苗條 / 瘦得好看
Sam goes running every day because he wants to be slim.

❷ 窈窕 / 曲線優美
Curvy women are often described as being sexy.
經常被說…

❸ 火辣
Different people have different ideas about what a sexy body looks like.
不同的人有不同的見解

❹ 身材勻稱
Fay has a shapely body; she's quite curvy.

❺ 魔鬼身材
She's got a killer body. She must exercise regularly.

學更多

❶ running〈run（跑步）的 ing 型態〉‧every day〈每天〉
❷ women〈woman（女人）的複數〉‧described〈describe（形容）的過去分詞〉
❸ different〈不同的〉‧idea〈見解〉‧look like〈看起來像…〉
❹ body〈身體〉‧quite〈很〉
❺ killer〈令人著迷之物〉‧must〈一定〉‧exercise〈運動〉‧regularly〈有規律地〉

中譯

❶ Sam 每天跑步，因為他希望變苗條。
❷ 曲線優美的女人經常被形容為性感。
❸ 每個人對於火辣身材的定義各有不同的見解。
❹ Fay 身材勻稱，她很窈窕。
❺ 她有一副魔鬼身材，她一定有規律地運動。

097 高矮胖瘦(1)

MP3 097

3
fat
[fæt]
(adj.) 肥胖

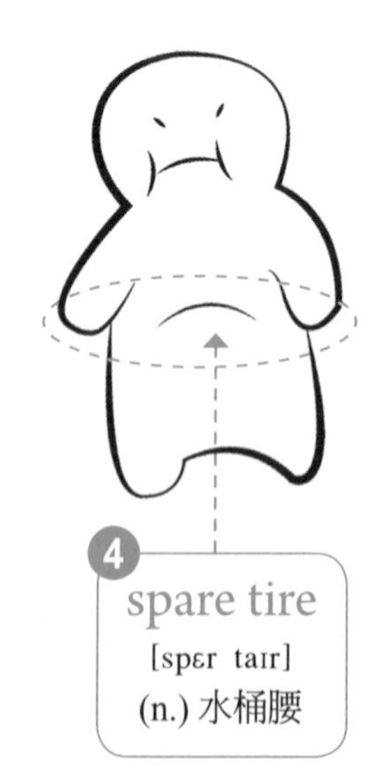

❶ 高

Most basketball players are very tall.

❷ 矮

The little boy is short, so he can't reach the cookies on the top shelf.

他拿不到餅乾

❸ 肥胖

Tom has to lose some weight; he's a little bit fat.

❹ 水桶腰

He's not really fat, but he does have a spare tire around his middle.

他的腰部有一圈水桶腰

❺ 肥肚皮

If you drink too much wine or beer, you might get a big, round potbelly.

得到一個大大圓圓的肥肚皮

學更多

❶ most〈多數的〉・basketball〈籃球〉・player〈運動員〉
❷ reach〈伸手拿到〉・cookie〈甜餅乾〉・top〈頂的〉・shelf〈架子〉
❸ have to〈必須〉・lose weight〈減肥〉・some〈一些〉・a little bit〈有點〉
❹ fat〈肥胖的〉・spare〈備用的〉・tire〈輪胎〉・around〈圍繞〉・middle〈腰部〉
❺ drink〈喝〉・wine〈葡萄酒〉・beer〈啤酒〉・round〈圓的〉

中譯

❶ 大部分的籃球員個子都很高。
❷ 那個小男孩個子矮，所以他拿不到放在架子頂端的甜餅乾。
❸ Tom 必須稍微減肥了，他有一點胖。
❹ 他並不是真的很胖，但是他的確有一圈水桶腰。
❺ 如果你喝太多葡萄酒或啤酒，你可能會有一個大大圓圓的肥肚皮。

098 高矮胖瘦(2)

MP3 098

4 overweight
[ˋovɚ͵wet]
(adj.) 過重

5 underweight
[ˋʌndɚ͵wet]
(adj.) 過輕

❶ 臃腫／微胖的
The little baby's round, chubby cheeks look so cute.
圓圓肉肉的臉頰

❷ 瘦得皮包骨
Rachel should eat more; she's too skinny.

❸ 健康／適當的
Dave isn't very fit; he needs to do more exercise.

❹ 過重
Stop eating fatty foods; you're already overweight.
停止吃油膩的食物

❺ 過輕
Being underweight is just as bad for you as being overweight.
對你的身體不好

學更多

❶ little〈幼小的〉・baby〈嬰兒〉・round〈圓的〉・cheek〈臉頰〉・cute〈可愛的〉
❷ should〈應該〉・eat〈吃〉・more〈更多〉
❸ need〈需要〉・exercise〈運動〉
❹ stop〈停止〉・eating〈eat（吃）的 ing 型態〉・fatty〈油膩的〉・already〈已經〉
❺ just〈就〉・as...as〈跟…一樣〉・bad〈不好的〉

中譯

❶ 小嬰兒圓圓、微胖的臉頰看起來好可愛。
❷ Rachel 應該多吃一點，她太瘦了。
❸ Dave 不太健康，他應該要多做運動。
❹ 停止吃那些油膩的食物，你已經過重了。
❺ 體重過輕跟過重一樣，對你的身體都不好。

099

日常數學(1)

MP3 099

1 Arabic numerals
[`ærəbɪk `njumərəlz]
(n.) 阿拉伯數字

0 1 2 3 4
5 6 7 8 9

2 odd number
[ɑd `nʌmbɚ]
(n.) 奇數

1、3、5、
7、9 ...

3 even number
[`ivən `nʌmbɚ]
(n.) 偶數

2、4、6、
8、10 ...

4 addition
[ə`dɪʃən]
(n.) 加法

2 + 2 = 4

5 subtraction
[səb`trækʃən]
(n.) 減法

2 - 2 = 0

2 X 2 = 4

6 multiplication
[ˌmʌltəplə`keʃən]
(n.) 乘法

2 ÷ 2 = 1

7 division
[də`vɪʒən]
(n.) 除法

❶ 阿拉伯數字
Arabic numerals are recognized by people in all different countries.
所有不同的國家

❷ 奇數
Odd numbers can't be divided by two.
被二整除

❸ 偶數
Even numbers can be divided by two.

❹ 加法
Addition involves adding things together.
把東西相加

❺ 減法
Subtraction means taking one number from another.

❻ 乘法
Multiplication is represented by a cross on most calculators.
大部分的計算機上

❼ 除法
Division is represented by a line with dots above and below it.
在線條上方和下方的圓點

學更多

❶ Arabic〈阿拉伯的〉・numeral〈數字〉・recognized〈recognize（認可）的過去分詞〉
❷ odd〈奇數的〉・divided〈divide（除）的過去分詞〉
❸ even〈偶數的〉・number〈數字、數量〉
❹ involve〈意味著〉・adding...together〈add... together（將⋯相加）的 ing 型態〉
❺ mean〈意味著〉・taking〈take（拿走）的 ing 型態〉・another〈另一個〉
❻ represented〈represent（表示）的過去分詞〉・cross〈叉號〉・calculator〈計算機〉
❼ line〈線〉・dot〈小圓點〉・above〈在上面〉・below〈在下面〉

中譯

❶ 各國人都採用阿拉伯數字。
❷ 奇數不能被二整除。
❸ 偶數可以被二整除。
❹ 加法意味著把東西相加。
❺ 減法意味著從一個數量裡拿走某些數量。
❻ 在大部份的計算機上，乘法是以叉號表示。
❼ 除法是以一條線和它的上下各有一個圓點來表示。

100 日常數學(2)

MP3 100

1 multiplication table
[ˌmʌltəpləˋkeʃən ˋtebl̩]
(n.) 九九乘法表

2x1=2	3x1=3
2x2=4	3x2=6
2x3=6	3x3=9
2x4=8	3x4=12
.	.
.	.
2x9=18	3x9=27

2 round up
[raʊnd ʌp]
round down
[raʊnd daʊn]
(phr.) 四捨五入

下圖表示「小數點第一位」四捨五入

12.9 = 13

3 decimal point
[ˋdɛsɪml̩ pɔɪnt]
(n.) 小數點

12.9

4 average
[ˋævərɪdʒ]
(n.) 平均值
(adj.) 平均的

(175+185) / 2
= 180

5 sum
[sʌm]
(n.) 總和

175+185
= 360

6 calculate
[ˋkælkjəˌlet]
(v.) 計算

175+185 = ?

❶ 九九乘法表
"Two times two is four, three times two is six," said the girl learning her multiplication tables.
（Two times two：二乘二）

❷ 四捨五入
If you round up 19.5, then it's 20. If you round down 19.4, then it's 19.

❸ 小數點
A decimal point separates whole numbers from smaller numbers.
（whole numbers：整數；smaller numbers：比整數小的數字）

❹ 平均值 / 平均的
One boy is 175cm tall, another is 185cm. Their average height is 180cm.

❺ 總和
The sum of two and two is four.

❻ 計算
Irene bought a lot of things for Rachel, so she wants to calculate how much she's owed.
（how much she's owed：她被欠了多少錢）

學更多

❶ times〈乘〉‧said〈say（說）的過去式〉‧multiplication〈乘法〉‧table〈表〉
❷ if〈如果〉‧up〈向上〉‧then〈那麼〉‧down〈向下〉
❸ decimal〈小數的〉‧point〈點〉‧separate〈分隔〉‧whole〈整數的〉‧smaller〈較小的，small（小的）的比較級〉
❹ tall〈有…高〉‧another〈另一個〉‧height〈身高〉
❺ two〈二〉‧four〈四〉
❻ bought〈buy（買）的過去式〉‧a lot of〈很多〉‧owed〈owe（欠錢）的過去分詞〉

中譯

❶ 正在學九九乘法表的女孩說：「二乘二等於四，三乘二等於六。」
❷ 如果你把 19.5 四捨五入，會變成 20；如果把 19.4 四捨五入，會是 19。
❸ 小數點把整數和小數區隔開來。
❹ 一個男孩身高 175 公分，另一個身高 185 公分，他們平均的身高是 180 公分。
❺ 二加二的總和為四。
❻ Irene 幫 Rachel 買了很多東西，她想計算 Rachel 欠了自己多少錢。

101 數學符號

MP3 101

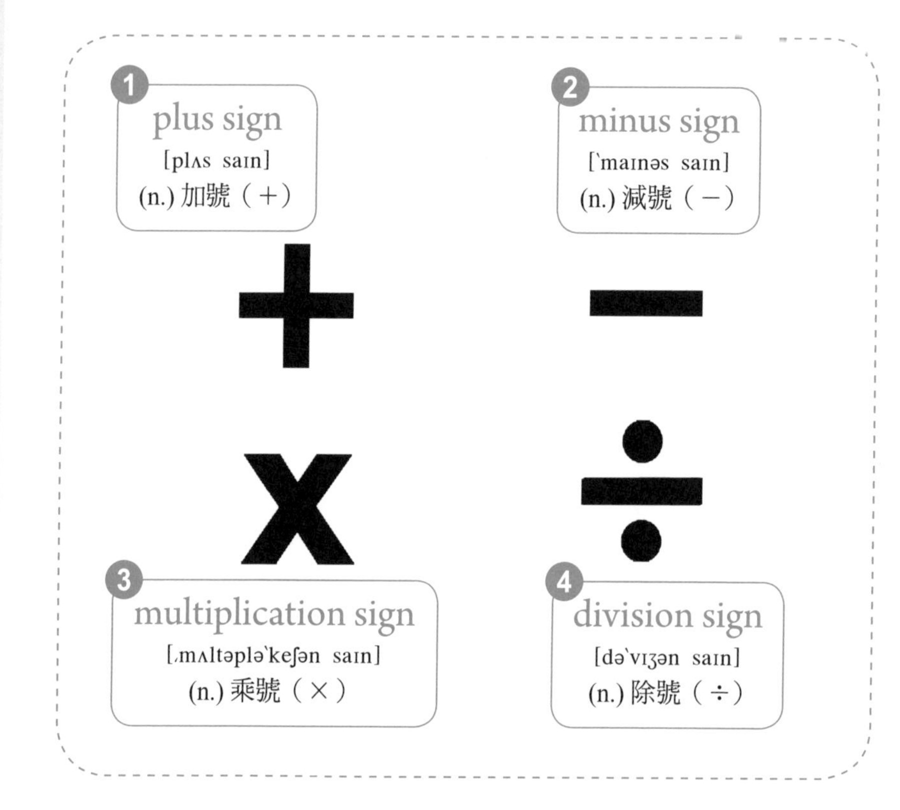

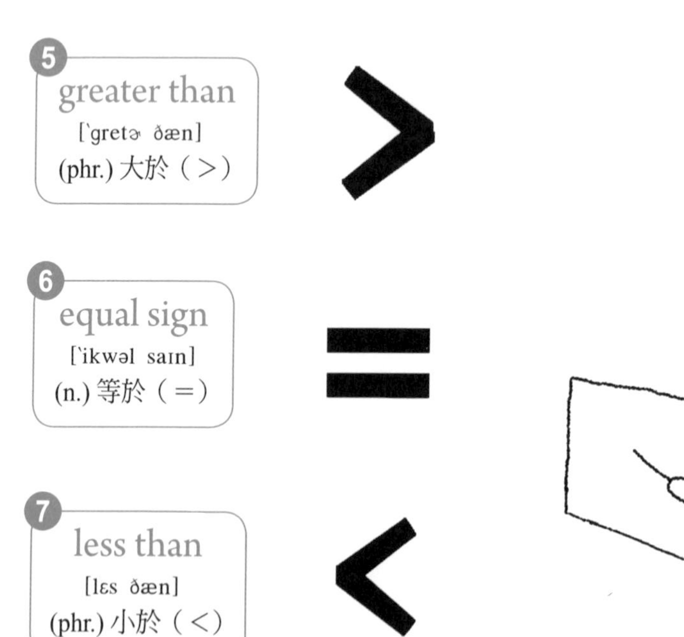

❶ 加號（＋）

Use the plus sign when you're doing any addition.
當你進行任何加法時

❷ 減號（－）

The minus sign is simply a short horizontal line.

❸ 乘號（×）

If you make an "x", you have a multiplication sign.

❹ 除號（÷）

When you need to divide numbers, you will use a division sign between them.
除以數字

❺ 大於（>）

The greater than sign is used in comparing two numbers. The larger number is on the left side of the sign.

❻ 等於（＝）

Following the equal sign is the result of your calculation.

❼ 小於（<）

Everyone knows that 10 is less than 20.

學更多

❶ plus〈加的、正的〉• sign〈符號〉• addition〈加法〉
❷ minus〈減去的、負的〉• simply〈僅僅〉• short〈短的〉• horizontal〈橫的〉
❸ make〈做〉• multiplication〈乘法〉
❹ divide〈除〉• division〈除法〉• between〈在…之間〉
❺ comparing〈compare（比較）的 ing 型態〉• left〈左的〉• side〈側〉
❻ following〈follow（接在…之後）的 ing 型態〉• result〈結果〉• calculation〈計算〉
❼ everyone〈大家〉• know〈知道〉• less〈較小的〉

中譯

❶ 當你進行任何加法時，要使用加號。
❷ 減號只是一條短短的橫線。
❸ 如果你打一個「x」，就有一個乘號。
❹ 當數字需要相除時，你會在數字之間使用除號。
❺ 大於符號用來比較兩個數字的大小。較大的數字會在符號左側。
❻ 等號的後面，就是你計算後的結果。
❼ 大家都知道：10 小於 20。

102 標點符號

MP3 102

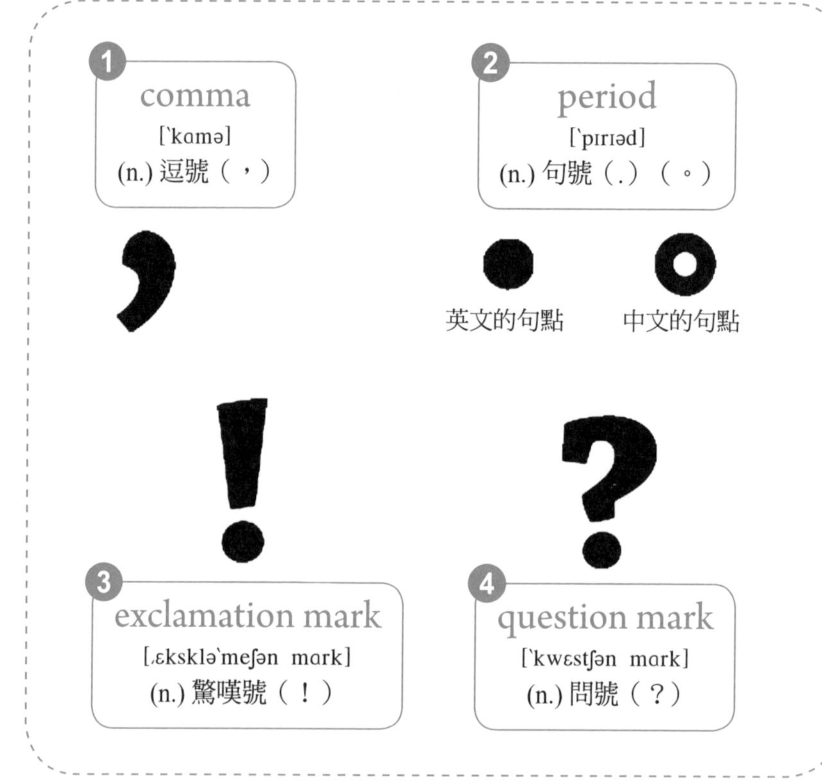

❶ 逗號（，）

Commas are used in writing to help separate clauses in sentences.

被用於 (are used in)

❷ 句號（。）

A period signals the end of a sentence.

❸ 驚嘆號（！）

If you want people to read what you write with more emotion, add an exclamation mark to your sentences!

看你寫的東西 (read what you write)

❹ 問號（？）

If you have a question, then you should end your sentence with a question mark, right?

❺ 括號（ ）

You can use parentheses in a sentence if you want to add a little comment in-between.

在中間加入一些意見 (add a little comment in-between)

❻ 引號（ “ ” ）

If you use someone's exact words in your writing, remember to use quotation marks around them.

他人說過的話語 (someone's exact words)

在前後使用引號 (use quotation marks around them)

❼ 斜線（／）

Slash signs are used in website addresses.

網址 (website addresses)

學更多

❶ writing〈寫作〉・separate〈分隔〉・clause〈子句〉・sentence〈句子〉
❷ signal〈表示〉・end〈結尾〉
❸ emotion〈情感〉・add〈增加〉・exclamation〈感嘆〉・mark〈符號〉
❹ question〈疑問〉・end〈作結束〉
❺ a little〈一點〉・comment〈意見〉・in-between〈中間的〉
❻ exact〈確切的〉・word〈話〉・remember〈記得〉・quotation〈引用〉・around〈周圍〉
❼ sign〈符號〉・website〈網站〉・addresses〈地址〉

中譯

❶ 書寫英文時，逗號用於區隔句中的子句。
❷ 句號表示一個句子的結束。
❸ 如果你希望讀者帶更多的情感來閱讀你的作品，就在句子裡加入驚嘆號！
❹ 如果你是提出問題，句子就該以問號結尾，對吧？
❺ 如果你想在句中加入一些意見，可以使用括號。
❻ 如果寫作時你要引用他人的言論，記得在那些內容前後加上引號。
❼ 網址中會有斜線符號。

103 度量衡(1)

MP3 103

1 millimeter
[ˋmɪlə͵mitɚ]
(n.) 公釐（mm）

10 公釐 = 1 公分

2 centimeter
[ˋsɛntə͵mitɚ]
(n.) 公分（cm）

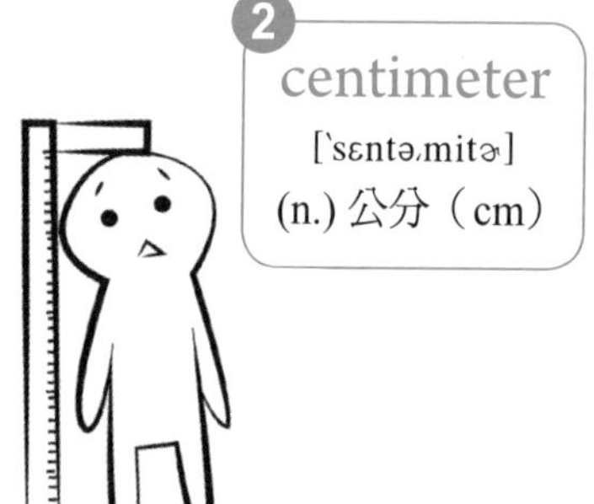

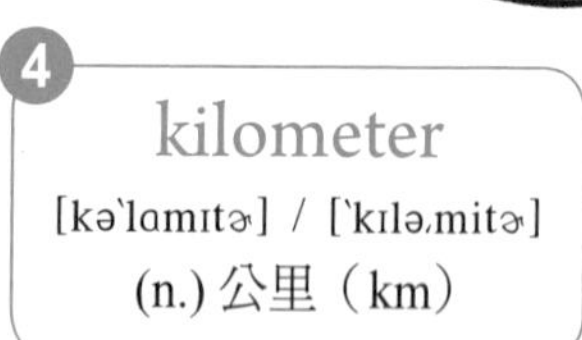

3 meter
[ˋmitɚ]
(n.) 公尺（m）

1 公尺 = 100 公分

4 kilometer
[kəˋlɑmɪtɚ] / [ˋkɪlə͵mitɚ]
(n.) 公里（km）

1 公里 = 1000 公尺
第一種是「美式發音」，第二種是「英式發音」。

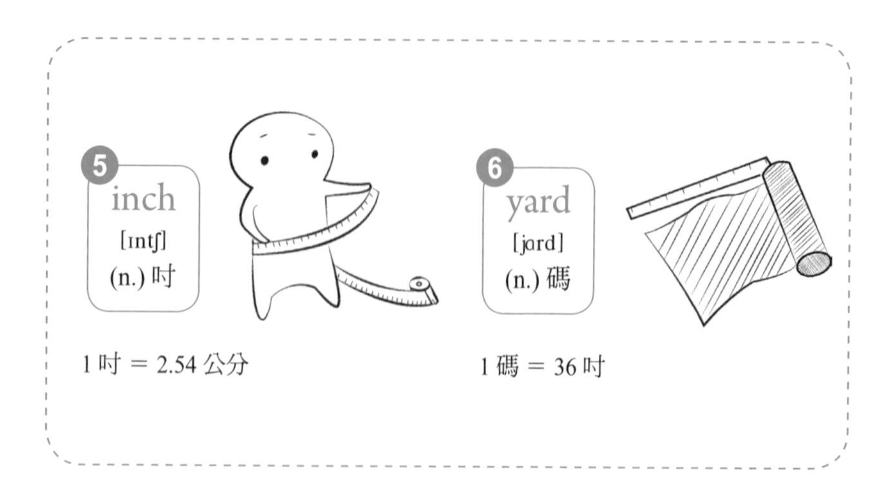

5 inch
[ɪntʃ]
(n.) 吋

1 吋 = 2.54 公分

6 yard
[jɑrd]
(n.) 碼

1 碼 = 36 吋

❶ 公釐（mm）
There are ten millimeters in a centimeter.

❷ 公分（cm）
The girl is only 150 centimeters tall.

❸ 公尺（m）
He is just less than two meters tall.
比 2 公尺少一點點

❹ 公里（km）
The speed limit here is 50 kilometers per hour.
每小時

❺ 吋
An inch is 2.54 centimeters.

❻ 碼
A yard equals three feet.

學更多

❶ there are〈有〉
❷ girl〈女孩〉・only〈只有〉・tall〈有…高〉
❸ just〈正好〉・less〈較少的〉
❹ speed limit〈速度限制〉・per〈每〉・hour〈小時〉
❺ centimeter〈公分〉
❻ equal〈等於〉・feet〈foot（呎）的複數〉

中譯

❶ 1 公分等於 10 公釐。
❷ 這個女孩的身高只有 150 公分。
❸ 他的身高接近 2 公尺。
❹ 這裡的速限是每小時 50 公里。
❺ 1 吋是 2.54 公分。
❻ 1 碼等於 3 呎。

104 度量衡(2)

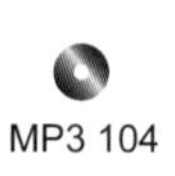

MP3 104

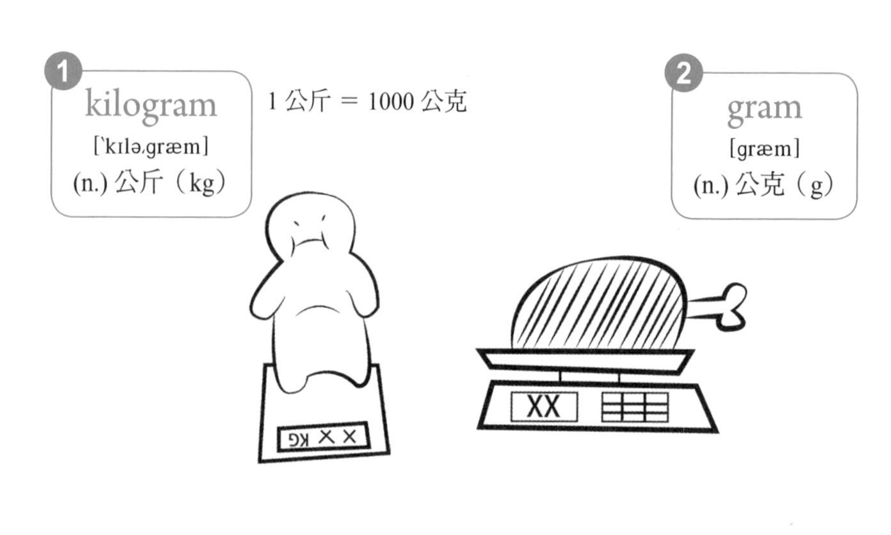

1 kilogram
[ˋkɪlə͵græm]
(n.) 公斤（kg）

1 公斤 = 1000 公克

2 gram
[græm]
(n.) 公克（g）

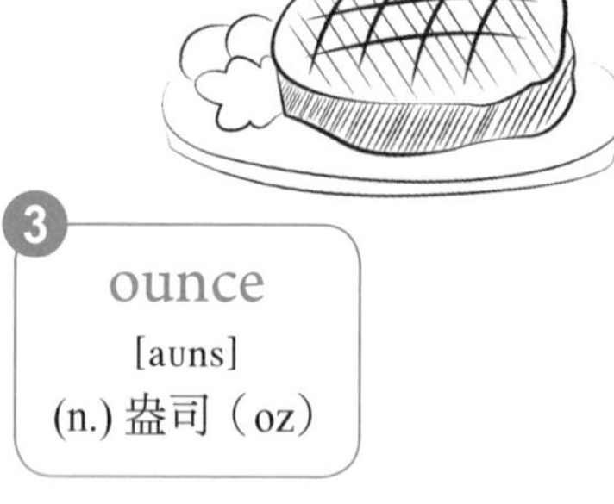

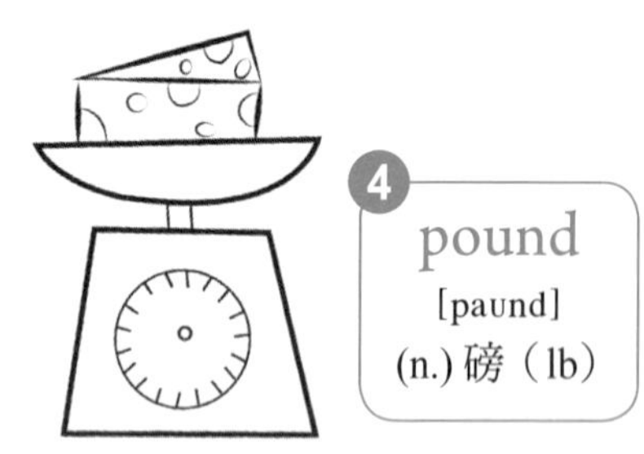

3 ounce
[aʊns]
(n.) 盎司（oz）

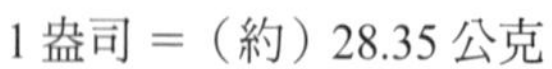

1 盎司 =（約）28.35 公克

4 pound
[paʊnd]
(n.) 磅（lb）

1 磅 =（約）0.45 公斤

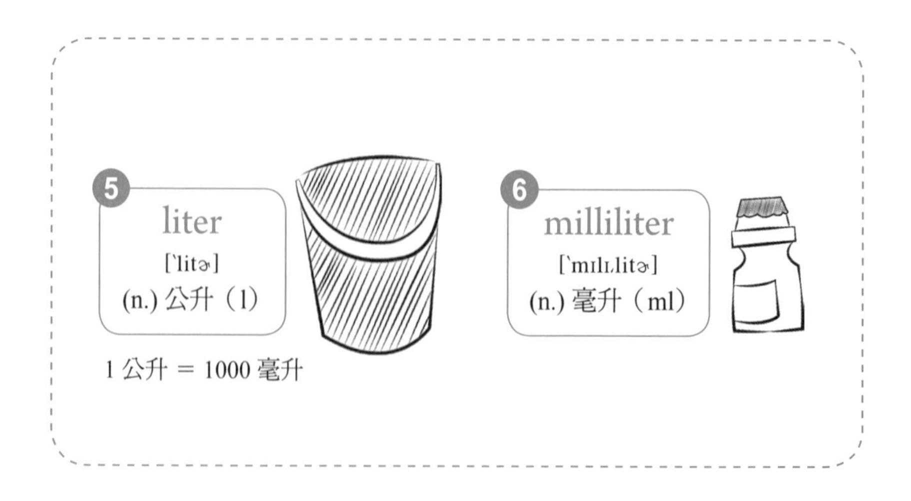

5 liter
[ˋlitɚ]
(n.) 公升（l）

1 公升 = 1000 毫升

6 milliliter
[ˋmɪlɪ͵litɚ]
(n.) 毫升（ml）

❶ 公斤（kg）
Danny weighs about 90 kilograms.
體重大約

❷ 公克（g）
I'd like 200 grams of that cheese, please.
我想要（= I would like）

❸ 盎司（oz）
There are 16 ounces in a pound.

❹ 磅（lb）
There are 2.2 pounds in a kilogram.

❺ 公升（l）
Can you get me a two-liter bottle of soda, please?
你可以為我買…嗎

❻ 毫升（ml）
This cup holds 700 milliliters.

學更多

❶ weigh〈有…重量〉・about〈大約〉
❷ cheese〈起司〉・please〈請〉
❸ there are〈有〉・pound〈磅〉
❹ kilogram〈公斤〉
❺ get〈為…買〉・bottle〈瓶〉・soda〈汽水〉
❻ cup〈杯子〉・hold〈容納〉

中譯

❶ Danny 的體重大約 90 公斤。
❷ 麻煩你，我要買那種起司 200 公克。
❸ 1 磅是 16 盎司。
❹ 1 公斤是 2.2 磅。
❺ 可以請你幫我買瓶 2 公升的汽水嗎？
❻ 這個杯子的容量有 700 毫升。

105 平面幾何圖形(1)

MP3 105

1 triangle

[ˋtraɪ͵æŋɡḷ]

(n.) 三角形

三條線段所組成的閉合平面圖形。

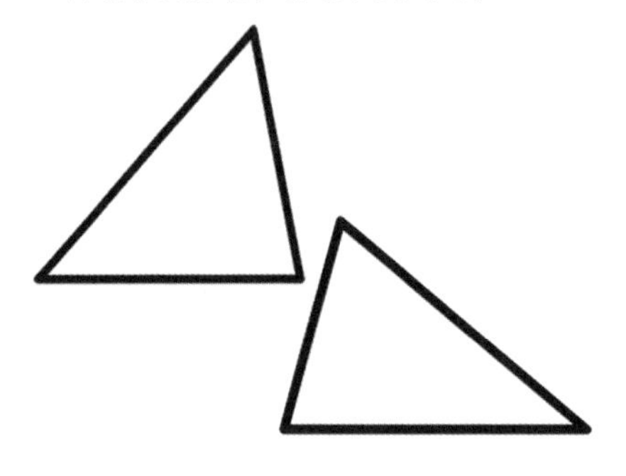

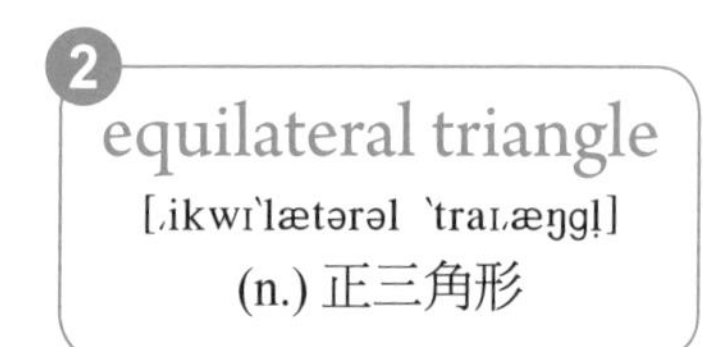

2 equilateral triangle

[͵ikwɪˋlætərəl ˋtraɪ͵æŋɡḷ]

(n.) 正三角形

三邊等長，三個角都是 60 度的三角形。

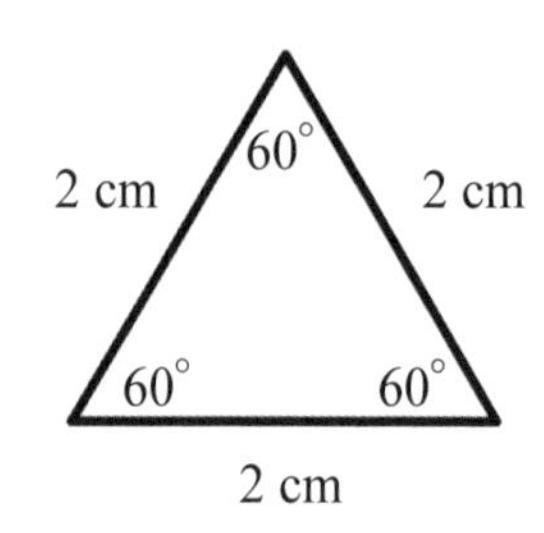

3 isosceles triangle

[aɪˋsɑsḷ͵iz ˋtraɪ͵æŋɡḷ]

(n.) 等腰三角形

至少有兩個邊等長的三角形。

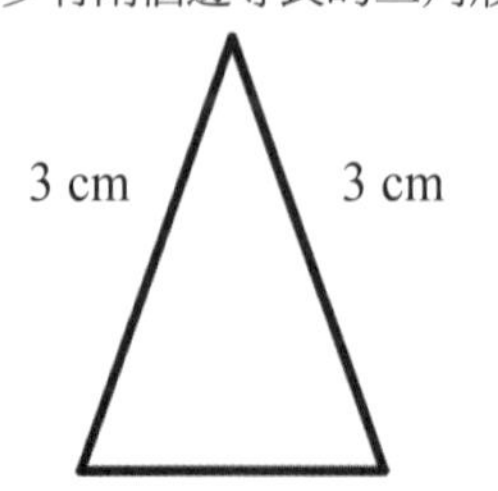

4 right triangle

[raɪt ˋtraɪ͵æŋɡḷ]

(n.) 直角三角形

有一個角為直角的三角形。

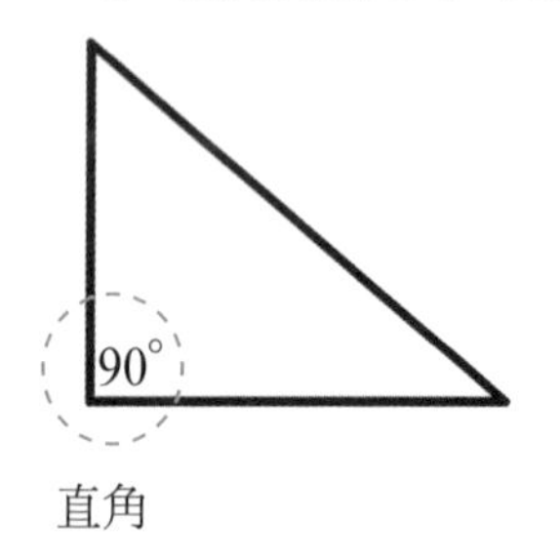

5 star

[stɑr]

(n.) 星形

❶ 三角形
A triangle is always three-sided.

❷ 正三角形
All three sides are equal on an equilateral triangle.

❸ 等腰三角形
With at least two equal sides and equal angles, you have what is called an isosceles triangle.
一個叫做等腰三角形的東西

❹ 直角三角形
A right triangle is a triangle with one 90-degree angle.
90 度角

❺ 星形
The shape of a star has five points.

學更多

❶ always〈永遠〉・sided〈…邊的〉
❷ all〈所有的〉・side〈邊〉・equal〈均等的〉・equilateral〈等邊的〉
❸ at least〈至少〉・called〈call（把…叫做）的過去分詞〉・isosceles〈二等邊的〉
❹ degree〈度數〉・angle〈角度〉
❺ shape〈形狀〉・point〈尖頭〉

中譯

❶ 三角形永遠是三個邊。
❷ 正三角形的三邊均等長。
❸ 只要至少有兩個等邊以及等角，就是等腰三角形。
❹ 直角三角形是指有一個 90 度角的三角形。
❺ 星形的形狀，是有五個尖角。

106 平面幾何圖形(2)

MP3 106

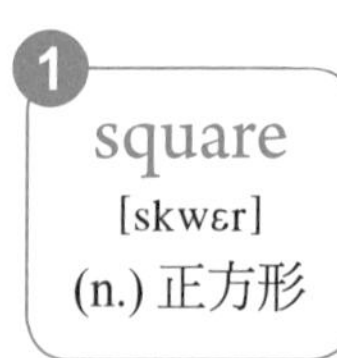

四邊等長，四個角都是直角的平面圖形。

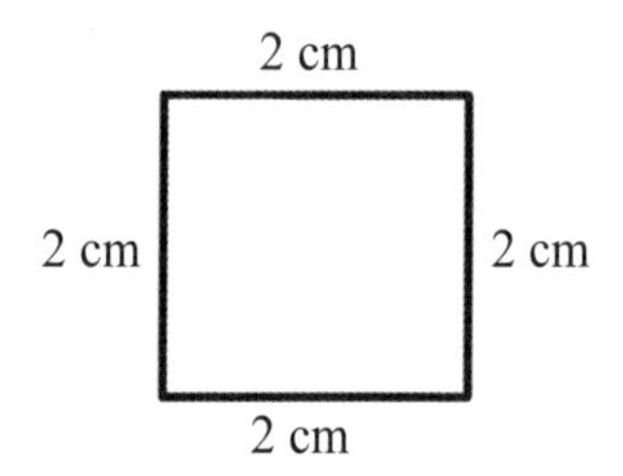

2 rectangle
[rɛkˋtæŋgḷ]
(n.) 矩形/長方形

四個角都是直角的平面圖形。正方形也是矩形的一種。

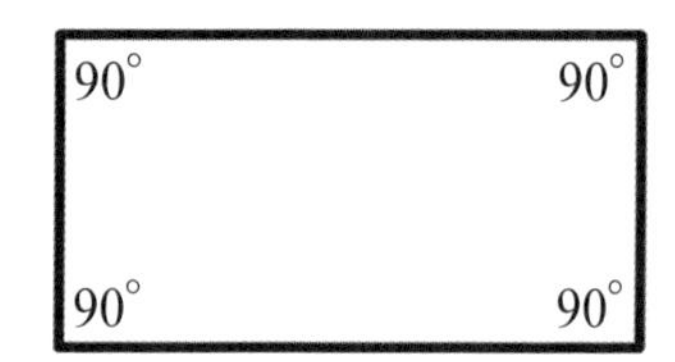

3 parallelogram
[ˌpærəˋlɛləˌgræm]
(n.) 平行四邊形

兩組對邊平行且等長的四邊形。

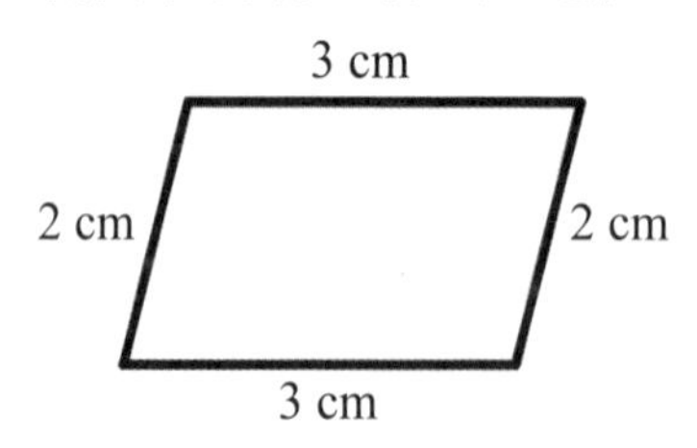

4 kite
[kaɪt]
(n.) 鳶形

兩鄰邊相等，對角線互相垂直的四邊形。

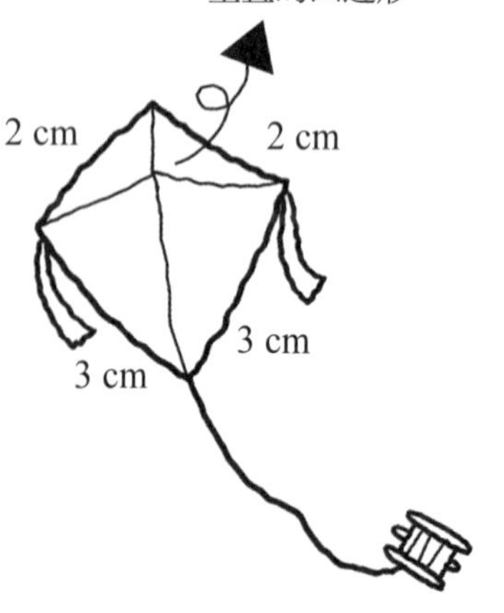

四邊相等，對角線互相垂直平分的四邊形。

5 diamond
[ˋdaɪəmənd]
(n.) 菱形

2 cm
2 cm
2 cm
2 cm

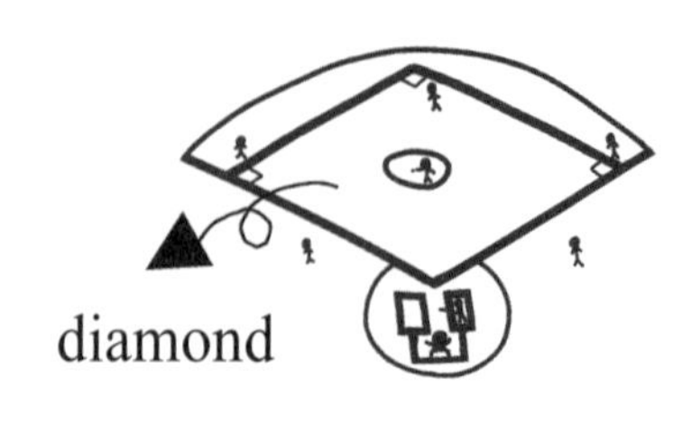

❶ 正方形

Max has a square jaw which makes him look very masculine.

方形下巴

❷ 矩形 / 長方形

My new eyeglass frames are in the shape of a rectangle.

形狀是長方形的

❸ 平行四邊形

A parallelogram is a shape you'll learn about when you study geometry.

❹ 鳶形

In geometry, a kite is defined as having two pairs of equal-length sides which are adjacent to each other.

被定義為

彼此相鄰

❺ 菱形

A baseball field is called a baseball diamond because it's in the shape of a diamond.

被稱為…

學更多

❶ jaw〈下巴〉・make〈使得〉・look〈看起來〉・masculine〈男子氣概的〉
❷ eyeglass〈鏡片〉・frame〈框架〉・shape〈形狀〉
❸ learn〈學習〉・study〈學習、研究〉・geometry〈幾何學〉
❹ defined〈define（為…定義）的過去分詞〉・pair〈一對〉・equal〈均等的〉・length〈長度〉・side〈邊〉・adjacent〈相鄰的〉・each other〈互相〉
❺ baseball〈棒球〉・field〈運動場〉・called〈call（把…叫做）的過去分詞〉

中譯

❶ Max 有一個正方形的下巴，這使他看起來很有男子氣概。
❷ 我的新眼鏡鏡框是長方形的。
❸ 平行四邊形是學習幾何學時，你會學到的形狀。
❹ 在幾何學中，鳶形的定義是有兩對等長的鄰邊。
❺ 棒球場被稱為「baseball diamond」，因為它是菱形的。

107 平面幾何圖形(3)

MP3 107

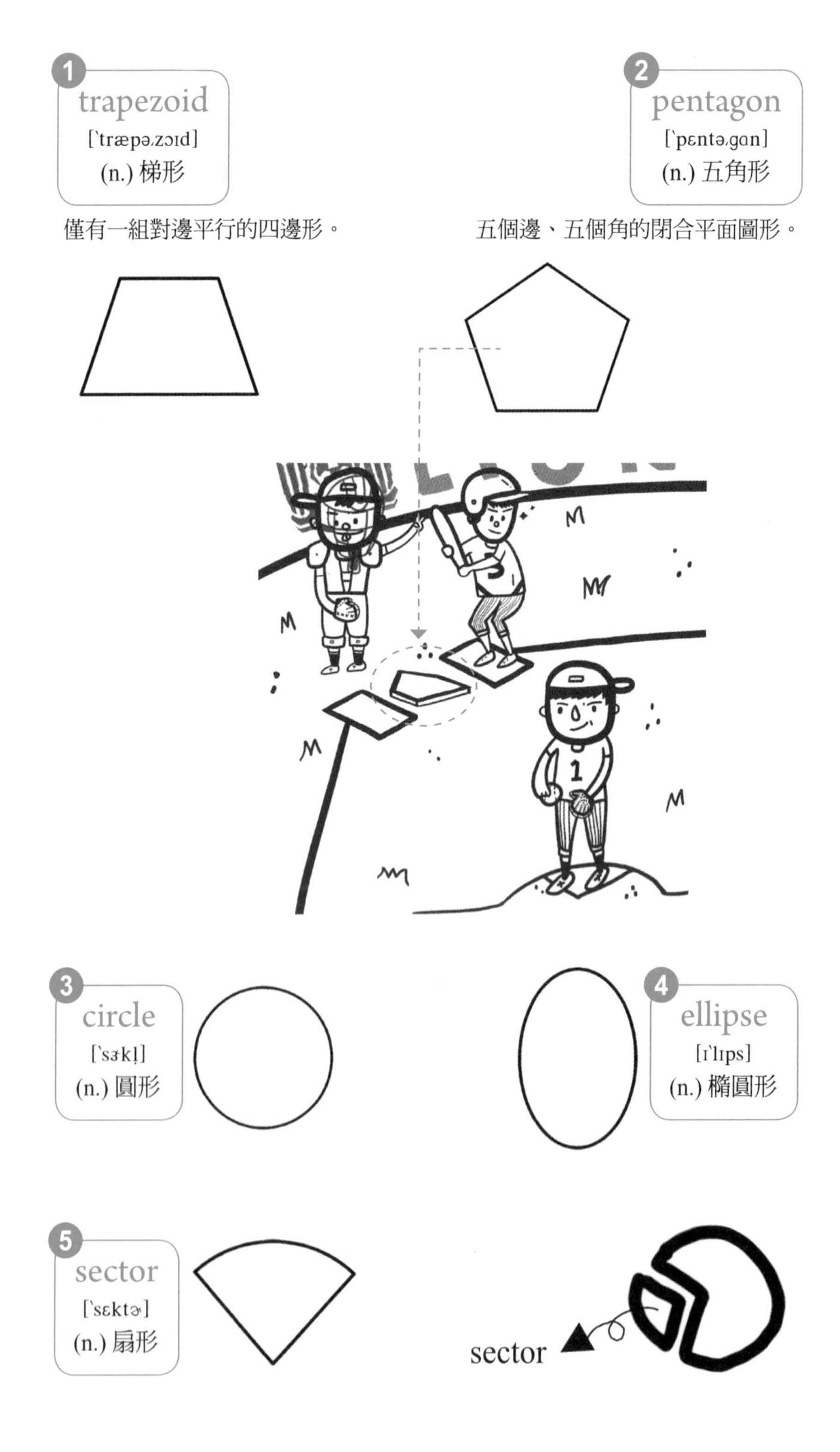

1 trapezoid
[ˋtræpə͵zɔɪd]
(n.) 梯形

僅有一組對邊平行的四邊形。

2 pentagon
[ˋpɛntə͵gɑn]
(n.) 五角形

五個邊、五個角的閉合平面圖形。

3 circle
[ˋsɝkḷ]
(n.) 圓形

4 ellipse
[ɪˋlɪps]
(n.) 橢圓形

5 sector
[ˋsɛktɚ]
(n.) 扇形

❶ 梯形
In geometry, we study trapezoids in order to measure their area.

❷ 五角形
The Pentagon (五角大廈) is the name of the building which houses the US Department of Defense (美國國防部). It's actually in the shape of a pentagon.

❸ 圓形
As we learned to waltz, the dancing instructor (舞蹈教練) told us to dance in a circle.

❹ 橢圓形
An ellipse occurs when there's intersection of a cone by a plane (由一個平面在圓錐體上形成的切面).

❺ 扇形
A sector is in the shape of a fan (扇子的形狀).

學更多

❶ geometry〈幾何學〉• in order to〈為了〉• measure〈測量〉• area〈面積〉
❷ building〈建築物〉• house〈提供空間給…〉• department〈部門〉• defense〈防禦〉• actually〈真的〉• shape〈形狀〉
❸ as〈當…時〉• waltz〈華爾滋舞〉• dancing〈跳舞〉• instructor〈教練〉• told〈tell（告訴）的過去式〉
❹ occur〈存在、出現〉• intersection〈橫斷〉• cone〈圓錐體〉• plane〈平面〉
❺ fan〈扇子〉

中譯

❶ 在幾何學中，我們研究梯形來測量它的面積。
❷ 美國國防部所在的那棟建築物稱為五角大廈。它的外形真的是五角形，真是名符其實。
❸ 在我們學習華爾滋時，舞蹈教練告訴我們跳舞時要畫圓轉圈。
❹ 當平面在圓錐體形成橫切面，就會出現橢圓形。
❺ 扇形就是扇子的形狀。

108 報紙各版新聞(1)

MP3 108

1 **headline** [ˋhɛd͵laɪn] (n.) 頭條

2 **anecdote** [ˋænɪk͵dot] (n.) 軼聞/趣事

3 **national** [ˋnæʃənḷ] (adj.) 國內

4 **international** [͵ɪntəˋnæʃənḷ] (adj.) 國際

5 **economy** [ɪˋkɑnəmɪ] (n.) 財經/經濟

6 **politics** [ˋpɑlətɪks] (n.) 政治

7 **life** [laɪf] (n.) 生活

8 **society** [səˋsaɪətɪ] (n.) 社會

❶ 頭條
Headlines are written in much bigger letters.

❷ 軼聞／趣事
Dave loves telling people anecdotes about the time he met Prince Charles.
他遇見查爾斯王子的那段經歷

❸ 國內
❹ 國際
Front pages of newspapers often contain both national and international news.
報紙頭版

❺ 財經／經濟
The economy is not doing well, and lots of businesses are having trouble.

❻ 政治
Don't ever discuss politics with cab drivers, especially in Taiwan.

❼ 生活
Pete has an interesting life. He's always doing fun things.

❽ 社會
Sometimes illegal immigration causes great damage to society.
非法移民

學更多

❶ written〈write（寫）的過去分詞〉• bigger〈比較大的，big（大的）的比較級〉• letter〈文字〉
❷ telling〈tell（告訴）的 ing 型態〉• time〈一段經歷〉• met〈meet（遇見）的過去式〉
❸ ❹ front page〈頭版〉• contain〈包含〉• both〈兩者皆〉• news〈新聞、消息〉
❺ doing well〈do well（興旺）的 ing 型態〉• business〈企業〉• trouble〈困難〉
❻ ever〈永遠〉• discuss〈討論〉• cab〈計程車〉• driver〈司機〉• especially〈尤其〉
❼ interesting〈有趣的〉• always〈總是〉• fun〈有趣的〉
❽ immigration〈移民〉• cause〈造成〉• great〈巨大的〉• damage〈傷害〉

中譯

❶ 頭條會使用比較大的字體。
❷ Dave 喜愛告訴人們關於他遇到查爾斯王子的趣事。
❸ ❹ 報紙的頭版上，通常有國內和國際新聞。
❺ 經濟情勢不好，很多企業都正面臨困難。
❻ 永遠不要和計程車司機談論政治，尤其是在台灣。
❼ Pete 的生活充滿樂趣，他總是做些有趣的事。
❽ 有時候，非法移民會對社會造成極大的傷害。

109 報紙各版新聞(2)

MP3 109

1 entertainment news
[ˌɛntəˋtenmənt njuz]
(n.) 影劇/娛樂新聞

2 tourism
[ˋturɪzəm]
(n.) 旅遊

3 the arts
[ðɪ ɑrts]
(n.) 藝文

4 technology
[tɛkˋnɑlədʒɪ]
(n.) 科技

5 sports
[spɔrts]
(n.) 運動

6 health
[hɛlθ]
(n.) 健康

❶ 影劇／娛樂新聞
Entertainment news is very popular in today's culture.

❷ 旅遊
France has a huge tourism industry. Millions of people go there on holiday.
旅遊產業　數百萬的…

❸ 藝文
Ray has a great interest in the arts and loves to go to the theater and art galleries.
對於藝文相當感興趣

❹ 科技
Hannah is interested in technology and loves reading about the newest machines.
對科技有興趣

❺ 運動
The most popular sports in Taiwan are baseball and basketball.
最流行的運動

❻ 健康
Gary has very bad health problems, so he's going to the doctor.
他要去看醫生

學更多

❶ entertainment〈娛樂〉‧news〈新聞〉‧today〈現今〉‧culture〈文化〉
❷ huge〈龐大的〉‧industry〈行業〉‧million〈百萬〉‧holiday〈假日〉
❸ great〈大的〉‧interest〈興趣〉‧theater〈劇場、電影院〉‧art gallery〈畫廊〉
❹ be interested in〈對…感興趣〉‧reading〈read（閱讀）的 ing 型態〉‧machine〈機器〉
❺ popular〈流行的〉‧baseball〈棒球〉‧basketball〈籃球〉
❻ bad〈壞的〉‧problem〈問題〉‧doctor〈醫生〉

中譯

❶ 在現今文化，娛樂新聞廣受歡迎。
❷ 法國擁有龐大的旅遊產業，好幾百萬的人都去那裡渡假。
❸ Ray 對藝文很感興趣，也喜歡去劇院和藝廊。
❹ Hannah 對科技感興趣，也喜歡閱讀關於最新機械的報導。
❺ 台灣最盛行的運動是棒球和籃球。
❻ Gary 的健康狀況非常差，所以他要去看醫生。

110 各種出版品(1)

MP3 110

1 newspaper / paper
[ˋnjuz͵pepɚ] / [ˋpepɚ]
(n.) 報紙

兩個單字都是「報紙」。

2 journal
[ˋdʒɝnl̩]
(n.) 週刊/期刊/日記

3 magazine
[͵mægəˋzin]
(n.) 雜誌

4 instruction manual
[ɪnˋstrʌkʃən ˋmænjʊəl]
(n.) 說明書

5 catalog
[ˋkætəlɔg]
(n.) 型錄

❶ 報紙

Tony used to have the paper delivered to his home; now he reads it online.

讓報紙送到他家

❷ 週刊 / 期刊 / 日記

Grandpa wrote in his journal every day before he died, so now his posterity can read all about his life.

❸ 雜誌

Once Jill finishes reading her fashion magazines, she shares them with her friends.

Jill 一旦看完她的時尚雜誌

❹ 說明書

Without an instruction manual, Harry would have no idea how to put together his DIY furniture.

如何組裝他的 DIY 家具

❺ 型錄

Angie wastes hours looking through clothes catalogs.

翻閱衣服型錄

學更多

❶ used to〈過去曾做〉‧delivered〈deliver（投遞）的過去分詞〉‧read〈閱讀〉‧online〈在網路上〉

❷ grandpa〈爺爺〉‧wrote〈write（寫）的過去式〉‧died〈die（死）的過去式〉‧posterity〈子孫〉‧life〈一生〉

❸ once〈一旦〉‧finish〈完成〉‧fashion〈時尚〉‧share〈分享〉

❹ instruction〈教導〉‧manual〈手冊〉‧put together〈組合〉‧furniture〈家具〉

❺ waste〈浪費〉‧looking through〈look through（瀏覽）的 ing 型態〉‧clothes〈衣服〉

中譯

❶ Tony 以前家裡有訂報紙，但現在他都在網路上看報。

❷ 直到過世前，爺爺每天寫日記；所以他的子孫現在能從日記裡閱讀關於他的一生。

❸ Jill 一旦看完自己的時尚雜誌，就會把它們分享給朋友。

❹ 沒有說明書的話，Harry 就完全不知道要如何組裝他的 DIY 家具。

❺ Angie 浪費好幾個小時翻閱衣物型錄。

111

各種出版品(2)

MP3 111

1 e-book
[ˋiˋbʊk]
(n.) 電子書

2 disk / disc
[dɪsk]
(n.) 光碟

兩個單字都是「光碟」。

3 audio book
[ˋɔdɪˏo bʊk]
(n.) 有聲書

4 dictionary
[ˋdɪkʃənˏɛrɪ]
(n.) 字典

5 illustrated book
[ˋɪləstretɪd bʊk]
(n.) 繪本

❶ 電子書
Reading e-books can help save trees!

❷ 光碟
Oh no! I scratched the disc. Do you think I ruined it?
刮到光碟了

❸ 有聲書
My sister is ill in bed, so I send her audio books to keep her entertained.
使她歡樂

❹ 字典
Although e-dictionaries are handy, Ms. Hsu still prefers her dictionary in book form.
電子字典很方便
書本形式的字典

❺ 繪本
Have you seen this illustrated book? The artist is so gifted!
這位畫家很有天賦

學更多

❶ reading〈read（閱讀）的 ing 型態〉・help〈幫助〉・save〈挽救、節省〉
❷ scratched〈scratch（刮）的過去式〉・ruined〈ruin（毀壞）的過去式〉
❸ sister〈姊妹〉・ill〈生病的〉・bed〈床〉・send〈寄送〉・audio〈聲音的〉・keep〈使保持在某一狀態〉・entertained〈entertain（使歡樂）的過去分詞〉
❹ although〈雖然〉・handy〈便利的〉・still〈仍然〉・prefer〈較喜歡〉・form〈形式〉
❺ seen〈see（看）的過去分詞〉・illustrated〈有插圖的〉・artist〈畫家〉・gifted〈有天賦的〉

中譯

❶ 閱讀電子書能有助於挽救樹木。
❷ 喔不！我刮到光碟了，你認為我把它弄壞了嗎？
❸ 我妹妹臥病在床，因此我寄給她有聲書，讓她開心。
❹ 雖然電子字典很方便，但徐小姐還是偏好使用實體書形式的字典。
❺ 你看過這本繪本嗎？這位畫家真有天賦！

112 各種學校(1)

MP3 112

❶ 托兒所
Little Debbie goes to daycare while her mom is working at Microsoft.
在微軟公司上班

❷ 幼稚園
In kindergarten, Sonia learned to tie her shoelaces all by herself!
全靠她自己綁鞋帶

❸ 中學
Are you performing with your junior high school band at the school concert Saturday?

❹ 小學
I met my best friend, Heather, in elementary school and we're still friends after 20 years!
20 年後我們仍然是朋友

❺ 高中
Sammy's favorite teacher while he was a student was his English teacher in senior high school.
在他還是學生時

學更多

❶ little〈幼小的〉・while〈當…的時候〉・working〈work（工作）的 ing 型態〉
❷ learned〈learn（學）的過去式〉・tie〈繫上〉・shoelace〈鞋帶〉・herself〈她自己〉
❸ performing〈perform（表演）的 ing 型態〉・band〈樂隊〉・concert〈演奏會〉
❹ met〈meet（認識）的過去式〉・best〈最好的〉・elementary〈基礎的〉・still〈仍然〉・after〈在…之後〉
❺ favorite〈特別喜愛的〉・teacher〈老師〉・student〈學生〉

中譯

❶ 當媽媽在微軟公司上班時，Debbie 小妹妹都會去托兒所。
❷ 讀幼稚園時，Sonia 學會了自己綁鞋帶。
❸ 週六的校園演奏會上，你會和你的中學樂隊一起演出嗎？
❹ 我和我最好的朋友 Heather 是讀小學時認識的，我們已經是交情 20 年的朋友。
❺ 當 Sammy 還是學生時，他最喜歡的老師是高中的英文老師。

113 各種學校(2)

MP3 113

1 **university**
[ˏjunəˋvɝsətɪ]
(n.) 大學

2 **graduate school**
[ˋgrædʒuˏet skul]
(n.) 研究所

3 **cram school**
[kræm skul]
(n.) 補習班

4 **public school**
[ˋpʌblɪk skul]
(n.) 公立學校

5 **private school**
[ˋpraɪvɪt skul]
(n.) 私立學校

❶ 大學
After university, Cindy decided to go to Europe for the summer.

❷ 研究所
Graduate school was difficult, but worth the effort!
值得努力

❸ 補習班
If you haven't done your homework, you can do it during cram school.
如果你還沒做你的功課

❹ 公立學校
Some public schools have really good quality teachers.

❺ 私立學校
Are you transferring Bobby to a private school next year?

學更多

❶ after〈在…之後〉・decided〈decide（決定）的過去式〉・summer〈夏天〉
❷ graduate〈大學畢業生〉・difficult〈難熬的〉・worth〈有…的價值〉・effort〈努力〉
❸ done〈do（做）的過去分詞〉・homework〈家庭作業〉・during〈在…期間〉・cram〈死記硬背〉
❹ some〈一些〉・public〈公立的、公眾的〉・really〈很〉・quality〈品質〉
❺ transferring〈transfer（使轉校）的 ing 型態〉・private〈私立的〉・next〈下一個〉

中譯

❶ 大學畢業後，Cindy 決定在暑期時去一趟歐洲。
❷ 讀研究所很辛苦，但辛苦是值得的！
❸ 如果你還沒有做功課，你可以在補習班做。
❹ 有些公立學校擁有相當優秀的師資。
❺ 明年你要把 Bobby 轉學去私立學校嗎？

114 各種學校(3)

MP3 114

1 military school
[ˋmɪlə͵tɛrɪ skul]
(n.) 軍校

2 music school
[ˋmjuzɪk skul]
(n.) 音樂學校

3 nursing school
[ˋnɝsɪŋ skul]
(n.) 護校

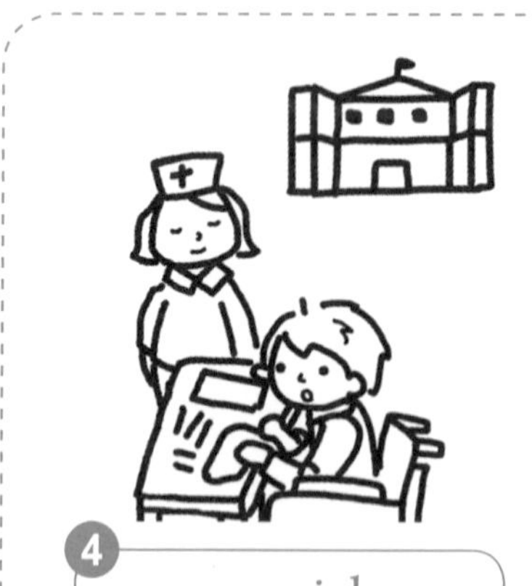

4 special education school
[ˋspɛʃəl ͵ɛdʒʊˋkeʃən skul]
(n.) 特殊教育學校

5 vocational school
[voˋkeʃənl̩ skul]
(n.) 職業學校

❶ 軍校

Ron is following in his dad's footsteps and is attending military school.

正追隨他的父親的腳步（效法他父親）

❷ 音樂學校

I've just been accepted into the finest music school in the world to study voice!

最優秀的音樂學校剛接受我入學

❸ 護校

Holly enrolled in nursing school this year, and is on her way to becoming a nurse.

在她成為護士的路上

❹ 特殊教育學校

Special education schools are set up to teach mentally and physically disabled children.

身心障礙的孩童

❺ 職業學校

Vocational schools offer specialized training in a variety of fields,

不同領域的專業訓練

including computer programming, electronics, fashion and art.

學更多

❶ footstep〈腳步〉・attending〈attend（上學）的 ing 型態〉・military〈軍人的〉

❷ accepted〈accept（接受）的過去分詞〉・finest〈最優秀的，fine（優秀的）的最高級〉・voice〈聲樂〉

❸ enrolled〈enroll（註冊）的過去式〉・nursing〈護理〉・on one's way to〈在去…的路上〉

❹ education〈教育〉・set up〈set up（開創）的過去分詞〉・teach〈教導〉・mentally〈心理上〉・physically〈身體上〉・disabled〈有缺陷的〉

❺ vocational〈職業的〉・offer〈提供〉・specialized〈專業的〉・a variety of〈各種各樣的〉・field〈領域〉・programming〈程式設計〉・electronics〈電子學〉

中譯

❶ Ron 目前正追隨父親的腳步就讀軍校。

❷ 我獲准進入全世界最優秀的音樂學校攻讀聲樂。

❸ Holly 在今年進入護校就讀，努力成為一名護士。

❹ 特殊教育學校是為了教育身心障礙的學童而設立的。

❺ 職業學校提供各領域的專業訓練，包含電腦程式設計、電子學、時尚、以及藝術。

115 哺乳動物(1)

MP3 115

1 lion [ˋlaɪən] (n.) 獅子

2 tiger [ˋtaɪgɚ] (n.) 老虎

3 leopard [ˋlɛpɚd] (n.) 豹

4 wolf [wʊlf] (n.) 狼

5 bear [bɛr] (n.) 熊

6 polar bear [ˋpolɚ bɛr] (n.) 北極熊

❶ 獅子
The male lion is the one with the long mane of hair.

❷ 老虎
Do you think I could adopt a baby tiger?

❸ 豹
Have you heard the saying that a leopard can't change his spots?
你有聽過一句諺語

❹ 狼
Wolves prefer to travel and hunt together in packs.
成群結隊

❺ 熊
When camping in the mountains, beware of any bears.

❻ 北極熊
Polar bears are being impacted by global warming.
正受到影響

學更多

❶ male〈公的〉・long〈長的〉・mane〈鬃毛〉・hair〈毛髮〉
❷ think〈認為〉・adopt〈收養〉・baby〈幼小的〉
❸ heard〈hear（聽）的過去分詞〉・saying〈諺語〉・change〈改變〉・spot〈斑點〉
❹ wolves〈wolf（狼）的複數〉・travel〈移動〉・hunt〈獵食〉・pack〈一群〉
❺ camping〈camp（露營）的 ing 型態〉・mountain〈山〉・beware〈小心〉
❻ polar〈北極的〉・impacted〈impact（產生影響）的過去分詞〉・global warming〈地球暖化〉

中譯

❶ 有長鬃毛的是公獅子。
❷ 你認為我可以認養一隻小老虎嗎？
❸ 你有聽過「豹無法改變牠的斑紋」（本性難移）這句諺語嗎？
❹ 狼喜歡群體行動和狩獵。
❺ 在山區露營時，要小心有熊出沒。
❻ 北極熊正受到地球暖化的影響。

116

哺乳動物(2)

MP3 116

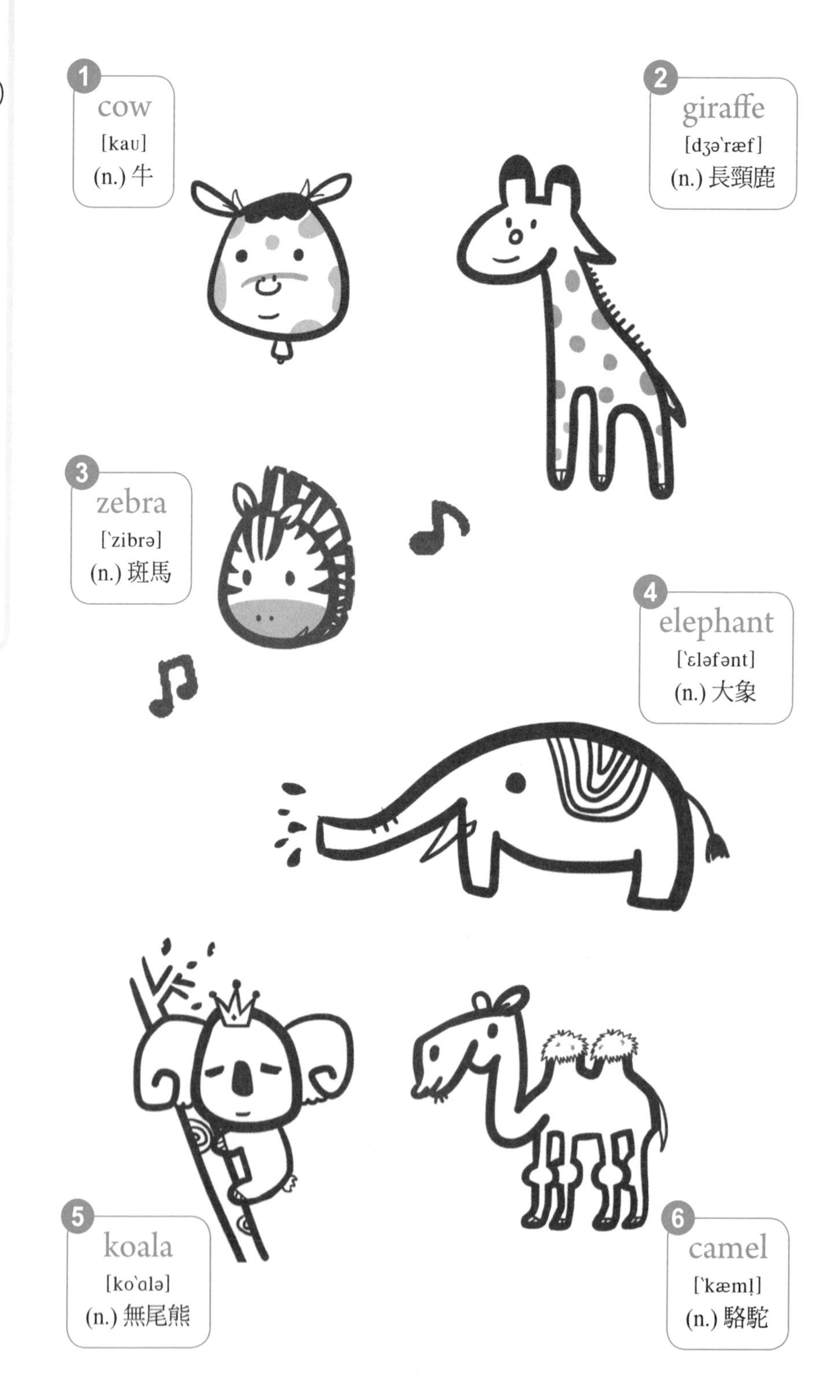

❶ 牛
I grew up on a farm and had to milk our cows as a young boy.
當我還是個小男孩的時候

❷ 長頸鹿
Girls everywhere would love to have long eyelashes like a giraffe.
所有女孩

❸ 斑馬
Zebras are beautiful animals with distinctive black and white stripes.
特殊的黑白條紋

❹ 大象
Elephants are tragically being killed for their ivory tusks.

❺ 無尾熊
Some of the most popular animals in zoos are the koalas.

❻ 駱駝
If you're planning a trip through the Sahara, you'd better take some camels along with you.
帶些駱駝一起去

學更多

❶ grew up〈grow up（成長）的過去式〉・farm〈農場〉・milk〈擠牛奶〉・our〈我們的〉
❷ everywhere〈每個地方〉・long〈長的〉・eyelash〈睫毛〉・like〈像〉
❸ animal〈動物〉・distinctive〈特殊的〉・stripe〈條紋〉
❹ tragically〈悲慘地〉・killed〈kill（殺害）的過去分詞〉・ivory〈象牙的〉・tusk〈長牙〉
❺ some〈一些〉・popular〈受歡迎的〉・zoo〈動物園〉
❻ planning〈plan（計劃）的 ing 型態〉・trip〈旅行〉・through〈在…各處〉・along with〈和…一起〉

中譯

❶ 我是在農場裡長大的，小時候還必須幫忙擠牛奶。
❷ 所有女孩都想要擁有像長頸鹿一樣的長睫毛。
❸ 斑馬是種美麗的動物，身上有與眾不同的黑白條紋。
❹ 大象因為它們的象牙，而遭到慘無人道的殺害。
❺ 動物園裡最受歡迎的動物之一，便是無尾熊。
❻ 如果你計劃去遊歷撒哈拉沙漠，最好帶些駱駝一起去。

117 天然災害(1)

MP3 117

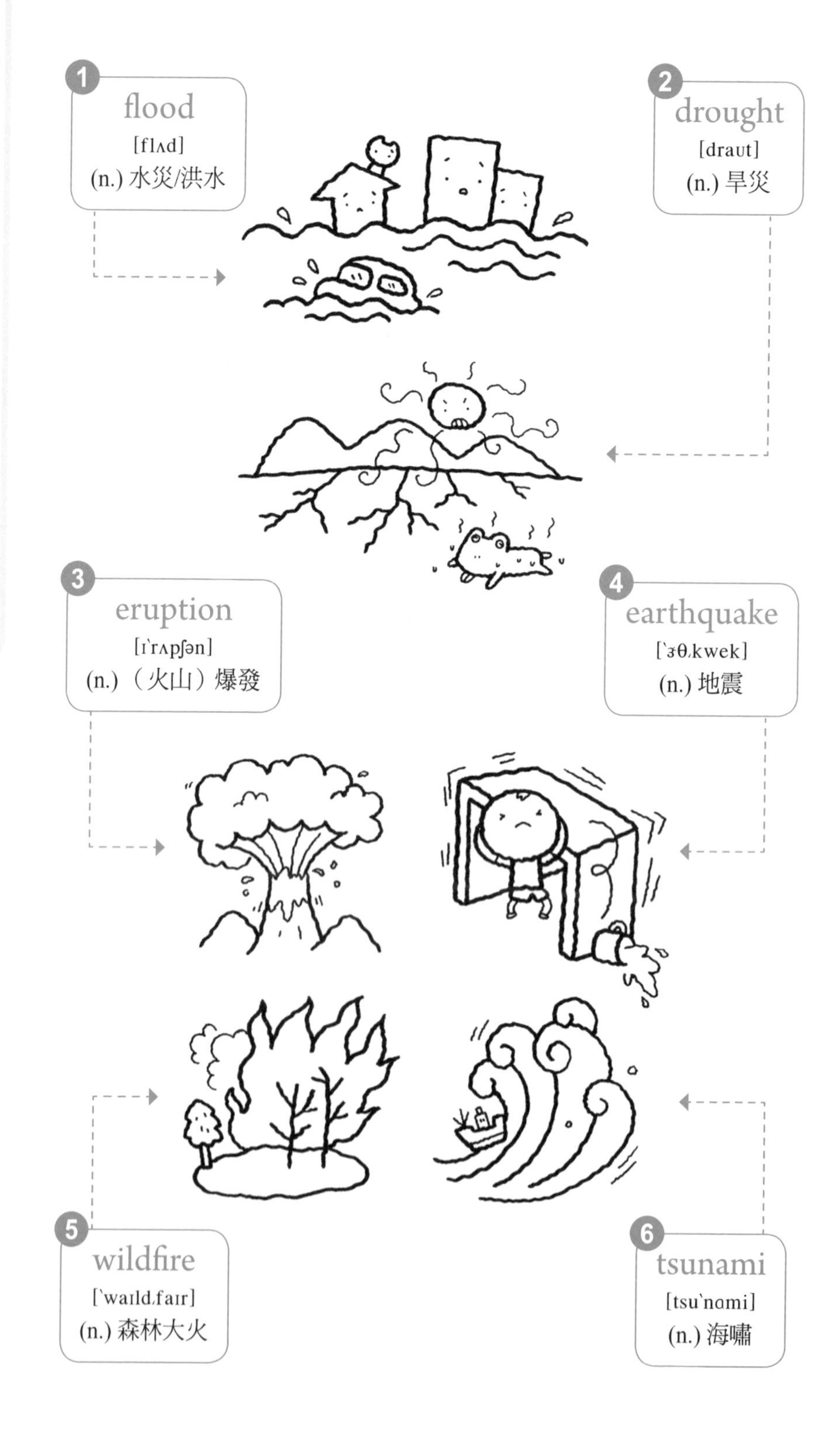

❶ 水災 / 洪水

Besides the strong winds and rains, typhoons often bring with them devastating floods. 強風和豪雨

❷ 旱災

Africa has been experiencing severe droughts, and now famine has become an issue. 最近經歷嚴重的旱災

❸（火山）爆發

The volcano eruption shocked the village's residents who ran for their lives! 為了他們的性命而逃跑

❹ 地震

The worst earthquake damage I've ever seen was in the 2010 earthquake in Haiti. 我看過最嚴重的地震災害

❺ 森林大火

Firefighters have been unable to put out the wildfires raging in the mountains.

❻ 海嘯

Scientists have reported that animals sense when a tsunami is coming and run for higher ground. 科學家們已報告過 何時會有海嘯來襲

學更多

❶ besides〈除…之外〉‧strong〈強大的〉‧bring〈帶來〉‧devastating〈毀滅性的〉
❷ experiencing〈experience（經歷）的 ing 型態〉‧severe〈嚴重的〉‧famine〈饑荒〉‧become〈become（變成）的過去分詞〉‧issue〈議題〉
❸ volcano〈火山〉‧shocked〈shock（震驚）的過去式〉‧village〈村莊〉‧resident〈居民〉‧ran〈run（跑）的過去式〉‧lives〈life（性命）的複數〉
❹ worst〈最壞的〉‧damage〈損害〉‧ever〈至今〉‧seen〈see（看）的過去分詞〉
❺ firefighter〈消防隊員〉‧put out〈熄滅〉‧raging〈rage（肆虐）的 ing 型態〉
❻ scientist〈科學家〉‧reported〈report（報告）的過去分詞〉‧sense〈感覺到〉

中譯

❶ 颱風除了帶來強風和豪雨，常會伴隨毀滅性的洪水。
❷ 非洲最近歷經嚴重的旱災，目前已經出現饑荒問題。
❸ 火山爆發嚇得村民倉皇逃生。
❹ 我看過最嚴重的地震災害，是 2010 年發生在海地的地震。
❺ 消防員遲遲無法撲滅肆虐山區的森林大火。
❻ 科學家指出，動物能察覺海嘯何時來襲，並逃往高處避難。

118

天然災害(2)

MP3 118

1 **twister / tornado**
[ˋtwɪstɚ] / [tɔrˋnedo]
(n.) 龍捲風

兩個單字都是「龍捲風」。

2 **typhoon**
[taɪˋfun]
(n.) 颱風

3 **hailstorm**
[ˋhel͵stɔrm]
(n.) 冰雹

對流雲系旺盛時，雲中水蒸氣凝結成冰粒降下。

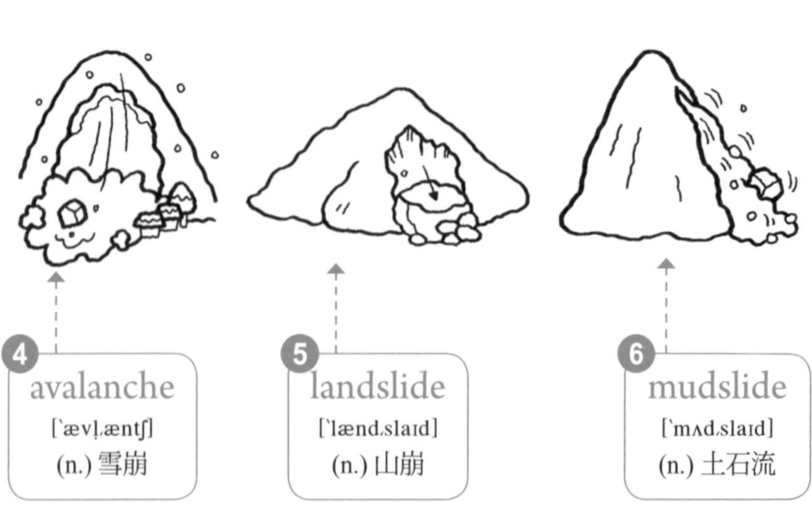

4 **avalanche**
[ˋævḷ͵æntʃ]
(n.) 雪崩

5 **landslide**
[ˋlænd͵slaɪd]
(n.) 山崩

6 **mudslide**
[ˋmʌd͵slaɪd]
(n.) 土石流

❶ 龍捲風
Did you see that cow in the twister? It was flying overhead!

❷ 颱風
Typhoon season is typically during summer and early autumn.
通常在夏季和初秋

❸ 冰雹
Were you in that hailstorm yesterday? My car window was broken by the huge hail stones.
被大冰雹砸破了

❹ 雪崩
Several skiers were killed in the avalanche in the Swiss Alps.
在雪崩中喪命

❺ 山崩
Typhoon Megi caused a huge landslide to cover part of Highway 3.
掩埋了部分的國道 3 號

❻ 土石流
The typhoon caused several mudslides to occur in the mountains.

學更多

❶ see〈看〉・cow〈牛〉・flying〈fly（飛）的 ing 型態〉・overhead〈在頭頂上〉
❷ season〈季節〉・typically〈典型地〉・early〈早的〉・autumn〈秋天〉
❸ window〈窗戶〉・broken〈break（打破）的過去分詞〉・huge〈龐大的〉・hail stone〈冰雹〉
❹ several〈幾個的〉・skier〈滑雪的人〉・Swiss〈瑞士的〉・Alps〈阿爾卑斯山脈〉
❺ caused〈cause（導致）的過去式〉・cover〈覆蓋〉・part〈部分〉・highway〈公路〉
❻ occur〈發生〉・mountain〈山〉

中譯

❶ 你看到了龍捲風裡的那頭牛嗎？牠從頭頂上飛過去了！
❷ 颱風季節通常是在夏季和初秋。
❸ 你昨天經歷了那場冰雹嗎？我的車窗被大冰雹砸破了。
❹ 有數名滑雪客命喪於瑞士阿爾卑斯山的雪崩中。
❺ 梅姬颱風造成了大山崩，掩蓋了國道 3 號的部分道路。
❻ 颱風導致山區發生了數次的土石流。

119 風&雨類型(1)

MP3 119

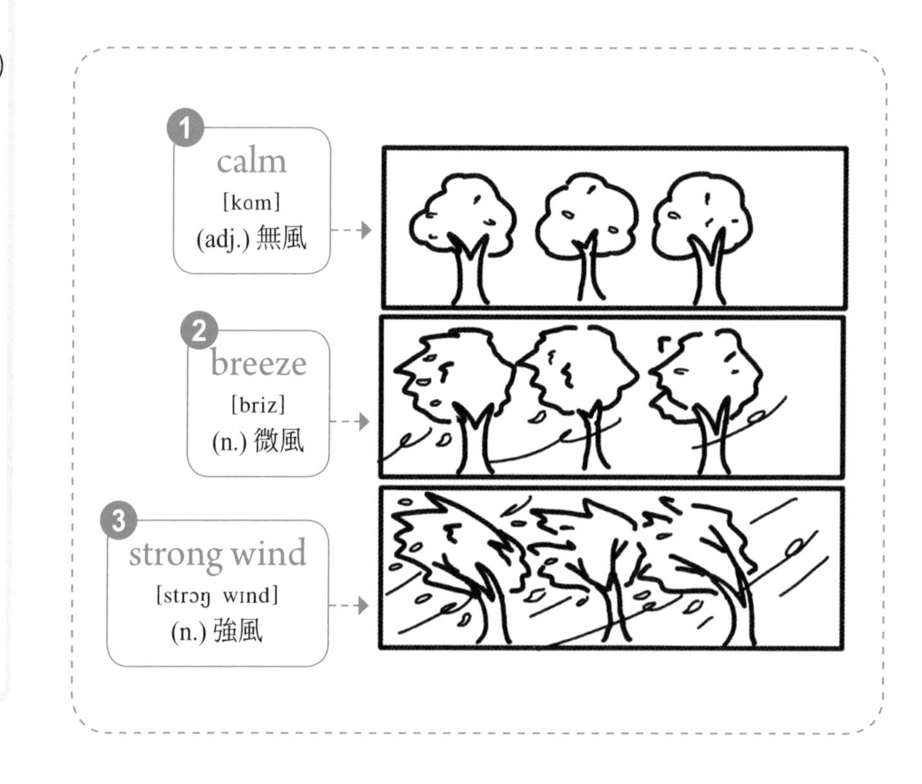

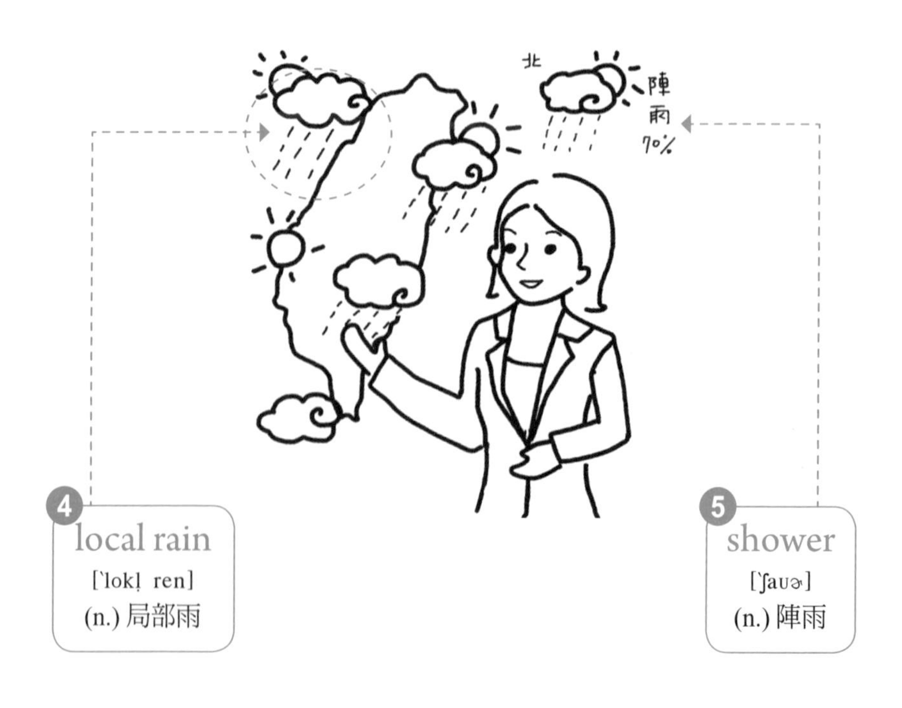

❶ 無風

The wind was so calm that sailing was out of the question.

乘船航行是不可能的

❷ 微風

There's nothing as lovely as a nice, cool breeze on a spring day.

像…一樣美好

❸ 強風

Strong winds and rain are expected over the weekend.

週末期間

❹ 局部雨

Local rain is expected this morning, though it will clear up by early afternoon.

在下午初期

❺ 陣雨

We're expecting some showers this afternoon.

學更多

❶ wind〈風〉・sailing〈航海〉・out of the question〈不可能的〉

❷ nothing〈沒什麼〉・lovely〈美好的〉・cool〈涼快的〉・spring〈春天〉

❸ strong〈強勁的〉・rain〈雨〉・expected〈預期要發生的〉・over〈在…期間〉・weekend〈週末〉

❹ local〈局部的〉・though〈不過〉・clear up〈放晴〉・early〈早的〉・afternoon〈下午〉

❺ expecting〈expect（預期）的 ing 型態〉・some〈一些〉

中譯

❶ 因為無風，所以乘船航行是不可能的。

❷ 沒有任何事物能像春天涼爽宜人的微風一樣美好。

❸ 週末期間預計會有強風豪雨。

❹ 今天早上預計各地區會有局部雨，不過一到下午就會放晴。

❺ 我們預期下午會有些零星陣雨。

120 風&雨類型(2)

MP3 120

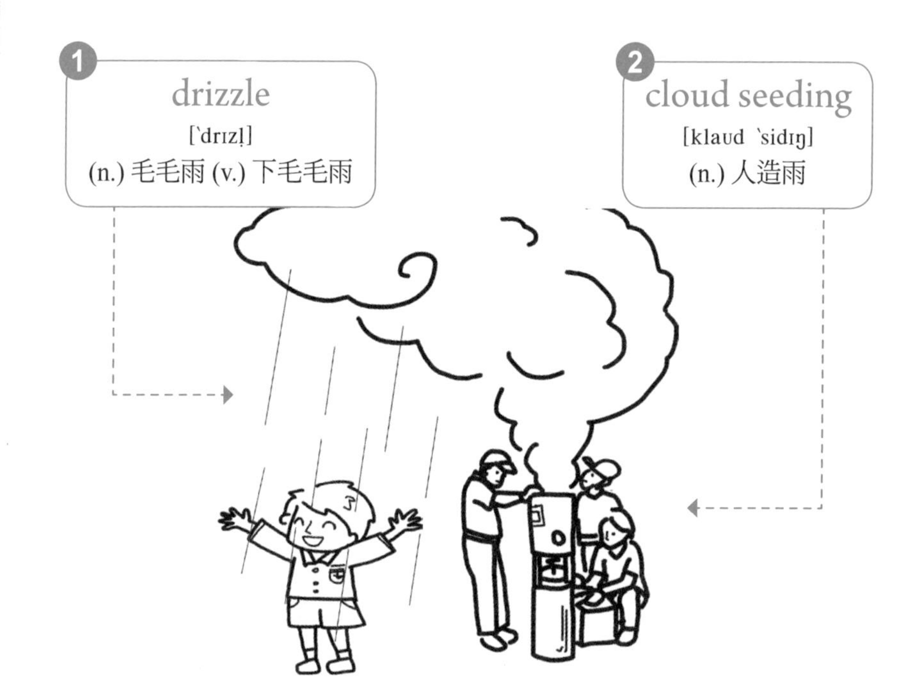

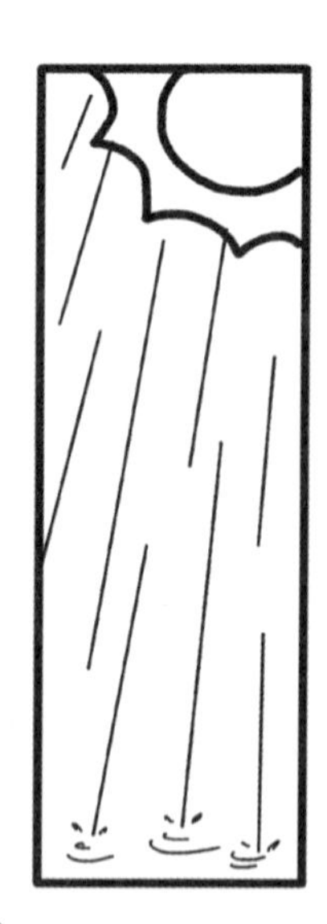

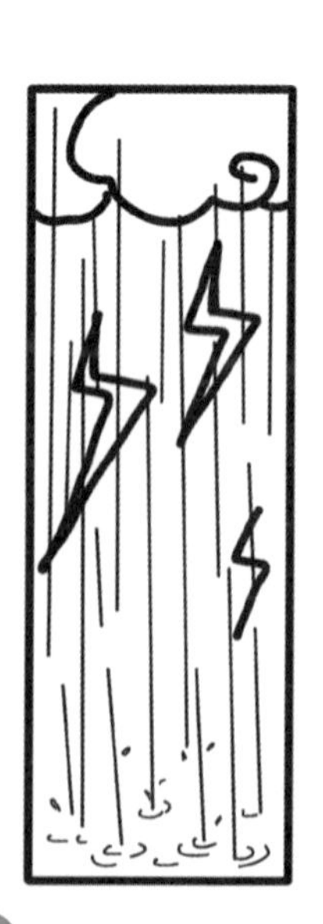

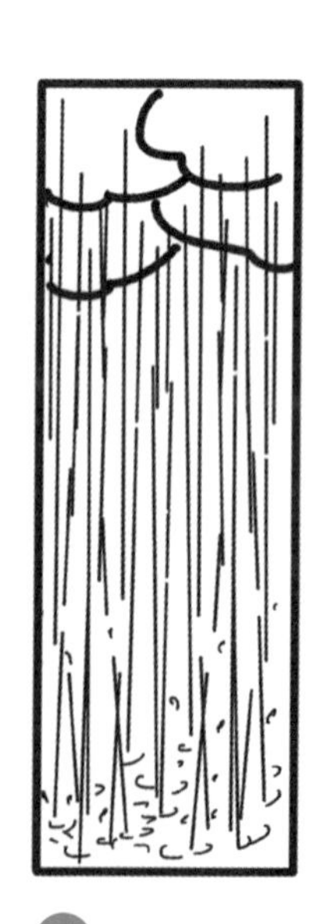

3 **sun shower**
[sʌn ˋʃaʊɚ]
(n.) 太陽雨

4 **thunderstorm**
[ˋθʌndɚˌstɔrm]
(n.) 雷雨

5 **downpour**
[ˋdaʊnˌpor]
(n.) 傾盆大雨

❶ 毛毛雨 / 下毛毛雨
You won't need an umbrella today because it's just drizzling.

❷ 人造雨
Cloud seeding is used to produce rain during dry seasons.
在乾季時

❸ 太陽雨
Sun showers catch you by surprise, so I never seem to have an umbrella
使你措手不及
when they happen.

❹ 雷雨
Lou loves thunderstorms, especially late at night.

❺ 傾盆大雨
During downpours, umbrellas are often of little use.
往往沒什麼用處

學更多

❶ umbrella〈雨傘〉・because〈因為〉・just〈只〉
❷ cloud〈雲〉・seeding〈催化〉・used〈use（使用）的過去分詞〉・produce〈製造〉・dry season〈乾季〉
❸ catch...by surprise〈使某人措手不及〉・happen〈發生〉
❹ especially〈尤其〉・late at night〈深夜〉
❺ during〈在…期間〉・often〈常常〉・of little use〈沒什麼用處〉

中譯

❶ 你今天不需要帶傘，因為只有下毛毛雨。
❷ 乾季時，會利用人造雨來增加降雨。
❸ 太陽雨使人措手不及，所以每次下太陽雨時，我幾乎都沒帶傘。
❹ Lou 喜愛雷雨，尤其是在深夜時。
❺ 傾盆大雨時，雨傘往往沒什麼用處。

121 水的型態

MP3 121

① **well** [wɛl] (n.) 水井

② **pond** [pand] (n.) 池塘

③ **waterfall** [ˋwɔtɚ͵fɔl] (n.) 瀑布

④ **ocean** [ˋoʃən] (n.) 海洋

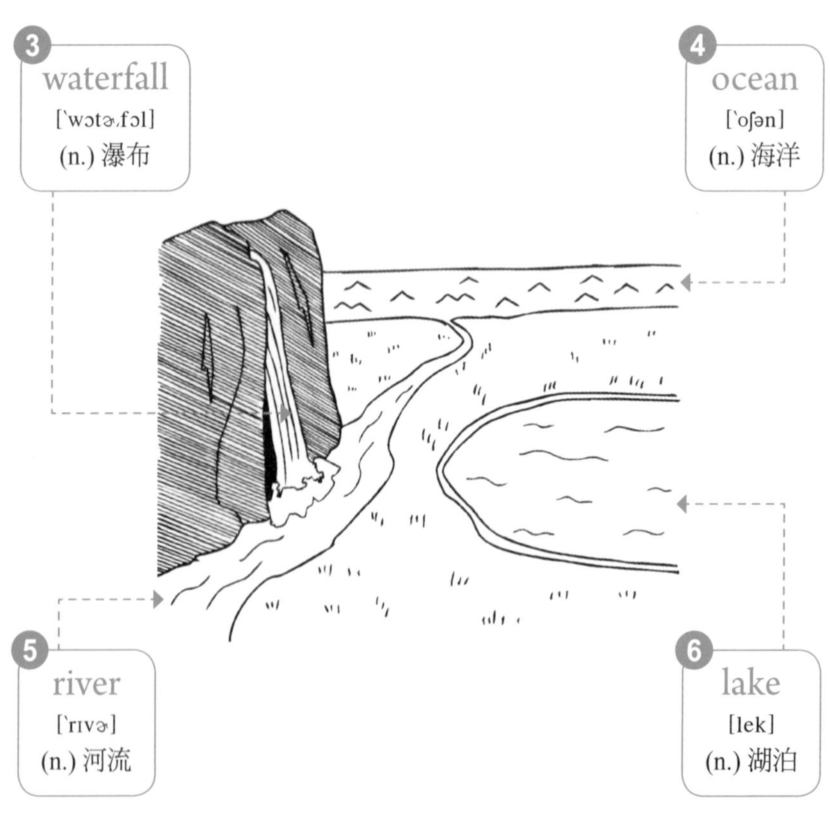

⑤ **river** [ˋrɪvɚ] (n.) 河流

⑥ **lake** [lek] (n.) 湖泊

❶ 水井

Terry's grandfather has a well in his backyard.

有一口井在他的後院裡

❷ 池塘

We have a pond in the backyard with goldfish!

❸ 瀑布

One of the world's most famous waterfalls is Iguazu Falls in South America.

世界上最有名的瀑布

❹ 海洋

The Pacific Ocean surrounds Hawaii.

❺ 河流

The Danshui River is known for its beautiful sunsets.

❻ 湖泊

Let's go water-skiing on the lake this afternoon.

去湖泊上滑水

學更多

❶ grandfather〈祖父〉• backyard〈後院〉
❷ have〈擁有〉• goldfish〈金魚〉
❸ famous〈出名的〉• world〈世界〉• falls〈瀑布〉• South America〈南美洲〉
❹ Pacific〈太平洋的〉• surround〈圍繞〉• Hawaii〈夏威夷〉
❺ known for〈因…而聞名〉• beautiful〈美麗的〉• sunset〈日落〉
❻ water-skiing〈滑水運動〉• afternoon〈下午〉

中譯

❶ Terry 的祖父家後院有一口井。
❷ 在我們的後院有一個養金魚的池塘。
❸ 南美的伊瓜蘇瀑布是世界上最有名的瀑布之一。
❹ 太平洋環繞著夏威夷。
❺ 淡水河以美麗的日落景色聞名。
❻ 今天下午我們去湖泊上滑水吧。

122
職稱(1)
MP3 122

1
shareholder
[ˋʃɛrˏholdɚ]
(n.) 股東
2
CEO / chief executive officer
[ˋsiˋiˋo] / [tʃif ɪgˋzɛkjʊtɪv ˋɔfəsɚ]
(n.) 執行長
縮寫為「CEO」。
3
board chairman
[bord ˋtʃɛrmən]
(n.) 董事長
4
manager
[ˋmænɪdʒɚ]
(n.) 經理
5
general manager
[ˋdʒɛnərəl ˋmænɪdʒɚ]
(n.) 總經理
6
supervisor
[ˏsupɚˋvaɪzɚ]
(n.) 主管
7
assistant general manager
[əˋsɪstənt ˋdʒɛnərəl ˋmænɪdʒɚ]
(n.) 副總經理

❶ 股東
How many shareholders does Data Services Inc. have?
幾位股東

❷ 執行長
IBM's chief executive officer (CEO) is Virginia Rometty.

❸ 董事長
Mr. Wu is the board chairman of the Singapore Power Company.

❹ 經理
I'd like to talk to your manager about your poor customer service!
關於你糟糕的客戶服務

❺ 總經理
Please ask the general manager if he'll be able to attend our meeting today.
他是否能出席我們今天的會議

❻ 主管
The supervisor is required to check on all employees during the day.
監督所有員工

❼ 副總經理
Though Linda is an assistant general manager now, she hopes to be promoted to general manager soon.
被晉升為總經理

學更多

❶ how many〈多少〉・Inc.〈incorporated（組成公司的）的縮寫〉・have〈有〉
❷ chief〈長官、領袖〉・executive〈執行的〉・officer〈高級職員〉
❸ board〈董事會〉・chairman〈董事長〉・Singapore〈新加坡〉・power〈電力〉
❹ talk〈談話〉・poor〈粗劣的〉・customer〈顧客〉・service〈服務〉
❺ ask〈詢問〉・general〈首席的〉・able〈能〉・attend〈參加〉・meeting〈會議〉
❻ required〈必須的〉・check on〈檢查〉・employee〈員工〉・day〈工作日〉
❼ though〈雖然〉・assistant〈輔助的〉・promoted〈promote（晉升）的過去分詞〉

中譯

❶ Data Services 公司有幾位股東？
❷ IBM 的執行長是 Virginia Rometty。
❸ 吳先生是新加坡電力公司的董事長。
❹ 我要跟你的經理談談你糟糕的客服！
❺ 請詢問總經理，他今天是否能夠出席我們的會議。
❻ 主管必須在工作時，監督所有的員工。
❼ Linda 現在雖然是副總經理，但她希望早點晉升為總經理。

123 職稱(2)

MP3 123

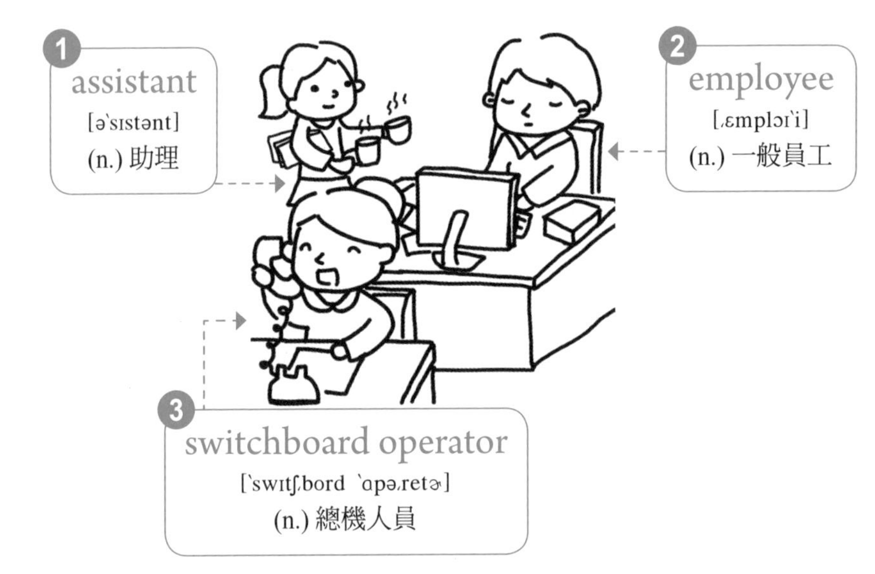

1 **assistant** [ə`sɪstənt] (n.) 助理

2 **employee** [ˏɛmplɔɪ`i] (n.) 一般員工

3 **switchboard operator** [`swɪtʃˏbord `ɑpəˏretɚ] (n.) 總機人員

4 **temporary employee** [`tɛmpəˏrɛrɪ ˏɛmplɔɪ`i] (n.) 派遣人員

5 **part-time employee** [`pɑrt`taɪm ˏɛmplɔɪ`i] (n.) 兼職人員

6 **project manager** [`prɑdʒɛkt `mænɪdʒɚ] (n.) 專案經理

7 **salesperson** [`selzˏpɝsn̩] (n.) 業務員

❶ 助理

Justin Timberlake's assistant always picks up his dry cleaning for him.

幫他拿他的乾洗衣物

❷ 一般員工

Hank is proud to be a long-time employee of Acer.

❸ 總機人員

Ask the switchboard operator to transfer your call.

轉接你的來電

❹ 派遣人員

Unfortunately, temporary employees do not get any benefits like pensions or sick leave.

像是退休金或病假

❺ 兼職人員

Some students can earn some cash for college by becoming a part-time employee either on or off campus.

賺些錢

不是校內就是校外

❻ 專案經理

Our project is running behind because the project manager isn't good at communicating.

我們的專案進度落後了

不擅長溝通

❼ 業務員

With Paul's outgoing personality, I bet he would make a great salesperson!

成為一名出色的業務員

學更多

❶ always〈總是〉・pick up〈拿起〉・dry cleaning〈乾洗過的衣物〉
❷ proud〈驕傲的〉・long-time〈長時間的〉
❸ switchboard〈電話總機〉・operator〈接線生〉・transfer〈轉換〉・call〈電話〉
❹ temporary〈暫時的〉・benefit〈好處〉・pension〈退休金〉・sick leave〈病假〉
❺ earn〈賺得〉・part-time〈兼職的〉・on campus〈在校內〉・off campus〈在校外〉
❻ running behind〈run behind（落後）的 ing 型態〉・project〈專案〉・good at〈擅長〉
❼ outgoing〈外向的〉・personality〈個性〉・bet〈確信〉・make〈成為〉

中譯

❶ Justin Timberlake 的助理都會幫他拿他的乾洗衣物。
❷ 作為一名 Acer 的長期員工，Hank 感到很驕傲。
❸ 交待總機為你轉接電話。
❹ 不幸地，派遣人員不享有任何福利，例如退休金或是病假。
❺ 有些學生可能會去做校內或校外的兼職人員，賺些錢來繳大學的學費。
❻ 我們的專案進度落後了，因為我們的專案經理不擅長溝通。
❼ Paul 的個性外向，我敢肯定他會成為一位出色的業務員！

124 各種判決(1)

MP3 124

1 in custody
[ɪn ˋkʌstədɪ]
(phr.) 羈押

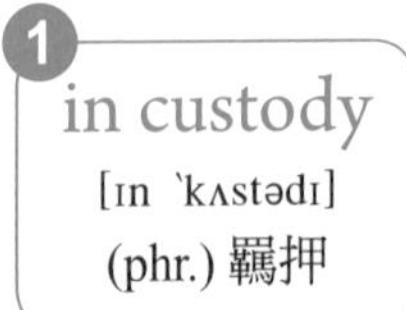

2 innocent
[ˋɪnəsn̩t]
(adj.) 無罪/清白的

3 release
[rɪˋlis]
(v.) 當庭釋放/釋放

4 imprisonment
[ɪmˋprɪzn̩mənt]
(n.) 有期徒刑/監禁

5 life imprisonment
[laɪf ɪmˋprɪzn̩mənt]
(n.) 無期徒刑

6 death penalty
[dɛθ ˋpɛnl̩tɪ]
(n.) 死刑

7 parole
[pəˋrol]
(n.) 假釋

❶ 羈押
The accused murderer is in custody and will be held without bail until his trial.
遭受控告的殺人犯 / 將會被拘留且不保釋

❷ 無罪 / 清白的
The accused told the judge that he was innocent of all charges.

❸ 當庭釋放 / 釋放
The convict was released from prison once he had served his sentence.
一旦他服滿了他的刑期

❹ 有期徒刑 / 監禁
The criminal's imprisonment was for a term of 15 years.

❺ 無期徒刑
The sentence for 1st degree murder is life imprisonment.

❻ 死刑
Not all countries support the death penalty, even in cases of murder.
即使是謀殺案

❼ 假釋
Is Tommy out on parole yet or is he still in prison?
假釋出獄

學更多

❶ custody〈監禁〉・held〈hold（拘留）的過去分詞〉・bail〈保釋〉・trial〈審判〉
❷ accused〈被告〉・told〈tell（告訴）的過去式〉・judge〈法官〉・charge〈指控〉
❸ convict〈囚犯〉・prison〈監獄〉・served〈serve（服刑）的過去分詞〉・sentence〈判刑〉
❹ criminal〈罪犯〉・term〈期限〉・year〈年〉
❺ degree〈等級〉・murder〈謀殺〉・life〈一生〉
❻ country〈國家〉・support〈贊成〉・penalty〈刑罰〉・even〈甚至、即使〉
❼ out〈在外面〉・yet〈已經〉・or〈或是〉・still〈仍然〉

中譯

❶ 遭受控告的殺人犯被羈押，直至審判前都將被拘留且不得交保。
❷ 被告告訴法官對於所有指控，他都是清白的。
❸ 囚犯一旦服滿刑期，就會被釋放。
❹ 那名罪犯被判了 15 年的有期徒刑。
❺ 一級謀殺罪的刑責是無期徒刑。
❻ 並非所有的國家都贊成死刑，即使是謀殺案。
❼ Tommy 已經假釋出獄了？或是還在獄中？

125 各種判決(2)

MP3 125

1 indictment
[ɪn`daɪtmənt]
(n.) 起訴

2 not prosecute
[nɑt `prɑsɪˏkjut]
(v.) 不起訴

3 suspended sentence
[sə`spɛndɪd `sɛntəns]
(n.) 緩刑

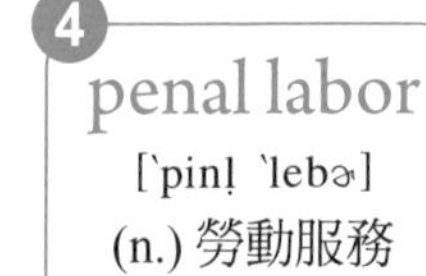

4 penal labor
[`pinḷ `lebɚ]
(n.) 勞動服務

5 commute a prison sentence to a fine
[kə`mjut ə `prɪzṇ `sɛntəns tu ə faɪn]
(phr.) 易科罰金

6 deprivation of civil rights
[ˏdɛprɪ`veʃən ɑv `sɪvḷ raɪts]
(phr.) 褫奪公權/剝奪公民權利

7 deportation
[ˏdipor`teʃən]
(n.) 驅逐出境

❶ 起訴

The indictment handed down was for armed robbery.

持槍搶劫

❷ 不起訴

I can't believe that con man was not prosecuted!

詐欺犯沒有被起訴

❸ 緩刑

If you're lucky, the judge will give you a suspended sentence.

❹ 勞動服務

Most prisons require all prisoners to take part in penal labor.

要求所有的囚犯

❺ 易科罰金

A judge has the authority to commute a prison sentence to a fine if he feels the prisoner warrants it.

牢刑

如果他覺得囚犯具有正當理由

❻ 褫奪公權 / 剝奪公民權利

During the US Civil War, the North was fighting the South to end the deprivation of civil rights for the slaves.

南北戰爭、美國內戰

❼ 驅逐出境

Illegal aliens face deportation if they are caught by the authorities.

非法移民 官方

學更多

❶ handed down〈hand down（正式宣布）的過去分詞〉• armed〈武裝的〉• robbery〈搶劫〉
❷ believe〈相信〉• con〈詐欺的〉• prosecuted〈prosecute（起訴）的過去分詞〉
❸ lucky〈幸運的〉• judge〈法官〉• suspended〈暫緩執行的〉• sentence〈判刑〉
❹ prisoner〈囚犯〉• take part in〈參加〉• penal〈受刑罰的〉• labor〈勞動〉
❺ authority〈權力〉• commute〈減輕〉• fine〈罰金〉• warrant〈證明…有正當理由〉
❻ end〈結束〉• deprivation〈剝奪〉• civil〈公民的〉• right〈權利〉• slave〈奴隸〉
❼ illegal〈非法的〉• alien〈外國人〉• caught〈catch（逮捕）的過去分詞〉

中譯

❶ 因為持槍搶劫被起訴。
❷ 我真不敢相信，那名詐欺犯居然沒有被起訴！
❸ 如果運氣好，法官會判你緩刑。
❹ 大多數的監獄都會要求所有囚犯參與勞動服務。
❺ 若是法官覺得囚犯有正當理由，他有權判予囚犯易科罰金。
❻ 美國南北戰爭期間，北方為了終結奴隸被剝奪公民權利的現象，和南方開戰。
❼ 非法移民若遭逮捕，將會面臨被官方驅逐出境的後果。

126 違法行為(1)

MP3 126

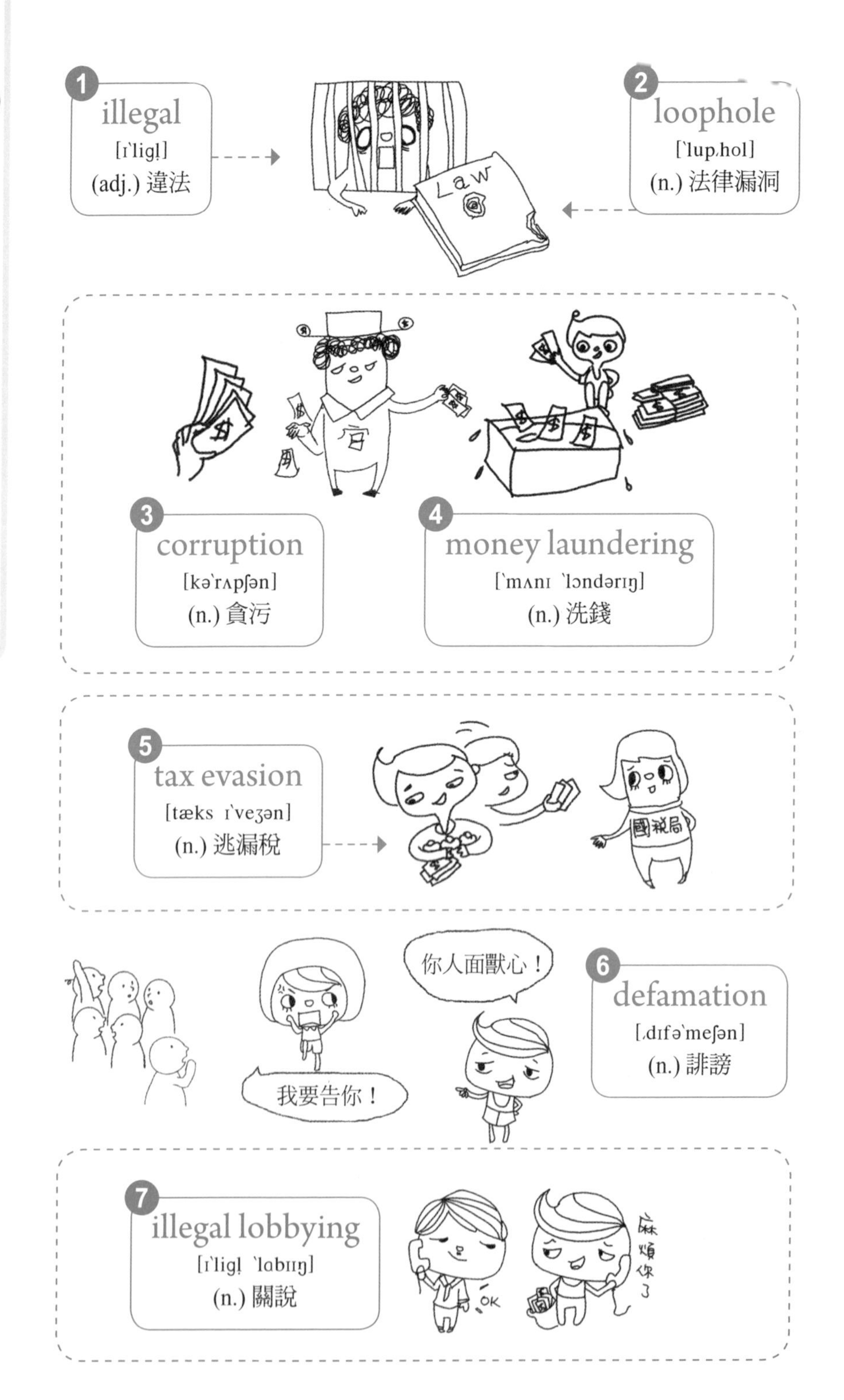

❶ 違法
It's illegal to sell or use marijuana in Taiwan.
販售或使用大麻

❷ 法律漏洞
There are some loopholes in the tax system.
有一些法律漏洞

❸ 貪污
Unfortunately, there is a lot of corruption in politics.

❹ 洗錢
Money laundering is an illegal activity popular among mobsters.
違法行為

❺ 逃漏稅
Tax evasion can result in a prison sentence, as well as a large fine.
除了…還有

❻ 誹謗
An actor sued a magazine for defamation after it alleged he was gay.
控告一份雜誌誹謗　沒有證據就宣稱他是同性戀

❼ 關說
The government is working hard to stop illegal lobbying from corrupting the system.
阻止關說行為，避免體制腐敗

學更多

❶ sell〈販售〉・use〈使用〉・marijuana〈大麻〉
❷ some〈一些〉・tax〈稅〉・system〈系統、制度〉
❸ unfortunately〈不幸地〉・a lot of〈許多〉・politics〈政治〉
❹ activity〈活動〉・popular〈流行的〉・among〈在…之中〉・mobster〈盜匪集團的成員〉
❺ evasion〈逃避〉・result in〈導致〉・prison〈監獄〉・sentence〈刑責〉・fine〈罰款〉
❻ sued〈sue（控告）的過去式〉・alleged〈allege（無充分證據而宣稱）的過去式〉
❼ government〈政府〉・lobbying〈遊說〉・corrupting〈corrupt（使腐敗）的 ing 型態〉

中譯

❶ 在台灣，販售或使用大麻都是違法。
❷ 稅務制度中，存在一些法律漏洞。
❸ 不幸地，政治中包含許多貪污。
❹ 洗錢是盜匪集團中常見的違法行為。
❺ 逃漏稅可能造成牢獄之災，以及巨額罰款。
❻ 一份雜誌胡亂斷言某位演員是同性戀之後，便遭到該名演員控告誹謗。
❼ 政府正努力遏止關說行為，避免體制腐敗。

127 違法行為(2)

MP3 127

1 counterfeit document
[ˋkaʊntɚ͵fit ˋdɑkjəmənt]
forged document
[ˋfɔrdʒd ˋdɑkjəmənt]
(n.) 偽造文書

兩個單字都是「偽造文書」。

2 copyright infringement
[ˋkɑpɪ͵raɪt ɪnˋfrɪndʒmənt]
(n.) 侵犯著作權

3 fraud
[frɔd]
(n.) 詐欺

4 drug abuse
[drʌg əˋbjus]
(n.) 吸毒

5 theft
[θɛft]
(n.) 偷竊

6 illegal immigration
[ɪˋligḷ ͵ɪməˋgreʃən]
(n.) 非法移民

7 smuggling
[ˋsmʌgḷɪŋ]
(n.) 走私

❶ 偽造文書

These forged documents are proof that the criminal is guilty.

❷ 侵犯著作權

It's a copyright infringement to play a song on the radio without paying a fee.
未付費

❸ 詐欺

Email fraud is becoming more and more common in today's world.
越來越常見

❹ 吸毒

Drug abuse can lead to a life of crime.
步入犯罪的一生

❺ 偷竊

Ryan was distraught after discovering the theft of his passport.
發現他的護照被偷

❻ 非法移民

Illegal immigration is a serious problem in many countries.

❼ 走私

There has been an increase in human smuggling this year.
人口走私增加

學更多

❶ forged〈偽造的〉・proof〈證據〉・guilty〈有罪的〉・counterfeit〈偽造的〉
❷ copyright〈著作權〉・infringement〈侵犯〉・play〈播放〉・fee〈費用〉
❸ email〈電子郵件〉・more and more...〈越來越⋯〉・common〈常見的〉
❹ drug〈毒品〉・abuse〈濫用〉・lead to〈導致〉・life〈一生〉・crime〈犯罪〉
❺ distraught〈極煩惱的〉・discovering〈discover（發現）的 ing 型態〉・passport〈護照〉
❻ immigration〈移民〉・serious〈嚴重的〉・problem〈問題〉・country〈國家〉
❼ increase〈增加〉・human〈人〉

中譯

❶ 這些偽造文書，就是那名嫌犯有罪的證據。
❷ 未付費而在廣播中播放歌曲，是侵犯著作權的行為。
❸ 電子郵件詐欺在現今環境下越來越常見。
❹ 吸毒會使人誤入歧途。
❺ Ryan 發現護照遭到偷竊後，就非常煩惱。
❻ 在許多國家，非法移民是一個嚴重的問題。
❼ 今年人口走私的數量增加了。

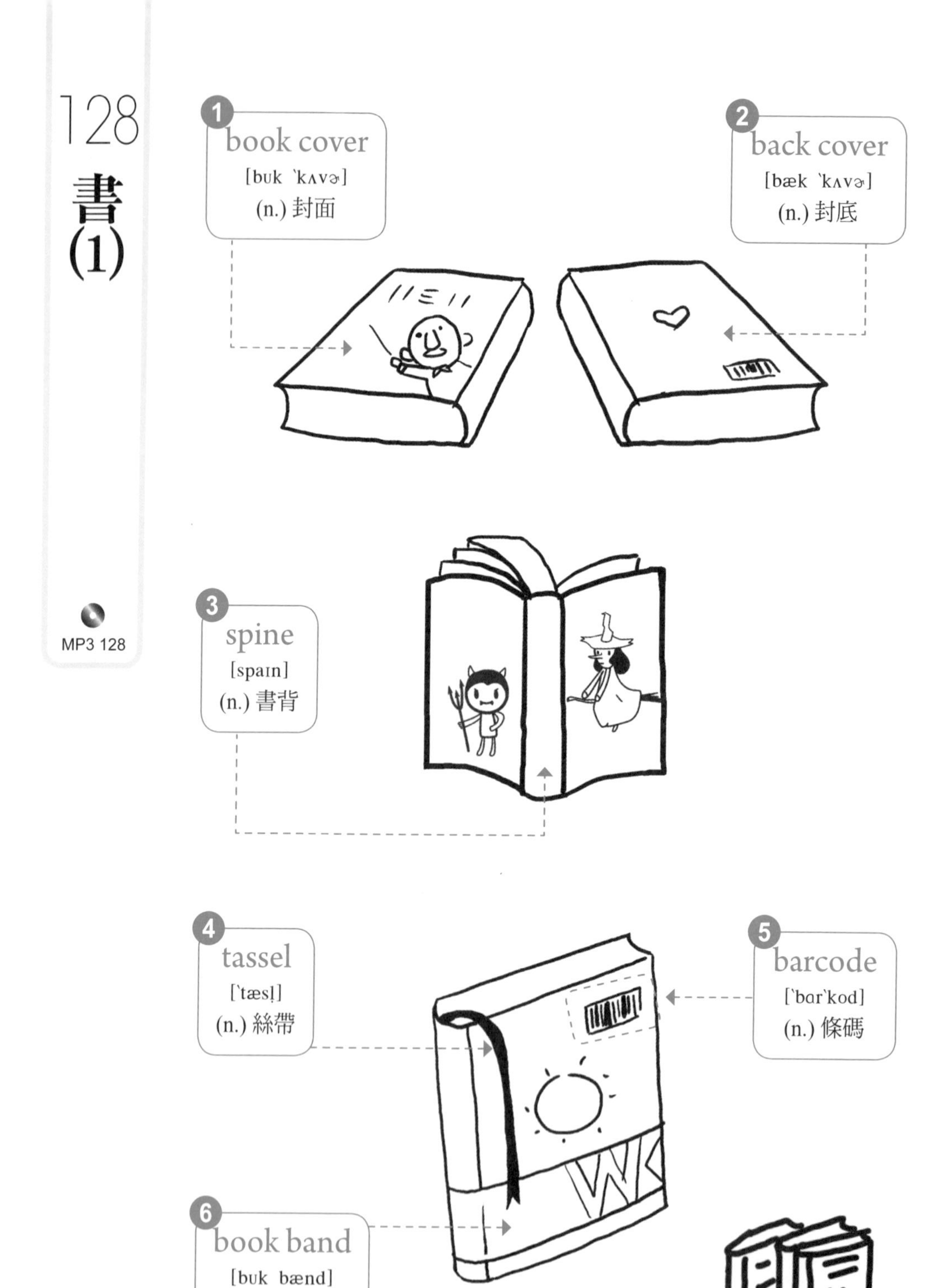
128
書(1)
MP3 128
1 book cover
[bʊk ˋkʌvɚ]
(n.) 封面
2 back cover
[bæk ˋkʌvɚ]
(n.) 封底
3 spine
[spaɪn]
(n.) 書背
4 tassel
[ˋtæsl̩]
(n.) 絲帶
5 barcode
[ˋbɑrˋkod]
(n.) 條碼
6 book band
[bʊk bænd]
(n.) 書腰

❶ 封面
Having an attractive book cover helps an author sell more copies.

❷ 封底
I like this book's back cover—it has the author's photo with his family.

❸ 書背
New books have a stiff spine because they've never been fully opened before.
之前它們從未被整個打開過

❹ 絲帶
Tassels on books are elegant, as well as being useful as bookmarks.
當作…是很有用的

❺ 條碼
At the cashier counter, Bill watched the clerk scan the book's barcode into her system.

❻ 書腰
The book bands can be removed after purchasing new books.

學更多

❶ attractive〈有吸引力的〉・author〈作者〉・sell〈賣〉・copy〈本〉
❷ like〈喜歡〉・photo〈照片〉・family〈家人〉
❸ stiff〈硬的〉・never〈從未〉・fully〈完全地〉・opened〈open（打開）的過去分詞〉
❹ elegant〈優美的〉・as well as〈不但…而且〉・useful〈有用的〉・bookmark〈書籤〉
❺ cashier counter〈收銀台〉・clerk〈店員〉・scan〈掃描〉・system〈系統〉
❻ removed〈remove（去掉）的過去分詞〉・purchasing〈purchase（買）的 ing 型態〉

中譯

❶ 有一個吸引人的封面，有助於作者多賣出幾本書。
❷ 我喜歡這本書的封底——上面放了作者和家人的合照。
❸ 新書的書背還很硬，因為它們還沒有被整個攤開過。
❹ 書本上的絲帶不但漂亮，當作書籤也很好用。
❺ 在收銀台，Bill 看著店員將書的條碼刷入她的電腦系統。
❻ 新書購買後，即可取下書腰。

129 書(2)

MP3 129

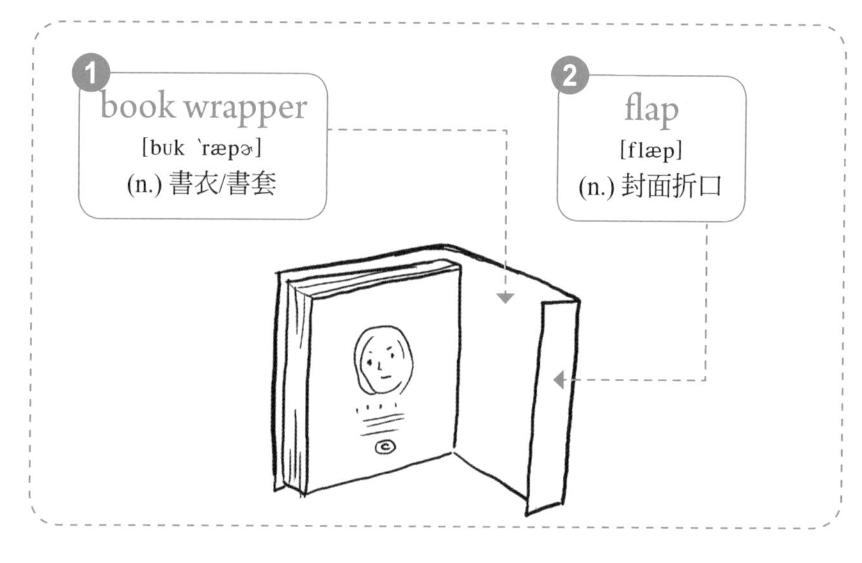

1. **book wrapper** [bʊk `ræpɚ] (n.) 書衣/書套
2. **flap** [flæp] (n.) 封面折口

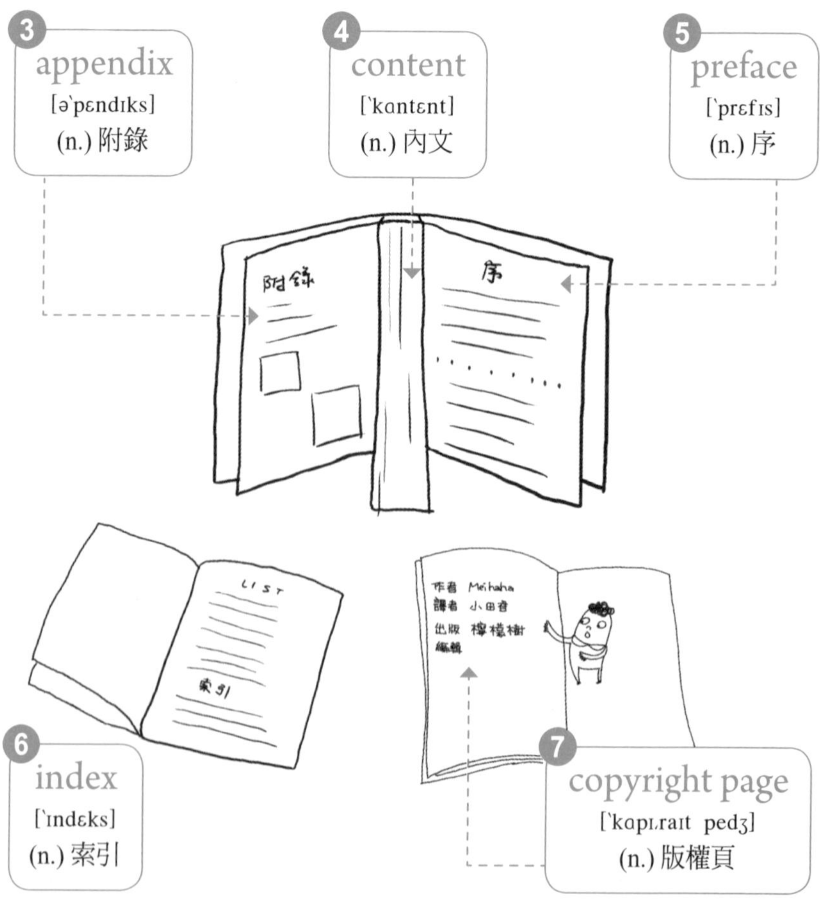

3. **appendix** [ə`pɛndɪks] (n.) 附錄
4. **content** [`kɑntɛnt] (n.) 內文
5. **preface** [`prɛfɪs] (n.) 序
6. **index** [`ɪndɛks] (n.) 索引
7. **copyright page** [`kɑpɪ͵raɪt pedʒ] (n.) 版權頁

❶ 書衣 / 書套

In order to protect a brand-new book, many are shipped to stores with book wrappers on them.
被運送去店裡

❷ 封面折口

The flaps on book covers are handy to use as quick bookmarks.
作為…使用

❸ 附錄

Authors put some additional information and references in the appendix.

❹ 內文

Is the content as good as you thought it would be?
和你想像的一樣好

❺ 序

Read the preface if you want to get a quick introduction to the book.

❻ 索引

After the dirty politician published a "tell-all", his colleagues quickly
出版一本「爆料書」

checked the index to see if their names were listed.
他們的名字被列出來

❼ 版權頁

A book's copyright page will have the date it was copyrighted.
書取得版權的日期

學更多

❶ in order to〈為了〉‧brand-new〈全新的〉‧shipped〈ship(運送)的過去分詞〉
❷ cover〈封面〉‧handy〈便利的〉‧as〈當作〉‧quick〈快的〉‧bookmark〈書籤〉
❸ author〈作者〉‧put〈放〉‧additional〈額外的〉‧reference〈參考文獻〉
❹ as...as...〈像…一樣〉‧thought〈think(想)的過去式〉
❺ read〈閱讀〉‧get〈得到〉‧introduction〈介紹〉
❻ dirty〈卑鄙的〉‧politician〈政客〉‧listed〈list(把…編入目錄)的過去分詞〉
❼ copyright〈版權〉‧date〈日期〉‧copyrighted〈copyright(為…取得版權)的過去分詞〉

中譯

❶ 為了保護全新的書籍，許多新書被運送到書店時，都會包著書套。
❷ 書封上的封面折口可以當作立即可用的書籤，相當方便。
❸ 作者會在附錄放一些補充資料及參考文獻。
❹ 內文有和你想像的一樣好嗎？
❺ 如果你想要快速地了解這本書，你可以閱讀它的序。
❻ 在那個卑鄙的政客出版「爆料書」之後，他的同事們都趕緊檢查索引，看看自己的名字是否被列入其中。
❼ 一本書的版權頁會有它的版權日期。

130 報紙(1)

MP3 130

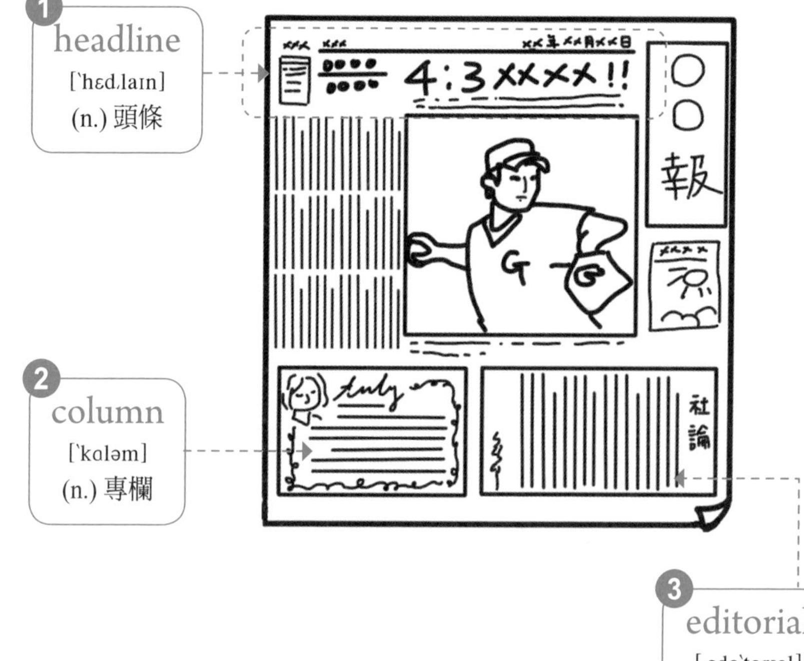

1. **headline** [ˋhɛd͵laɪn] (n.) 頭條

2. **column** [ˋkɑləm] (n.) 專欄

3. **editorial** [͵ɛdəˋtɔrɪəl] (n.) 社論

4. **feature** [fitʃɚ] (n.) 專題報導

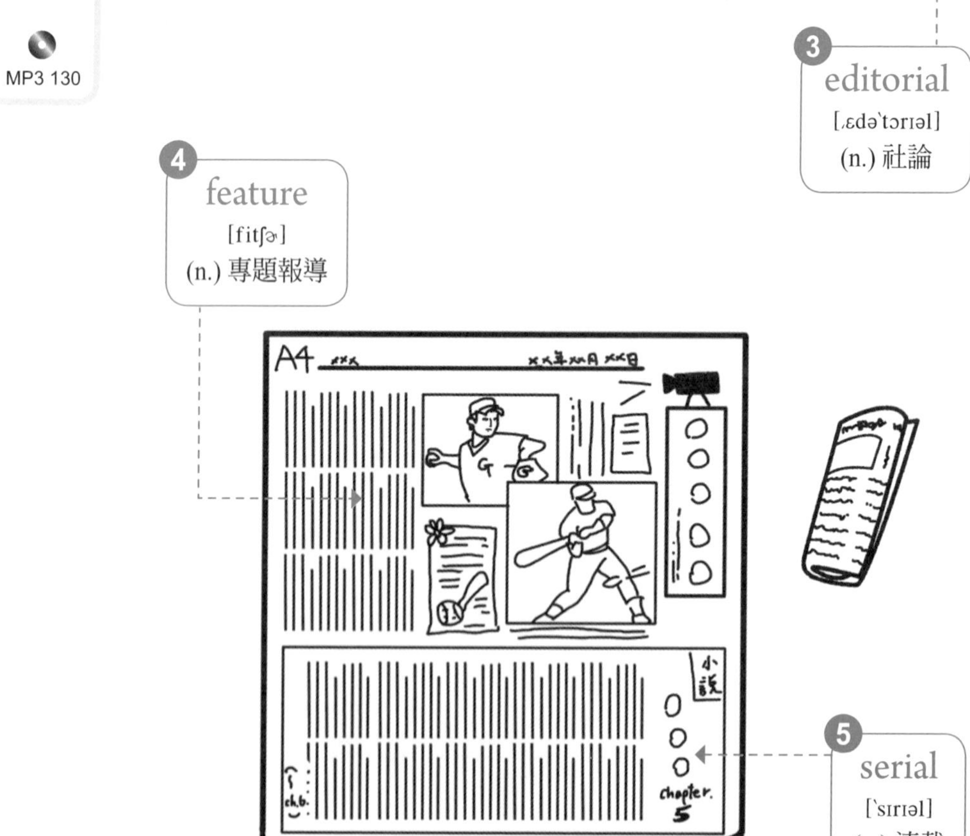

5. **serial** [ˋsɪrɪəl] (n.) 連載

❶ 頭條
Terry was stunned when she saw the newspaper's headline!

❷ 專欄
I love this political writer's column in the Sunday paper.
星期天出版的報紙

❸ 社論
Editorial views of the newspaper are typically either conservative or liberal, as far as politics are concerned.
關於政治方面

❹ 專題報導
Jane is a fashion reporter, and is writing a feature about Vera Wang's success.
時尚記者

❺ 連載
John Brown's new book is being published in serial form in the newspaper.
新書被刊登

學更多

❶ stunned〈震驚的〉・saw〈see（看）的過去式〉・newspaper〈報紙〉
❷ political〈政治的〉・writer〈作家〉・paper〈報紙〉
❸ view〈觀點〉・typically〈通常〉・either...or...〈不是…就是…〉・conservative〈保守的〉・liberal〈開放的〉・as far as...be concerned〈關於某方面〉
❹ fashion〈時尚〉・reporter〈記者〉・success〈成功〉
❺ published〈publish（刊登）的過去分詞〉・form〈形式〉

中譯

❶ Terry 看到報紙的頭條時非常震驚！
❷ 我很喜歡這位政治專欄作家在星期天報紙的專欄。
❸ 報紙裡關於政治的社論觀點，通常不是很保守，就是很開放。
❹ Jane 是一名時尚記者，最近正在撰寫關於 Vera Wang 成功歷程的專題報導。
❺ John Brown 的新書以連載的形式刊載於報紙上。

131 報紙(2)

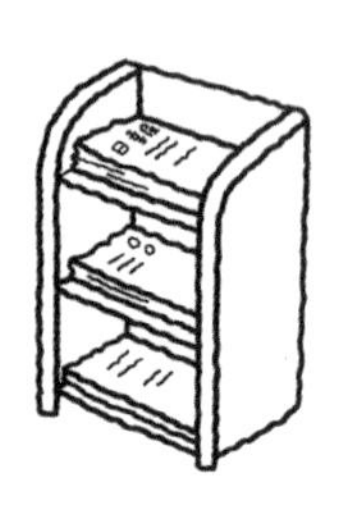

MP3 131

❶ **full-page advertisement**
[ˋfulpedʒ ˌædvɚˋtaɪzmənt]
full-page ad
[ˋfulpedʒ æd]
(n.) 全版廣告

兩個單字都是「全版廣告」。

兩個單字都是「分類廣告」。

❷ **classified advertisement**
[ˋklæsəˌfaɪd ˌædvɚˋtaɪzmənt]
classified ad
[ˋklæsəˌfaɪd æd]
(n.) 分類廣告

❸ **public apology**
[ˋpʌblɪk əˋpɑlədʒɪ]
(n.) 道歉啟事

❹ **correction**
[kəˋrɛkʃən]
(n.) 更正啟事

❺ **advice column**
[ədˋvaɪs ˋkɑləm]
(n.) 讀者來函專欄

❶ 全版廣告

British Petroleum paid for a full-page ad in The New York Times, apologizing for the oil spill in the Gulf of Mexico.

花錢刊登全版廣告　紐約時報

❷ 分類廣告

The classified ads last week had a 2002 BMC sedan for sale for only $NT400,000!

❸ 道歉啟事

After the corrupt politician was thrown out of office, he had a public apology to the citizens of his country printed in the leading newspaper.

被罷免職務　給全國民眾的道歉啟事

❹ 更正啟事

The newspaper reported someone's age incorrectly and printed a correction in the next issue.

❺ 讀者來函專欄

Dear Abby is a famous advice column that appears in newspapers around the world.

刊登在全球各地的報紙上

學更多

❶ British〈英國的〉・petroleum〈石油〉・full-page〈滿版的、全頁的〉・apologizing〈apologize（道歉）的 ing 型態〉・spill〈溢出〉・gulf〈海灣〉

❷ classified〈分類的〉・sedan〈轎車〉・sale〈賣〉・only〈只〉

❸ corrupt〈腐敗的〉・thrown out〈throw out（逐出）的過去分詞〉・office〈職務〉・public〈公眾的〉・apology〈道歉〉・citizen〈公民〉・country〈國家〉・printed〈print（刊登）的過去分詞〉・leading〈最重要的〉

❹ reported〈report（報導）的過去式〉・incorrectly〈錯誤地〉・issue〈期〉

❺ famous〈知名的〉・advice〈建議〉・appear〈發表〉・around〈在…四處〉

中譯

❶ 英國石油公司花錢在紐約時報刊登全版廣告，為墨西哥灣漏油事件道歉。

❷ 上週的分類廣告中，有一台 2002 BMC 的轎車居然只賣台幣四十萬元！

❸ 那位腐敗的政客被罷免後，在最具影響力的報紙上刊登了一篇給全國民眾的道歉啟事。

❹ 那份報紙刊錯某人的年紀之後，就在下一期刊登了更正啟事。

❺ Dear Abby 是能在全球各地報紙中看到的知名讀者來函專欄。

132 報紙(3)

MP3 132

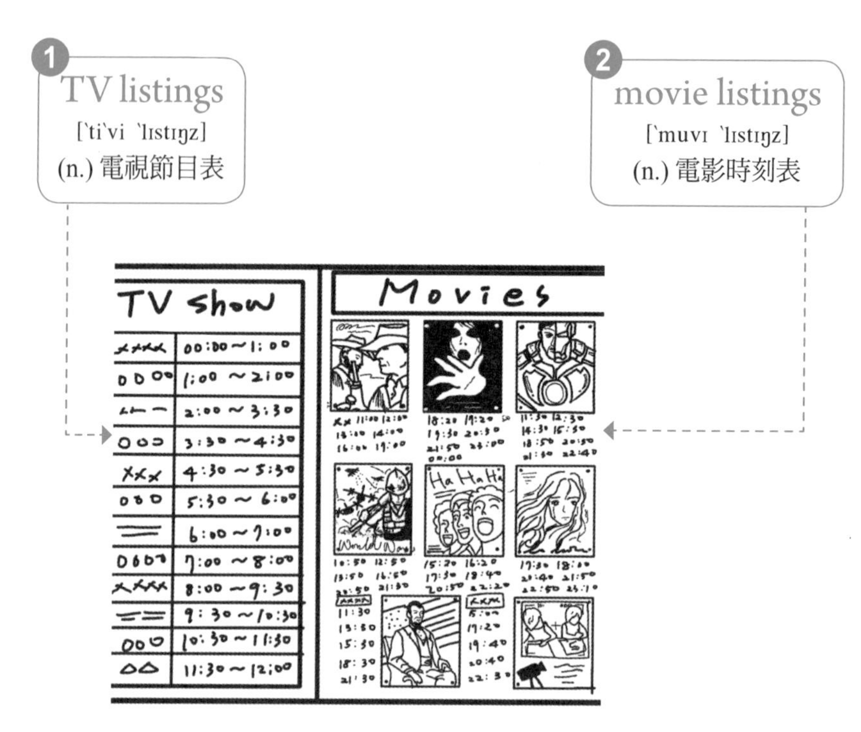

1. **TV listings** [ˋtiˋvi ˋlɪstɪŋz] (n.) 電視節目表
2. **movie listings** [ˋmuvɪ ˋlɪstɪŋz] (n.) 電影時刻表

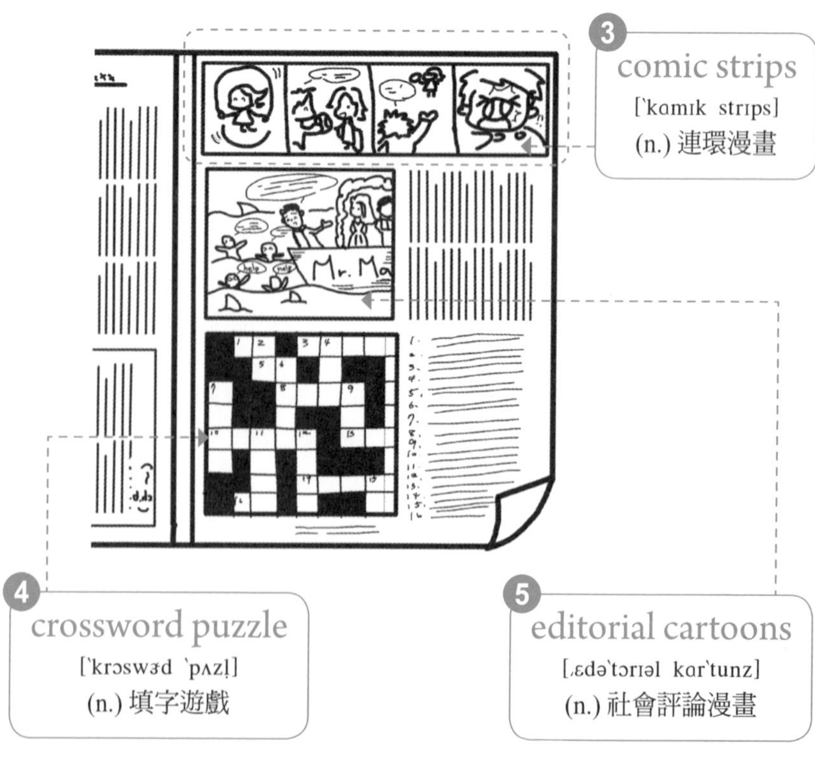

3. **comic strips** [ˋkɑmɪk strɪps] (n.) 連環漫畫
4. **crossword puzzle** [ˋkrɔswɝd ˋpʌzl̩] (n.) 填字遊戲
5. **editorial cartoons** [ˌɛdəˋtɔrɪəl kɑrˋtunz] (n.) 社會評論漫畫

❶ 電視節目表

Where are the TV listings? I want to see what's on right now.

現在正在上演什麼

❷ 電影時刻表

Sam, I checked the movie listings and *Mission Impossible* is playing at 7:30 pm.

在晚間七點半放映

❸ 連環漫畫

Kelly's favorite comic strips are *Charlie Brown* and *Garfield*.

❹ 填字遊戲

People say that doing crossword puzzles keeps your brain sharp.

保持你的腦袋靈活

❺ 社會評論漫畫

Some editorial cartoons have been so controversial the artist's life has been threatened.

被威脅

學更多

❶ listing〈列表〉・want〈想〉・see〈看〉・on〈在進行中〉・right now〈就是現在〉

❷ checked〈check（檢查）的過去式〉・movie〈電影〉・mission〈任務〉・impossible〈不可能的〉・playing〈play（上演）的 ing 型態〉

❸ favorite〈特別喜愛的〉・comic〈好笑的、連環漫畫〉・strip〈連環漫畫〉

❹ crossword〈縱橫填字謎〉・puzzle〈猜謎〉・brain〈頭腦〉・sharp〈敏銳的〉

❺ editorial〈社論的〉・cartoon〈以政治、時事為題材的諷刺畫〉・controversial〈有爭議的〉・life〈性命〉・threatened〈threaten（威脅）的過去分詞〉

中譯

❶ 電視節目表在哪？我想看一下現在有什麼節目。

❷ Sam，我查了電影時刻表，晚間七點半有一場「不可能的任務」。

❸ Kelly 最喜歡的連環漫畫是史奴比和加菲貓。

❹ 人們說，玩填字遊戲可以保持腦袋靈活。

❺ 有些社會評論漫畫非常具爭議性，畫家的性命甚至受到威脅。

133 雜誌(1)

MP3 133

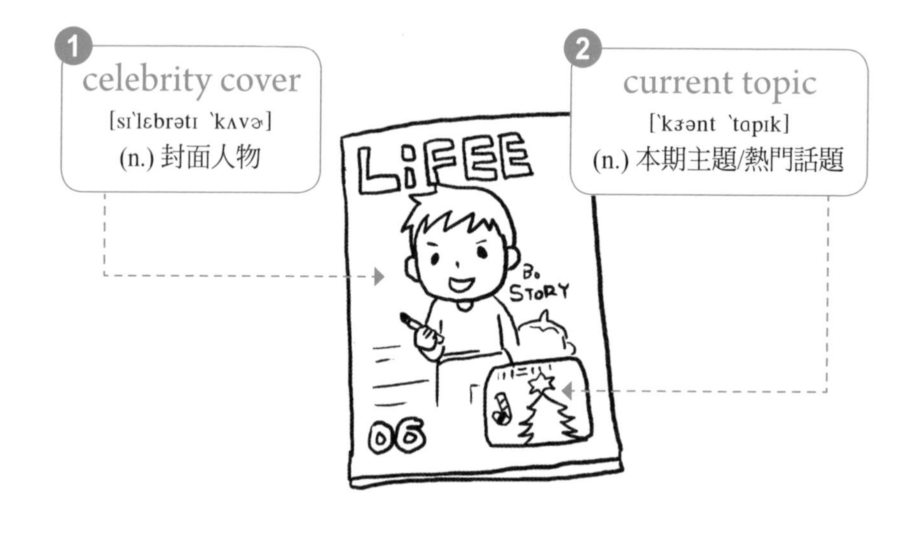

1. celebrity cover [sɪˋlɛbrətɪ ˋkʌvɚ] (n.) 封面人物
2. current topic [ˋkɝənt ˋtɑpɪk] (n.) 本期主題/熱門話題

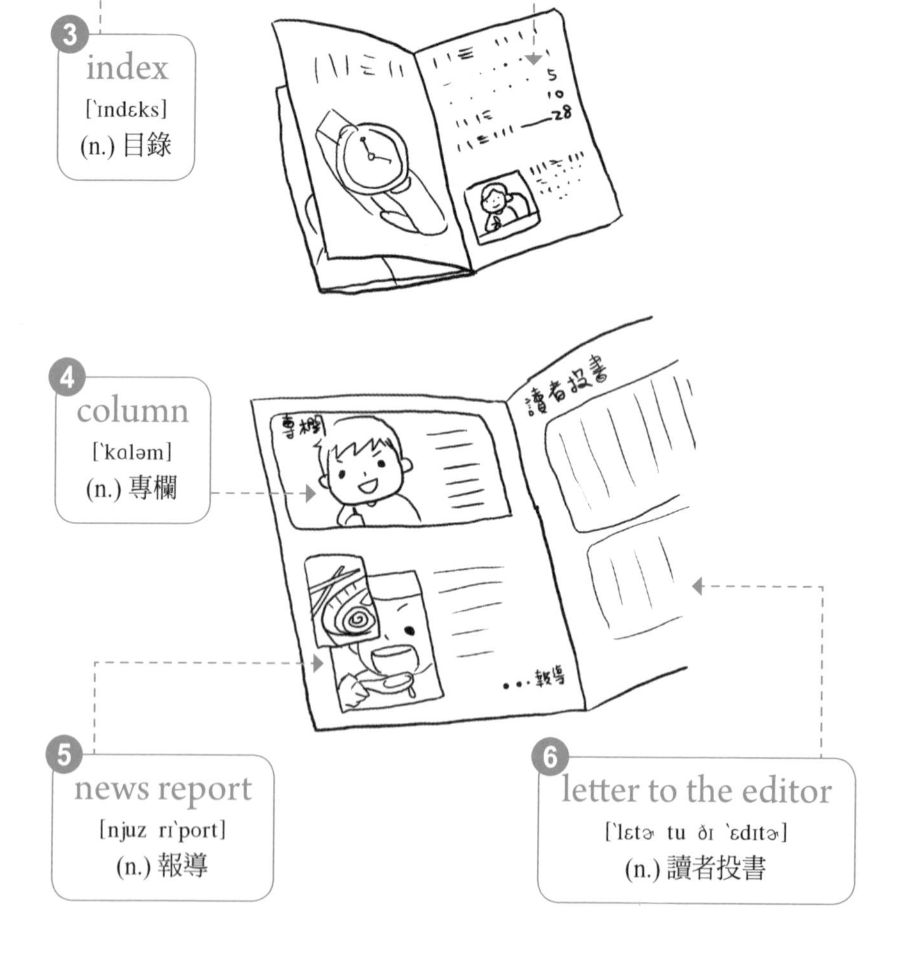

3. index [ˋɪndɛks] (n.) 目錄
4. column [ˋkɑləm] (n.) 專欄
5. news report [njuz rɪˋport] (n.) 報導
6. letter to the editor [ˋlɛtɚ tu ðɪ ˋɛdɪtɚ] (n.) 讀者投書

❶ 封面人物

The magazines that sell the most copies are those that have celebrity covers.

銷售最多本

❷ 本期主題 / 熱門話題

The sluggish global economy continues to be a current topic in most circles.

仍然是熱門話題

❸ 目錄

The index in a magazine is in the front, and lists the various articles inside.

在前面

❹ 專欄

I really enjoy reading my favorite sportswriter's column every week in *Sports Illustrated.*

❺ 報導

There was an in-depth news report on Whitney Houston's career in *Newsweek.*

深入的報導

❻ 讀者投書

The New York Times was flooded with letters to the editor from angry readers when they published an inaccurate report.

充滿⋯ 從生氣的讀者們

學更多

❶ magazine〈雜誌〉‧sell〈賣〉‧copy〈本〉‧celebrity〈名人〉‧cover〈封面〉

❷ sluggish〈蕭條的〉‧global〈全球的〉‧economy〈經濟〉‧continues〈持續〉‧current〈當前的〉‧circle〈圈子、範圍、界〉

❸ list〈把⋯編入目錄〉‧various〈各種各樣的〉‧article〈文章〉‧inside〈在裡面〉

❹ enjoy〈喜愛〉‧favorite〈特別喜愛的〉‧sportswriter〈體育專欄作者〉

❺ in-depth〈深入的〉‧career〈生涯〉

❻ flooded〈flood（充滿）的過去分詞〉‧letter〈信〉‧editor〈編輯〉‧published〈publish（刊登）的過去式〉‧inaccurate〈不正確的〉

中譯

❶ 銷售最好的雜誌，都是那些有封面人物的。

❷ 全球經濟蕭條仍是大多數圈子裡的熱門話題。

❸ 雜誌的目錄通常在前面幾頁，並列出雜誌內的各類文章。

❹ 我真的很喜歡閱讀我最喜歡的體育專欄作家每星期在 Sports Illustrated 的專欄。

❺ Newsweek 刊載了一篇關於 Whitney Houston 生涯的深入報導。

❻ 當紐約時報刊登了一篇不正確的報導，來自憤怒讀者的讀者投書，就如同雪片般飛來。

134 雜誌(2)

MP3 134

1. **next issue** [ˋnɛkst ˋɪʃju] (n.) 下期預告
2. **ad** [æd] (n.) 廣告
3. **magazine submission request** [ˌmægəˋzin sʌbˋmɪʃən rɪˋkwɛst] (n.) 徵稿啟事

4. **sweepstake** [ˋswipˌstek] (n.) 抽獎活動
5. **discount subscription** [ˋdɪskaʊnt səbˋskrɪpʃən] (n.) 訂購優惠
6. **winner's list** [ˋwɪnɚs lɪst] (n.) 中獎名單
7. **free gift / free giveaway** [fri gɪft] / [fri ˋgɪvəˌwe] (n.) 隨書贈品

兩個單字都是「隨書贈品」。

❶ 下期預告
In *Vogue*'s next issue, there will be a fashion spread of Jason Wu's clothes.
將有一個整版的時尚專題

❷ 廣告
Much of a magazine's profit comes from the ads.

❸ 徵稿啟事
Aspiring writers are often encouraged to send their stories in when
常常受到鼓勵
magazine submission requests are published in various publications.
被刊載在各種出版品上

❹ 抽獎活動
Magazine sweepstakes offer prizes like trips, jewelry and even cash awards.

❺ 訂購優惠
The Economist offered Tim a discount subscription to entice him to subscribe.
誘使他訂閱

❻ 中獎名單
Next month, *Elle* will print the winner's list from their sweepstakes this year.

❼ 隨書贈品
Many magazines offer free gifts to their readers.

學更多

❶ issue〈期〉‧fashion〈時尚〉‧spread〈整版〉‧clothes〈衣服〉
❷ magazine〈雜誌〉‧profit〈利潤〉‧come from〈來自〉
❸ aspiring〈有抱負的〉‧encouraged〈encourage（鼓勵）的過去分詞〉‧submission〈提交〉
❹ offer〈提供〉‧prize〈獎品〉‧trip〈旅行〉‧jewelry〈珠寶〉‧award〈獎品〉
❺ discount〈折扣〉‧subscription〈訂閱〉‧entice〈誘使〉‧subscribe〈訂閱〉
❻ month〈月〉‧print〈刊登〉‧winner〈獲勝的人〉‧list〈表〉
❼ many〈許多的〉‧free〈免費的〉‧gift〈禮物〉‧reader〈讀者〉‧giveaway〈贈品〉

中譯

❶ Vogue 雜誌的下期預告提到，將有整版的時尚專題介紹 Jason Wu 設計的衣服。
❷ 雜誌的利潤，大多來自廣告。
❸ 當徵稿啟事刊登在各種出版品上時，常會鼓舞有抱負的作家投稿他們的作品。
❹ 雜誌的抽獎活動會提供獎品，例如旅遊、珠寶、甚至於現金獎項。
❺ 經濟學人雜誌提供 Tim 訂購優惠，藉此吸引他訂閱。
❻ 下個月， Elle 雜誌會刊登今年抽獎活動的中獎名單。
❼ 許多雜誌會提供隨書贈品給讀者。

135 桌上型電腦

MP3 135

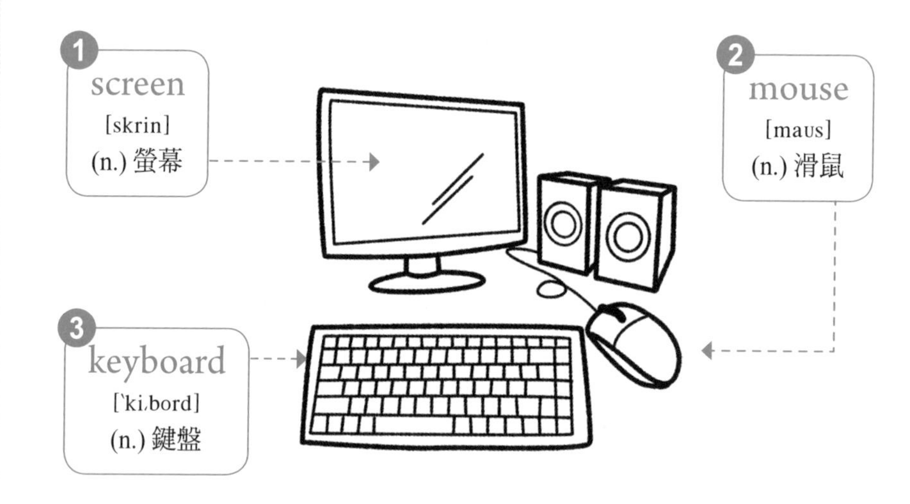

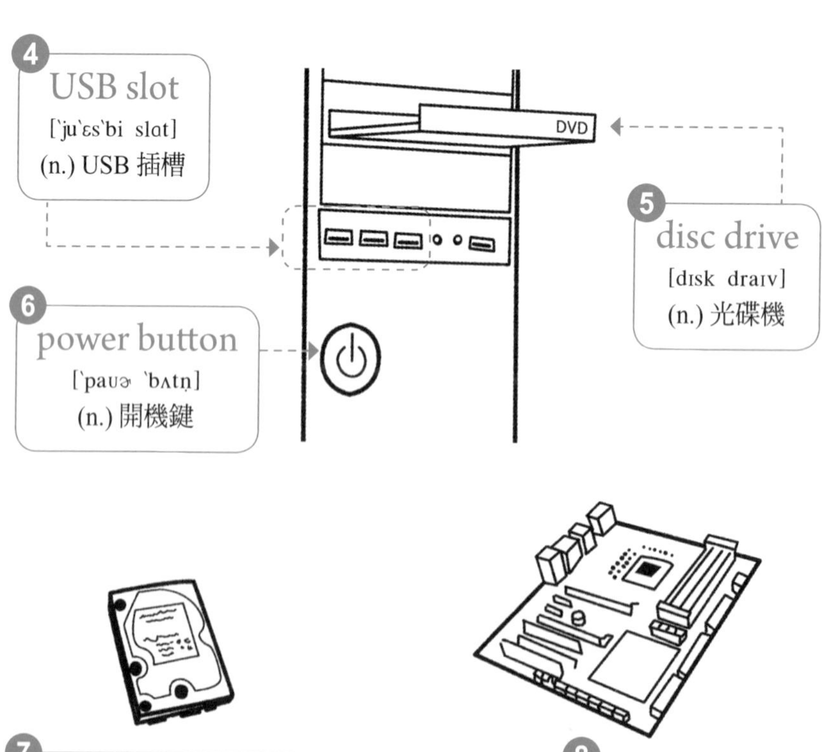

❶ 螢幕

The mini notebook computers come with screens that are 9 or 10 inches.

具備有

❷ 滑鼠

Wendy doesn't use a mouse with her laptop.

❸ 鍵盤

Darn it! There's a key that's stuck on my keyboard.

真討厭

❹ USB 插槽

How many USB slots does your computer have?

❺ 光碟機

My computer has a DVD disc drive that I watch movies on.

❻ 開機鍵

Use the power button to turn on your computer.

開啟你的電腦

❼ 硬碟

Johnny bought a new computer that had a huge hard disc drive for storage.

超大容量的硬碟

❽ 主機板

At the repair shop, they told me I'd ruined the motherboard with the soda I spilled all over my computer.

到處都是

學更多

❶ mini〈小型的〉・notebook computer〈筆記型電腦〉・inch〈吋〉
❷ use〈使用〉・laptop〈筆記型電腦〉
❸ key〈鍵〉・stuck〈stick（阻塞）的過去分詞〉
❹ slot〈狹縫〉・computer〈電腦〉
❺ disc〈磁盤〉・drive〈磁碟機〉・watch〈觀看〉・movie〈電影〉
❻ use〈用〉・power〈電力〉・button〈按鈕〉・turn on〈打開〉
❼ bought〈buy（買）的過去式〉・huge〈龐大的〉・storage〈儲存量〉
❽ repair〈修理〉・ruined〈ruin（毀壞）的過去分詞〉・spilled〈spill（濺出）的過去式〉

中譯

❶ 小筆電通常配備 9 或 10 吋的螢幕。
❷ Wendy 使用筆電時，不使用滑鼠。
❸ 討厭！我的鍵盤上有一個按鍵卡住了。
❹ 你的電腦有幾個 USB 插槽？
❺ 我的電腦有一個 DVD 光碟機，我可以用來觀賞電影。
❻ 用開機鍵開啟你的電腦。
❼ Johnny 買了一台配備超大容量硬碟的新電腦。
❽ 維修站的人員告訴我，被我打翻潑灑到電腦上的汽水，弄壞了主機板。

136 腳踏車(1)

MP3 136

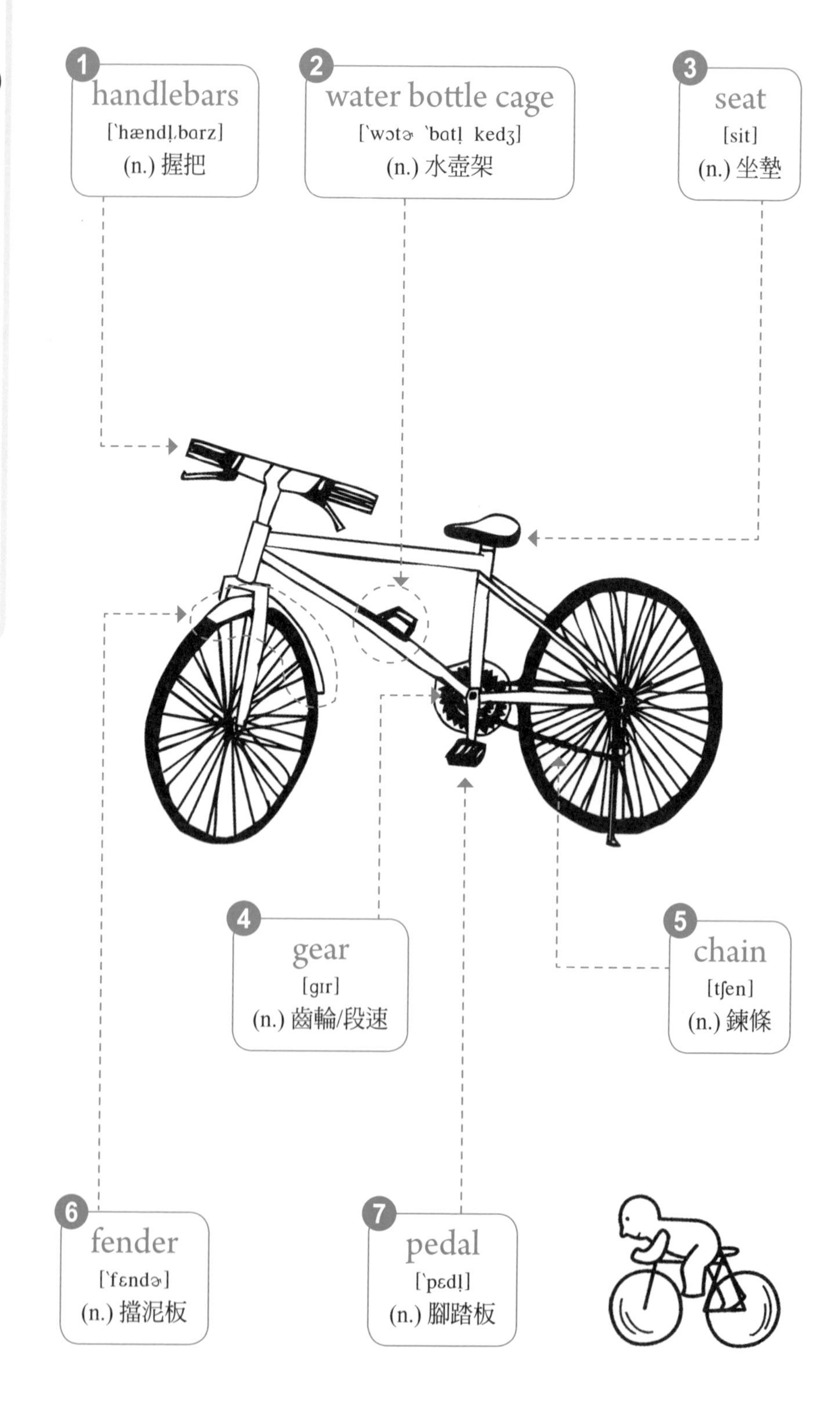

❶ 握把
While riding his bike, Steve let go of the handlebars to impress his girlfriend.
刻意放開握把

❷ 水壺架
A water bottle cage is a handy bike accessory.

❸ 坐墊
Let's buy this seat. It will be comfortable on long rides.
在長途騎乘時

❹ 齒輪 / 段速
I have a 10-speed bike which means it has 10 gears.

❺ 鍊條
Why does my bicycle chain keep falling off?
一直脫落

❻ 擋泥板
Roger had an accident on his bike and bent the fender.
騎他的腳踏車時出了意外

❼ 腳踏板
If you want to go faster, you need to step on the pedals.

學更多

❶ while〈當…的時候〉・riding〈ride（騎車）的 ing 型態〉・impress〈給…極深的印象〉
❷ bottle〈瓶子〉・cage〈籠子〉・handy〈便利的〉・accessory〈配件〉
❸ comfortable〈舒適的〉・long〈長的〉・ride〈乘車旅行〉
❹ speed〈變速裝置〉・mean〈意味著〉
❺ keep〈繼續不斷〉・falling off〈fall off（脫落）的 ing 型態〉
❻ accident〈意外〉・bent〈bend（折彎）的過去式〉
❼ faster〈比較快的，fast（快的）的比較級〉・step〈踩〉

中譯

❶ 為了給女友留下深刻印象，Steve 騎單車時刻意讓雙手放開握把。
❷ 水壺架是一個很方便的腳踏車配件。
❸ 我們買這個坐墊吧，長途騎乘時會比較舒服。
❹ 我有一部 10 段變速的腳踏車，這意味著它有 10 種段速。
❺ 為何我的腳踏車的鍊條一直脫落呢？
❻ Roger 騎腳踏車時出了意外，還撞彎了擋泥板。
❼ 如果你想加速，你需要踩腳踏板。

137 腳踏車(2)

MP3 137

❶ 電線桿
Many light poles were blown down when the typhoon came, causing a serious black out.
被吹倒

❷ 腳踏車鎖
A good bicycle lock is essential if you don't want your bike to be stolen.

❸ 停車腳架
Use the kickstand to keep your bike from falling over when you park it.
當你停放它時

❹ 輔助輪
When Katie was four, she rode a bike with training wheels.
在 Katie 4 歲的時候

❺ 車輪
Wow, the wheels on your bike are so tiny!

學更多

❶ light〈燈光〉・pole〈柱、桿〉・blown down〈blow down（吹倒）的過去分詞〉・typhoon〈颱風〉・causing〈cause（導致）的 ing 型態〉・serious〈嚴重的〉・black out〈斷電〉
❷ bicycle〈腳踏車〉・lock〈鎖〉・essential〈必要的〉・stolen〈steal（偷）的過去分詞〉
❸ keep A from B〈防止 A 免於 B〉・falling over〈fall over（倒下）的 ing 型態〉・park〈停放〉
❹ rode〈ride（騎車）的過去式〉・bike〈腳踏車〉・training〈訓練〉
❺ so〈多麼〉・tiny〈極小的〉

中譯

❶ 颱風來襲時許多電線桿被吹倒，造成嚴重的斷電。
❷ 如果你不希望腳踏車被偷，一個好的腳踏車鎖是必要的。
❸ 停車時，要使用停車腳架避免腳踏車倒下來。
❹ 在 Katie 4 歲時，她騎有輔助輪的腳踏車。
❺ 哇，你這台腳踏車的車輪好小喔！

138

汽車外觀(1)

MP3 138

❶ 後視鏡
Tom adjusted the rearview mirror before backing the car up.
在倒車之前

❷ 擋風玻璃
There are so many dead bugs on your windshield. You should clean it.

❸ 雨刷
Your windshield wipers need to be replaced.
需要被更換

❹ 引擎蓋
Lift up the hood and check the oil, please.
打開引擎蓋

❺ 保險桿
Hey! That guy just hit my back bumper.

❻ 大燈
It's dark. You should turn on your headlights!
天黑了

學更多

❶ adjusted〈adjust（調整）的過去式〉・rearview〈後視的〉・mirror〈鏡子〉・backing up〈back up（倒車）的 ing 型態〉
❷ dead〈死的〉・bug〈蟲子〉・clean〈弄乾淨〉
❸ wiper〈雨刷〉・need〈需要〉・replaced〈replace（更換）的過去分詞〉
❹ lift up〈舉起〉・check〈檢查〉・oil〈汽油〉
❺ guy〈傢伙〉・hit〈hit（碰撞）的過去式〉・back〈後面的〉
❻ dark〈暗的〉・should〈應該〉・turn on〈打開〉

中譯

❶ Tom 倒車前，先調整了後視鏡。
❷ 你的擋風玻璃上有很多死掉的蟲子，你應該把它清理乾淨。
❸ 你的雨刷需要換新了。
❹ 請打開引擎蓋，並檢查汽油。
❺ 嘿！那傢伙剛剛撞到了我的後保險桿。
❻ 天黑了。你應該打開你的大燈。

139
汽車外觀(2)

MP3 139

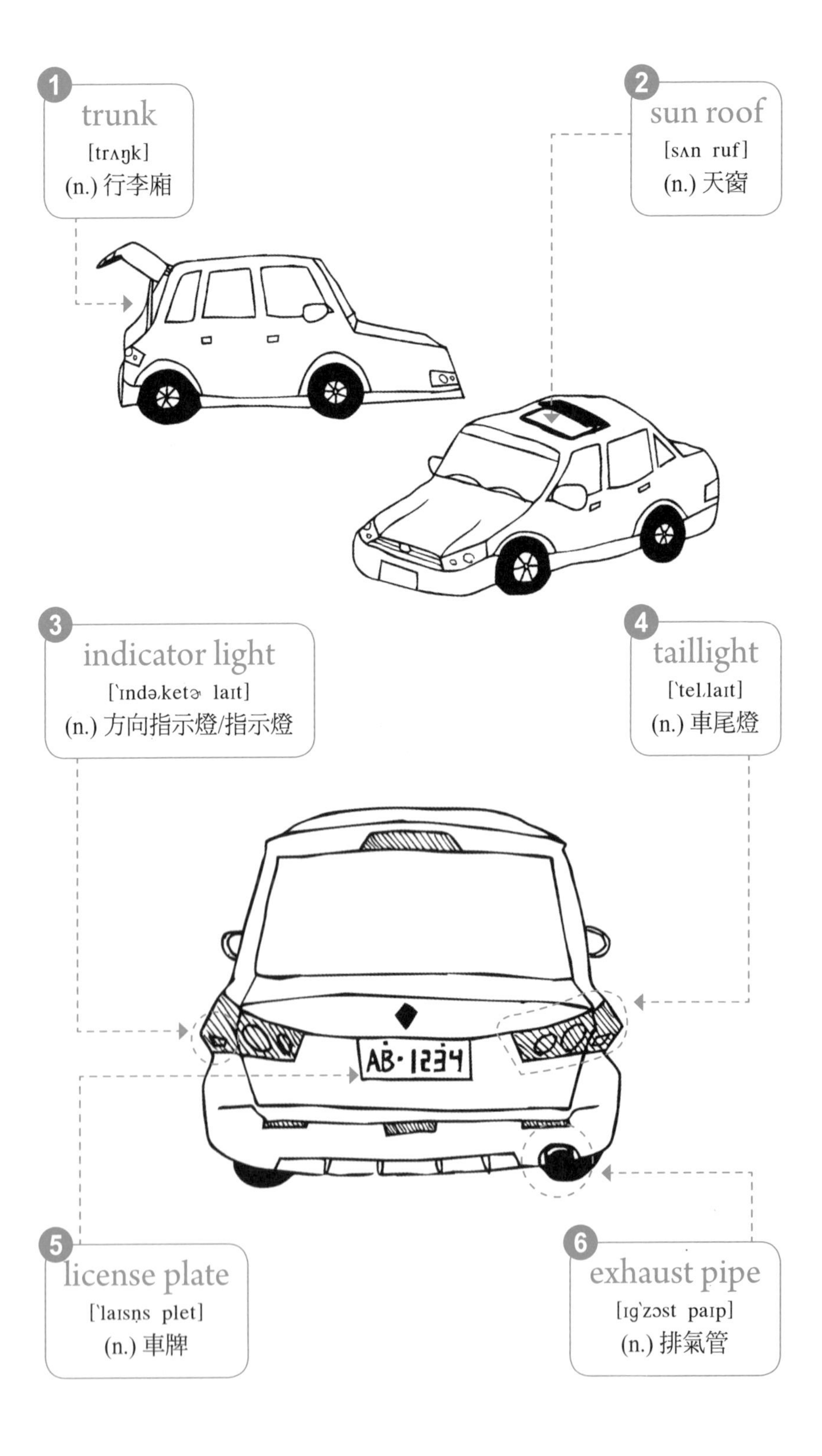

❶ 行李廂

Put the luggage in the trunk.

❷ 天窗

Jeff splurged and bought a car with a sun roof.

有天窗的汽車

❸ 方向指示燈 / 指示燈

The indicator light is on, so something must be wrong with the engine.

指示燈亮起了　一定出了問題

❹ 車尾燈

I'm sorry, officer, I was unaware that one of my taillights was broken.

我沒有察覺到

❺ 車牌

Hurry! Write down that guy's license plate number. He just robbed that bank.

❻ 排氣管

Lots of dirty exhaust is coming out of that lady's exhaust pipe.

骯髒的廢氣

學更多

❶ put〈放〉．luggage〈行李〉

❷ splurged〈splurge（揮霍）的過去式〉．bought〈buy（買）的過去式〉．roof〈車頂〉

❸ indicator〈指示器〉．light〈燈〉．wrong〈不正常的、出毛病的〉．engine〈引擎〉

❹ officer〈警官〉．unaware〈未察覺到的〉．broken〈損壞的〉

❺ hurry〈趕緊〉．write down〈把…寫下〉．guy〈傢伙〉．license〈牌照〉．plate〈車牌〉．robbed〈rob（搶劫）的過去式〉．bank〈銀行〉

❻ exhaust〈排出的氣〉．coming out〈come out（傳出來）的 ing 型態〉．pipe〈輸送管〉

中譯

❶ 把行李放進行李廂。

❷ Jeff 揮霍了一回，買了一輛有天窗的車。

❸ 指示燈亮了，這表示引擎一定出了問題。

❹ 對不起，警官，我不知道我有一個車尾燈壞了。

❺ 快點！把那傢伙的車牌號碼記下來。他剛剛搶劫銀行。

❻ 許多髒廢氣正從那位女士的排氣管裡排出來。

140 飛機

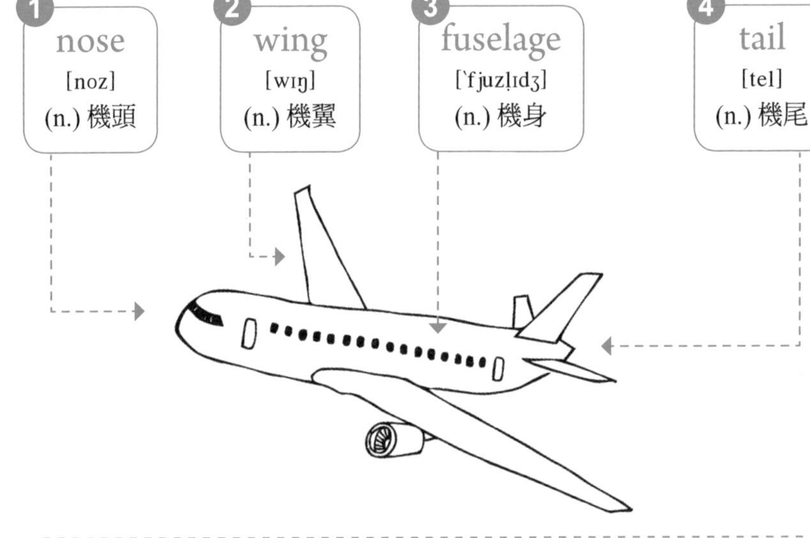

1. **nose** [noz] (n.) 機頭
2. **wing** [wɪŋ] (n.) 機翼
3. **fuselage** [`fjuzḷɪdʒ] (n.) 機身
4. **tail** [tel] (n.) 機尾

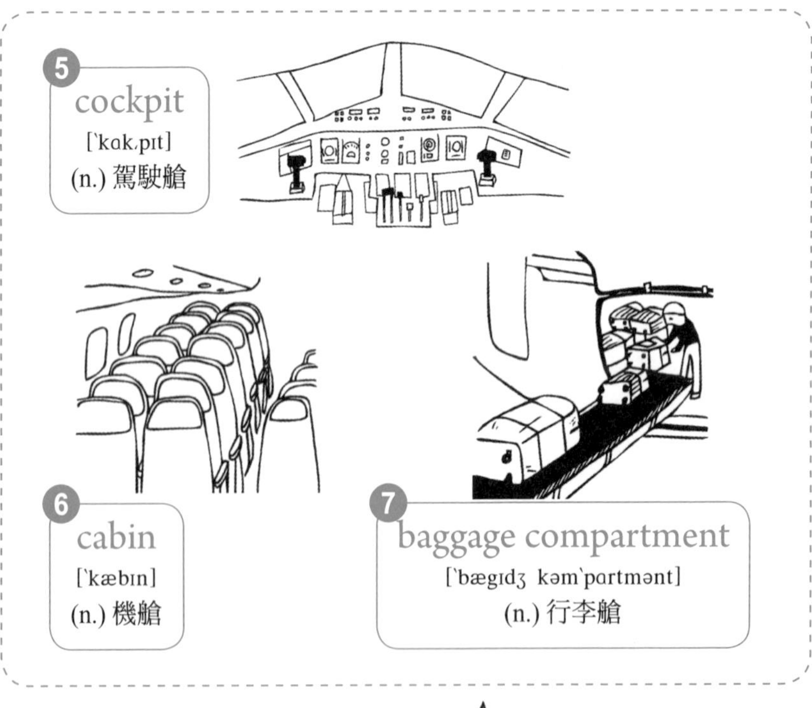

5. **cockpit** [`kɑk͵pɪt] (n.) 駕駛艙
6. **cabin** [`kæbɪn] (n.) 機艙
7. **baggage compartment** [`bægɪdʒ kəm`pɑrtmənt] (n.) 行李艙

8. **landing gear** [`lændɪŋ gɪr] (n.) 起落架

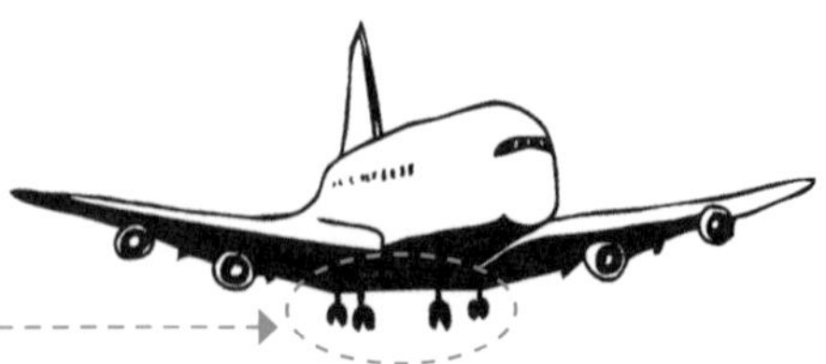

MP3 140

❶ 機頭

As a plane takes off, its nose is pointed upward.

它的機頭會被朝向上方

❷ 機翼

Danny walked out onto the wings of the plane to do some repair work.

❸ 機身

After the plane crashed, rescuers found the fuselage in several pieces.

發現機身斷成好幾節

❹ 機尾

Investigators determined that the crash was due to a missing piece on the tail.

由於

❺ 駕駛艙

The cockpit contains the controls to fly the plane.

❻ 機艙

The most comfortable seat in the plane's cabin is always in 1st class.

在頭等艙

❼ 行李艙

If you check in your luggage at the airport, the airline will put it in the plane's baggage compartment.

把你的行李辦理託運

❽ 起落架

The pilot put the landing gear down as he prepared to land the plane.

當他準備降落飛機時

學更多

❶ as〈當…時〉・take off〈起飛〉・pointed〈point（指向）的過去分詞〉・upward〈向上〉
❷ walked out〈walk out（走出去）的過去式〉・repair〈維修〉・work〈工作〉
❸ crashed〈crash（墜毀）的過去式〉・rescuer〈援救者〉・several〈數個的〉
❹ investigator〈調查員〉・determined〈determine（判定）的過去式〉・missing〈缺掉的〉
❺ contain〈包含〉・control〈操控裝置〉・fly〈駕駛飛機〉・plane〈飛機〉
❻ comfortable〈舒適的〉・seat〈座位〉・always〈總是〉・class〈等級〉
❼ check in〈到達並登記〉・airport〈機場〉・airline〈航空公司〉・compartment〈艙〉
❽ pilot〈駕駛員〉・gear〈裝置〉・put down〈put down（放下）的過去式〉・land〈降落〉

中譯

❶ 當飛機起飛時，機頭會朝上。
❷ Danny 走到機翼上，做些維修的工作。
❸ 飛機墜毀後，搜救人員發現機身斷成好幾節。
❹ 調查員研判墜機原因是機尾少了一塊。
❺ 駕駛艙裡有駕駛飛機的操控裝置。
❻ 機艙內最舒服的座位，永遠都在頭等艙。
❼ 如果你在機場辦理行李託運，航空公司會將你的行李放進飛機的行李艙。
❽ 準備降落時，駕駛員放下了飛機的起落架。

141 機車(1)

MP3 141

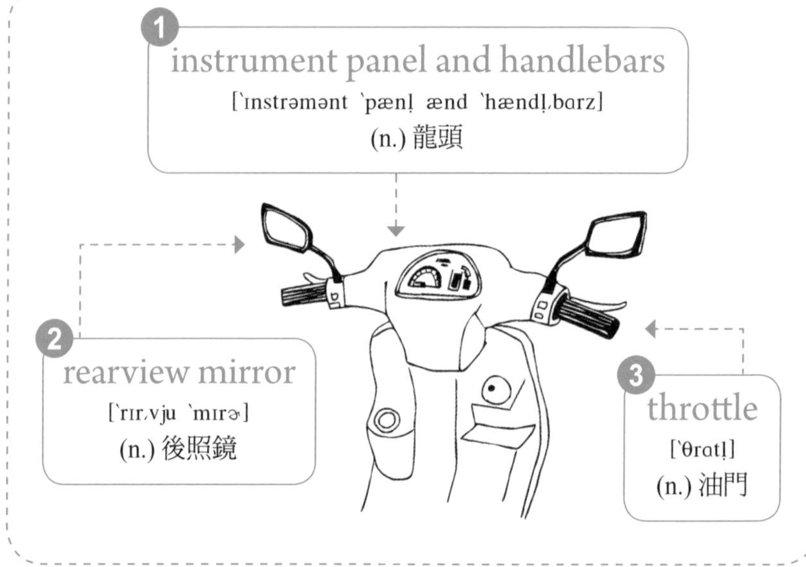

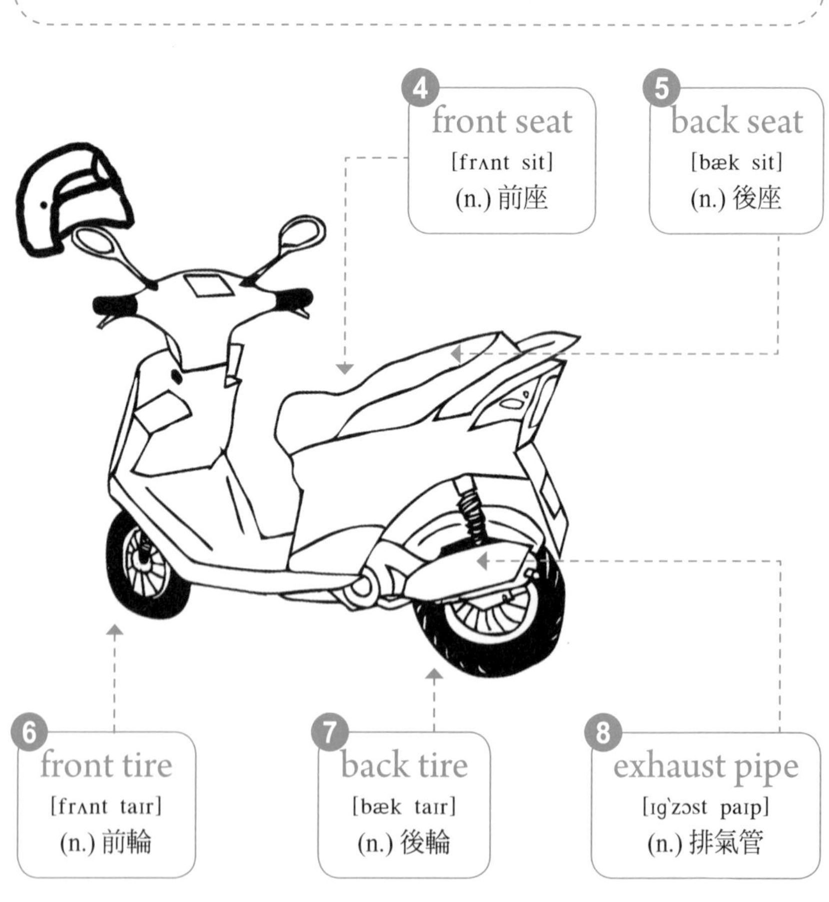

❶ 龍頭

Motor scooters have an instrument panel and handlebars at the front of the bike.

儀表板　在機車的前面

❷ 後照鏡

On his way to a hot date, Logan checked his hair in his rearview mirror.

在他去一個重要約會的途中

❸ 油門

Where is the throttle located on a motorcycle?

❹ 前座

❺ 後座

Jason takes his girlfriend to work on his motorcycle. He sits on the front seat, and she sits on the back seat.

帶他女朋友去上班

❻ 前輪

❼ 後輪

After checking the front tire and back tire for air, Jack paid for his gas and rode away.

付了他的油錢

❽ 排氣管

You'd better check your exhaust pipe. It looks cracked.

你最好…（＝ You had better）

學更多

❶ motor scooter〈速克達，腳可以放在前方平台的機車〉‧bike〈機車〉

❷ hot〈火熱的〉‧date〈約會〉‧hair〈頭髮〉‧rearview〈後視的〉

❸ located〈位於的〉‧motorcycle〈騎車時腳放在兩側的機車〉

❹❺ girlfriend〈女朋友〉‧sit〈坐〉‧front〈前面的〉‧seat〈座位〉‧back〈後面的〉

❻❼ checking〈check（檢查）的 ing 型態〉‧tire〈輪胎〉‧air〈空氣〉‧paid〈pay（支付）的過去式〉‧rode〈ride（騎車）的過去式〉‧away〈離開〉

❽ exhaust〈排氣裝置〉‧pipe〈輸送管〉‧cracked〈破裂的〉

中譯

❶ 速克達機車的前面有一個龍頭。

❷ 在前往一個重要約會的途中， Logan 用後照鏡檢查自己的髮型。

❸ 機車的油門位在哪裡？

❹❺ Jason 騎機車載女朋友去上班。他坐前座，女朋友坐後座。

❻❼ 檢查完前輪和後輪的含氣量之後， Jack 付了油錢，然後把車騎走了。

❽ 你最好檢查一下排氣管，它看起來好像裂開了。

142 機車(2)

MP3 142

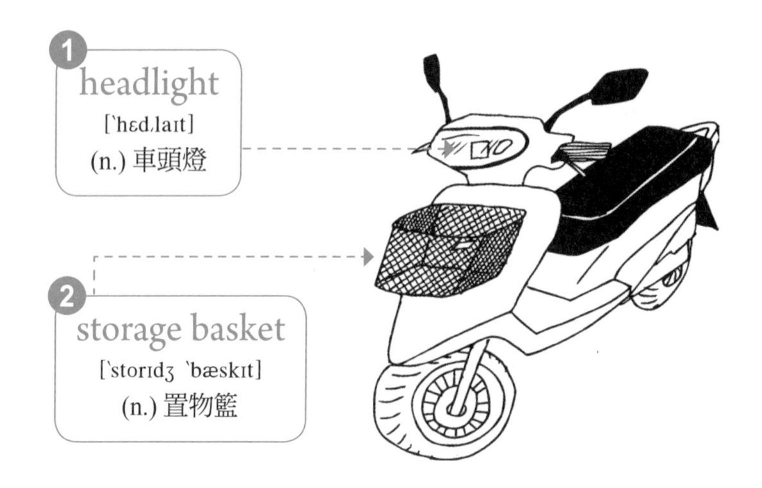

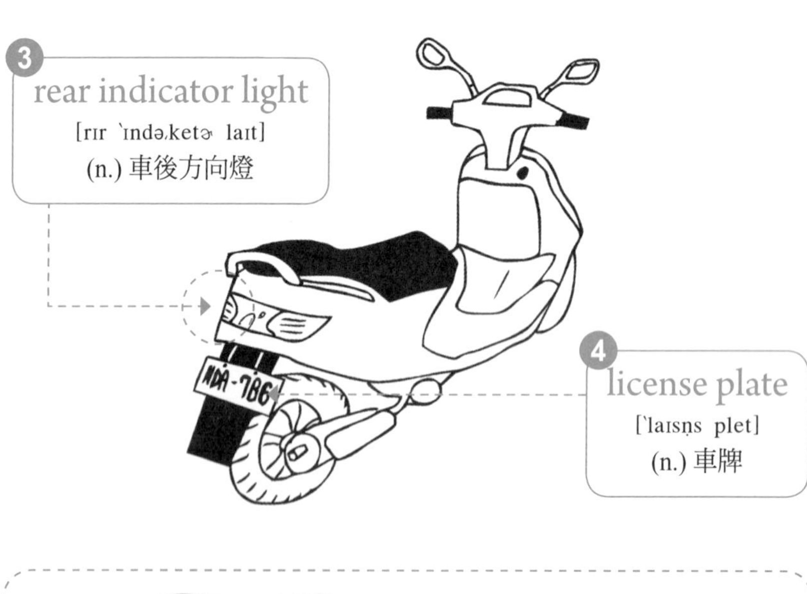

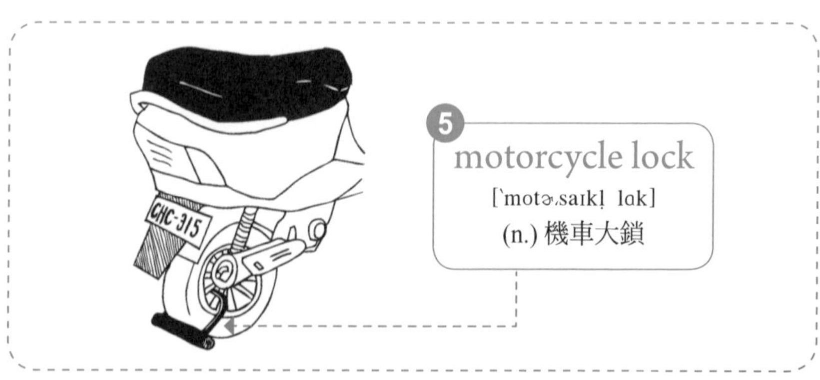

❶ 車頭燈

This road is really dark; turn on your headlights.

實在是很暗

❷ 置物籃

Isn't it convenient having this storage basket to carry things around?

帶著東西到處走

❸ 車後方向燈

The police officer issued the man a ticket because his rear indicator lights were out.

開給那個男人一張罰單　他的車後方向燈不亮

❹ 車牌

The police caught the thief by using his license plate number.

❺ 機車大鎖

Make sure your motorcycle lock is secure before walking away.

機車大鎖有鎖好

學更多

❶ road〈路〉・really〈很〉・dark〈暗的〉・turn on〈打開〉

❷ convenient〈方便的〉・storage〈貯藏〉・basket〈籃子〉・carry〈攜帶〉・around〈到處〉

❸ police officer〈警察〉・issued〈issue（發給）的過去式〉・ticket〈罰單〉・rear〈後面的〉・indicator light〈指示燈〉・out〈熄滅〉

❹ caught〈catch（逮捕）的過去式〉・thief〈小偷〉・license〈牌照〉・plate〈車牌〉

❺ make sure〈確定〉・lock〈鎖〉・secure〈牢固的〉・before〈在…之前〉・walking〈walk（走）的 ing 型態〉・away〈離開〉

中譯

❶ 這條路好暗，打開你的車頭燈。

❷ 有這個置物籃可以裝著東西到處走，不是很方便嗎？

❸ 警察開了一張罰單給那個男人，因為他的車後方向燈不亮了。

❹ 警方利用小偷的車牌號碼逮到他。

❺ 離開前，要確認你的機車大鎖有鎖好。

143 手機(1)

MP3 143

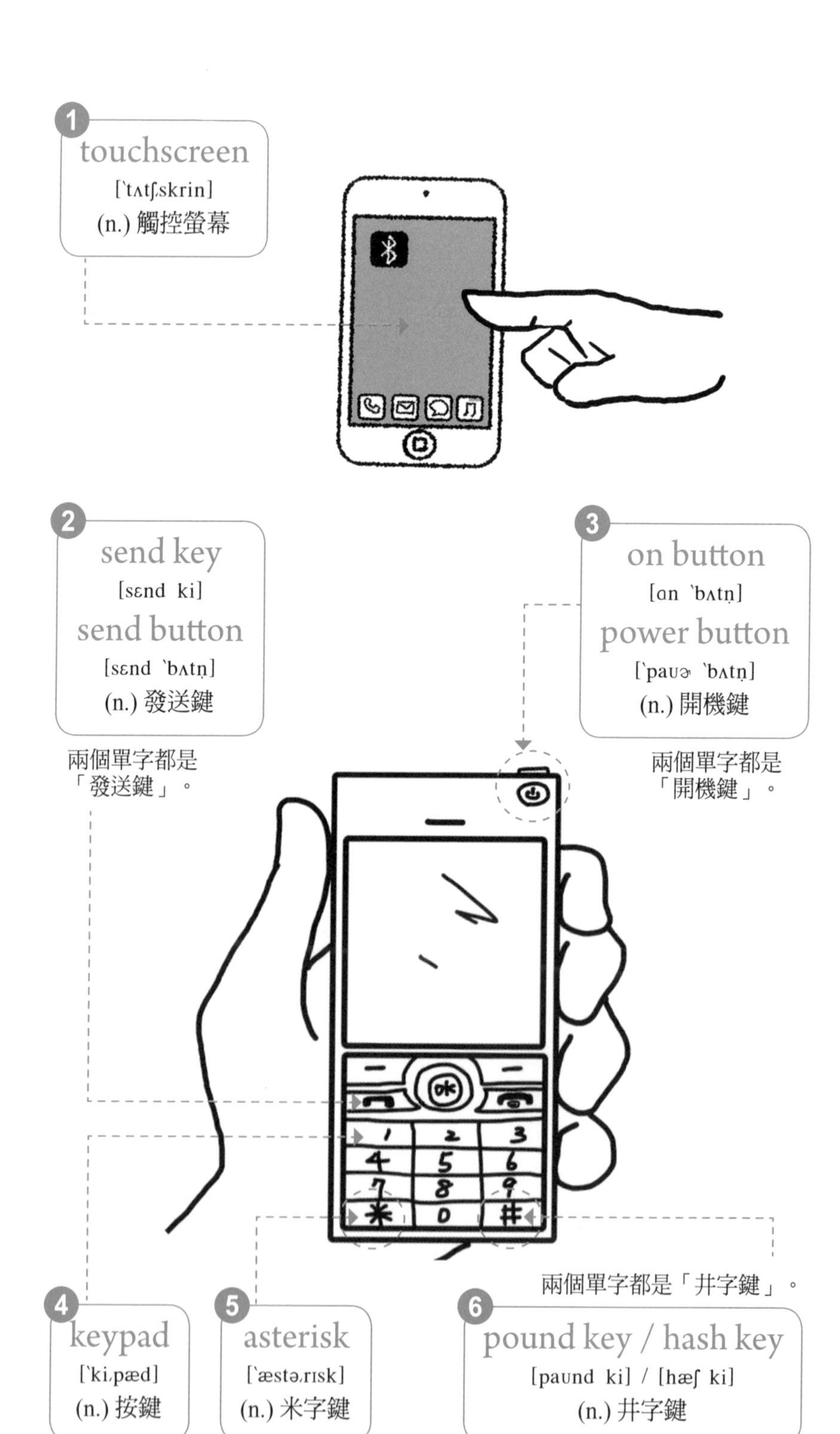

❶ 觸控螢幕

Smartphones today all have touchscreens which means you can use your fingers to interact with it instead of a stylus or keyboard.

你可以用你的手指和觸控螢幕互動

❷ 發送鍵

Once you dial the number, just press the send key.

一旦你按好號碼

❸ 開機鍵

Use the on button to turn on your phone.

❹ 按鍵

The keypad on cell phones can be used to either dial a number or send a text message.

打電話

❺ 米字鍵

I press the asterisk button when I need to add a symbol to my text message.

在我的簡訊裡加上符號

❻ 井字鍵

Sometimes, callers are asked to press the pound key when they are listening to recorded messages.

他們正在聽語音訊息

學更多

❶ smartphone〈智慧型手機〉・mean〈意味著〉・finger〈手指〉・interact〈互動〉・instead of〈代替〉・stylus〈觸控筆〉・keyboard〈鍵盤〉
❷ once〈一旦〉・dial〈打電話〉・press〈按〉・send〈發送〉・key〈按鍵〉
❸ use〈使用〉・button〈按鈕〉・turn on〈打開〉・phone〈電話〉
❹ cell phone〈手機〉・used〈use（使用）的過去分詞〉・either...or...〈不是…就是…〉
❺ add〈加〉・symbol〈符號〉・text message〈簡訊〉
❻ sometimes〈有時〉・asked〈ask（要求）的過去分詞〉・recorded message〈語音訊息〉

中譯

❶ 現今的智慧型手機都具備觸控螢幕，這表示你不需要觸控筆或鍵盤，用手指就能和螢幕互動。
❷ 當你輸入好電話號碼，按下發送鍵即可。
❸ 用開機鍵開啟你的手機。
❹ 手機上的按鍵，可以用來打電話或發送簡訊。
❺ 當我需要在簡訊裡加入符號時，我會按下米字鍵。
❻ 有時候，在聽語音訊息時，撥打者會被要求按下井字鍵。

144
手機(2)

MP3 144

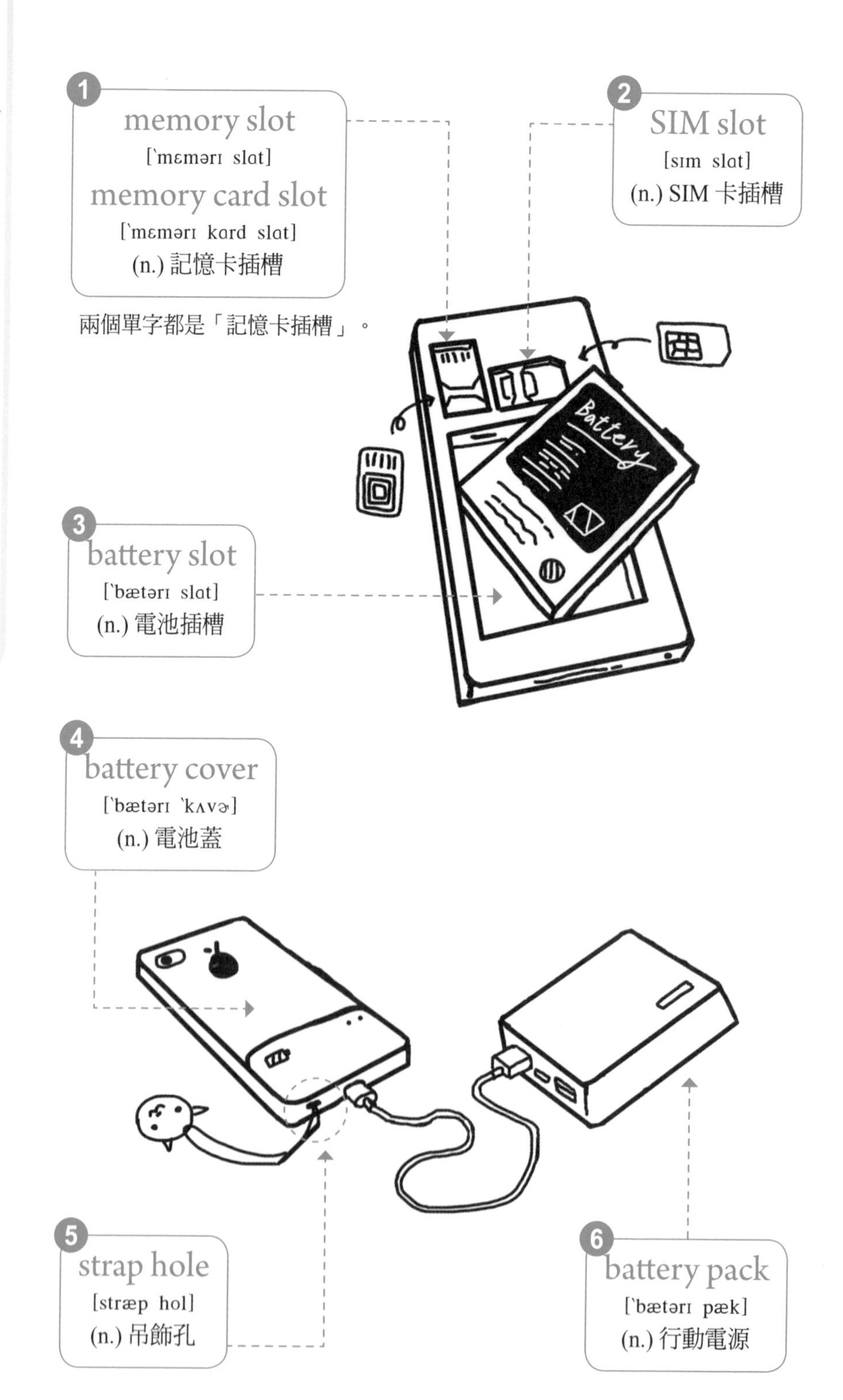
1 memory slot
[ˋmɛmərɪ slɑt]
memory card slot
[ˋmɛmərɪ kɑrd slɑt]
(n.) 記憶卡插槽
兩個單字都是「記憶卡插槽」。
2 SIM slot
[sɪm slɑt]
(n.) SIM 卡插槽
Battery
3 battery slot
[ˋbætərɪ slɑt]
(n.) 電池插槽
4 battery cover
[ˋbætərɪ ˋkʌvɚ]
(n.) 電池蓋
5 strap hole
[stræp hol]
(n.) 吊飾孔
6 battery pack
[ˋbætərɪ pæk]
(n.) 行動電源

❶ 記憶卡插槽

If you want more memory, just buy a new memory card and put it in the memory slot.

❷ SIM 卡插槽

After buying a new cell phone, Alice inserted her previous SIM card into the SIM slot.

之前的 SIM 卡

❸ 電池插槽

Batteries for mobile phones are set inside the battery slot.

手機

❹ 電池蓋

When I dropped my cell phone, the battery cover flew off and broke.

❺ 吊飾孔

Mary bought a cute strap for her cell and attached it using the strap hole.

利用吊飾孔把它裝上去

❻ 行動電源

I always carry my battery pack with me when I travel for extra power.

作為額外的電源

學更多

❶ more〈更多的〉‧memory〈記憶體〉‧put〈放〉‧slot〈狹縫〉

❷ after〈在…之後〉‧inserted〈insert（插入）的過去式〉‧previous〈以前的〉

❸ battery〈電池〉‧mobile〈移動的〉‧set〈set（安裝）的過去分詞〉‧inside〈在裡面〉

❹ dropped〈drop（掉下）的過去式〉‧flew off〈fly off（脫落）的過去式〉‧broke〈break（破裂）的過去式〉

❺ bought〈buy（買）的過去式〉‧strap〈吊飾〉‧attached〈attach（裝上）的過去式〉

❻ carry〈攜帶〉‧travel〈旅行〉‧extra〈額外的〉‧power〈電力〉

中譯

❶ 如果你需要更多記憶體，只要買一張新的記憶卡，並放入記憶卡插槽即可。

❷ 買了新手機之後，Alice 就將她之前的 SIM 卡插入 SIM 卡插槽。

❸ 手機的電池都裝在電池插槽裡。

❹ 當我摔落手機時，電池蓋不但脫落還裂開了。

❺ Mary 為她的手機買了一個可愛的吊飾，並把它穿進吊飾孔。

❻ 當我出遊時，我都會攜帶行動電源作為備用。

145 相機外觀(1)

MP3 145

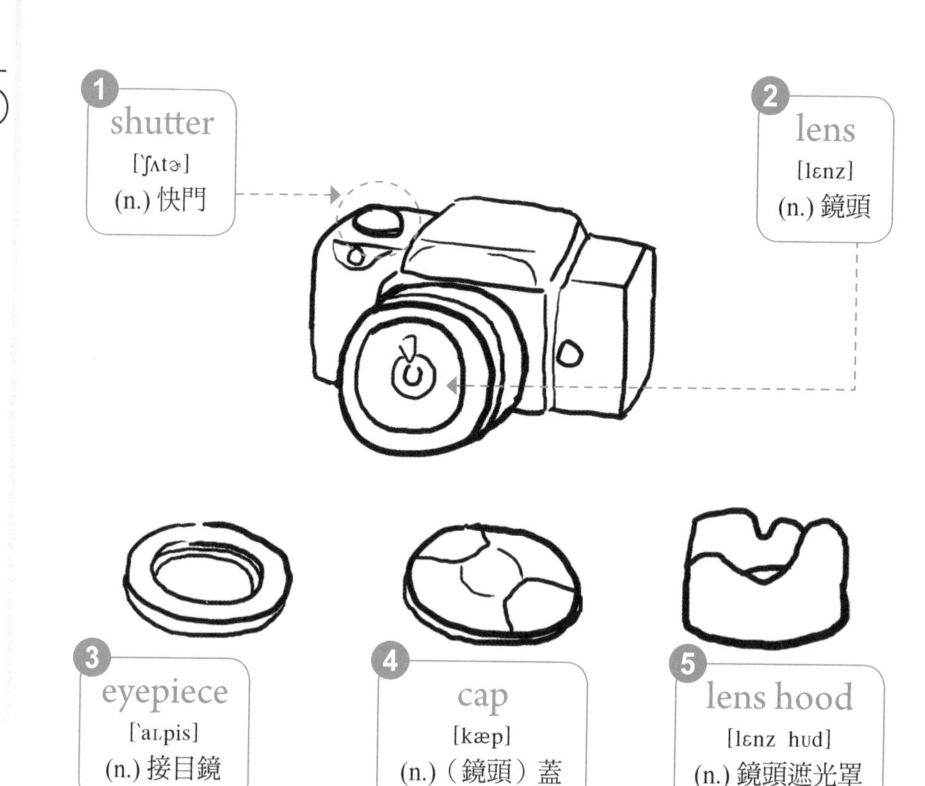

透過調整焦距，達到放大影像的功能。

套在照相機鏡頭前，用來阻擋多餘的光線。

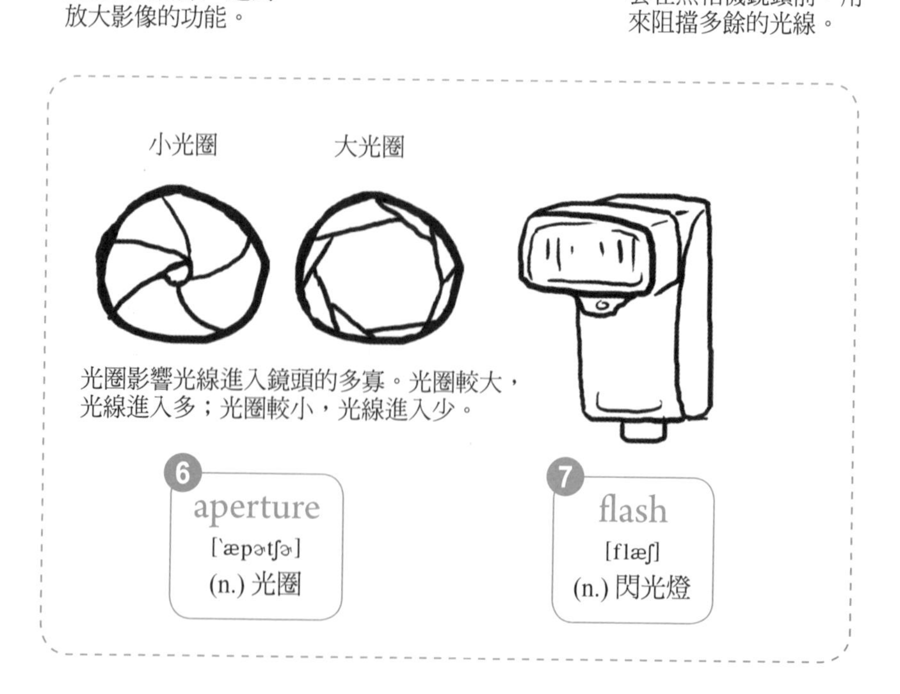

❶ 快門

A slower shutter speed is very important in low light.

在低光源環境下

❷ 鏡頭

Most professional photographers invest a lot of money in different camera lenses.

耗費許多錢

❸ 接目鏡

The eyepiece is the device used for looking through a camera.

透過相機

❹（鏡頭）蓋

What happened to the cap on my lens? It's gone!

我的鏡頭蓋

❺ 鏡頭遮光罩

A lens hood is used to prevent glare from ruining a photo.

防止強光毀壞相片

❻ 光圈

The aperture on a camera is an opening where the light passes through.

光線通過

❼ 閃光燈

This room's too dark for a photo without a flash.

沒有閃光燈

學更多

❶ slower〈比較慢的，slow（慢的）的比較級〉・speed〈速度〉・important〈重要的〉
❷ professional〈職業的〉・photographer〈攝影師〉・invest〈耗費〉・different〈不同的〉
❸ device〈裝置〉・through〈憑藉〉・camera〈相機〉
❹ happened〈happen（發生）的過去式〉・gone〈遺失了的〉
❺ hood〈蓋子〉・prevent〈防止〉・glare〈強光〉・ruining〈ruin（毀壞）的 ing 型態〉
❻ opening〈孔〉・light〈光線〉・pass through〈通過〉
❼ dark〈暗的〉・photo〈照片〉・without〈沒有〉

中譯

❶ 在低光源環境下，使用較慢的快門速度是很重要的。
❷ 大多數的專業攝影師，會花大筆錢購買不同的相機鏡頭。
❸ 接目鏡是透過相機觀看景物的裝置。
❹ 我的鏡頭蓋怎麼了？它不見了！
❺ 鏡頭遮光罩用來防止強光影響相片品質。
❻ 相機上的光圈，是光線通過的洞孔。
❼ 這個房間太暗了，沒有閃光燈就不好拍照。

146 相機外觀(2)

MP3 146

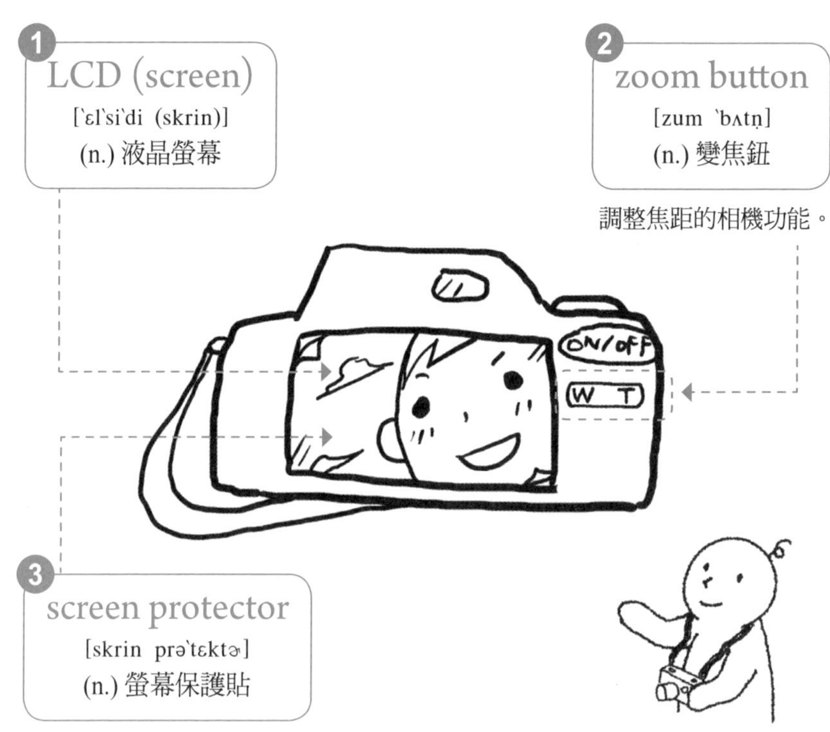

1 **LCD (screen)**
[ˋɛlˋsiˋdi (skrin)]
(n.) 液晶螢幕

2 **zoom button**
[zum ˋbʌtn̩]
(n.) 變焦鈕

調整焦距的相機功能。

3 **screen protector**
[skrin prəˋtɛktɚ]
(n.) 螢幕保護貼

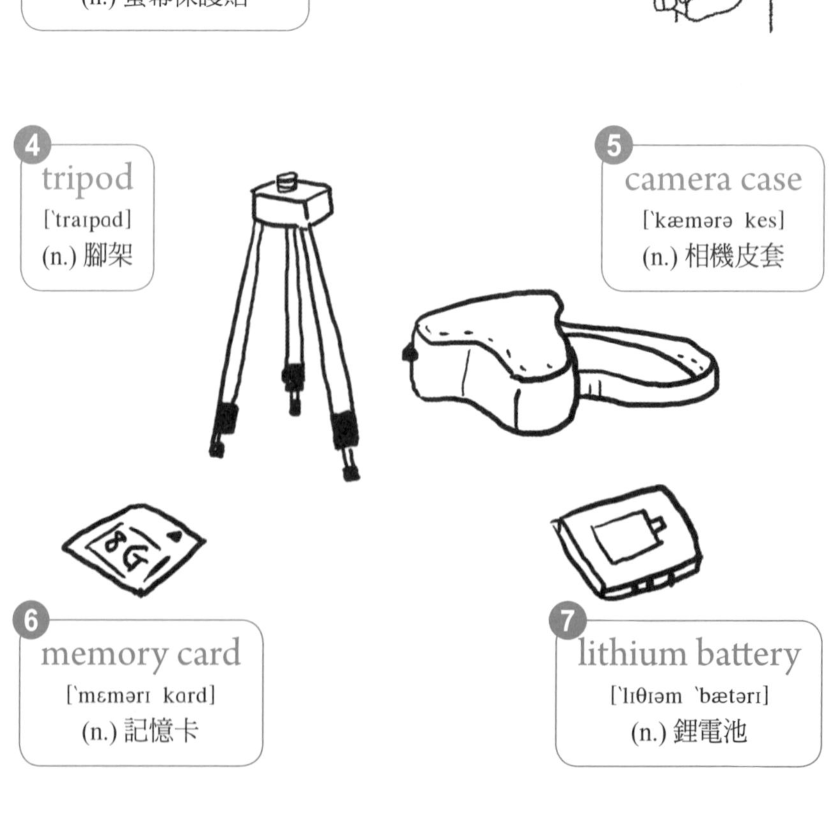

4 **tripod**
[ˋtraɪpɑd]
(n.) 腳架

5 **camera case**
[ˋkæmərə kes]
(n.) 相機皮套

6 **memory card**
[ˋmɛmərɪ kɑrd]
(n.) 記憶卡

7 **lithium battery**
[ˋlɪθɪəm ˋbætərɪ]
(n.) 鋰電池

❶ 液晶螢幕

LCD stands for liquid crystal display.
液晶顯示器

❷ 變焦鈕

Push the zoom button to get a closer shot.
拍近照

❸ 螢幕保護貼

I need to get a screen protector while we're out shopping today.
當我們出去購物時

❹ 腳架

A tripod will hold your camera still.
保持你的相機靜止不動

❺ 相機皮套

Oliver's camera case is the perfect size, isn't it?

❻ 記憶卡

Tim needs to buy a new memory card for his camera.

❼ 鋰電池

Most portable consumer products use rechargeable lithium batteries
消費品
like cell phones, laptops and MP3 players.

學更多

❶ stand for〈代表〉‧liquid〈液體〉‧crystal〈結晶體〉‧display〈顯示〉
❷ zoom〈將畫面拉近或拉遠〉‧closer〈比較近的，close（近的）的比較級〉‧shot〈照片〉
❸ get〈買〉‧screen〈螢幕〉‧protector〈保護裝置〉‧out〈出外〉
❹ hold〈保持〉‧camera〈照相機〉‧still〈不動的〉
❺ case〈套〉‧perfect〈理想的〉‧size〈大小〉
❻ need〈需要〉‧buy〈買〉‧new〈新的〉‧memory〈記憶體〉
❼ portable〈便於攜帶的〉‧rechargeable〈可再充電的〉‧lithium〈鋰〉

中譯

❶「LCD」表示液晶顯示器。
❷ 想要拍近照，就按變焦鈕。
❸ 今天我們出去購物時，我需要買個螢幕保護貼。
❹ 腳架可以固定你的相機。
❺ Oliver 的相機皮套大小恰到好處，對吧？
❻ Tim 需要幫他的相機買一張新的記憶卡。
❼ 大部分的可攜式消費品都使用可充電的鋰電池，如手機、筆電、以及 MP3 播放器。

147 建築物(1)

MP3 147

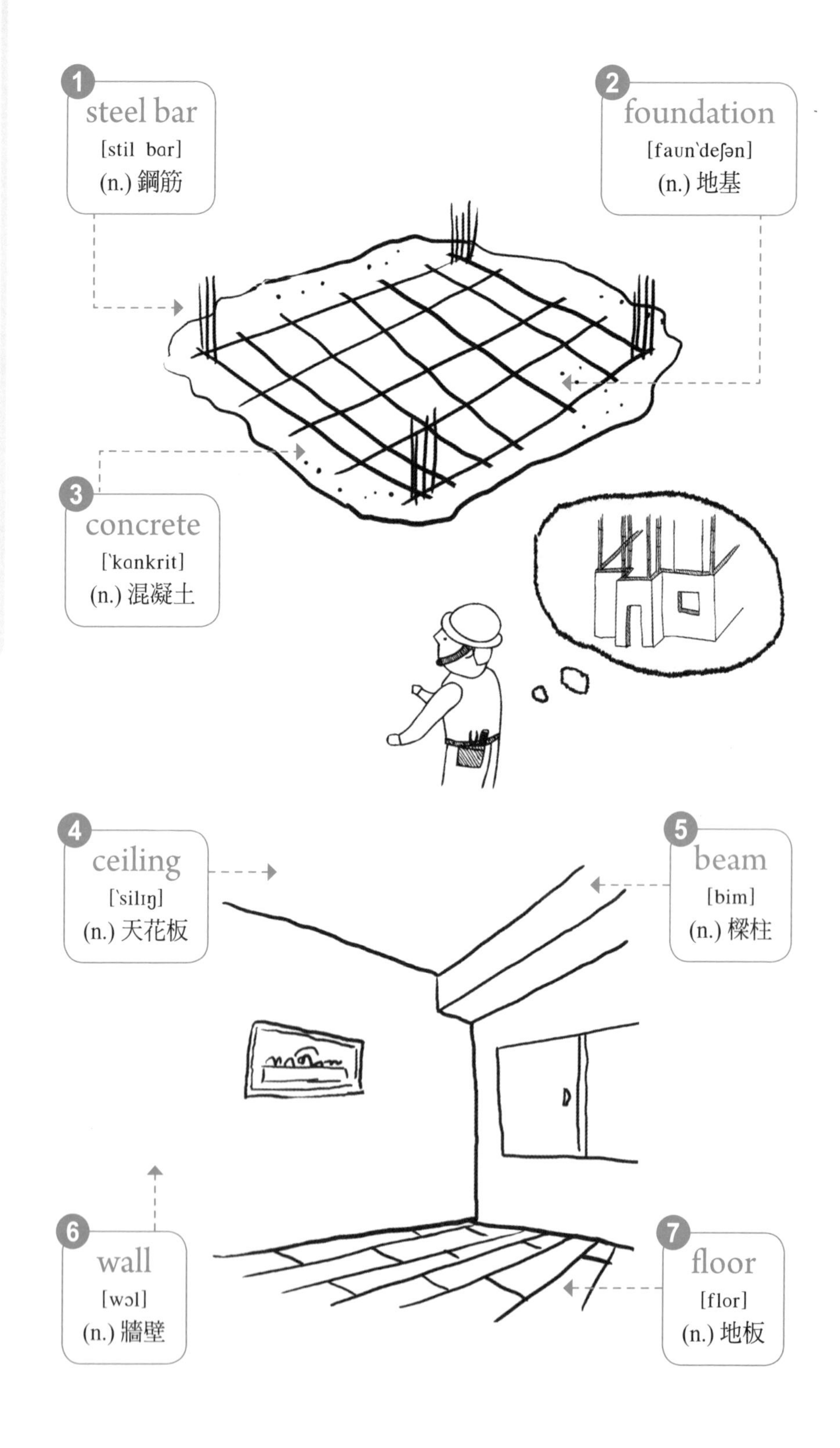

❶ 鋼筋
Steel bars are used to construct strong buildings.
被用來

❷ 地基
All buildings need solid foundations before walls can be constructed.
在牆壁可以被建造之前

❸ 混凝土
The construction workers poured the concrete today for the new floor.
作為新的樓層

❹ 天花板
High ceilings are very popular in New York City apartments.
在…非常流行

❺ 樑柱
The workers are using wooden beams to construct the roof.

❻ 牆壁
My dream house has all glass walls. Of course, I couldn't have any neighbors nearby!
當然

❼ 地板
Wayne doesn't have a bed yet; he just sleeps on the floor.
還沒有一張床

學更多

❶ steel〈鋼〉・bar〈條狀物〉・construct〈建造〉・strong〈堅固的〉・building〈建築物〉
❷ all〈所有的〉・solid〈堅固的〉・constructed〈construct（建造）的過去分詞〉
❸ construction〈建造〉・worker〈工人〉・poured〈pour（倒）的過去式〉・floor〈樓層〉
❹ high〈高的〉・popular〈流行的〉・apartment〈公寓〉
❺ using〈use（使用）的 ing 型態〉・wooden〈木製的〉・roof〈屋頂〉
❻ dream〈理想的〉・glass〈玻璃〉・neighbor〈鄰居〉・nearby〈在附近〉
❼ bed〈床〉・yet〈還〉・sleep〈睡〉

中譯

❶ 鋼筋被用來建造堅固的建築物。
❷ 所有的建築物在可以建造牆壁之前，都需要有堅固的地基。
❸ 今天建築工人灌入了混凝土，建造新的樓層。
❹ 紐約市的公寓非常流行採用挑高的天花板。
❺ 工人正使用木頭的樑柱建造屋頂。
❻ 我夢想中的房子擁有整面的玻璃牆。當然，我附近不能有任何鄰居！
❼ Wayne 還沒有床舖，他直接睡在地板上。

148

建築物(2)

MP3 148

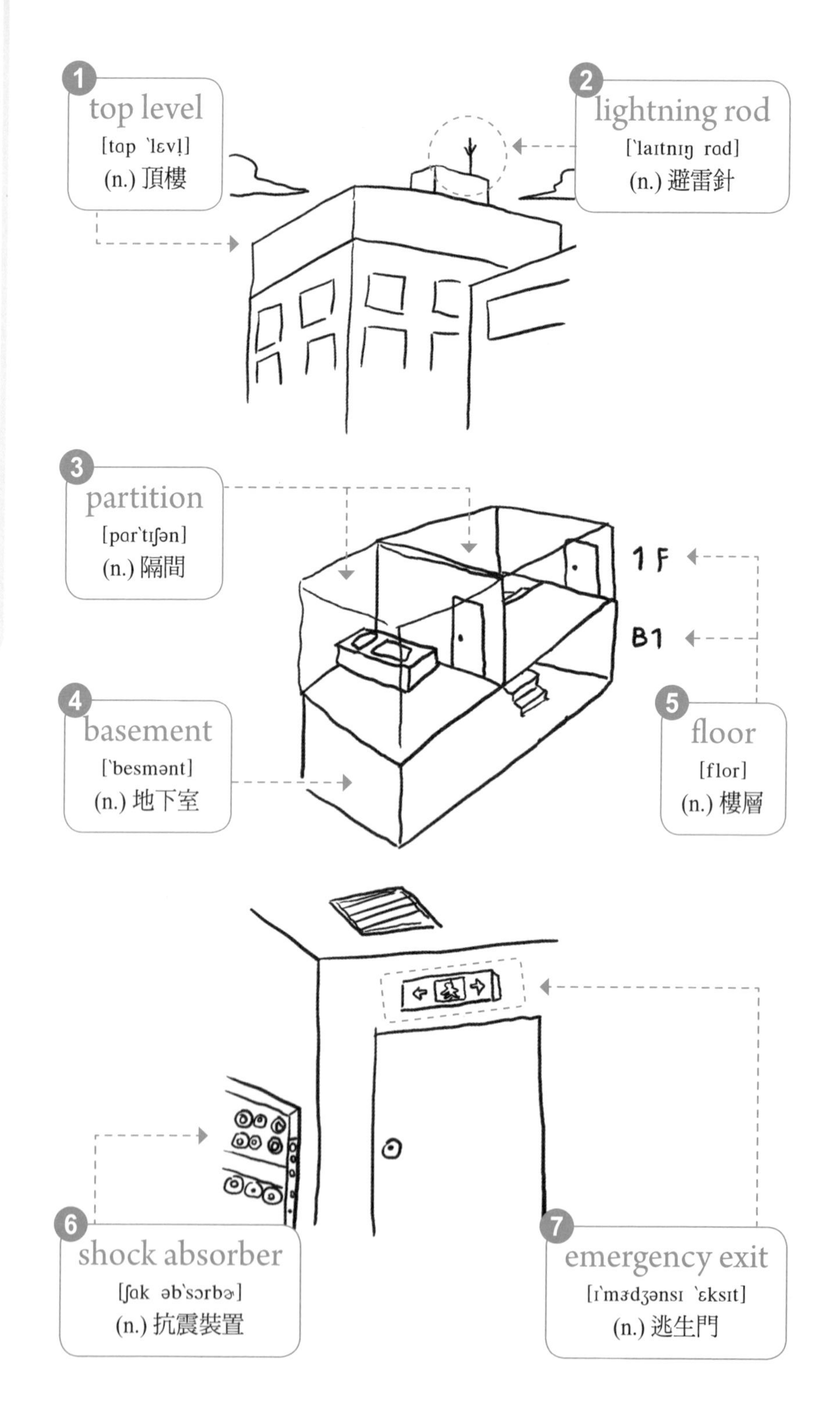

❶ 頂樓
The space on the top level of Nathan's building is very warm in the summer.
頂樓的區域

❷ 避雷針
Lightning rods on the roofs of buildings protect them against lightning strikes.
保護它們不受雷擊

❸ 隔間
It's easy to divide a large room into two spaces by using partitions.
把一間大房間劃分成兩個區塊

❹ 地下室
A basement apartment doesn't have much light.
沒什麼採光

❺ 樓層
Does this apartment building have more than 10 floors?

❻ 抗震裝置
With all the earthquake activity in Taiwan, it's essential that all buildings be constructed with shock absorbers.
因應每一次的地震活動

❼ 逃生門
All hotels must have instructions posted for guests regarding the emergency exit.
必須張貼說明

學更多

❶ space〈空間〉‧top〈頂的〉‧level〈層〉‧building〈建築物〉‧warm〈溫暖的〉
❷ lightning〈閃電〉‧rod〈竿〉‧protect A against B〈保護 A 避免 B〉‧strike〈攻擊〉
❸ easy〈容易的〉‧divide〈劃分〉‧large〈大的〉
❹ apartment〈公寓〉‧much〈很大程度的〉‧light〈光線〉
❺ apartment building〈公寓大樓〉‧more than〈多於〉
❻ essential〈必要的〉‧constructed〈construct（建造）的過去分詞〉‧absorber〈吸收器〉
❼ instructions〈說明、指南〉‧posted〈post（張貼）的過去分詞〉‧regarding〈關於〉

中譯

❶ 夏天時，Nathan 住的那棟建築物的頂樓區域非常熱。
❷ 屋頂的避雷針，可以保護建築物不受雷擊。
❸ 利用隔間就能輕易地將一個大房間劃分成兩個空間。
❹ 地下室的公寓沒什麼採光。
❺ 這棟公寓大樓有超過 10 個樓層嗎？
❻ 因應台灣每一次的地震活動，所有建築物建造時都必須有抗震裝置。
❼ 所有的飯店都必須張貼緊急逃生門的相關說明給旅客看。

149 郵件&包裹(1)

MP3 149

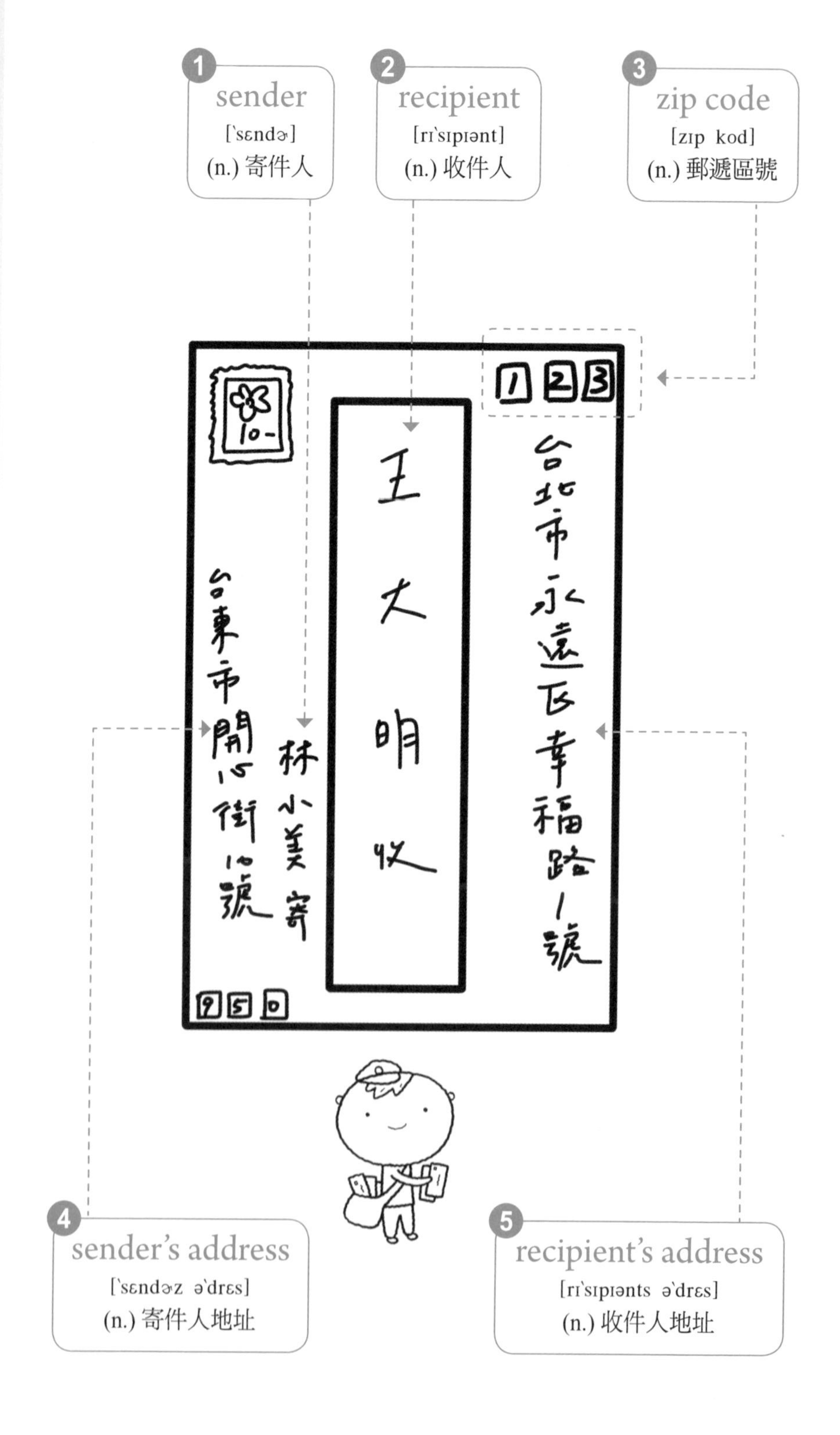

❶ 寄件人

The post office couldn't find the address written on the letter, so it was stamped, "return to sender."
被寫在信上的地址

❷ 收件人

Renee was the lucky recipient of a big box of cookies her mom sent.
她媽媽寄的

❸ 郵遞區號

Steve's zip code is 10670. He lives in the Da-An area.
他住在

❹ 寄件人地址

The sender's address on the letter is in Japan.

❺ 收件人地址

The recipient's address on the package is in Taiwan.

學更多

❶ post office〈郵局〉・find〈找到〉・written〈write（寫）的過去分詞〉・stamped〈stamp（蓋章）的過去分詞〉・return〈退回〉

❷ lucky〈幸運的〉・box〈盒〉・cookie〈甜餅乾〉・sent〈send（寄）的過去式〉

❸ zip〈zone improvement plan（區域改善計劃）的縮寫〉・code〈代碼〉・live〈住〉・area〈地區〉

❹ address〈地址〉・letter〈信件〉・Japan〈日本〉

❺ package〈包裹〉・Taiwan〈台灣〉

中譯

❶ 郵局找不到信上的地址，所以信件被蓋上「退回寄件人」的章。

❷ Renee 就是那個幸運的收件人，她收到媽媽寄的大盒餅乾。

❸ Steve 家的郵遞區號是 10670。他住在大安區。

❹ 信件上的寄件人地址位於日本。

❺ 包裹上的收件人地址位於台灣。

150
郵件&包裹(2)
MP3 150

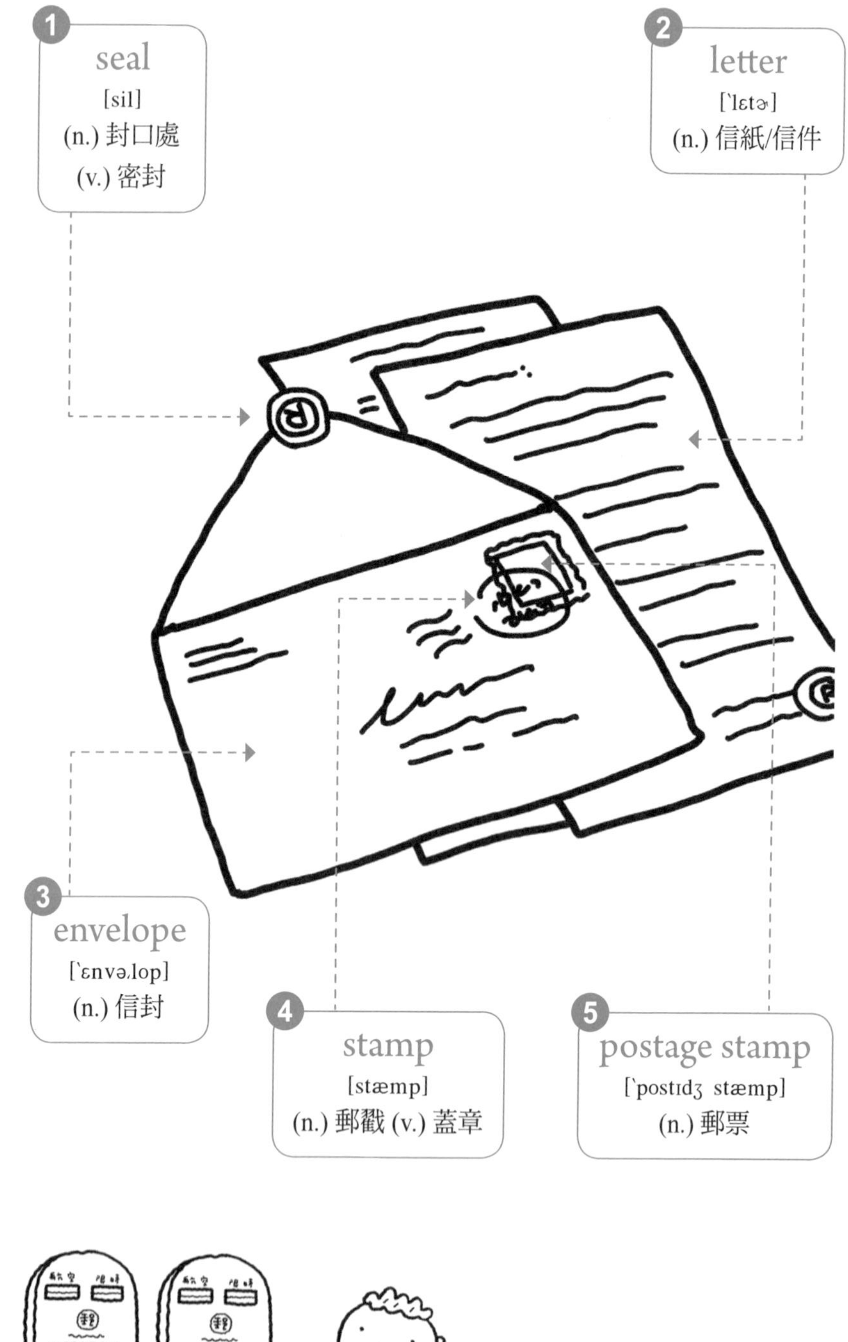
1 seal
[sil]
(n.) 封口處
(v.) 密封
2 letter
[`lɛtɚ]
(n.) 信紙/信件
3 envelope
[`ɛnvə͵lop]
(n.) 信封
4 stamp
[stæmp]
(n.) 郵戳 (v.) 蓋章
5 postage stamp
[`postɪdʒ stæmp]
(n.) 郵票

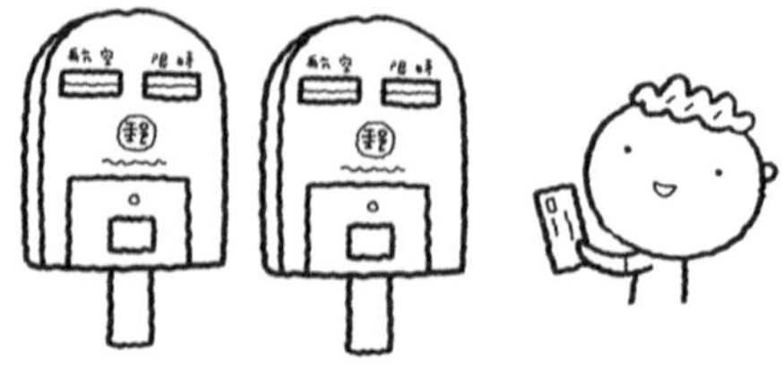

❶ 封口處 / 密封

You'd better seal that envelope well so the letter doesn't fall out.

你最好…（= You had better）

❷ 信紙 / 信件

Wow, did you see how many letters you got today?

❸ 信封

I need an envelope to mail my parents a letter.

寄一封信給我父母

❹ 郵戳 / 蓋章

The post office stamped my package with a "fragile, handle with care" warning.

小心輕放

❺ 郵票

It's possible to buy postage stamps at the hotel counter.

有可能

學更多

❶ well〈徹底地〉・fall out〈脫落〉

❷ see〈看〉・how many〈多少〉・got〈get（得到）的過去式〉・today〈今天〉

❸ need〈需要〉・mail〈郵寄〉・parents〈父母〉

❹ post office〈郵局〉・package〈包裹〉・fragile〈容易損壞的〉・handle〈對待〉・care〈小心〉・warning〈警告〉

❺ possible〈可能的〉・postage〈郵資〉・stamp〈戳記〉・hotel〈飯店〉・counter〈櫃檯〉

中譯

❶ 你最好把信封密封好，信件才不會掉出來。

❷ 哇，你有看到你今天收到了多少封信件嗎？

❸ 我需要一個信封寄信給父母。

❹ 郵局在我的包裹上蓋章，警告「內有易碎品，小心輕放」。

❺ 在飯店櫃檯可能買得到郵票。

151
郵件&包裹(3)

MP3 151

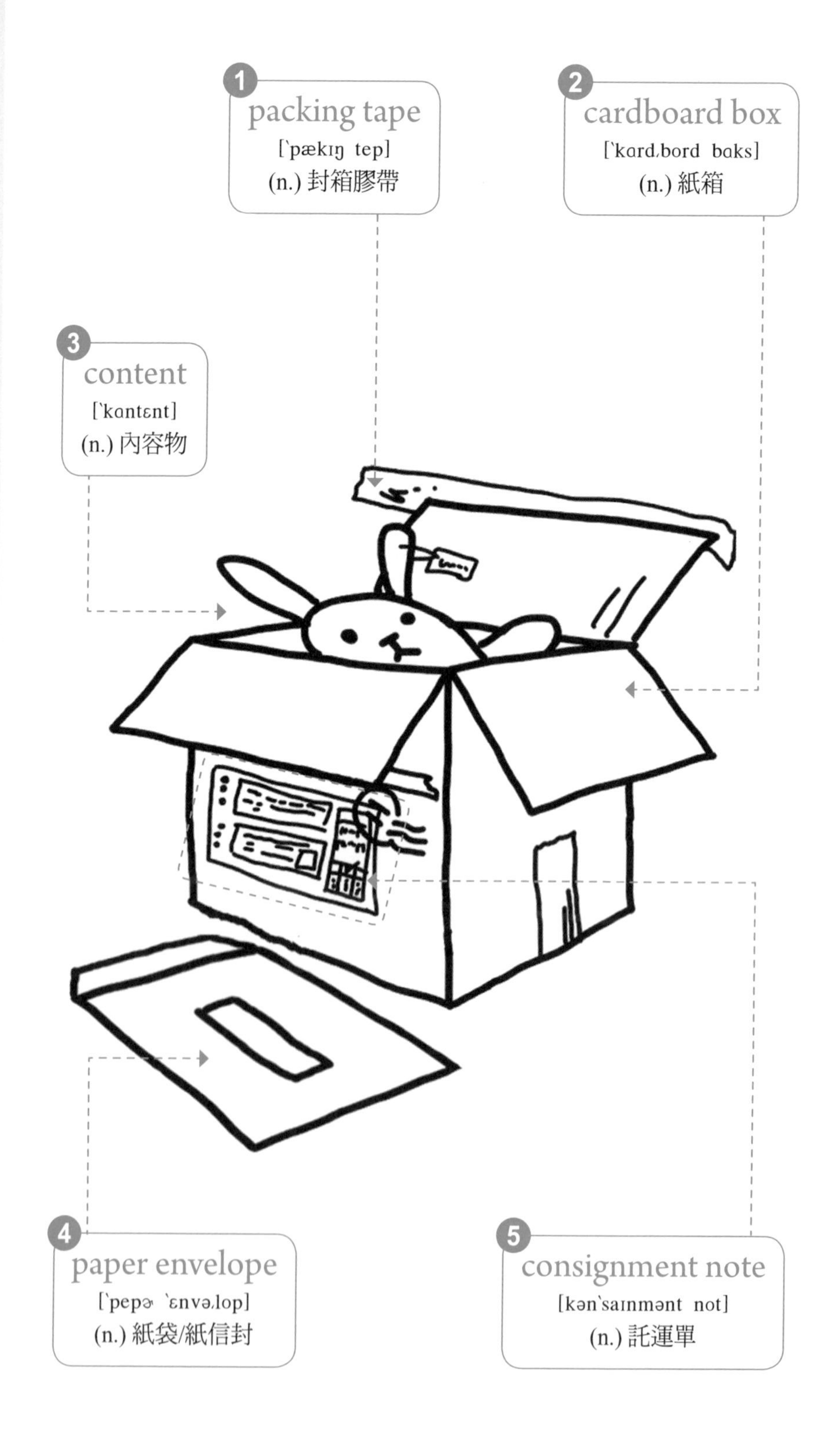
1 packing tape
[ˋpækɪŋ tep]
(n.) 封箱膠帶
2 cardboard box
[ˋkɑrd͵bord bɑks]
(n.) 紙箱
3 content
[ˋkɑntɛnt]
(n.) 內容物
4 paper envelope
[ˋpepɚ ˋɛnvə͵lop]
(n.) 紙袋/紙信封
5 consignment note
[kənˋsaɪnmənt not]
(n.) 託運單

❶ 封箱膠帶
Good, strong packing tape will keep packages sealed well during transit.
保持包裹密封良好

❷ 紙箱
Cardboard boxes are strong enough to ship goods internationally.

❸ 內容物
You must declare the content of any packages you mail abroad.
你寄往國外

❹ 紙袋 / 紙信封
Paper envelopes are really not sturdy enough to ship goods in.

❺ 託運單
A consignment note is issued by a shipping carrier with details and
由貨運公司所核發
instructions for a shipment of goods.

學更多

❶ strong〈堅固的〉・packing〈包裝〉・tape〈膠帶〉・keep〈保持某一狀態〉・sealed〈密封的〉・during〈在…期間〉・transit〈運送〉
❷ cardboard〈硬紙板製的〉・enough〈足夠〉・ship〈運送、裝運〉・goods〈貨物〉・internationally〈在國際間〉
❸ declare〈申報〉・package〈包裹〉・mail〈郵寄〉・abroad〈到國外〉
❹ paper〈紙製的〉・envelope〈信封〉・really〈實在〉・sturdy〈堅固的〉
❺ consignment〈委託貨物〉・issued〈issue（核發、發行）的過去分詞〉・carrier〈運輸公司〉・detail〈細節〉・instructions〈用法說明〉・shipment〈裝運〉

中譯

❶ 品質優良且牢固的封箱膠帶，能使包裹在運送途中保持密封良好。
❷ 紙箱夠堅固，適用於跨國的貨物運輸。
❸ 所有寄往國外的包裹，你都必須申報包裹中的內容物。
❹ 紙袋實在不夠堅固，不適合用來裝運貨物。
❺ 貨運公司開立的託運單，會詳列運送物品的細節和說明。

152
冰箱(1)

MP3 152

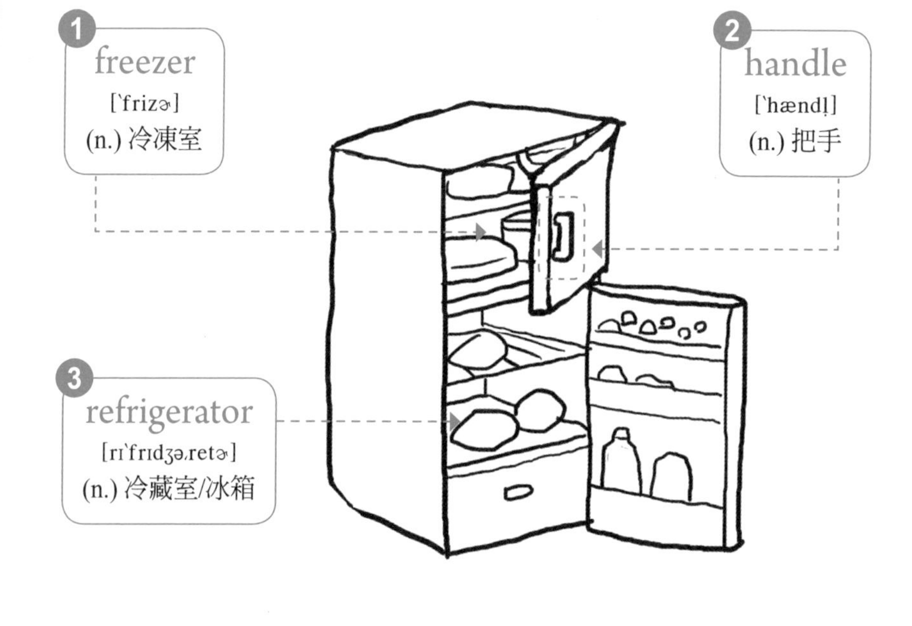
1 freezer
[ˋfrizɚ]
(n.) 冷凍室
2 handle
[ˋhændl̩]
(n.) 把手
3 refrigerator
[rɪˋfrɪdʒə͵retɚ]
(n.) 冷藏室/冰箱

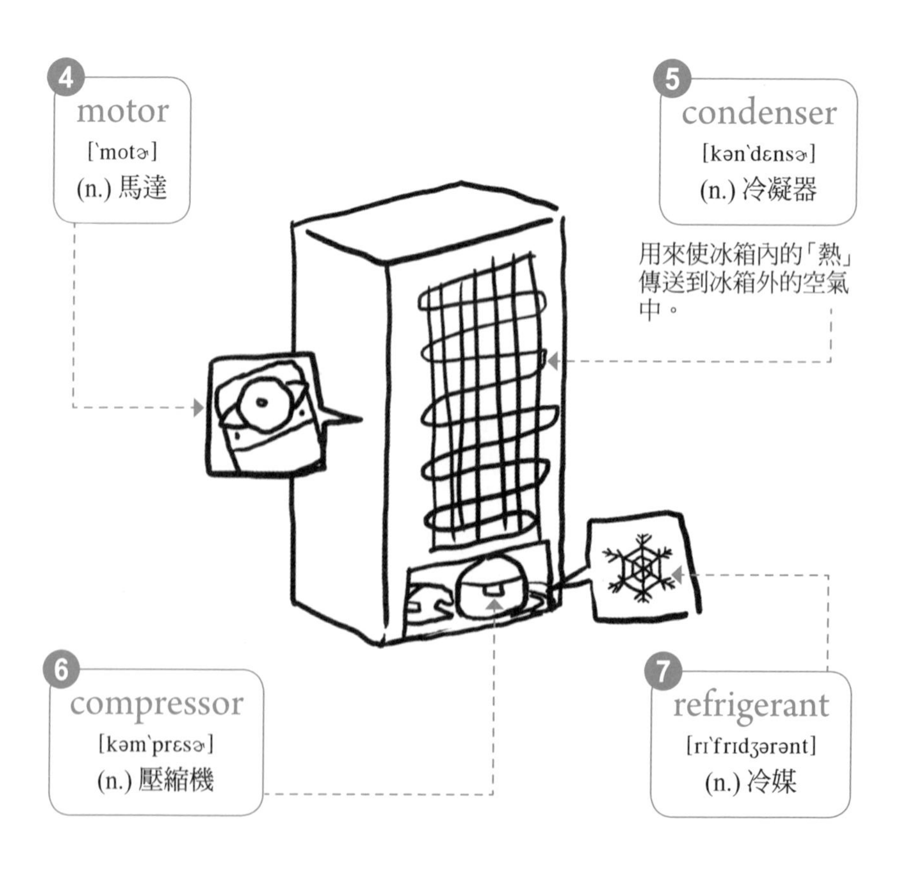
4 motor
[ˋmotɚ]
(n.) 馬達
5 condenser
[kənˋdɛnsɚ]
(n.) 冷凝器
用來使冰箱內的「熱」傳送到冰箱外的空氣中。
6 compressor
[kəmˋprɛsɚ]
(n.) 壓縮機
7 refrigerant
[rɪˋfrɪdʒərənt]
(n.) 冷媒

❶ 冷凍室

I keep a lot of ice cream in my freezer.

存放許多冰淇淋

❷ 把手

Oh no! Dad pulled on the refrigerator door handle too hard, and it broke off.

拉斷了

❸ 冷藏室 / 冰箱

Put the fresh vegetables in the refrigerator so they don't spoil.

❹ 馬達

The food's spoiled in the refrigerator. Is the motor not running?

沒有運作

❺ 冷凝器

A refrigerator condenser plays an important role in the cooling system.

扮演重要的角色

❻ 壓縮機

George, call the repairman! We need to get the refrigerator compressor replaced.

讓冰箱的壓縮機被取代

❼ 冷媒

You should add refrigerant to your refrigerator in order to keep it cooling properly.

為了讓它正常地冷卻

學更多

❶ keep〈存放〉・a lot of〈許多〉・ice cream〈冰淇淋〉
❷ pulled on〈pull on（用力拉）的過去式〉・broke off〈break off（折斷）的過去式〉
❸ put〈放〉・fresh〈新鮮的〉・vegetable〈蔬菜〉・spoil〈腐敗〉
❹ spoiled〈spoil（腐敗）的過去分詞〉・running〈run（運轉）的 ing 型態〉
❺ play〈扮演〉・important〈重要的〉・role〈角色、作用〉・cooling〈冷卻的〉
❻ call〈打電話〉・repairman〈修理工〉・replaced〈replace（取代）的過去分詞〉
❼ in order to〈為了〉・cooling〈cool（冷卻）的 ing 型態〉・properly〈正確地〉

中譯

❶ 我的冷凍室裡存放了許多冰淇淋。
❷ 喔不！爸爸太用力拉冰箱門的把手，把它拉斷了。
❸ 將新鮮蔬菜放進冷藏室，這樣它們才不會腐壞。
❹ 冰箱裡的食物都腐壞了，馬達沒有在運作嗎？
❺ 冰箱的冷凝器在冷卻系統中扮演重要的角色。
❻ George，打電話給維修員！我們需要更換冰箱的壓縮機。
❼ 為了讓冰箱能夠正常冷卻，你應該添加冷媒到冰箱裡。

153 冰箱(2)

MP3 153

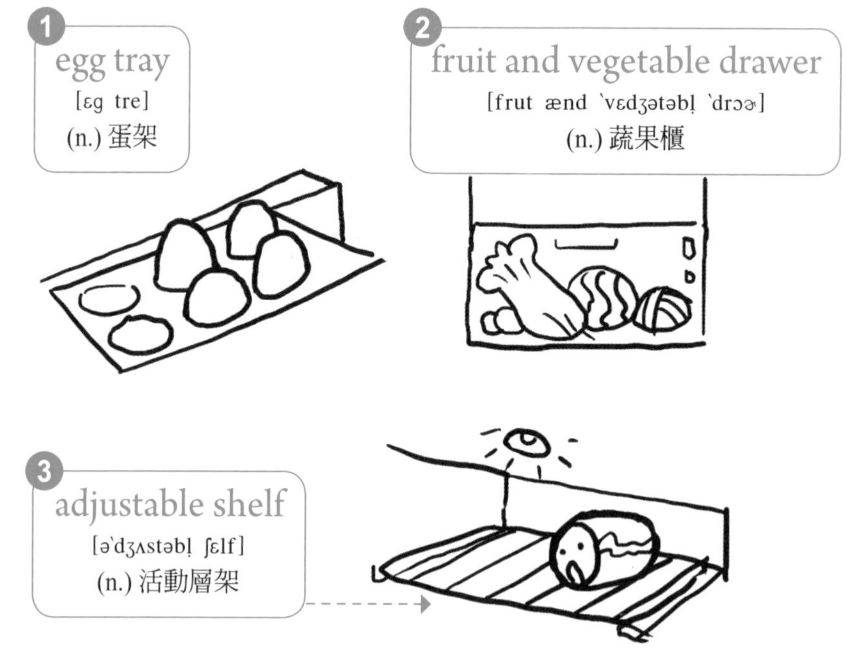

1 egg tray
[ɛg tre]
(n.) 蛋架

2 fruit and vegetable drawer
[frut ænd ˋvɛdʒətəbḷ ˋdrɔɚ]
(n.) 蔬果櫃

3 adjustable shelf
[əˋdʒʌstəbḷ ʃɛlf]
(n.) 活動層架

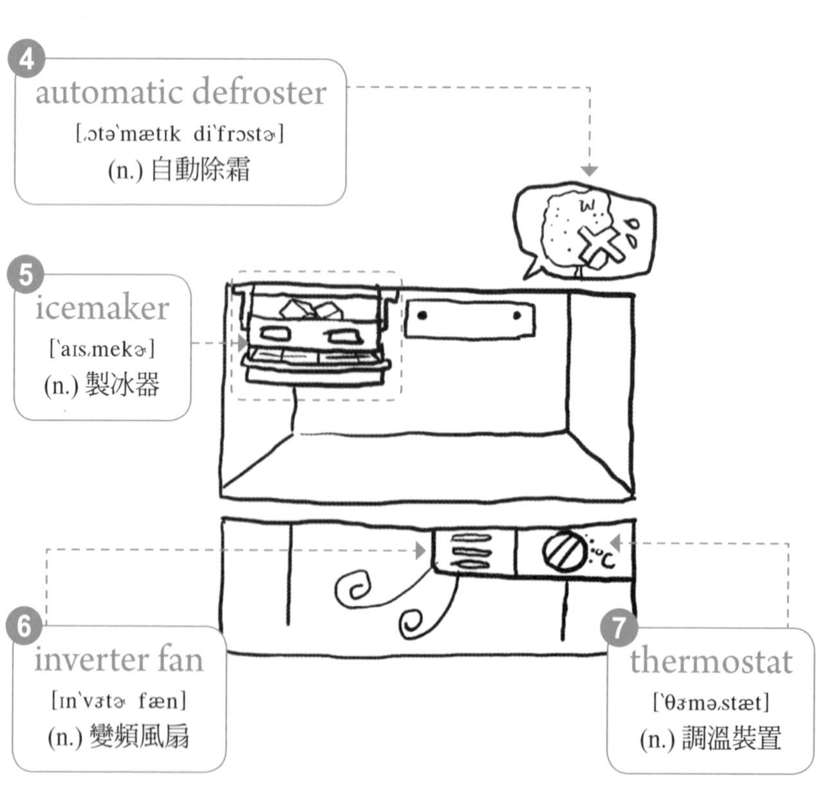

4 automatic defroster
[ˏɔtəˋmætɪk diˋfrɔstɚ]
(n.) 自動除霜

5 icemaker
[ˋaɪsˏmekɚ]
(n.) 製冰器

6 inverter fan
[ɪnˋvɝtɚ fæn]
(n.) 變頻風扇

7 thermostat
[ˋθɝməˏstæt]
(n.) 調溫裝置

❶ 蛋架

Put the eggs you bought in the egg tray, Jenny.

你買的蛋

❷ 蔬果櫃

Wow, this refrigerator is huge. It has two fruit and vegetable drawers.

❸ 活動層架

Put the adjustable shelf lower to make more room for the watermelon.

製造更多空間

❹ 自動除霜

Henry wants to buy a refrigerator with an automatic defroster.

有自動除霜功能的冰箱

❺ 製冰器

I don't have an icemaker in my freezer. I just use ice trays and make the ice cubes myself.

自己製作冰塊

❻ 變頻風扇

Hmm...I don't think the fridge's inverter fan is working.

我不認為 正在運作

❼ 調溫裝置

The refrigerator isn't cold enough—check the thermostat. What's it set at?

學更多

❶ egg〈蛋〉．bought〈buy（買）的過去式〉．tray〈盤子〉
❷ huge〈龐大的〉．fruit〈水果〉．vegetable〈蔬菜〉．drawer〈抽屜〉
❸ adjustable〈可調整的〉．shelf〈架子〉．lower〈比較低的〉．make〈製造〉
❹ refrigerator〈冰箱〉．automatic〈自動的〉．defroster〈除霜裝置〉
❺ freezer〈冷凍庫〉．ice tray〈製冰盒〉．ice cube〈冰塊〉．myself〈我自己〉
❻ fridge〈電冰箱〉．inverter〈變頻器〉．fan〈風扇〉．working〈work（運轉）的 ing 型態〉
❼ cold〈冷的〉．enough〈足夠〉．check〈檢查〉．set〈設定〉

中譯

❶ Jenny，把你買的蛋放到蛋架上。
❷ 哇，這台冰箱好大。它有兩個蔬果櫃。
❸ 把活動層架降低一點，挪出更多空間來放西瓜。
❹ Henry 想買一台具有自動除霜功能的冰箱。
❺ 我的冷凍庫裡沒有製冰器，我都用製冰盒自製冰塊。
❻ 嗯……我覺得冰箱的變頻風扇壞了。
❼ 冰箱不夠冷。檢查一下調溫裝置，看看它設定在幾度？

154 上衣

MP3 154

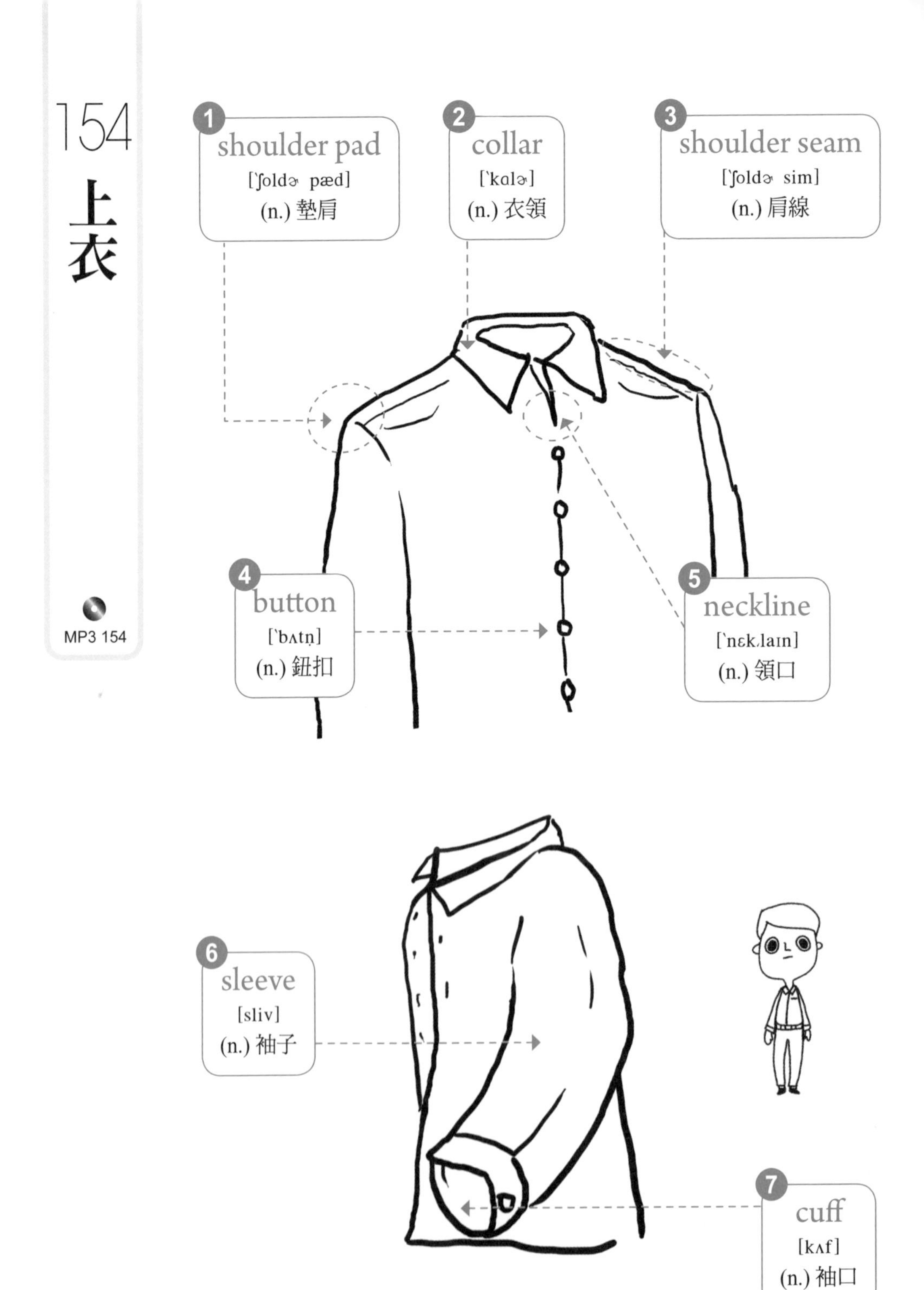

❶ 墊肩
Shoulder pads were really popular in the 80's.
在八零年代

❷ 衣領
Mike likes collar-less shirts like T-shirts.
沒有衣領

❸ 肩線
Can you recommend a tailor? The shoulder seams need to be taken in.
被改窄

❹ 鈕扣
Zoe lost a button on her coat.

❺ 領口
Can you raise the neckline? It's a bit low.

❻ 袖子
I only wear short sleeves in the summer.

❼ 袖口
Dad was very happy with the cuff links my brother gave him.
我弟弟送給他

學更多

❶ shoulder〈肩膀〉‧pad〈墊子〉‧really〈很〉‧popular〈流行的〉
❷ shirt〈汗衫〉‧like〈像〉
❸ recommend〈推薦〉‧tailor〈裁縫師〉‧seam〈縫合處〉‧take in〈改小、改窄〉
❹ lost〈lose（丟失）的過去式〉‧coat〈外套〉
❺ raise〈提高〉‧a bit〈有點〉‧low〈低的〉
❻ only〈只〉‧wear〈穿著〉‧short〈短的〉
❼ happy〈高興的〉‧link〈袖口鍊扣〉‧gave〈give（給）的過去式〉

中譯

❶ 在八零年代，墊肩相當風行。
❷ Mike 喜歡像 T 恤那樣沒有衣領的汗衫。
❸ 你能推薦裁縫師嗎？這裡的肩線需要改窄一點。
❹ Zoe 弄丟了自己外套上的一顆鈕扣。
❺ 你可以把領口弄高一點嗎？它有點低。
❻ 只有夏天時，我才會穿短袖。
❼ 弟弟送給爸爸袖扣，讓爸爸非常高興。

155
褲子

MP3 155

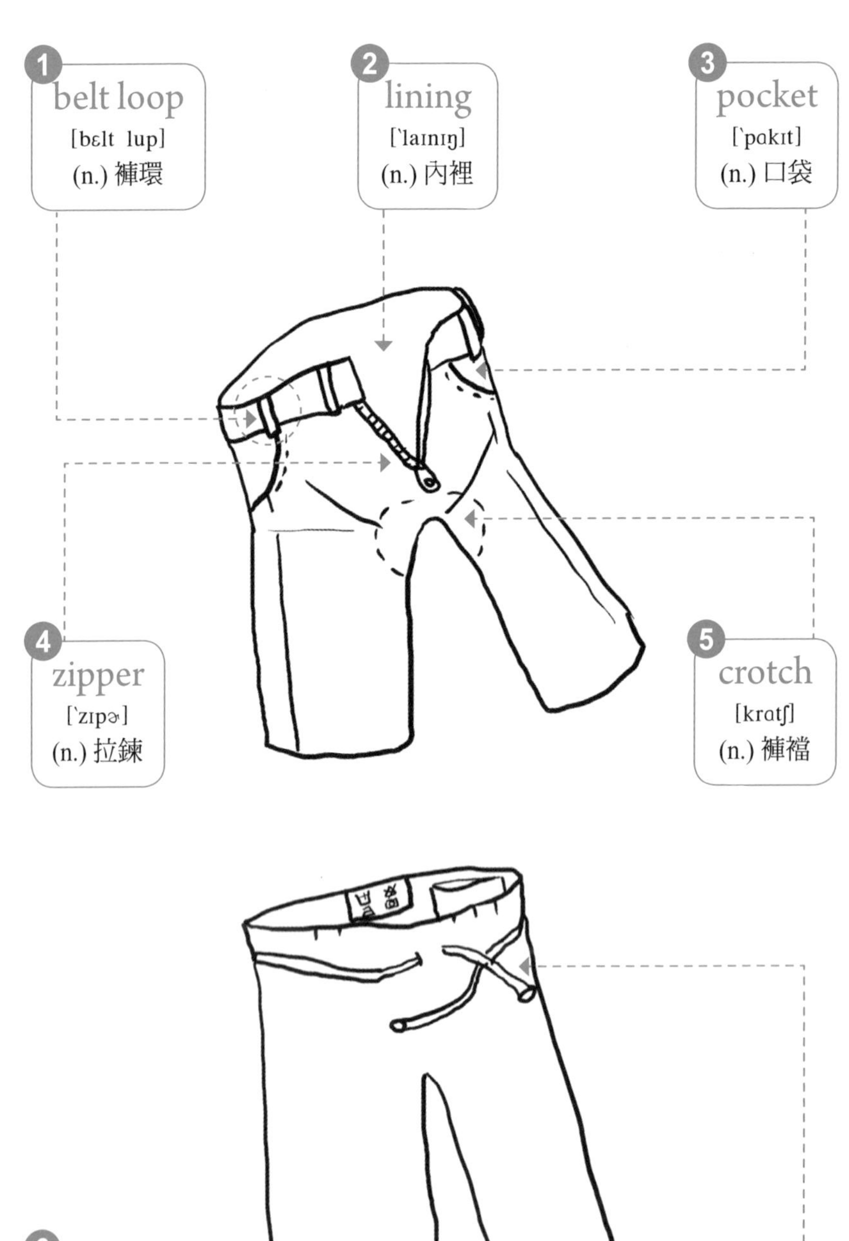

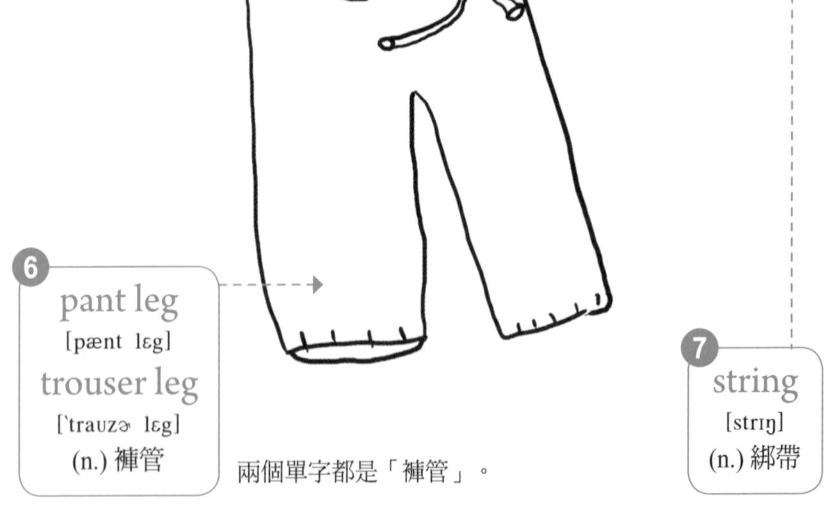

❶ 褲環
My little brother always misses a belt loop or two on his pants when he puts his belt on.
當他要繫皮帶時

❷ 內裡
A sheer dress usually has lining sewn into it.

❸ 口袋
I need pants with pockets so I can have a place to put my keys.
有個地方放我的鑰匙

❹ 拉鍊
Lori prefers jackets with zippers rather than buttons.

❺ 褲襠
Mom, can we shorten the crotch on these pants for me? It's way too long.
太長了

❻ 褲管
Her right pant leg is too long. You need to hem it up.

❼ 綁帶
Your mom lets you wear that tiny string bikini?

學更多

❶ little〈幼小的〉‧miss〈遺漏〉‧belt〈腰帶〉‧loop〈環形〉
❷ sheer〈極薄的〉‧dress〈洋裝〉‧usually〈通常〉‧sewn〈sew（縫）的過去分詞〉
❸ pants〈褲子〉‧place〈地方〉‧put〈放〉‧key〈鑰匙〉
❹ prefer〈更喜歡〉‧jacket〈夾克〉‧rather than〈而不是〉‧button〈鈕扣〉
❺ shorten〈使變短〉‧long〈長的〉
❻ right〈右邊的〉‧hem〈縫邊〉‧up〈向上〉‧trouser〈褲子〉
❼ wear〈穿著〉‧tiny〈極小的〉‧bikini〈比基尼泳裝〉

中譯

❶ 我那年幼的弟弟要繫皮帶時，總會漏穿一兩個褲環。
❷ 薄洋裝通常都縫有內裡。
❸ 我需要有口袋的褲子，我才有地方可以放鑰匙。
❹ 比起鈕扣式的夾克，Lori 更喜歡拉鍊式的。
❺ 媽媽，我們可以把這條褲子的褲襠改短一點嗎？它太長了。
❻ 她右腳的褲管太長了，你需要把它往上縫起。
❼ 妳媽媽讓妳穿那件細綁帶的比基尼？

156 鞋子(1)

MP3 156

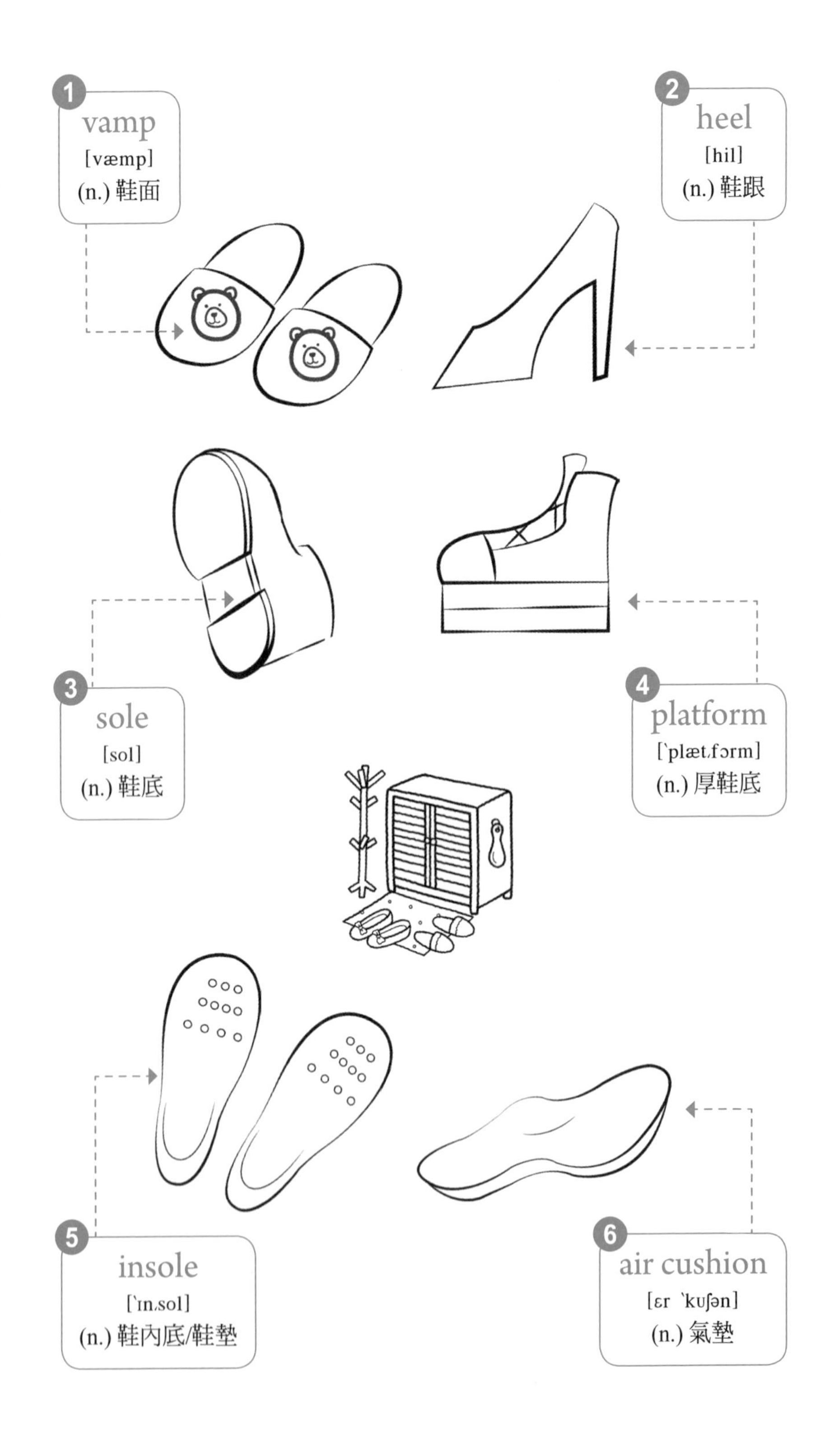

❶ 鞋面

The vamp on a shoe is the upper part which can cover toes and the top of the foot.

腳背

❷ 鞋跟

Those heels are so high! Are you sure you can walk in them?

妳可以穿著它們走路

❸ 鞋底

The soles of John's shoes are worn down and need replacing.

被磨壞

❹ 厚鞋底

Platform shoes are becoming popular again.

又變得流行起來了

❺ 鞋內底 / 鞋墊

These insoles are very comfortable.

❻ 氣墊

Aunt Jenny uses air cushions to make her feet feel better inside her shoes.

讓她的腳感覺比較舒服

學更多

❶ upper〈上面的〉・part〈部分〉・cover〈覆蓋〉・toe〈腳趾〉・top〈上方〉

❷ high〈高的〉・sure〈確信的〉・walk〈走〉

❸ worn down〈wear down（磨損）的過去分詞〉・replacing〈replace（取代）的 ing 型態〉

❹ becoming〈become（變得）的 ing 型態〉・popular〈流行的〉・again〈再一次〉

❺ very〈很〉・comfortable〈舒適的〉

❻ aunt〈阿姨〉・air〈空氣〉・cushion〈墊子〉・make〈使得〉・
feet〈foot（腳）的複數〉・better〈更好的〉・inside〈在裡面〉

中譯

❶ 鞋子的鞋面是指鞋子上方能夠覆蓋腳趾及腳背的部分。

❷ 那些鞋跟好高！妳確定妳能穿著它們走路嗎？

❸ John 那雙鞋的鞋底已經磨壞了，需要更換。

❹ 厚鞋底的鞋又開始流行起來。

❺ 這些鞋墊很舒適。

❻ Jenny 阿姨會在鞋內放氣墊，讓她穿鞋的腳感覺比較舒服。

157 鞋子(2)

MP3 157

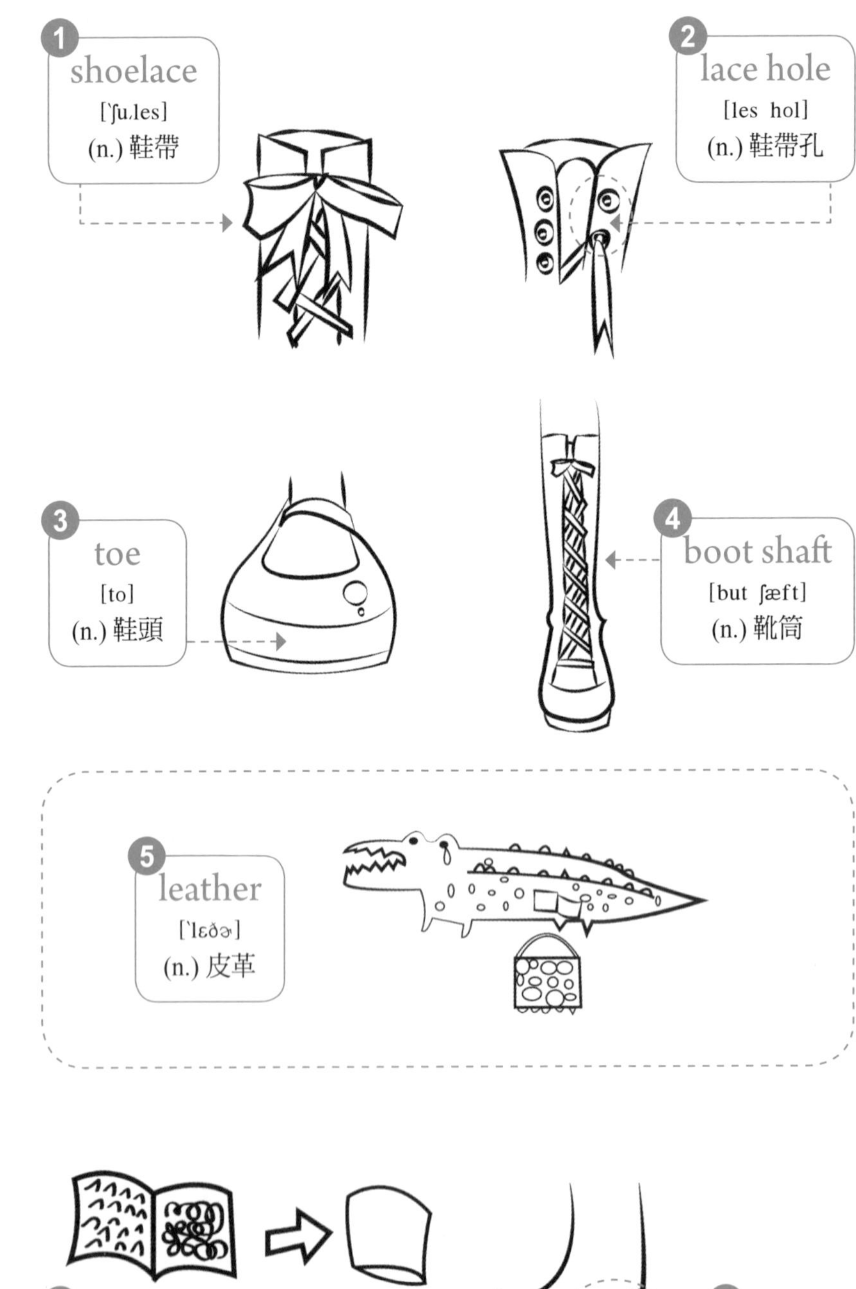

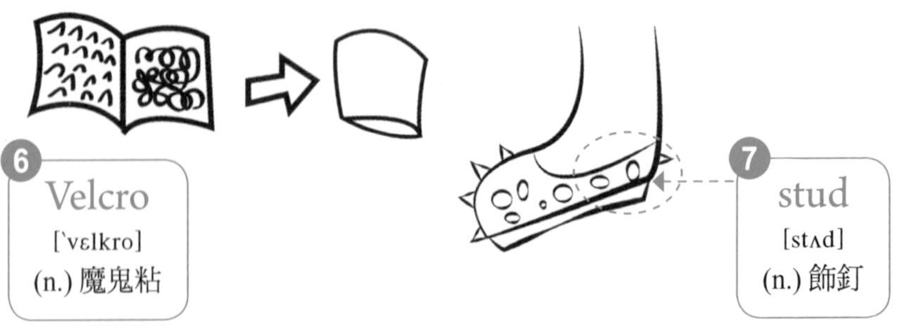

❶ 鞋帶
Oh darn! My shoelace just broke. I need to buy a new one.
討厭

❷ 鞋帶孔
I'll help you thread your shoelaces through your lace holes.
把你的鞋帶穿過你的鞋帶孔

❸ 鞋頭
His boots are very sturdy. They even have steel toes.
鋼鐵般堅硬的鞋頭

❹ 靴筒
If you want new boots to fit right, you should measure your calf and then find the right-sized boot shafts for you.
合腳
大小合適的靴筒

❺ 皮革
Italy is famous for its beautiful leather shoes.

❻ 魔鬼粘
Children's sneakers often have Velcro instead of shoelaces.

❼ 飾釘
Studs on shoes and clothes are considered stylish right now.

學更多

❶ broke〈break（斷裂）的過去式〉・buy〈買〉・new〈新的〉
❷ thread〈穿線〉・through〈通過〉・lace〈鞋帶〉・hole〈洞〉
❸ boot〈靴子〉・sturdy〈堅固的〉・even〈甚至〉・steel〈鋼鐵般的、堅硬的〉
❹ fit〈合身〉・right〈恰好〉・measure〈測量〉・calf〈小腿〉・find〈找到〉
❺ Italy〈義大利〉・famous〈出名的〉・beautiful〈美麗的〉
❻ children〈child（小孩）的複數〉・sneaker〈運動鞋〉・instead of〈代替〉
❼ clothes〈衣服〉・considered〈consider（視為）的過去分詞〉・stylish〈流行的〉

中譯

❶ 討厭！我的鞋帶斷了，我需要買一條新的。
❷ 我會幫你把鞋帶穿過鞋帶孔。
❸ 他的靴子很堅固，甚至還有鋼鐵般堅硬的鞋頭。
❹ 如果想要一雙合腳的新靴子，你應該先測量你的小腿圍，再去找大小合適的靴筒。
❺ 義大利以其美麗的皮鞋聞名。
❻ 小孩子的運動鞋通常會使用魔鬼粘，而非鞋帶。
❼ 鞋子及衣物上的飾釘，現今被視為流行。

158 身體外觀

MP3 158

1. **shoulders** [ˋʃoldɚz] (n.) 肩膀
2. **chest** [tʃɛst] (n.) 胸部
3. **waist** [west] (n.) 腰部
4. **abdomen** [ˋæbdəmən] (n.) 腹部
5. **torso** [ˋtɔrso] (n.) 軀幹 

人體除了頭、頸、四肢外，皆屬軀幹。

6. **back** [bæk] (n.) 背部
7. **hip** [hɪp] (n.) 臀部

❶ 肩膀

Danny carries his little girl on his shoulders when she gets tired at the zoo.

his little girl：他的女兒　gets tired：感到疲倦

❷ 胸部

❻ 背部

Lifting weights has helped strengthen Jack's chest and back.

❸ 腰部

❹ 腹部

Belly dancing has slimmed down Vivien's waist and abdomen.

❺ 軀幹

The torso is the central part of the human body.

central part：中心部位

❼ 臀部

Grandma broke one of her hips when she fell down the stairs.

fell down the stairs：摔下樓梯

學更多

❶ carry〈抱〉・get〈變得〉・tired〈疲倦的〉・zoo〈動物園〉

❷ ❻ lifting weight〈lift weight（舉重）的 ing 型態〉・helped〈help（幫助）的過去分詞〉・strengthen〈增強〉

❸ ❹ belly dancing〈肚皮舞〉・slimmed down〈slim down（縮小某物的大小）的過去分詞〉

❺ central〈中心的〉・part〈部分〉・human〈人〉・body〈身體〉

❼ broke〈break（斷裂）的過去式〉・fell down〈fall down（摔下）的過去式〉・stairs〈樓梯〉

中譯

❶ 在動物園時，當女兒覺得累了， Danny 就會把她抱到肩膀上。

❷ ❻ 舉重幫助 Jack 強化胸部及背部。

❸ ❹ 跳肚皮舞讓 Vivien 的腰部和腹部都瘦了。

❺ 軀幹是人體的中心部位。

❼ 祖母摔下樓梯時，一側的臀部骨折了。

159
四肢(1)

MP3 159

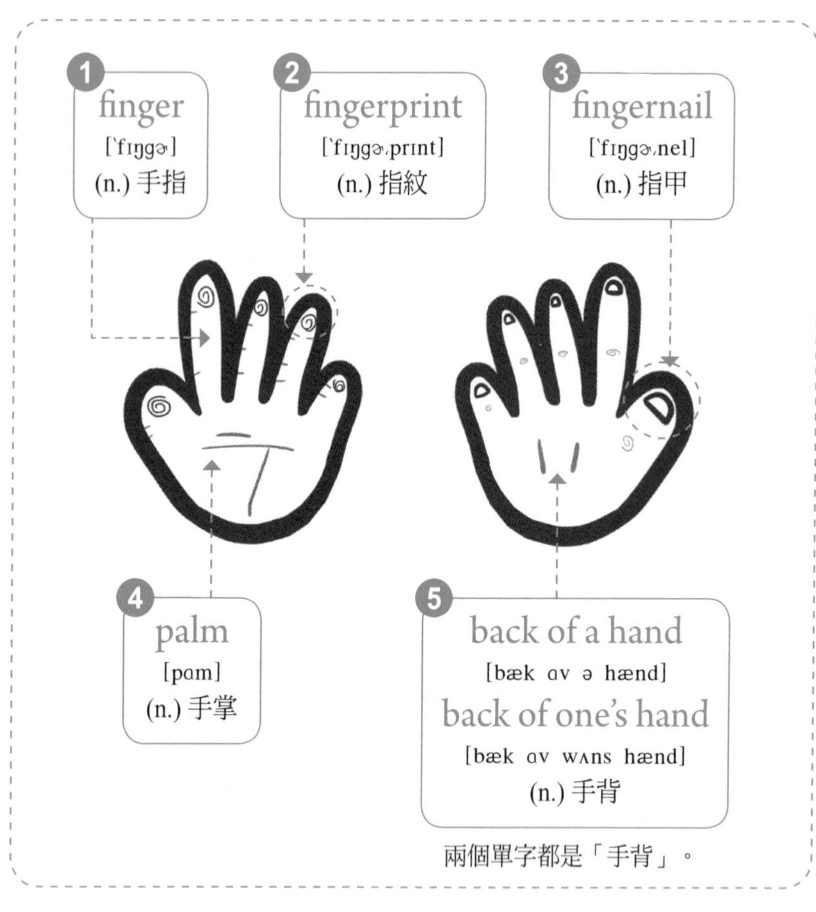

兩個單字都是「手背」。

❶ 手指
In kindergarten today, we learned to wiggle our wrists and fingers.

❷ 指紋
The police took Eric's fingerprints when he was arrested.

❸ 指甲
Your fingernails are beautiful. Do you get them painted at a salon?
讓它們被畫

❹ 手掌
Can you really read my palm and predict my future?
預測我的未來

❺ 手背
Jake has a big scar on the back of his hand from playing baseball.
有一個大疤痕

❻ 手腕
John broke his wrist yesterday when he crashed on his scooter.

❼ 手肘
❽ 手臂
Jaime hit his elbow and his whole arm felt tingly.
整個手臂感覺刺痛

學更多

❶ kindergarten〈幼稚園〉・learned〈learn（學）的過去式〉・wiggle〈擺動〉
❷ police〈警察〉・took〈take（採取）的過去式〉・arrested〈arrest（逮捕）的過去分詞〉
❸ beautiful〈美麗的〉・painted〈著色的〉・salon〈沙龍〉
❹ really〈確實〉・read〈讀〉・predict〈預言〉・future〈未來〉
❺ scar〈疤痕〉・back〈背部〉・playing〈play（打球）的 ing 型態〉・baseball〈棒球〉
❻ broke〈break（斷裂）的過去式〉・crashed〈crash（撞擊）的過去式〉・scooter〈機車〉
❼ ❽ hit〈hit（碰撞）的過去式〉・whole〈整個的〉・tingly〈有刺痛感的〉

中譯

❶ 今天在幼稚園，我們學會擺動我們的手腕跟手指。
❷ 警方逮捕 Eric 之後，採得了他的指紋。
❸ 妳的指甲好美。妳是去沙龍給人家畫的嗎？
❹ 你真的可以解讀我的手掌，然後預測我的未來嗎？
❺ Jake 的手背上有一個打棒球留下的大疤痕。
❻ John 昨天騎機車發生衝撞時，一隻手的手腕骨折了。
❼ ❽ Jaime 撞到了手肘，整個手臂感覺刺痛。

160
四肢(2)
MP3 160

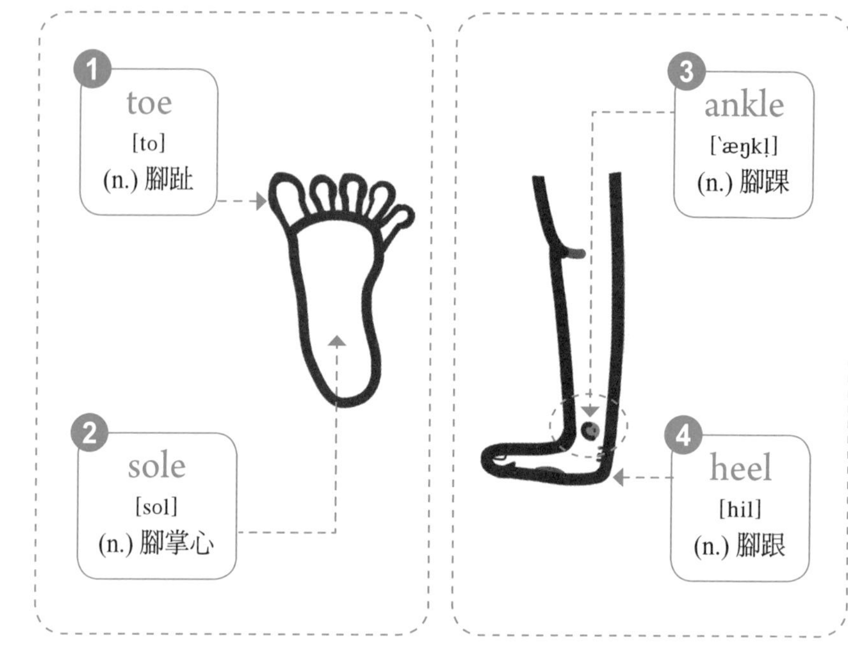

1
toe
[to]
(n.) 腳趾
2
sole
[sol]
(n.) 腳掌心
3
ankle
[ˋæŋkḷ]
(n.) 腳踝
4
heel
[hil]
(n.) 腳跟

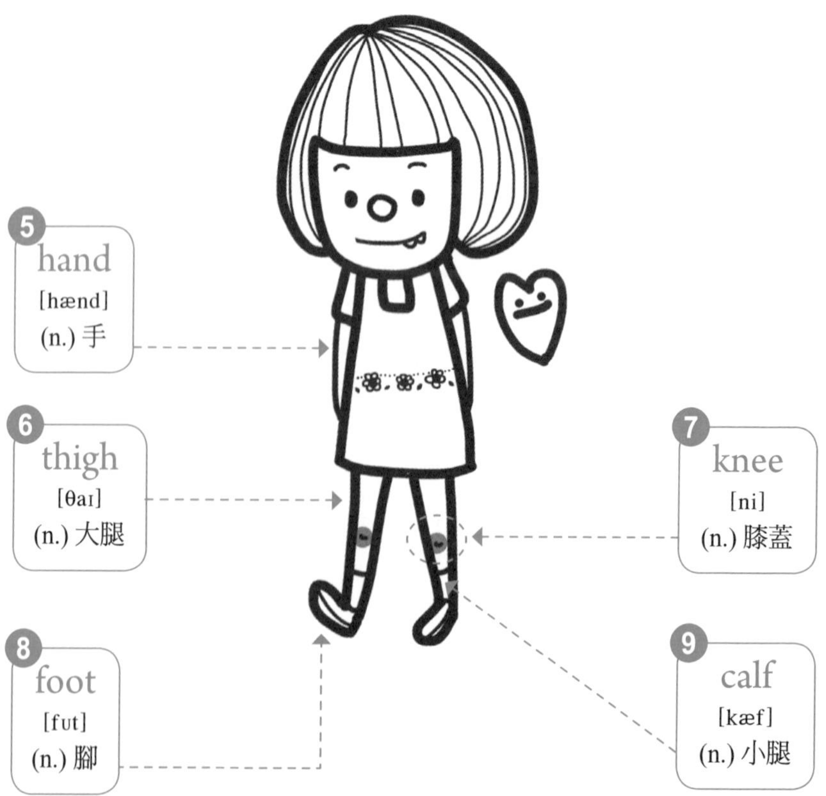

5
hand
[hænd]
(n.) 手
6
thigh
[θaɪ]
(n.) 大腿
7
knee
[ni]
(n.) 膝蓋
8
foot
[fʊt]
(n.) 腳
9
calf
[kæf]
(n.) 小腿

❶ 腳趾
Pointing your toes is very important in ballet.
壓腳背

❷ 腳掌心
The soles of your feet are so smooth.

❸ 腳踝
Jill has a butterfly tattoo on her right ankle.
蝴蝶圖案的刺青

❹ 腳跟
Carrie's heels are rough, so she's going to use some pumice stone on them.
使用一些浮石來磨它們

❺ 手
❽ 腳
I'm getting a hand and foot massage tonight.
得到一個手部和腳部的按摩服務

❻ 大腿
❾ 小腿
My whole body aches from hiking all weekend—especially my thighs and calves.
整個週末都在健行

❼ 膝蓋
Grandpa's knees are bad, I wonder if he'll need surgery soon?
是否不久後他需要開刀

學更多

❶ pointing〈point（指向、弄尖）的 ing 型態〉・important〈重要的〉・ballet〈芭蕾舞〉
❷ feet〈foot（腳）的複數〉・smooth〈平滑的〉
❸ butterfly〈蝴蝶〉・tattoo〈刺青〉・right〈右邊的〉
❹ rough〈粗糙的〉・use〈用〉・pumice stone〈浮石〉
❺❽ massage〈按摩〉・tonight〈今晚〉
❻❾ whole〈整個的〉・ache〈疼痛〉・hiking〈hike（健行）的 ing 型態〉・especially〈尤其〉
❼ bad〈不好的〉・wonder〈想知道〉・surgery〈手術〉・soon〈很快地〉

中譯

❶ 在芭蕾中，壓腳背（將腳趾用力向下伸展）這個動作是非常重要的。
❷ 妳的腳掌心的皮膚好平滑。
❸ 在 Jill 的右腳踝上，有一個蝴蝶圖案的刺青。
❹ Carrie 的腳跟很粗糙，所以她打算用浮石來磨它們。
❺❽ 我今晚要去讓人幫我按摩手跟腳。
❻❾ 因為整個週末都在健行，所以我現在全身痠痛——尤其是大腿跟小腿。
❼ 祖父的膝蓋不好，我想知道是否不久後他需要開刀？

161 頭部

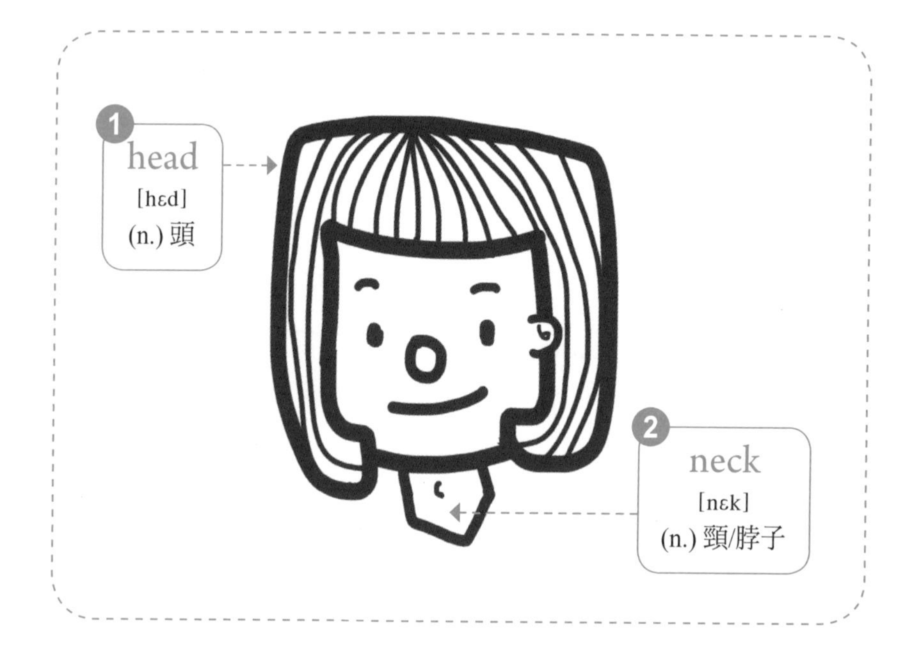

1
head
[hɛd]
(n.) 頭
2
neck
[nɛk]
(n.) 頸/脖子

MP3 161

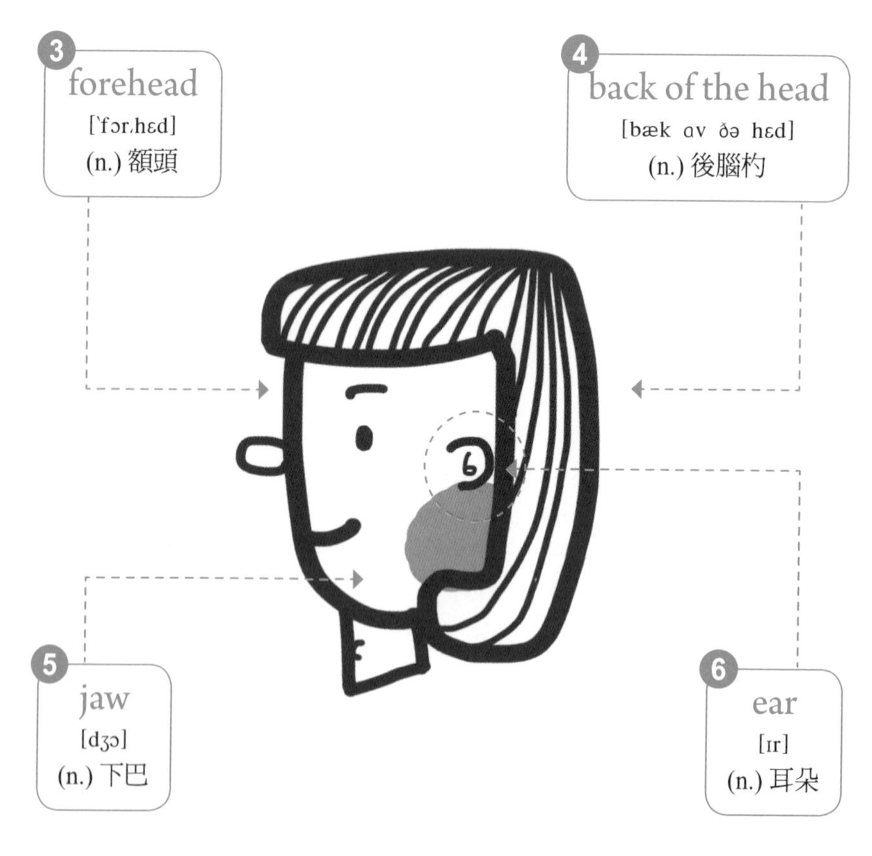

3
forehead
[ˋfɔr͵hɛd]
(n.) 額頭
4
back of the head
[bæk ɑv ðə hɛd]
(n.) 後腦杓
5
jaw
[dʒɔ]
(n.) 下巴
6
ear
[ɪr]
(n.) 耳朵

❶ 頭

❷ 頸 / 脖子

The neck supports the head.

❸ 額頭

He has a big forehead. I heard that represents wisdom.

我聽說…

❹ 後腦杓

As the toddler was walking around, he slipped and hit the back of his head on the floor.

當學走路的小孩到處走動時　他的後腦杓撞到地板

❺ 下巴

Larry got into a fist fight and broke a guy's jaw!

參與了一場鬥毆

❻ 耳朵

Tess is getting her ears pierced for her birthday.

讓她的耳朵被穿洞

學更多

❶ ❷ support〈支撐〉

❸ heard〈hear（聽說）的過去式〉・represent〈象徵〉・wisdom〈智慧〉

❹ toddler〈學步的小孩〉・walking around〈walk around（四處走動）的 ing 型態〉・slipped〈slip（滑倒）的過去式〉・hit〈hit（碰撞）的過去式〉・back〈後部〉

❺ got into〈get into（參與某事）的過去式〉・fist fight〈鬥毆〉・broke〈break（打破）的過去式〉

❻ pierced〈pierce（穿洞）的過去分詞〉・birthday〈生日〉

中譯

❶ ❷ 脖子支撐著頭。

❸ 他有個大額頭，我聽說這象徵很有智慧。

❹ 學走路的小孩到處走動時滑倒了，他的後腦杓撞到了地板。

❺ Larry 跟人互毆，還打掉了一個人的下巴。

❻ Tess 打算在生日時去穿耳洞。

162 眼睛

MP3 162

1 eye
[aɪ]
(n.) 眼睛

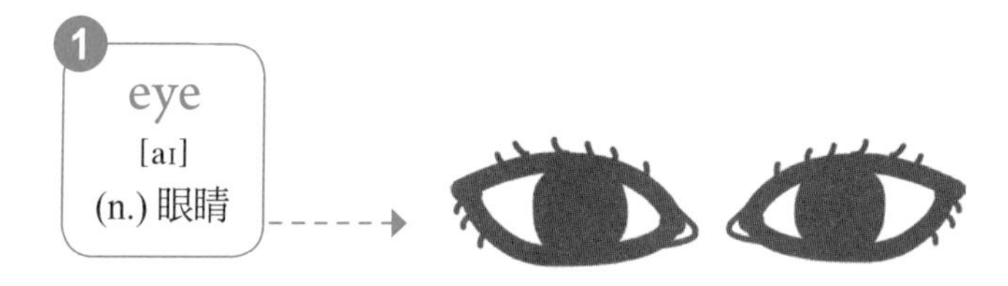

2 eyeball
[`aɪ͵bɔl]
(n.) 眼球

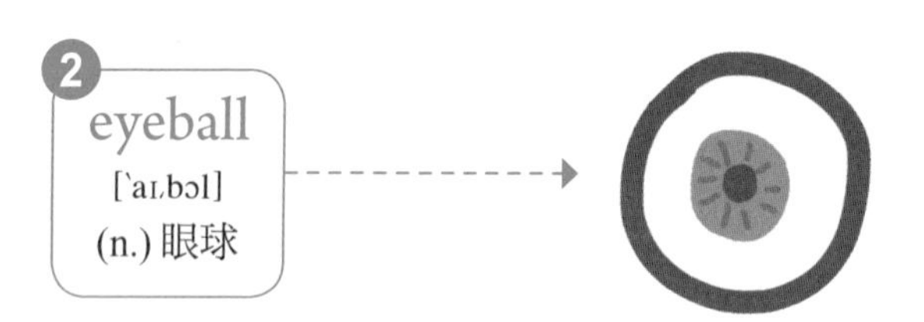

3 pupil
[`pjupḷ]
(n.) 瞳孔

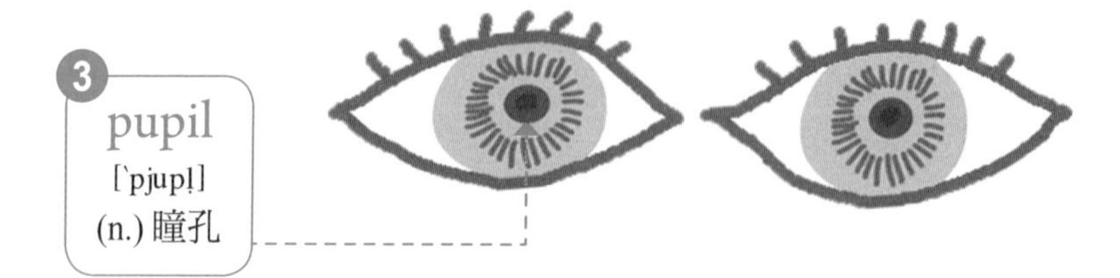

4 eyelid
[`aɪ͵lɪd]
(n.) 眼皮

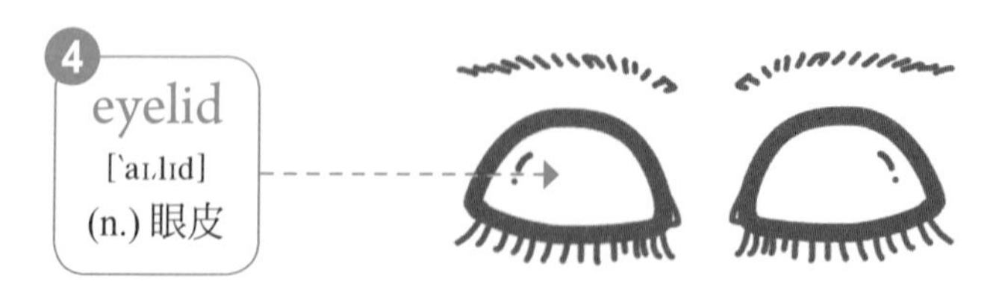

5 eyelash
[`aɪ͵læʃ]
(n.) 眼睫毛

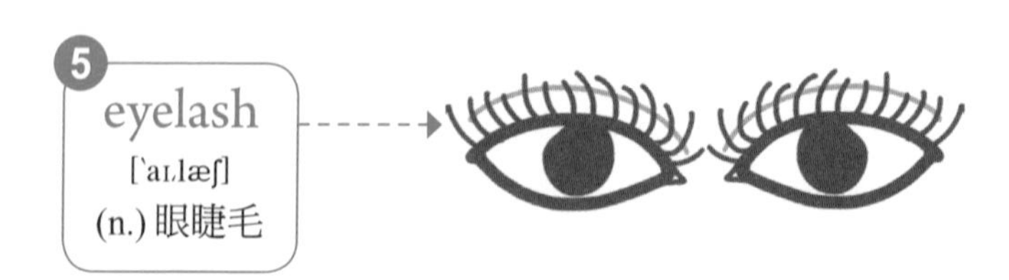

❶ 眼睛
My father has green eyes and my mother has blue, so mine are mixed.

❷ 眼球
David's teammate's finger jabbed his eyeball during basketball practice.
手指戳到他的眼球

❸ 瞳孔
Some types of medicines can make your pupils appear larger.
讓你的瞳孔看起來比較大

❹ 眼皮
When you blink, you close both eyelids at the same time.
兩邊的眼皮會同時闔起來

❺ 眼睫毛
Lady Gaga always wears very long fake eyelashes.
總是戴著

學更多

❶ green〈綠色的〉・blue〈藍色的〉・mine〈我的〉・mixed〈混合的〉
❷ teammate〈隊友〉・finger〈手指〉・jabbed〈jab（戳）的過去式〉・practice〈練習〉
❸ type〈類型〉・medicine〈藥〉・make〈使得〉・appear〈看起來〉・larger〈比較大的，large（大的）的比較級〉
❹ blink〈眨眼〉・close〈闔上〉・both〈兩者〉・at the same time〈同時〉
❺ always〈總是〉・wear〈配戴〉・long〈長的〉・fake〈假的〉

中譯

❶ 我父親的眼睛是綠色的，母親是藍色的，所以我的是兩者的混合。
❷ David 的籃球隊友在進行練習時，用手指戳到他的眼球。
❸ 有些藥物會讓你的瞳孔看起來比較大。
❹ 當你眨眼時，兩邊的眼皮會同時合起來。
❺ 女神卡卡總是戴著非常長的假睫毛。

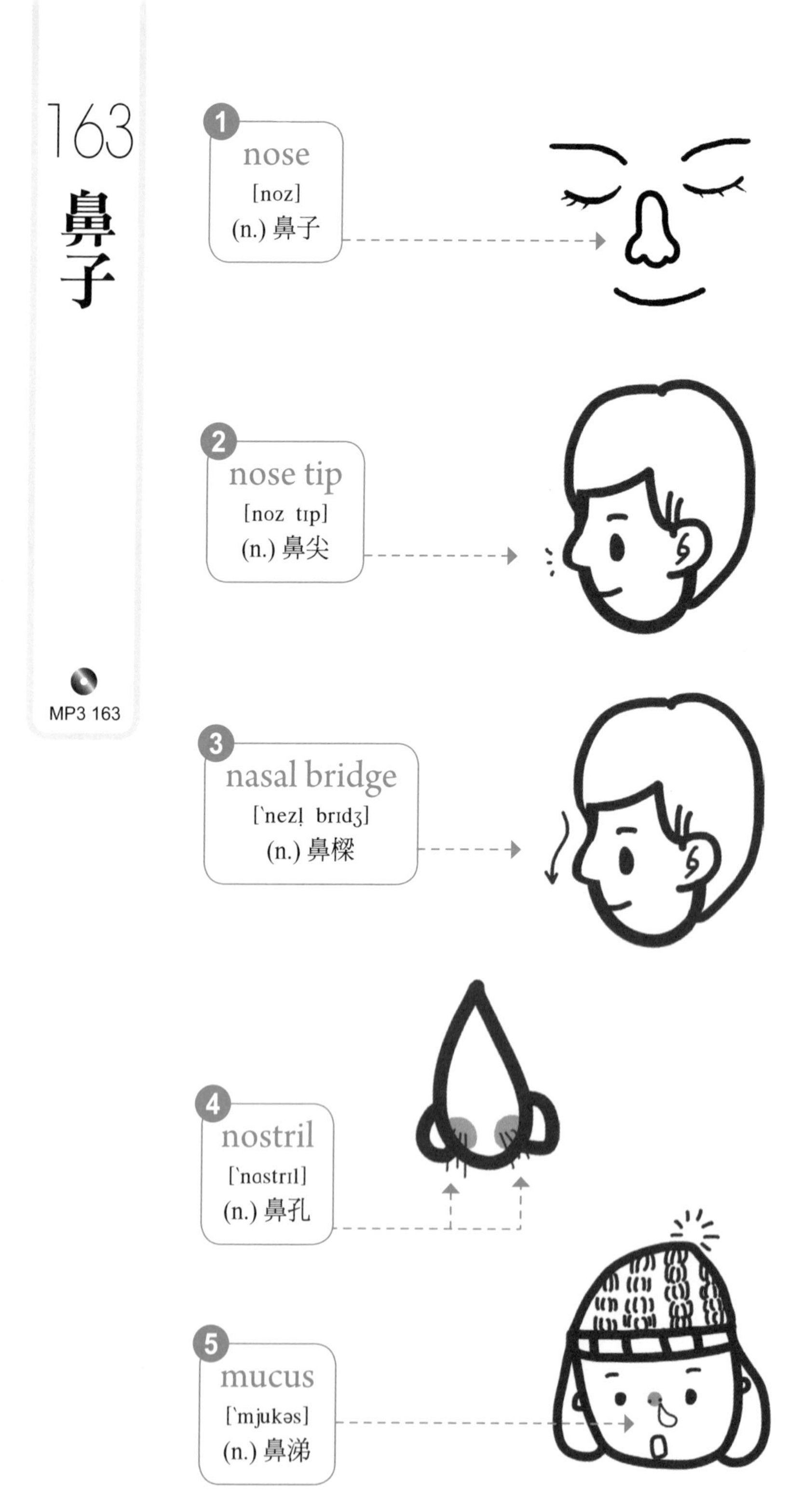
163
鼻子
MP3 163
1
nose
[noz]
(n.) 鼻子
2
nose tip
[noz tɪp]
(n.) 鼻尖
3
nasal bridge
[ˋnezl̩ brɪdʒ]
(n.) 鼻樑
4
nostril
[ˋnɑstrɪl]
(n.) 鼻孔
5
mucus
[ˋmjukəs]
(n.) 鼻涕

❶ 鼻子
Jill's friend doesn't like her nose, so she's getting plastic surgery to fix it.
她要去做整型手術

❷ 鼻尖
His nose tip is flat and round.

❸ 鼻樑
Foreigners tend to have very high nasal bridges.

❹ 鼻孔
During a fire, it's best to plug your nostrils to keep out the smoke.
不讓煙霧進入

❺ 鼻涕
Colds produce a lot of mucus, so drinking more water is important.
喝更多的水

學更多

❶ friend〈朋友〉・plastic surgery〈整型手術〉・fix〈修理〉
❷ tip〈尖端〉・flat〈平的〉・round〈圓的〉
❸ foreigner〈外國人〉・tend to〈有…的傾向〉・high〈高的〉・nasal〈鼻的〉・bridge〈橋梁〉
❹ fire〈火災〉・plug〈把…塞住〉・keep out〈使不進入〉・smoke〈煙霧〉
❺ cold〈感冒〉・produce〈產生〉・drinking〈drink（喝）的 ing 型態〉・important〈重要的〉

中譯

❶ Jill 的朋友不喜歡她的鼻子，所以她要去做整形手術改變它。
❷ 他的鼻尖又扁又圓。
❸ 外國人通常有很高的鼻梁。
❹ 火災時最好堵住你的鼻孔，以防吸入濃煙。
❺ 感冒會流很多鼻涕，所以多喝水是很重要的。

164 嘴巴

MP3 164

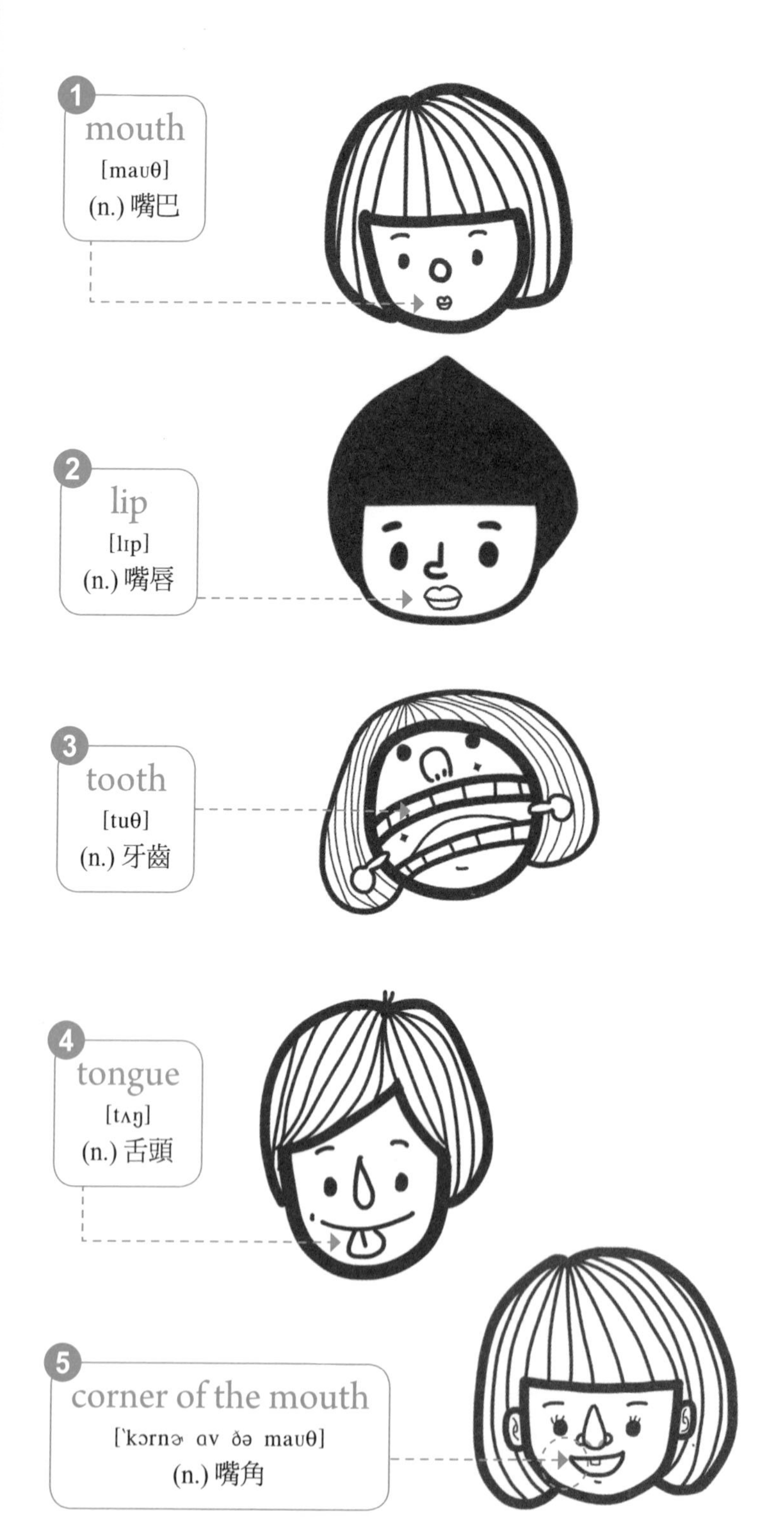

1. **mouth** [mauθ] (n.) 嘴巴
2. **lip** [lɪp] (n.) 嘴唇
3. **tooth** [tuθ] (n.) 牙齒
4. **tongue** [tʌŋ] (n.) 舌頭
5. **corner of the mouth** [ˋkɔrnɚ ɑv ðə mauθ] (n.) 嘴角

❶ 嘴巴

You'd better keep your mouth shut and not tell anyone our secret!

你最好…

❷ 嘴唇

If your lips become dry, just try some lip balm to soften them.

試試護唇膏來滋潤它們

❸ 牙齒

I had to get a tooth pulled after it became infected.

讓一顆牙齒被拔掉

❹ 舌頭

Don't stick out your tongue at others. It's rude!

吐舌頭

❺ 嘴角

He has a sore on the corner of his mouth. He needs some ointment to heal it.

需要一些藥膏治療它

學更多

❶ keep〈保持某一狀態〉‧shut〈shut（閉上）的過去分詞〉‧tell〈告訴〉‧secret〈秘密〉
❷ become〈變得〉‧dry〈乾燥的〉‧lip balm〈護唇膏〉‧soften〈使變柔軟〉
❸ had to〈have to（必須）的過去式〉‧pulled〈pull（拔）的過去分詞〉‧became〈become（變得）的過去式〉‧infected〈受感染的〉
❹ stick out〈伸出〉‧others〈其他人〉‧rude〈無禮的〉
❺ sore〈痛處、瘡、潰瘍〉‧corner〈角落〉‧ointment〈藥膏〉‧heal〈治癒〉

中譯

❶ 你最好閉上你的嘴，不要告訴任何人我們的秘密！
❷ 如果你的嘴唇變得乾燥，試著擦點護唇膏來滋潤它們。
❸ 在一顆牙齒發炎之後，我必須去拔掉它。
❹ 不要對別人吐舌頭，那很沒有禮貌！
❺ 他的嘴角有個傷口，他需要擦些藥膏治療它。

165 人體組成(1)

MP3 165

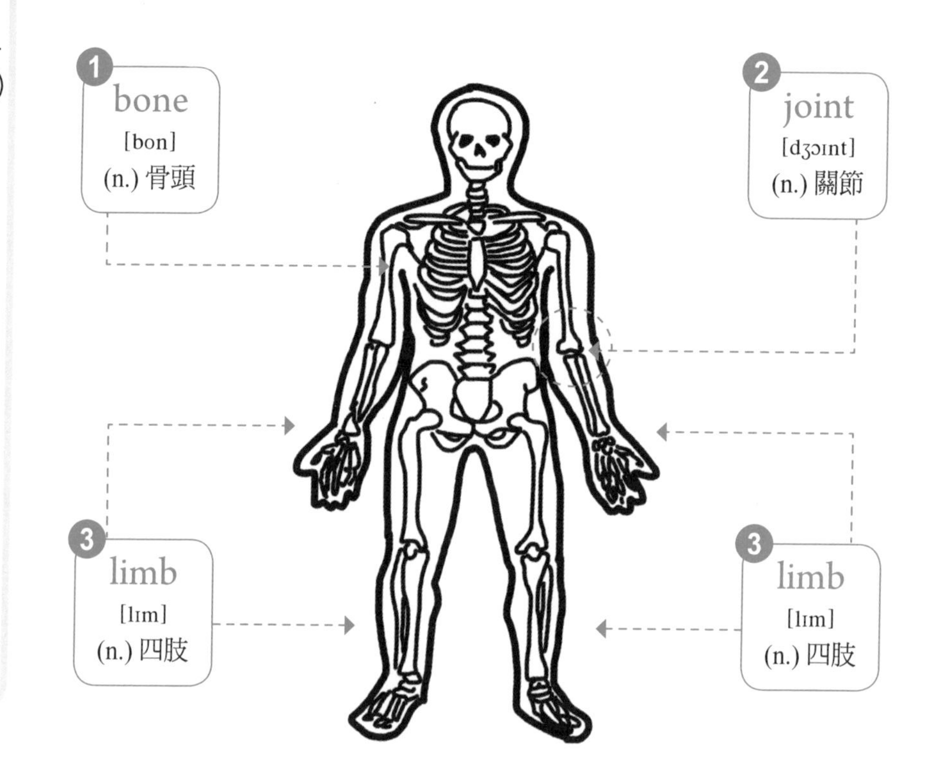

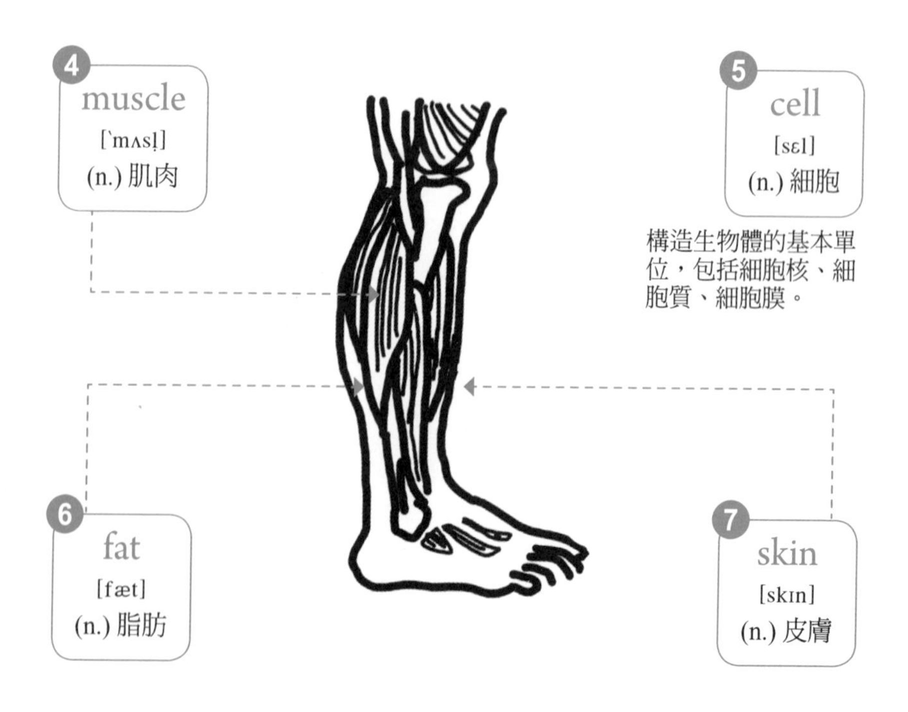

❶ 骨頭

Be careful on that skateboard, or you may end up breaking a bone!

最終會變成骨折

❷ 關節

Arthritis can affect the joints and cause pain for the sufferer.

造成疼痛

❸ 四肢

Nick Vujicic is an inspirational speaker who was born without limbs.

出生時就沒有四肢

❹ 肌肉

After lifting weights for 2 hours, Andy's muscles tired.

❺ 細胞

Our bodies contain trillions of cells.

❻ 脂肪

Too much belly fat during middle age can lead to strokes or heart attacks.

腹部的脂肪太多 心臟病發作

❼ 皮膚

Sarah's skin was really sunburned after playing on the beach all day.

在海灘上玩整天

學更多

❶ skateboard〈滑板〉· end up〈以…終結〉· breaking〈break(折斷)的 ing 型態〉
❷ arthritis〈關節炎〉· affect〈影響〉· cause〈引起〉· pain〈疼痛〉· sufferer〈患病者〉
❸ inspirational〈鼓舞人心的〉· speaker〈演講者〉· be born〈出生〉
❹ lifting weight〈lift weight(舉重)的 ing 型態〉· tired〈tire(感到疲勞)的過去式〉
❺ our〈我們的〉· contain〈包含〉· trillion〈萬億〉
❻ belly〈肚子〉· middle age〈中年〉· lead to〈導致〉· stroke〈中風〉
❼ sunburned〈sunburn(曬傷)的過去分詞〉· beach〈海灘〉· all day〈整天〉

中譯

❶ 玩滑板要小心,否則你可能會骨折!
❷ 關節炎可能影響關節,並造成患者的疼痛。
❸ Nick Vujicic 是個激勵人心的演說者,他在出生時便沒有四肢。
❹ 舉重兩個鐘頭之後, Andy 的肌肉感到疲勞。
❺ 我們的身體裡,有好幾萬億的細胞。
❻ 中年時腹部脂肪太多,可能導致中風或心臟病。
❼ 在海灘上玩了一整天後, Sarah 的皮膚就曬傷了。

166 人體組成(2)

MP3 166

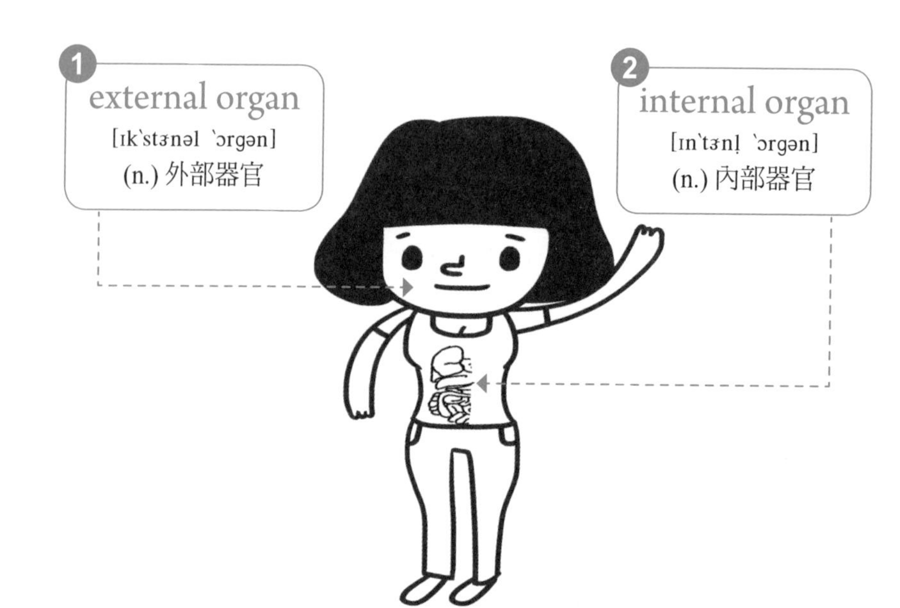

1 external organ [ɪkˋstɝnəl ˋɔrgən] (n.) 外部器官

2 internal organ [ɪnˋtɝnḷ ˋɔrgən] (n.) 內部器官

3 artery [ˋɑrtərɪ] (n.) 動脈

從心臟運送血液到全身的血管。

4 vein [ven] (n.) 靜脈

運送血液回心臟的血管。

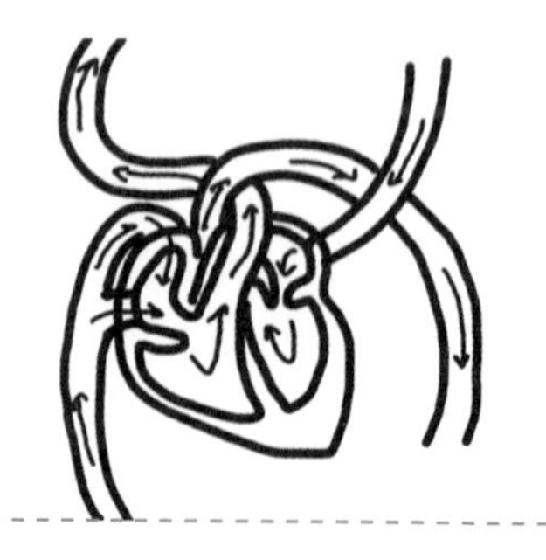

5 blood [blʌd] (n.) 血液

6 water [ˋwɔtɚ] (n.) 水分

7 nerve [nɝv] (n.) 神經

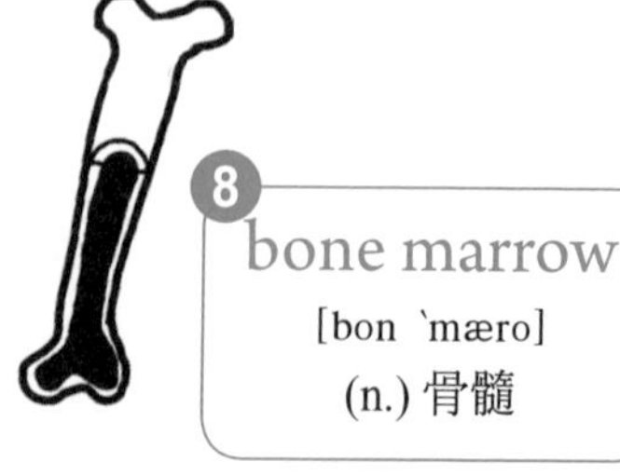

8 bone marrow [bon ˋmæro] (n.) 骨髓

❶ 外部器官
Did you know skin is an external organ?

❷ 內部器官
Your lungs, heart and kidneys are just a few of your internal organs.
你的內部器官的其中一小部分

❸ 動脈
❹ 靜脈
Arteries are blood vessels that carry blood away from the heart, while veins carry blood back to the heart.
運送血液離開心臟
運送血液回到心臟

❺ 血液
❻ 水分
Drinking lots of water helps blood do its job and carry oxygen to cells.
運作

❼ 神經
Messages are carried between the brain and the rest of the body by nerves.
在腦部和身體其他部位之間

❽ 骨髓
Tony has leukemia, and he will need a bone marrow transplant.

學更多

❶ know〈知道〉‧skin〈皮膚〉‧external〈外部的〉‧organ〈器官〉
❷ lung〈肺〉‧heart〈心臟〉‧kidney〈腎臟〉‧a few〈為數不多的〉‧internal〈內部的〉
❸❹ blood vessel〈血管〉‧carry〈運送〉‧away〈離開〉‧back〈往回〉
❺❻ help〈幫助〉‧job〈工作〉‧oxygen〈氧氣〉‧cell〈細胞〉
❼ message〈訊息〉‧between〈在…之間〉‧brain〈腦〉‧rest〈其餘部分〉
❽ leukemia〈白血病〉‧need〈需要〉‧bone〈骨頭〉‧marrow〈髓、骨髓〉‧transplant〈移植〉

中譯

❶ 你知道皮膚是一個外部器官嗎？
❷ 肺、心臟和腎臟，只是你的內部器官中的一小部分。
❸❹ 動脈是運送血液離開心臟的血管，而靜脈是運送血液回到心臟的血管。
❺❻ 多喝水有助於血液運作，以及運送氧氣到細胞。
❼ 透過神經，可以在腦部及身體其他部位之間傳遞訊息。
❽ Tony 罹患白血病，他將需要進行骨髓移植。

167 蛋糕

MP3 167

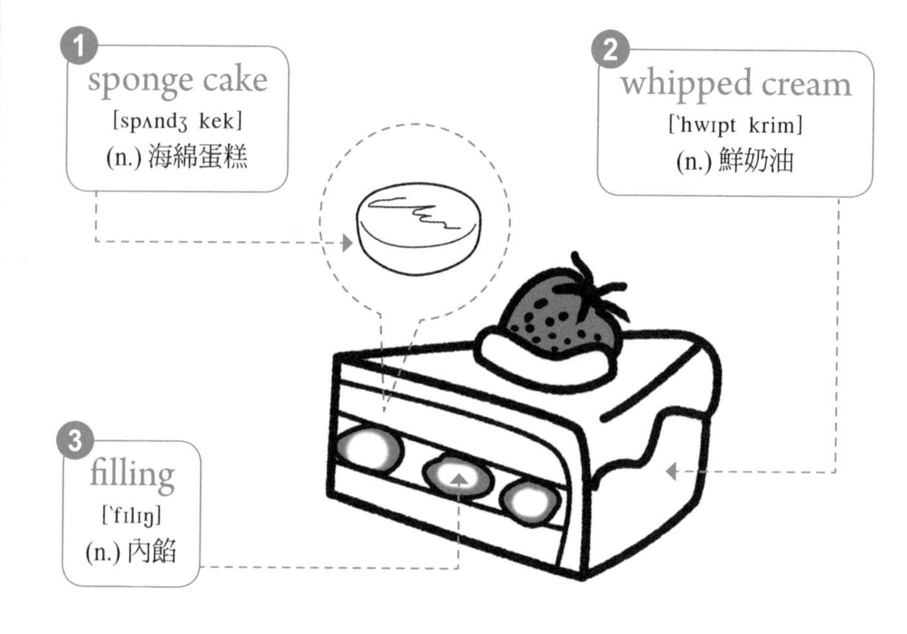

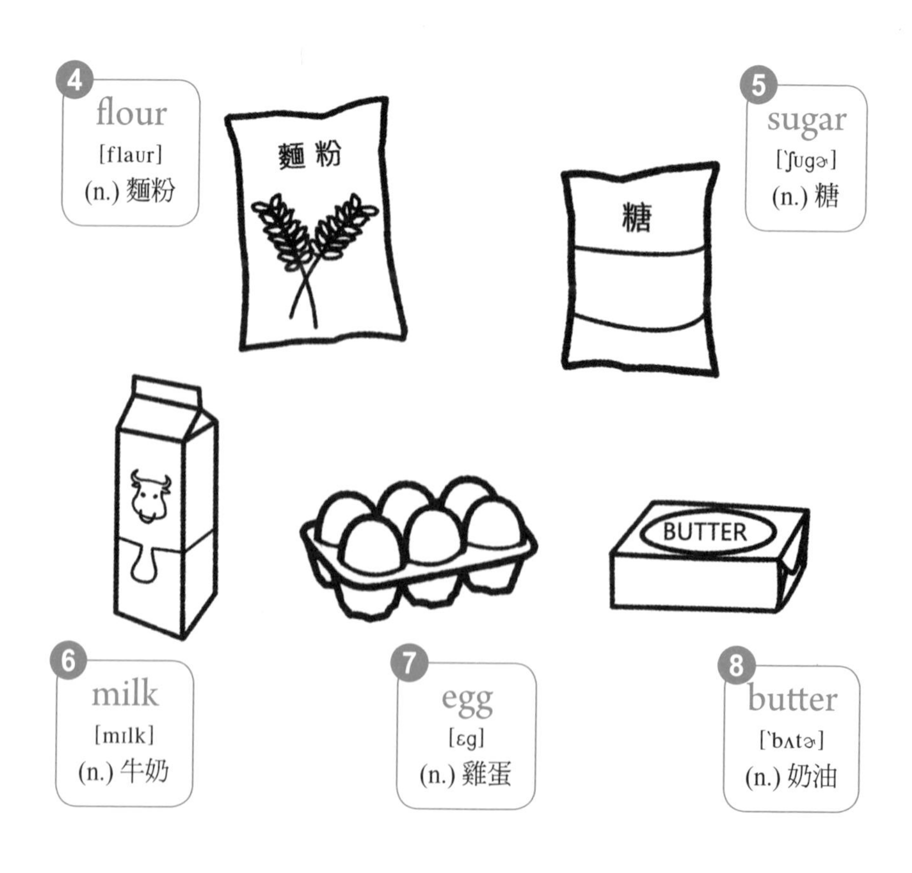

❶ 海綿蛋糕

I bought a yellow sponge cake at the bakery with strawberries on top.

上面放著草莓

❷ 鮮奶油

There is a lot of whipped cream on top of the dessert.

❸ 內餡

The chocolate filling in the cake was smooth and tasty.

蛋糕內的巧克力夾餡

❹ 麵粉

I need to buy some flour before I can bake some bread.

❺ 糖

The dentist said eating too much sugar would damage their teeth.

❻ 牛奶

Drinking milk is essential for kids who need healthy bones.

需要骨骼健康的孩童

❼ 雞蛋

Every morning, Johnny buys an egg sandwich for breakfast.

❽ 奶油

Susie doesn't eat butter anymore because she is trying to lose weight.

學更多

❶ bought〈buy（買）的過去式〉・sponge〈海綿〉・bakery〈麵包店〉・strawberry〈草莓〉
❷ whipped〈攪打過的〉・cream〈奶油〉・top〈表面〉・dessert〈甜點〉
❸ chocolate〈巧克力〉・smooth〈香醇的〉・tasty〈可口的〉
❹ some〈一些〉・bake〈烤〉・bread〈麵包〉
❺ dentist〈牙醫〉・damage〈損害〉・teeth〈tooth（牙齒）的複數〉
❻ essential〈必要的〉・healthy〈健康的〉・bone〈骨骼〉
❼ sandwich〈三明治〉・breakfast〈早餐〉
❽ anymore〈再也〉・trying〈try（試圖、努力）的 ing 型態〉・lose weight〈減輕體重〉

中譯

❶ 我在麵包店買了一個上面有草莓的黃色海綿蛋糕。
❷ 那道甜點上面有很多鮮奶油。
❸ 蛋糕內的巧克力內餡，口感香醇又好吃。
❹ 在烤麵包之前，我需要去買一些麵粉。
❺ 牙醫說，吃太多糖會損害他們的牙齒。
❻ 對於需要健康骨骼的孩童來說，喝牛奶很重要。
❼ 每天早上， Johnny 都會買一個雞蛋三明治當早餐。
❽ Susie 不再吃奶油了，因為她正在努力減肥。

168 熱狗麵包(1)

MP3 168

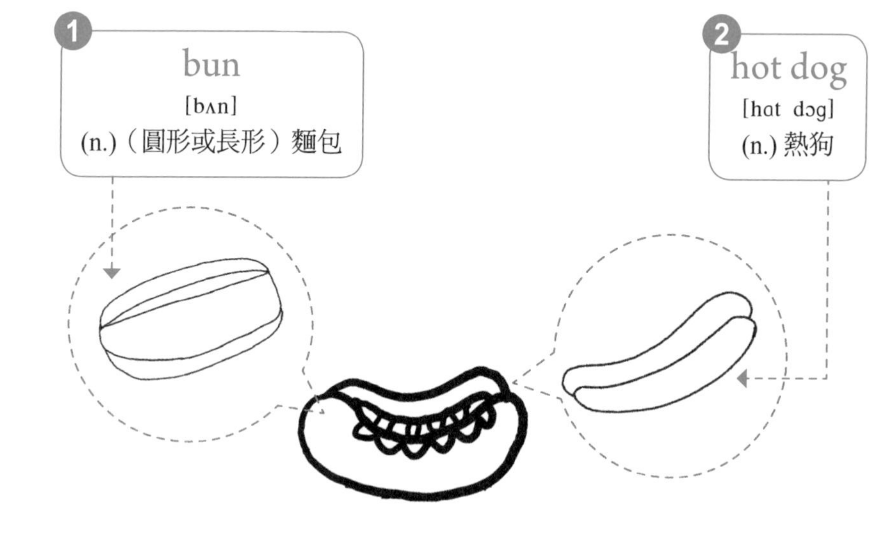

1. **bun**
[bʌn]
(n.)（圓形或長形）麵包

2. **hot dog**
[hɑt dɔg]
(n.) 熱狗

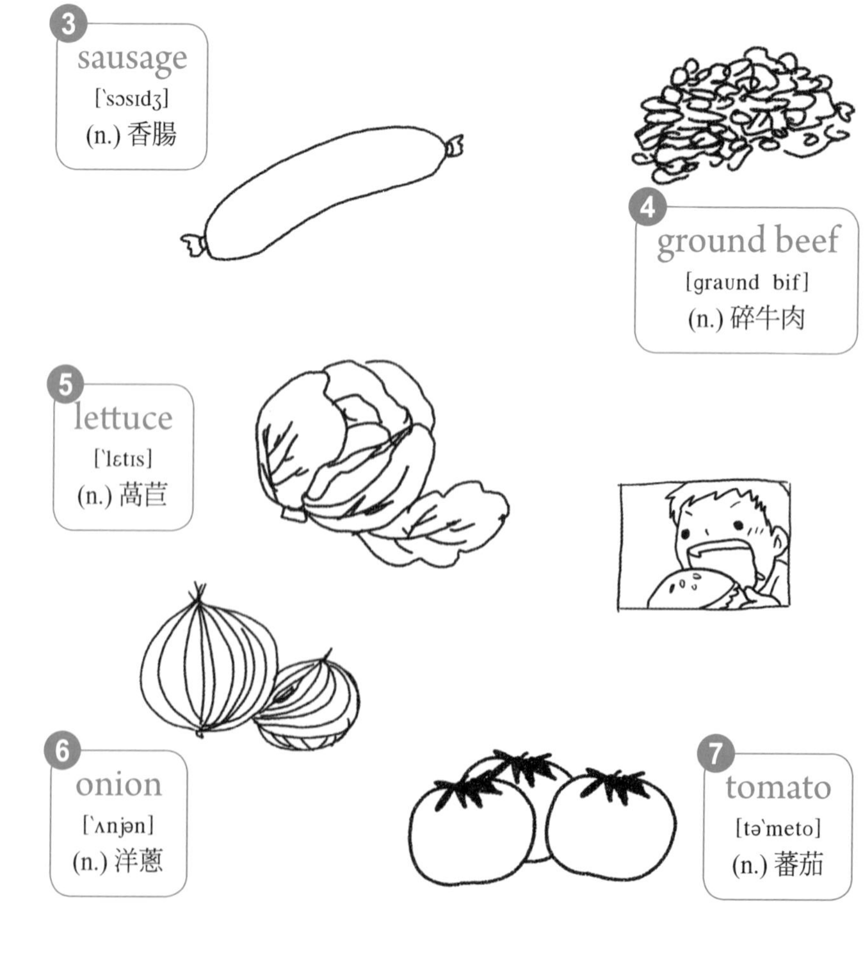

3. **sausage**
[ˋsɔsɪdʒ]
(n.) 香腸

4. **ground beef**
[graʊnd bif]
(n.) 碎牛肉

5. **lettuce**
[ˋlɛtɪs]
(n.) 萵苣

6. **onion**
[ˋʌnjən]
(n.) 洋蔥

7. **tomato**
[təˋmeto]
(n.) 蕃茄

❶（圓形或長形）麵包

Shelly likes to toast her hamburger bun for a nice, crispy texture.

酥脆的口感

❷ 熱狗

Hot dogs sold on the streets of New York City are a convenient and inexpensive meal.

方便又便宜的餐點

❸ 香腸

Pork sausage is very tasty with pancakes and syrup in the morning.

❹ 碎牛肉

Ground beef is used to make hamburgers, among other dishes.

❺ 萵苣

I eat at least two heads of lettuce every week in my salads.

至少兩顆萵苣

❻ 洋蔥

I hate cutting up onions because they make my eyes water.

讓我眼睛流淚

❼ 蕃茄

Fresh tomatoes straight out of the garden are such a delicious treat.

從菜園現摘　如此美味的享受

學更多

❶ toast〈烤〉・crispy〈酥脆的〉・texture〈結構、質地〉
❷ sold〈sell（賣）的過去分詞〉・inexpensive〈價錢低廉的〉・meal〈餐點〉
❸ pork〈豬肉〉・tasty〈可口的〉・pancake〈鬆餅、薄煎餅〉・syrup〈糖漿〉
❹ ground〈磨碎的〉・beef〈牛肉〉・hamburger〈漢堡牛排〉・among〈在…之中〉
❺ at least〈至少〉・head〈顆〉・salad〈沙拉〉
❻ hate〈討厭〉・cutting up〈cut up（切開）的 ing 型態〉・water〈流淚〉
❼ straight〈立刻〉・out of〈自…離開〉・garden〈菜園〉・treat〈難得的樂事或享受〉

中譯

❶ Shelly 喜歡烤一下她的漢堡麵包，讓它有酥脆的好口感。
❷ 紐約市街頭所販賣的熱狗，是既方便又便宜的餐點。
❸ 早晨時，吃豬肉香腸搭配鬆餅和糖漿，是非常美味的。
❹ 碎牛肉被用來製作漢堡牛排，以及其他料理。
❺ 在每週的沙拉中，我至少會吃掉兩顆萵苣。
❻ 我痛恨切洋蔥，因為它們會讓我流淚。
❼ 菜園現摘的新鮮番茄，是如此美味的享受。

169

熱狗麵包(2)

MP3 169

1 pickle
[`pɪkḷ]
(n.) 酸黃瓜

2 cheese
[tʃiz]
(n.) 起司

3 sauerkraut
[`saur͵kraut]
(n.) 德國酸菜

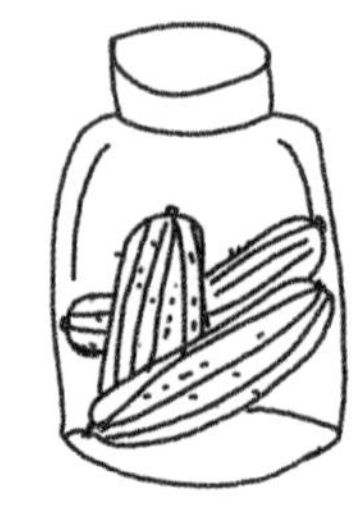

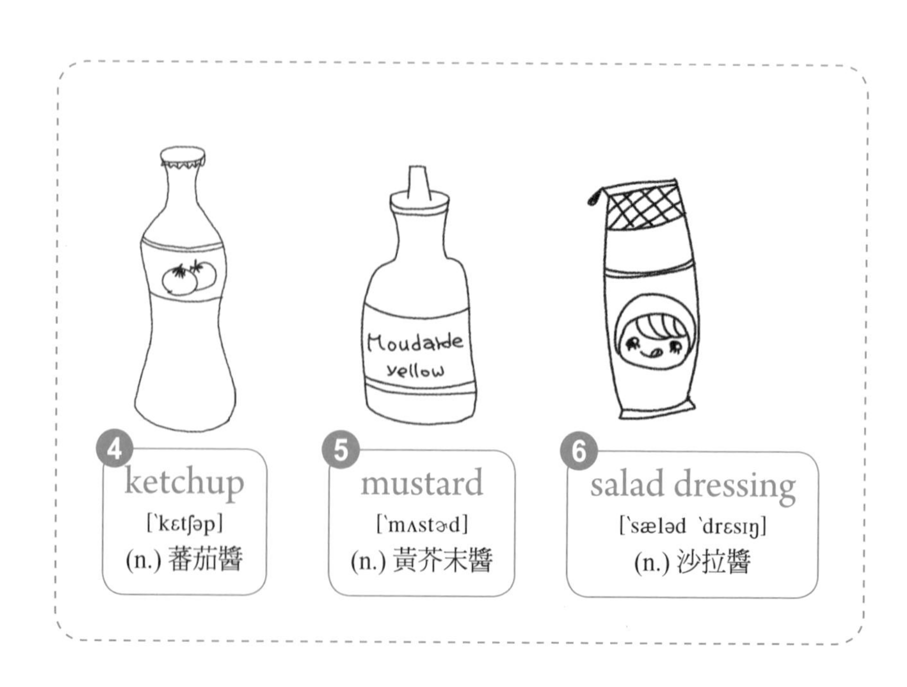

4 ketchup
[`kɛtʃəp]
(n.) 蕃茄醬

5 mustard
[`mʌstəd]
(n.) 黃芥末醬

6 salad dressing
[`sæləd `drɛsɪŋ]
(n.) 沙拉醬

❶ 酸黃瓜
The most popular types of pickles are sweet pickles and dill pickles.

❷ 起司
When John orders pizza, he always asks for extra cheese.
加點額外的起司

❸ 德國酸菜
Sauerkraut means sour cabbage in German, and is a popular topping on hot dogs.
在德文裡是指酸的白菜

❹ 蕃茄醬
Ketchup is made using tomatoes, sugar, and various spices.
用…製成的

❺ 黃芥末醬
One of the condiments used on hamburgers and some types of sandwiches is mustard.
被用在漢堡跟一些三明治上

❻ 沙拉醬
Sally is on a diet, so she always gets salad dressing on the side when she orders salads at restaurants.
讓沙拉醬放在旁邊

學更多

❶ popular〈受歡迎的〉‧type〈類型〉‧sweet〈甜的〉‧dill〈蒔蘿〉
❷ order〈點餐〉‧always〈總是〉‧ask〈要求〉‧extra〈額外的〉
❸ mean〈意謂〉‧sour〈酸的〉‧cabbage〈甘藍菜〉‧German〈德語〉‧topping〈配料〉
❹ sugar〈糖〉‧various〈各種各樣的、許多的〉‧spice〈香料〉
❺ condiment〈佐料〉‧some〈一些〉‧sandwich〈三明治〉
❻ on a diet〈節食〉‧dressing〈拌沙拉用的調醬〉‧on the side〈放在旁邊〉

中譯

❶ 最受歡迎的兩種酸黃瓜，是甜酸黃瓜以及蒔蘿酸黃瓜。
❷ John 點披薩時，總會要求多加一點起司。
❸ 在德文中， sauerkraut 是指酸的白菜；它也是很受歡迎的熱狗配料。
❹ 番茄醬是用番茄、糖和許多香料製成的。
❺ 一種會用於漢堡和一些三明治的醬料，是黃芥末醬。
❻ Sally 正在減肥，所以她在餐廳點沙拉時，都會讓沙拉醬放在旁邊。

170 義大利麵

MP3 170

1 **macaroni**
[ˌmækəˋronɪ]
(n.) 通心粉

2 **spaghetti**
[spəˋgɛtɪ]
(n.) 義大利麵條

3 **herb**
[hɝb]
(n.) 香料

4 **olive oil**
[ˋɑlɪv ɔɪl]
(n.) 橄欖油

5 **tomato sauce**
[təˋmeto sɔs]
(n.) 茄汁

6 **grated cheese**
[ˋgretɪd tʃiz]
(n.) 起司粉

❶ 通心粉
Macaroni is a type of noodle that is short and hollow.
一種又短又空心的麵條

❷ 義大利麵條
Spaghetti with meatballs is the chef's special at *Cosi*, an Italian restaurant.
主廚的拿手菜

❸ 香料
Herbs and spices can add a lot of flavor to dishes without adding calories.
添加許多風味

❹ 橄欖油
My doctor advised that I use olive oil in my cooking, instead of butter.
我的醫生建議…

❺ 茄汁
If you want to make really yummy spaghetti, always make your own tomato sauce.
製作你自己的茄汁

❻ 起司粉
The chef finished off the fresh pasta dish by adding some grated cheese on top.
完成剛料理好的義大利麵食

學更多

❶ type〈類型〉．noodle〈麵條〉．short〈短的〉．hollow〈中空的〉
❷ meatball〈肉糰〉．chef〈主廚、廚師〉．special〈拿手菜〉．Italian〈義大利的〉
❸ spice〈調味品〉．add〈添加〉．flavor〈味道〉．calorie〈卡路里〉
❹ advised〈advise（建議）的過去式〉．olive〈橄欖〉．cooking〈烹調〉．instead of〈代替〉．butter〈奶油〉
❺ yummy〈好吃的〉．always〈總是〉．own〈自己的〉
❻ finished off〈finish off（完成）的過去式〉．pasta〈義大利麵〉．dish〈菜餚〉．adding〈add（添加）的 ing 型態〉．grated〈磨碎的〉

中譯

❶ 通心粉是一種又短又空心的麵條。
❷ 肉丸義大利麵是義大利餐廳 Cosi 的一道主廚拿手菜。
❸ 香料和調味品都可以為菜餚增添風味，而且不會增加卡路里。
❹ 我的醫師建議我在烹調時，要使用橄欖油來代替奶油。
❺ 如果你想做出很好吃的義大利麵，一定要自己製作茄汁。
❻ 主廚在上面撒了一些起司粉，就完成了這道剛料理好的義大利麵。

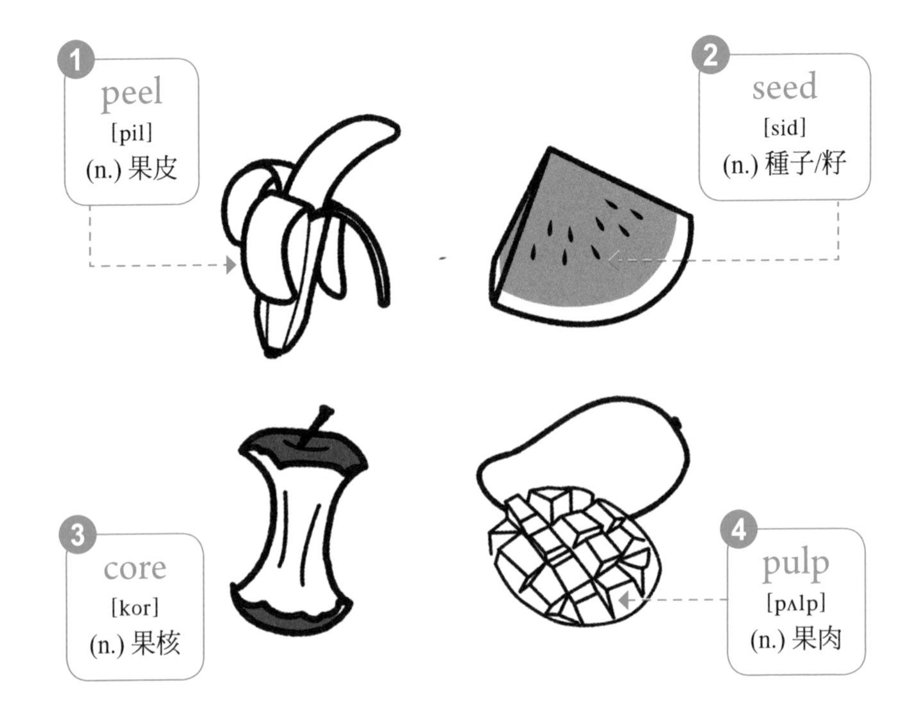

❶ 果皮
Don't eat the peel of oranges because it's too bitter!
柳丁皮

❷ 種子 / 籽
Stop spitting the watermelon seeds all over the floor!
地上到處都是

❸ 果核
The core of an apple isn't usually eaten.
通常不會被吃

❹ 果肉
I prefer fresh-squeezed orange juice with pulp in it.

學更多

❶ orange〈柳橙〉・too〈太〉・bitter〈苦的〉
❷ spitting〈spit（吐）的 ing 型態〉・all over〈到處〉・floor〈地板〉
❸ usually〈通常〉・eaten〈eat（吃）的過去分詞〉
❹ prefer〈更喜歡〉・fresh-squeezed〈現榨的〉・squeezed〈squeeze（榨）的過去分詞〉

中譯

❶ 不要吃柳丁的果皮，它太苦了！
❷ 不要把西瓜籽吐得地上到處都是！
❸ 通常沒人會吃蘋果的果核。
❹ 我喜歡現榨且含果肉的柳橙汁。

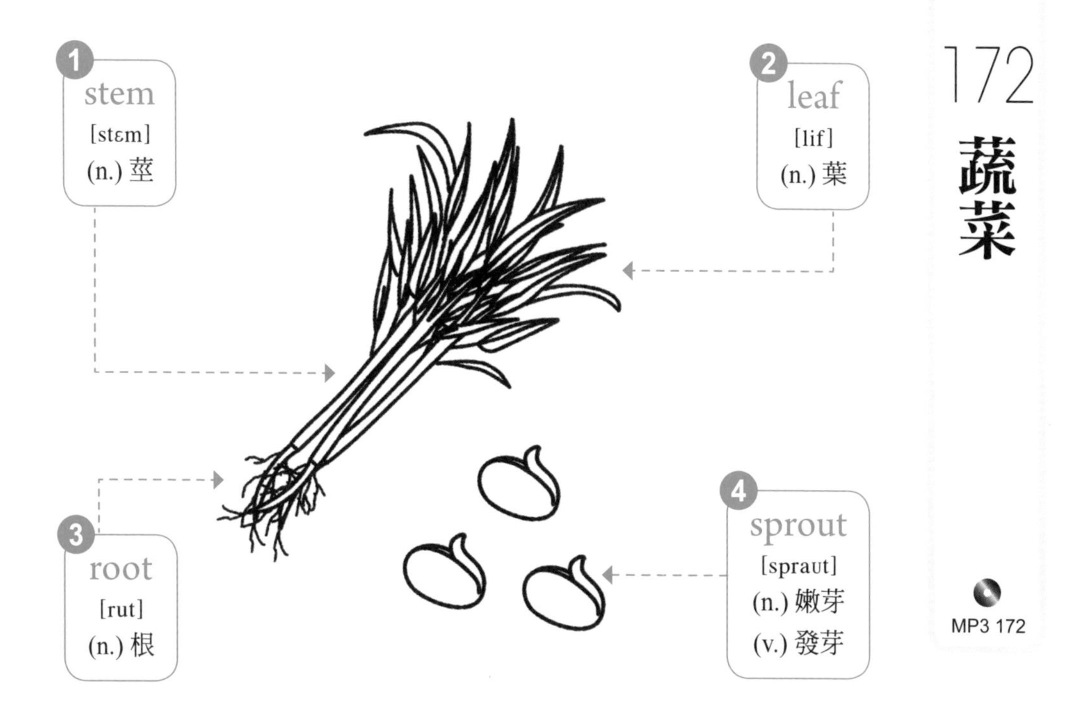

❶ 莖

The stems on roses have thorns that are very sharp!

❷ 葉

The leaves are falling off my dying plant due to lack of water.

falling off my dying plant：從我那棵垂死的植物上掉落

lack of water：缺水

❸ 根

The roots on that old tree aren't getting enough water.

❹ 嫩芽 / 發芽

The seeds Jenny planted in her garden are just beginning to sprout.

planted in her garden：播種在她的花園裡

學更多

❶ rose〈玫瑰〉・thorn〈刺〉・sharp〈尖的〉

❷ falling off〈fall off（脫離）的 ing 型態〉・dying〈垂死的〉・lack〈欠缺〉

❸ old〈老的〉・getting〈get（得到）的 ing 型態〉・enough〈足夠的〉

❹ seed〈種子〉・planted〈plant（栽種、播種）的過去式〉・garden〈花園〉

中譯

❶ 玫瑰的莖上有很尖銳的刺。

❷ 我那棵垂死的植物因為缺水，葉子不斷掉落。

❸ 那棵老樹的根，沒有得到足夠的水分。

❹ Jenny 播種在自己花園的種子，剛開始發芽了。

173 企業構成(1)

MP3 173

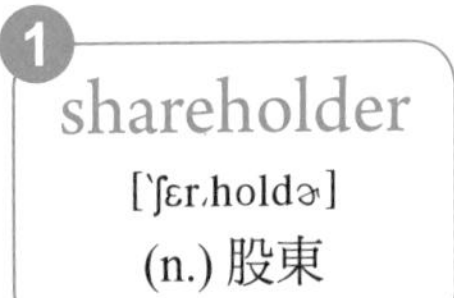

1 shareholder
[ˋʃɛrˏholdɚ]
(n.) 股東

2 employer
[ɪmˋplɔɪɚ]
(n.) 雇主

3 employee
[ˏɛmplɔɪˋi]
(n.) 員工

4 superior
[səˋpɪrɪɚ]
(n.) 上級

5 subordinate
[səˋbɔrdn̩ɪt]
(n.) 下屬

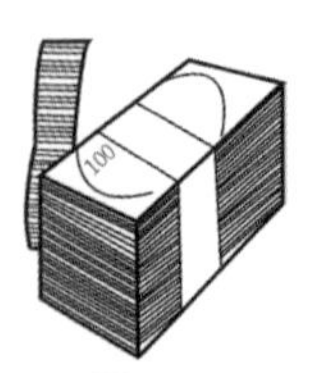

6 office and equipment
[ˋɔfɪs ænd ɪˋkwɪpmənt]
(n.) 廠辦設備/辦公室和設備

7 asset
[ˋæsɛt]
(n.) 資產

8 cash
[kæʃ]
(n.) 現金

❶ 股東
I am a shareholder of HTC stock.

❷ 雇主
Andy is self-employed, so he is his own boss; he doesn't have an employer.
他是他自己的老闆

❸ 員工
If you want a promotion, then be a responsible, hard-working employee.
想要升遷

❹ 上級
❺ 下屬
Although Frank is not my boss, he is my superior at our firm, and I am his subordinate.
他在我們公司裡是我的上級

❻ 廠辦設備 / 辦公室和設備
Before a company moves into a new office, they need to purchase some equipment.
搬到新的辦公室

❼ 資產
Apple Computer's greatest asset was Steve Jobs's creative mind.
創意頭腦

❽ 現金
Will you pay by cash or credit card?

學更多

❶ stock〈股票、股份〉
❷ self-employed〈自己經營的、自雇的〉‧own〈自己的〉
❸ promotion〈升遷〉‧responsible〈認真負責的〉‧hard-working〈努力工作的〉
❹ ❺ although〈雖然〉‧boss〈老闆〉‧firm〈公司〉
❻ move into〈搬進〉‧purchase〈購買〉
❼ greatest〈最優秀的，great（優秀的）的最高級〉‧creative〈有創造力的〉‧mind〈頭腦〉
❽ pay〈付款〉‧credit card〈信用卡〉

中譯

❶ 我是 HTC 股份的股東之一。
❷ Andy 屬於自雇的性質，所以自己就是老闆，他沒有雇主。
❸ 如果你想升遷，就得當一位認真負責且努力工作的員工。
❹ ❺ 雖然 Frank 不是我的老闆，但他在我們公司是我的上級，我是他的下屬。
❻ 一間公司搬到新辦公室之前，需要先購買一些設備。
❼ 蘋果電腦最有價值的資產，是 Steve Jobs 的創意頭腦。
❽ 你要用現金付款，還是刷卡？

174 企業構成(2)

MP3 174

❶ 企業形象

Building a good corporate image can take time and money.
花費時間跟金錢

❷ 產品

High-quality products usually cost more, but last longer than low-quality items.
花費更多 更耐久

❸ 生產
❹ 銷售

After the earthquake in 2011, Japan was unable to produce and sell as many goods as usual.
像往常一樣多的產品

❺ 行銷

Without good marketing, customers won't know about your product or services.
顧客不會知道

❻ 發行通路

Apple Computer likes to sell directly to customers, while other
直接銷售給顧客
companies prefer to use sales channels to reach more people.
觸及更多的人

❼ 供應商

Our company uses a vendor to handle all of our IT needs.
處理我們所有的 IT 需求

❽ 合作廠商 / 合夥

The partnership between Larry Page and Sergey Brin resulted in the founding of Google.
導致

學更多

❶ building〈build（建立）的 ing 型態〉• corporate〈公司的〉• image〈形象〉• take〈花費〉
❷ quality〈品質〉• cost〈花費〉• last〈持久、保持良好的狀態〉• item〈物品〉
❸ ❹ earthquake〈地震〉• unable〈沒有辦法的〉• goods〈商品〉• as...as...〈像…一樣〉
❺ without〈沒有〉• customer〈顧客〉• product〈產品〉• service〈服務〉
❻ directly〈直接地〉• while〈然而〉• prefer〈更喜歡〉• sales〈銷售的〉• reach〈到達〉
❼ company〈公司〉• handle〈處理〉• all〈所有的〉• IT〈資訊科技〉• need〈需求〉
❽ resulted〈result（導致）的過去式〉• founding〈found（創辦）的 ing 型態〉

中譯

❶ 建立良好的企業形象，需要花費時間跟金錢。
❷ 高品質的產品通常成本高，但比低品質的產品更持久耐用。
❸ ❹ 在 2011 年的地震之後，日本無法生產及銷售跟往常一樣多的產品。
❺ 沒有好的行銷，顧客就無法獲得你的產品或服務的相關訊息。
❻ 蘋果電腦喜歡對顧客進行直接銷售，而其他公司則較喜歡利用發行通路讓產品觸及更多人。
❼ 我們公司利用一家供應商來處理我們所有的 IT 需求。
❽ Larry Page 和 Sergey Brin 的合夥，造就了 Google 的創立。

175 人口結構

MP3 175

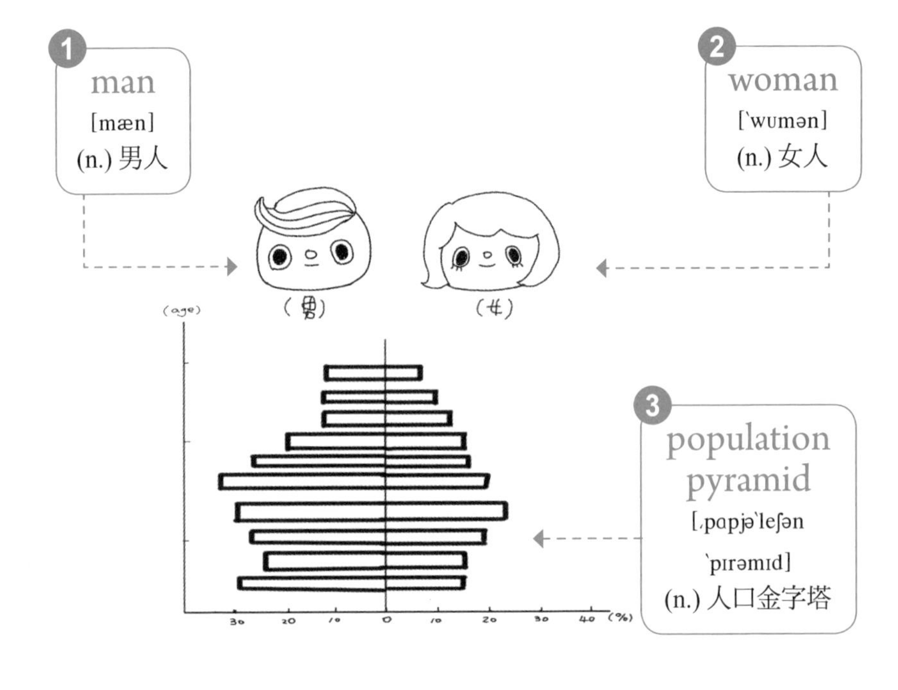

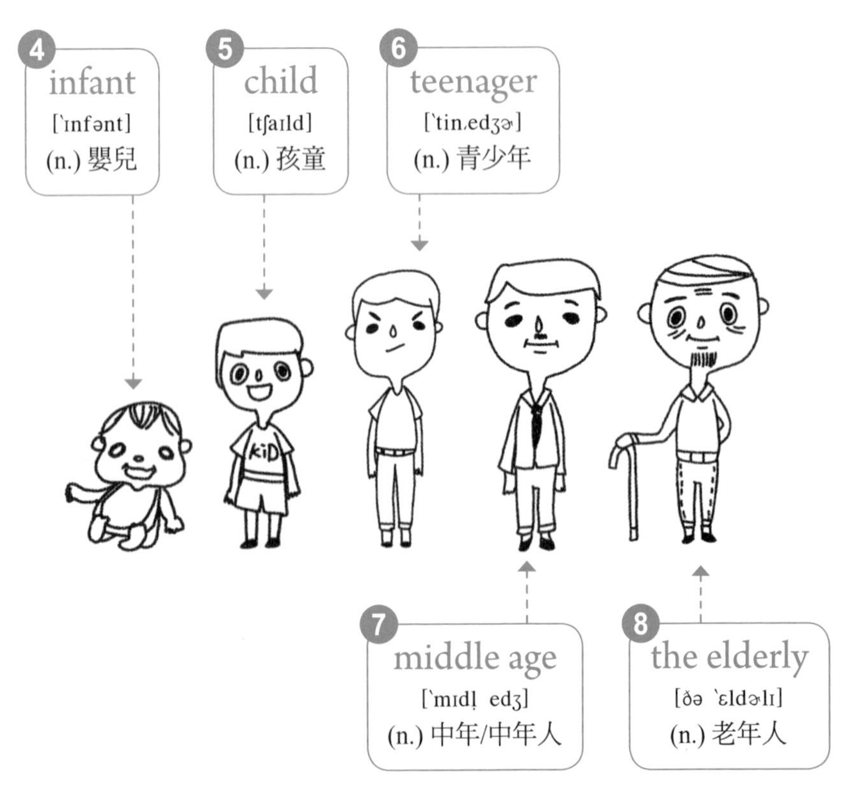

❶ 男人
❷ 女人
That man loves to flirt, but he never gets serious with a single woman!
從來沒有變得認真

❸ 人口金字塔
The population pyramid is a chart that shows the distribution of male and female age groups.
男性和女性的年齡層分布

❹ 嬰兒
An infant just sleeps and eats most of the time.
大多數的時間

❺ 孩童
He's only a child, so let him have some fun.
讓他玩

❻ 青少年
After becoming a teenager, David turned rebellious.
變得叛逆

❼ 中年 / 中年人
Middle age is usually considered to start around 45-50 years old.
大約 45 到 50 歲左右

❽ 老年人
It's important for society to take care of the elderly.
照顧老年人

學更多

❶ ❷ love〈喜愛〉・flirt〈調情〉・never〈從未〉・serious〈認真的〉・single〈單一的〉
❸ population〈人口〉・pyramid〈金字塔〉・chart〈圖表〉・distribution〈分布〉
❹ just〈只〉・sleep〈睡覺〉・eat〈吃〉・most〈大部分的〉
❺ only〈只〉・let〈讓〉・have fun〈玩得開心〉
❻ turned〈turn（變得）的過去式〉・rebellious〈難以控制的〉
❼ middle〈中間的〉・age〈年齡〉・considered〈consider（認為）的過去分詞〉・start〈起始於〉
❽ important〈重要的〉・society〈社會〉・take care of〈照顧〉

中譯

❶ ❷ 那個男人愛調情，但他從來沒有認真和單一女性交往過。
❸ 人口金字塔是一個顯示男性與女性年齡層分布的圖表。
❹ 嬰兒大多數的時間都是睡覺和吃東西。
❺ 他只是個孩子，就讓他玩得開心吧！
❻ 成為青少年後，David 就變得很叛逆。
❼ 一般認為中年大約是從 45 到 50 歲左右開始。
❽ 就社會而言，對老年人的照顧是很重要的。

附錄

詞性分類 × 字母排序

名詞 單元

詞性分類 × 字母排序

詞性分類 × 字母排序

詞性分類 × 字母排序

Fly 飛系列 11

圖解生活實用英語：人事物的種類構造（附 1MP3）

初版一刷　2015 年 10 月 23 日

作者　檸檬樹英語教學團隊
英語例句　Stephanie Buckley、張馨匀
插畫　許仲綺、陳博深、陳琬瑜、吳怡萱、鄭菀書、周奕伶、葉依婷、朱珮瑩、沈諭、巫秉旂、王筑儀
封面設計　陳文德
版型設計　洪素貞
英語錄音　Stephanie Buckley
責任編輯　沈祐禎、黃冠禎

發行人　江媛珍
社長・總編輯　何聖心
出版者　檸檬樹國際書版有限公司 檸檬樹出版社
E-mail：lemontree@booknews.com.tw
地址：新北市235中和區中安街80號3樓
電話・傳真：02-29271121・02-29272336
會計・客服　方靖淳
法律顧問　第一國際法律事務所 余淑杏律師
北辰著作權事務所 蕭雄淋律師

全球總經銷・印務代理　知遠文化事業有限公司
網路書城　http://www.booknews.com.tw 博訊書網
電話：02-26648800　傳真：02-26648801
地址：新北市222深坑區北深路三段155巷25號5樓

港澳地區經銷　和平圖書有限公司
電話：852-28046687　傳真：850-28046409
地址：香港柴灣嘉業街12號百樂門大廈17樓

定價　台幣380元／港幣127元
劃撥帳號　戶名：19726702・檸檬樹國際書版有限公司
・單次購書金額未達300元，請另付40元郵資
・信用卡・劃撥購書需7-10個工作天

版權所有・侵害必究　本書如有缺頁、破損，請寄回本社更換

圖解生活實用英語：人事物的種類構造 /
檸檬樹英語教學團隊著. -- 初版. -- 新北市：
檸檬樹, 2015.09
面；　公分. --（Fly 飛系列；11）
ISBN 978-986-6703-96-6（平裝附光碟片）
1.英語　2.詞彙
805.12　　104013173

圖解生活實用英語
圖解生活實用日語

全套訂購 優惠方案

圖解生活實用英語：全套三冊

系統化整合大量英文單字

舉目所及
的人事物

以【眼睛所見人事物插圖】
對應學習單字

十字路口周遭

交通警察（traffic police）
行人（pedestrian）
斑馬線（zebra crossing）
紅綠燈（traffic light）
人行道（sidewalk）
地下道（underpass）

碼頭邊

燈塔（lighthouse）
碼頭（marina）
船錨（anchor）
起重機（crane）
堆高機（forklift）
貨櫃（cargo container）

腦中延伸
的人事物

以【大腦所想人事物插圖】
對應學習單字

畢業

畢業證書（diploma）
學士服（academic robes）
畢業論文（dissertation）
畢業旅行（graduation trip）
畢業紀念冊（yearbook）
畢業照（yearbook photo）

看電影

上映日期（release date）
電影分級（movie rating）
票房（box office）
爛片（bad movie）
熱門鉅片（blockbuster）
字幕（subtitle）

人事物的
種類構造

以【種類、構造插圖】
對應學習單字

身體損傷【種類】

淤青（bruise）
擦傷（abrasion）
凍傷（frostbite）
拉傷（stretch）
扭傷（sprain）
骨折（fracture）

腳踏車【構造】

握把（handlebars）
坐墊（seat）
齒輪（gear）
鍊條（chain）
擋泥板（fender）
腳踏板（pedal）

圖解生活實用日語：全套三冊

系統化整合大量日文單字

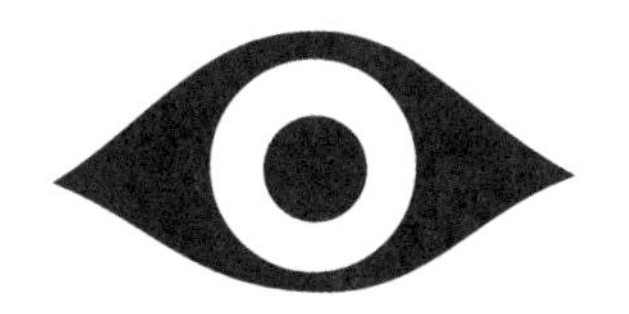

舉目所及的人事物

以【眼睛所見人事物插圖】對應學習單字

十字路口周遭

行人（歩行者）
斑馬線（横断歩道）
紅綠燈（信号）
人行道（歩道）
地下道（地下道）

碼頭邊

燈塔（灯台）
碼頭（港）
船錨（錨）
起重機（クレーン）
貨櫃（コンテナ）

腦中延伸的人事物

以【大腦所想人事物插圖】對應學習單字

畢業

畢業證書（卒業証書）
學士服（学士ガウン）
畢業論文（卒業論文）
畢業旅行（卒業旅行）
畢業照（卒業写真）

看電影

上映日期（公開日）
票房（興行収入）
爛片（ワースト映画）
熱門鉅片（人気超大作）
字幕（字幕）

人事物的種類構造

以【種類、構造插圖】對應學習單字

身體損傷【種類】

淤青（青痣）
擦傷（擦傷）
凍傷（凍傷）
扭傷（捻挫）
骨折（骨折）

腳踏車【構造】

握把（ハンドル）
坐墊（サドル）
齒輪（ギア）
鍊條（チェーン）
擋泥板（泥よけ）

訂購單

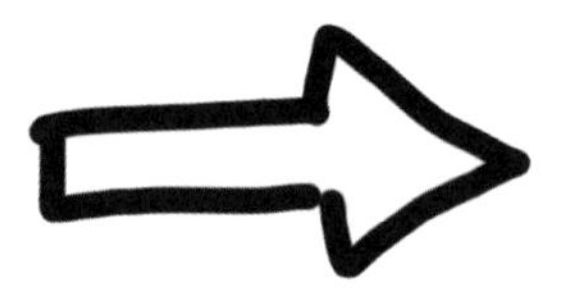

填寫後請沿虛線裁下傳真至出版社。傳真號碼，請見此頁背面。

1 圖解生活實用英語

☐ 選擇 1：以 *999* 元（原價 1229 元）購買全套三冊

☐ 選擇 2：已購買其中一本（請勾選），補差額買全套

☐ 圖解生活實用英語：舉目所及的人事物（399元）

☐ 圖解生活實用英語：腦中延伸的人事物（450元）

☐ 圖解生活實用英語：人事物的種類構造（380元）

補差額 *999* 元－ ______ 元 ＝ ______ 元 購買其他兩本

2 圖解生活實用日語

☐ 選擇 1：以 *999* 元（原價 1229 元）購買全套三冊

☐ 選擇 2：已購買其中一本（請勾選），補差額買全套

☐ 圖解生活實用日語：舉目所及的人事物（399元）

☐ 圖解生活實用日語：腦中延伸的人事物（450元）

☐ 圖解生活實用日語：人事物的種類構造（380元）

補差額 *999* 元－ ______ 元 ＝ ______ 元 購買其他兩本

3 種訂購方法：

信用卡

持卡人姓名______________ 電話___________ 手機_____________

卡別 ☐VISA ☐Master ☐聯合 卡號______-______-______-______

有效月年_____月_____年　末三碼____________（簽名欄末三碼）

金額_______元　持卡人簽名____________________（需與卡片一致）

收件人姓名______________ 電話___________ 手機_____________

收件地址☐☐☐____

統一編號______________ 抬頭_____________________________

郵政劃撥

帳號：19726702　戶名：檸檬樹國際書版有限公司。

【劃撥單通訊欄】請填寫購買的書名、數量。

貨到付款

請電洽檸檬樹出版社 (02) 2927-1121 分機 19。

貨到付款需另付 30 元手續費。

其他須知

◎海外及大陸地區郵資另計。台灣本島以外地區加收 50 元郵資。

◎購書寄送需 7-10 個工作天（不含周末假日）。

◎單次購書金額未達 300 元需另付 40 元郵資。

◎退貨郵資及退款手續費由購買方負擔。

◎本優惠方案之暫停、中斷，本公司保留最終決定權，且不另行通知。

24小時傳真（02）2927-2336

讀者服務專線（02）2927-1121

週一～週五　9:30~12:30　13:30~18:30

（例假日除外）